HOW TO
HAVE
A SHIT
RELATIONSHIP

J. L. DENT

First published in the UK in 2024 by Anatta books

Copyright © J. L. Dent 2024

All rights reserved.

www.jldent.com

ISBN no: 978-1-0687299-0-4

Contemporary fiction

Dedicated to my mum whose love of books was an inspiration, and my son River, who through his love of life, saw in me, something I'd been unable to see in myself.

HOW TO HAVE A SHIT RELATIONSHIP

Part One

ONE

The cell door closes
Key turning inside the lock
I am free at last
Haiku by Troy

Liam

When busting for a shit, it's a case of get there or suffer the consequences.

No time to avoid the pockmark cavities, Liam's backside was sporadically flung into the air as the old LDV swiftly bobbed its way along the uneven track.

The bouncing was torture. Bowels rapidly loosening, sphincter straining to hold on for a moment longer, each second excruciatingly long, distorting time.

Passing Bentley's house, the track dipped down into a secluded, wooded swale. On the absolute brink of an unfortunate explosion, beige variety, the van skidded to a halt. Liam jumped out, legging it to the compost loo—a stone's throw from his caravan.

Crouching over a hole cut into plywood, propped up by pallets, the relief began.

Heaven did exist.

Three sides of green tarp curtain surrounded the structure with the front looking out onto open fields beneath a sapphire sky. Venus, temptress of the night, had risen, clocking his face awash with serenity, the kind you feel whilst taking a good dump.

Bats were out to-ing and fro-ing, flittering on the hunt.

Colours vivid with intensity, made lucid from twilight.

What a beautiful night.

"Ah, splendid, you must be Liam," came a chirpy aristocratic voice from out of the fading light. Liam almost fell off the toilet. *Who the fuck could that be?*

A tall silhouette of a man a few yards away was looking at him. Not having wiped his arse yet, he remained squatting.

"Who's that?"

"Daniel Bloomberg."

Fuck me! thought, Liam. "Oh, y'alright." This was not a chin-wagging moment, and what a Bloomberg wanted with him was anybody's guess.

Thankfully, there was a drainage ditch with some low-growing holly bushes and bramble between them, preventing the shadowy shape from getting closer.

He remained standing there.

"I've been meaning to contact you. Marvellous evening," boomed Mr Bloomberg.

"Gorgeous." *Should I tell him I'm taking a dump?* thought Liam, his spidery hand creeping towards a damp toilet roll.

"I would have phoned but I needed to see Graham. He mentioned you're normally back around this time. Said your phone has no reception down here."

Daniel Bloomberg was the local squire, owning the land that Graham Bentley rented off him. Possibly one of the wealthiest people in Falindon. Everyone knew about the Bloombergs, but Liam had never met any of them.

"So, um, how can I help you?" said Liam, desperate for Lord Bloomberg, or whatever he was, to leave so he could wipe his bum in private.

Thankfully, the dark was closing in fast, concealing his predicament.

"Ah, yes of course," he said, as though forgetting why he'd gone there in the first place. "I saw your flyer in the mailbox and thought, ah-ha, I like the sound of this chap."

Would it be possible to surreptitiously wipe his arse without being noticed? "Oh, right, so you'd like me to do some gardening."

The flyer had been posted in the Bloomberg mailbox beside the domineering, electronic steel gates, just for a laugh—never in a million years expecting anything other than it to be crumpled up and thrown in the bin.

Under the stealth of darkness, the soggy tissue was administered. Job done, kegs pulled up, and down he climbed off the rickety construction, just in time, before a torch was switched on, aimed directly at his eyes.

"Yes, when would you be able to start?"

"I can come and have a look tomorrow," said Liam, squinting through the cracks of his fingers, trying to protect his eyes from the blinding glare.

"Splendid."

They agreed on a time before Mr Bloomberg marched off, following a tiny disk of light.

Liam dipped his hands in a bucket of cold water, wiped them on his trousers and headed to his caravan.

* * *

Falindon lay between Woking and Guildford. Woking was better, Guildford being way more up-market, its poshness only adding to feeling like a pariah. Woking wasn't posh. If they were books, Guildford would be *Pride and Prejudice* whilst Woking might be Alan Sugar's autobiography.

Most of his time was spent in the woodland, his private Virgin Island, surrounded by a pastoral sea of farmland and moorland, no houses in sight, secluded from the excruciating world of socialising.

It seemed a bit pathetic that his only friends were customers, the odd one or two coming out to do some gardening with him along with a cup of tea and a natter. Posh old people with old money. Mainly old women, men being prone to end up in the compost bin a little sooner, but they were friendly, motherly even, although somewhat condescending with their hoity-toity voices. Tories probably, but you can't be too fussy—good to keep an open mind.

Being a gardener had just sort of happened, drifted into, picking bits up here and there. Toffs know their plants, what to do with them, and are only too happy to share this information. With going online at Woking Library and his nose constantly wedged between charity shop books, his green fingers were coming on nicely.

Besides, outdoors always felt better than indoors.

The flyer read as follows:

Organic gardener. Eco spaces, meadows, ponds, compost systems, native hedges, be the change you want to see! Call Liam 07700 900878

Originally, the idea was to attract those with something in common, with his ethical values, open to the alternative, but this was Surrey and a dumbing down of expectations had been necessary.

On a good day, he fancied himself as the wild man of the woods, dancing naked under the stars, half-man, half-beast, like Pan. On a bad day, the fantasy changed to creepy loner, or at best, naïve, dope-smoking hippy. The truth is, he was neither: it was a case of living in a caravan was better than being homeless.

Chicken and egg as to whether living in a wood made him an outsider or Woking made him want to live in a wood. The woods were safe, unsnarled from the cogs of industry. Same reason he worked for himself, no one dishing out orders like the mind-numbing dishwashing job in London lasting about three weeks. Five minutes late one day and given a verbal warning. "Seriously, what is this, school?" he'd snapped back, apron thrown to the floor, walking out.

But the Bloombergs were a different breed altogether. Having a cuppa with Lord and Lady Bloomberg would be something else.

Opening the wood burner door, he struck a match, lit a candle and then put the match to a pile of scrunched up paper, onto which kindling had been methodically placed. The paper crackled, biting towards the wood, its yellowy tongue swaddling the dry sticks.

The Bloombergs were like royalty. It'd be like having a cuppa with Prince Charles—maybe like Charley, Daniel Bloomberg was also into talking to plants, he speculated, gently tipping molten wax from the candle, the fire feeding off it, ravenous for more.

* * *

Like a snail, Liam's head protruded from beneath an assortment of duvets squishing his body to the bed. Over the years, a variety of tricks had been learnt whilst living off-grid: covering hot coals with ash in the burner, keeping it smouldering through the night, mummifying both hot-water bottles in towels to keep them warm, wearing multiple layers in bed, and the pièce de resistance, a woolly hat.

Before prising himself from the leaden covers, his condensation barometer—an exaggerated, breathy exhalation into the air—was put to the test. Yup, it was concluded, spring had finally arrived. Heading to the burner, hot ashes were prodded with a poker, kindling and coal added, then blown to a flame. For good measure, the oven was lit, making the caravan extra toasty.

Sunlight mingled with smoke flooded the oblong space, head bowed to avoid the ceiling as breakfast was made. Outside, a great tit chirped, resembling a rusty, old bicycle wheeling around the tree canopy. In the distance, a woodpecker's staccato drummed a hollow trunk, carousing the morning.

The silver birch, ready to be tapped for her sweet, rising sap, invited him out into the day. It was always a relief to see the back of winter. Days stretching out. Body unfurling from tightly bound spiral frond into a light-loving fern. No longer having to dress Inuit style.

Leaving the caravan, there was the hint of a skip in his step, like a kid—not the child he remembered, worried, lost, but a happy kid, carefree. A flutter of butterflies rippled up his spine as he jumped in the van, setting off to the Bloombergs'.

The LDV chugged its way along narrow lanes, the radio belting out love songs from yesteryear, the same old tired, cliché-ridden ones endlessly played as if to keep everyone in some narcotic coma. Turning the dial, Radio Four news was on with the ubiquitous voice of Nigel Farage, the UKIP leader who, as ever, was presenting himself as a man of the people. *Despite his private education and his offshore funds to avoid paying tax*, thought Liam, who despised him. The polls predicted UKIP would do well in the local elections, just a few weeks away.

As Farage spoke about the need to leave the EU, the interviewer, pointing out implications, was reminded of Enoch Powell's *Rivers of Blood* speech from the late sixties. *Enoch who?* thought Liam.

It was interesting listening to the news, but ultimately as depressing as the music. Liam switched it off.

Crossing Falindon Moor, the Bloomberg Mansion swelled into view as it always had, imposing and austere. He'd seen it a million times before, its ashen, stony face peering down its nose on anyone approaching.

Why would anyone need to live anywhere so big?

The Mansion held a demeanour that the aristocracy prided itself on, standing detached, restrained and superior. Huge blocks of cut stone casting a solemn, grey shadow against the sky. Everything symmetrical, precise, devoid of softness. Three rows of four tall sash windows stared out across the drive, beyond which lay the road and open common. Liam parked his van on the grass verge and walked to the entrance.

Electric gates towered above as he rang the intercom. A stern female voice crackled from a tiny black speaker, her face flashing onto the screen, appearing as though reflected on the back of a spoon, her nose commanding attention.

"Can I help you?" she said in a haughty voice.

"Hi there. I'm here to see Mr Bloomberg."

"Ah, yes. You must be the gardener. Very well, push the gate."

The woman disappeared. There was a loud buzzing sound, and Liam pushed the smaller side gate and entered. A second later, the gate automatically closed with a loud clang and an electronic locking click, reminiscent of a documentary he'd watched about prisoners on death row. The world just disappeared, ceased to exist, as though stepping through a portal into a sphere where poverty was anathema. A place that had never known any other way. Where money and land, since feudal times, had surged the arteries of all its inhabitants. He pictured in contrast his mum in Barnsley, sat in her council flat, smoking roll-ups, totting up coins from the change jar kept for an emergency. Turning his attention to the grounds, her face was scrubbed away, leaving only a stain.

Liam wandered around, slack-jawed: The Georgian mansion depicted a world gone by. Judging by the size, there must have been twenty rooms, plus a dining hall too, he bet. Across the expansive lawn, a walled outdoor swimming pool, tennis courts and summer house that alone was big enough to live in quite easily.

Everything impeccable in a deadened sort of way. All neat and tidy. What would there be to do? Polish individual gravel stones in the drive? Seek out unruly blades of grass using nail scissors to put them back in line with the rest?

It was kind of going up in the world. Always nice getting a new job, but he'd never really known anyone this flush: the rich normally kept themselves apart. It was another planet: Planet lah-di-dah.

TWO

Maya

Propping open the double doors of Hampstead Secondary School for Girls with a speaker, spinning on her heels, Maya boomeranged back to the car to fetch more things. Lugging the speaker had been a considerable strain on her upper arms.

The *crew* hadn't arrived yet. The crew being only Ian this week. Looking at her mobile, there was nothing: no texts, no voicemail.

Racing back to the car, manically swiping the phone for Ian's number whilst grabbing a box of fairy lights and candles, she called him—there was no answer.

Conscious Movement evenings needed to be just right, not only the music that was assiduously selected throughout the week, but the ambiance needed to be tranquil, a cushioned, fluffy harem.

There was only an hour to set up before people started arriving. The evening sun gave the hall a celestial tinge.

Maybe the fairy lights and candles could be skipped to save some time. Again, she sped back to the car and was relieved to see

Ian pushing his bike through the gate; he looked oddly misshapen in his tight cycling pants, hi-viz jacket and streamlined helmet, like a bendy toy pink panther she used to have as a child.

"Sorry, sorry. Got stuck at work. Lost track of time."

"Hi, gorgeous." Maya walked over, dispensing a hug.

Ian's face lit up. He had a bit of a thing for her, but it was never going to happen. Not her type. Nice but no edge; smooth as a pebble. He'd be frustrating. Similar to a cagoule: safe, useful but belonging to the vestibule with the wellies, not in the house and certainly not in the bedroom—a sly once-over—definitely not in the bed.

"Okay, so we need to get on with it. If you grab the speaker, sweep the hall and then hang the lights," said Maya, no time for chat. Ian followed her, bearing a hefty speaker, still wearing his helmet like some freaky giant ant.

The mixer jack was inserted into the laptop, headphones placed over the ears.

Conscious Movement evenings could still be a bit nerve-wracking. It had been a year since completing the training in California, and though getting used to it, an anticipation of it all going tits up had tumoured itself to her brain.

The three-year training had been a twenty-eighth birthday gift from the parents, coinciding with a Saturn return, all inspired by her guru who'd said *it was time to be of service to both others and her higher self. To be only one was out of balance. Only a path that brings joy is truly worth following.*

As far as the parents were concerned, it was dance therapy training, which it was—sort of—though more New Age.

Indian devotional music floated through headphones as she glanced around the hall. Hampstead Secondary School for Girls was probably built in the 1960s. Its prefab architecture couldn't be any more different from the school she'd attended. There were, thankfully, no portraits of old men in gowns looking down their noses from high, panelled walls. No great oak timber beams, from which she could picture herself in a noose, hanging, as teachers and girls entered morning assembly—a fond fantasy often played with. The curtain wall windows looked out into the world, as opposed to high and unreachable, as if preventing escape.

She tested her mic.

"One two, to—fu, three four, Ian's-a-whore."

Turning up a piece of music by Coldplay, she continued. "Hello. One two, Ian-stinks-of-poo. How does it sound, Ian?"

"Maybe your mic could be a bit quieter," he shouted back, sounding nonplussed from across the hall, up some ladders, hanging the fairy lights. Why he hadn't laughed perplexed Maya.

Dials were turned until the sound was agreeable.

As dusk began to creep in, Ian switched on the fairy lights and Maya lit the candles.

Ian situated himself at the door to take entry fees. People began trickling in. The usual disparate crowd were instantly recognisable, undressing around the edge of the hall, putting on their dance clothes. The skinny looking Buddhist guy with an unpronounceable name that was equally impossible to remember sat in the corner, cross-legged, meditating. *For fuck's sake!* It wasn't that she'd never meditated, but why the fuck would anyone meditate here. *Fucking narcissist.*

"Welcome everybody," said Maya, her voice breathy and perhaps a little over sincere.

Twenty people, or thereabouts, were spread around the hall. Several chatting, others hugging, the odd newcomer looking a bit anxious, waiting to be told what to do, a few yoga stretches here and there, some already moving to the music. The word *dance* was never used: people associated dance with something you had to get right whereas everyone knows how to move.

"Find yourself a space in the room," Maya crooned.

Conscious Movement evenings always began with a warm-up, helping the group connect with their bodies. A little buzz of pride swirled around her when everyone did what they were told. Hanging onto each word as though steeped in wisdom. She felt wise, when all the bullshit conditioning got out of the way.

The group dropped into a flow.

It was like being a celebrity, or was that egotistical? Maybe quite narcissistic. Okay, more like a spiritual guide, everyone here to be taken on a journey. No matter what anyone said, this was not dee-jaying as one guy once put it—which he soon regretted—this was so much more: it was riding on the back of an eagle, waking up from samsara; it was aligning all the chakras and connecting to the core sacred truth.

Surveying the hall, there were a couple of tasty men, both in relationships of course. All the best men were. It had been weeks since she'd had sex.

The Buddhist guy who'd been meditating was now moving to the music, his eyes closed, tentacle arms like seaweed drifting around him. Still just as irritating. She wanted to like him but it just wasn't happening.

Being good or bad are both the same. When you are free, these no longer matter, her guru had said.

Maya enjoyed thinking of guru Swami Gandalih. He was like the perfect father: attentive, warm, loving. Whenever self-flagellating thoughts got her on the whipping post, there was nothing more alleviating than conjuring up his soft, silky voice.

Was she an enlightened being or another deluded New Age hippy? The latter being her mother's very words.

About twenty minutes into the evening there was a loud banging on the door. The door was locked. Ian had stopped taking fees and joined the others, his eyes closed, his body swaying to the music. Through the glass door, a beefy looking man stood waiting. The banging grew louder, catching Ian's attention, prompting a gallop to the door, letting him in, taking his fee.

Ian went back into his movement. The man looked around the place, not fixing his gaze on anywhere in particular. His face was unfamiliar. He rubbed the back of his neck, standing there, looking like he'd come to the wrong event, wondering what to do now. Maya spoke into the mic.

"Gently, let yourself soften to the music, brain taking a rest, body surrendering to the rhythm of whatever is going on inside you right now," her voice a bit breathier than before.

The man took his jacket off, hanging it over the back of a chair. Having not brought any other clothes to change into, he stuck out, checked shirt conspicuously tucked tightly into belted jeans, still wearing shoes irrespective of the hordes of naked feet surrounding him. He began to step, soldier-like, to the music. Undoubtedly on the shorter side, though at least six inches taller than Maya, which didn't say much as she was often referred to as *pocket-sized*, probably said in the nicest way but still fucking annoying.

The man must have been in his late thirties, about five foot seven. Muscles bulging through his shirt like an Action Man toy, his physique moving robotically to the music, a face hardened, said, *Don't fuck with me.*

For heaven's sake, loosen up. He looked constipated. Maya found herself preoccupied with him.

"Move towards another person," she instructed. "Through movement, tell this person how your day has been. Let them know what kind of day you've had. Don't hold back, unless you've had a really held-back day, in which case exaggerate it."

Following the instructions, each person gravitated towards someone else, forming couples, sharing their day through a myriad of intense body movements. Sounds of laughter erupted across the hall.

Action Man ended up with a woman sensually snaking around him—either she'd had a day of multiple orgasms or was just letting Action Man know she found him hot. Action Man's movements suggested his day had involved being held hostage by a coven of witches intending to stick his magic wand into their bubbling cauldron.

"Change partners."

The sexy snake woman bowed and saluted Action Man with a prayer sign. Action Man was instantly approached by another hot, young nubile. He clearly had something that the women wanted. Again, he did his *please-don't-torture-me* moves, which included wide *get-me-the-hell-out-of-here* eyes. His new partner clearly hadn't had such a great day, though, as she huffed and puffed around him, gesticulating with sharp sword-like moves, brow set like a bald eagle ready to strike a kill.

Poor Action Man looked totally out of his depth.

"Okay, let this person go, and come back to yourself."

Everyone did their own thing, solo. Maya encouraged the group to be authentic, to trust and allow whatever emotions surfaced. House music pummelled the air with a fast repetitive beat, the group (except Action Man) became wildly animated, throwing themselves into distorted shapes. Buddhist guy screamed in the manner of someone being disembowelled alive. Others joined in, escalating, until the hall became a sea of emotional release, guttural screams, shameless shouts of primal liberation, freeing a menagerie of exotic animals from their cages. Arms flying uncontrollably, turbocharged bobbleheads, bodies jerking back and forth. A revolution of divine madness.

Action Man glanced at his watch, bouncing from his left foot to his right, nodding his head.

Eventually, Maya calmed everything down, wafting pink cirrus melodies across humid thermals. Ian's limbs were spaghettied around a woman on the floor. Buddhist guy lay dreamily on his back, eyes closed, performing the backstroke in slow motion.

Action Man was in the same place he'd been stood all evening but, wow, his eyes were closed too, face softened, muscular arms floating out in front, as though filled with helium. It was a small victory to get someone to a place they feared and then realise it's a place that offers nourishment and joy.

As the evening drew to an end, everyone was invited into a closing circle. A candle placed on the floor in the middle of the hall. Revellers, intoxicated, collected coats and blankets to stay warm, clustering together around the tiny, flickering light.

Action Man wound up sitting next to Maya. A strong whiff of aftershave and testosterone—though the latter may have been imagined—cloaked itself around her. On the other side was Ian who smelt funky. The glow from the candle reflected off his forehead. Hand in hand with the woman he'd been cuddling.

"Take a hand either side of you," said Maya, taking hold of both Action Man's and Ian's hand. Action Man's palm was clammy with a firm grip. Ian's was limp, difficult to tell if he was actually there.

"Let's close our eyes and take a moment to be present."

Everyone closed their eyes, including Maya.

As the group sat there, eyes shut, holding hands in the circle, Action Man gave a gentle stroke with his thumb: it was tiny, but it prompted her heart to race a little faster. It happened again. Was he hitting on her? A flirtatious tease? He wouldn't be getting anything back. Maybe it was nerves, a twiddling thumb looking for its twin.

"And opening your eyes, turn to thank each person and then let them go."

Maya turned towards Action Man. His eyes were puddled and dewy, betraying the hardness of his jaw and body.

"Thank you," she said.

"No worries," he replied, permitting himself a quick anatomical shufti.

Clearly not that shy after all. Frankly, his manner quite disconcerting, there was no thank you back. Her hand sat in his, waiting for a letting go, but only inertia. Peeling herself away from both his grasp and penetrating gaze, she used her liberated finger to scratch the side of her nose. Who was this feral-looking fish in her pond?

"Oh, yeah, sorry. Thanks," he said.

"Maya turned to thank Ian, whose hand had become superglued to hers, suffocating, longing, caging fingers. Loosening her grip urged him to set her free.

Being liked and admired was a real dopamine hit, but clingy men were the ultimate turn off.

"Thank you," he said, emitting a sigh that conveyed a bit too much meaning.

"Does anyone have anything they'd like to share? And please add your name," said Maya.

This was the part where people could bring up any insights they'd experienced for themselves over the course of the evening.

The girl who'd been cuddled up with Ian went first.

"Hi. I'm Asenka. There's so much love in this room tonight, such a beautiful evening, Maya. You hold a beautiful space. I don't know what I'd do without this. I wish we could all run off and live together in a community."

Nods of agreement echoed around the circle. Maya smiled inwardly, a warm glow in her belly.

Buddhist guy chipped in, "Candrasurya. For the sake of authenticity, I'd like to share something. I had a rubbish evening and I hate everyone, but I'll be coming back next week. Maybe."

A chorus of laughter sang out at Buddhist guy's comment, except for Action Man, who appeared puzzled. Maya laughed too but was fucked if she'd remember his name. Authenticity is precious in a world dominated by selfies showing only the best side. Buddhist guy was being playful. Maybe he wasn't so bad after all. People, largely newbies, in the personal growth world could be so irritating with their pseudo niceness that paraded itself as spirituality. The shadow was much more interesting. Truth and honesty kept you alert and alive.

As a child, and even now, truth was unwelcome at home. Boarding school was even worse: honesty sacrificed for courtesy, which in essence was dominance over free will, albeit diplomatic. Only the semblance of free spirit was permissible. Thank God for Suzy.

At school, the head had written to the parents suggesting Maya visit the counsellor, Suzy, to deal with some *emotional issues.* It wasn't just about being caught smoking weed when the distinctive aromatic smell had wafted up the nostrils of a particularly annoying despot prefect who happened to be passing nearby. Nor was it the shaved head after discovering feminism. Or getting caught having sex with another girl in the dorm when fifteen.

It was the answering back, arguing over the rules and the belief that her exorbitant education was worth jack shit.

Ian had a go at sharing, saying how he'd been feeling down lately with all the crap happening to the planet: global warming, rain forests being chopped down, too much plastic, oil spills in the ocean, overfishing. This topic never failed to get others chipping in with their own virtuous lamentations.

She was set to bring the group to a close, in need of a glass of wine and some Netflix escapism, when Action Man leant towards Ian, on the other side of Maya. "Don't you have a car then?"

"I have a car, yes, but I cycle most places."

"But you have a car, eh. Do you eat fish?"

Buddhist guy stepped in. "Hey listen, no one's here to judge anyone, okay. Keep it personal."

"Well, I'm hearing a load of judgment going on. Just 'cos I eat meat doesn't make me some murderer."

Fuck! Who was this loose cannon? This was not how the sharing was meant to go. All eyes were on Action Man. His eyes hardened, his lower jaw jutting forward.

"Maybe you could share something about how it was for you this evening, erm ... sorry, you didn't say your name," said Maya, attempting to nip any potential brawl in the bud.

"Troy."

"Hi Troy. Welcome." Maya gave her best pacifying smile. She meant it too. Even if disinclined to referee a scarp, his edginess was refreshing. None of that trying to fit in. "So, how was this evening for you?"

"Yeah, alright. Thanks. Bit weird, not the kind of thing I normally do, but hey, gotta try new things, ain't yer." He then looked at Ian. "Sorry mate, lost it a bit there."

Ian did a bowing pose and prayer sign; Maya cringed inwardly.

* * *

Deciding to leave unpacking the car until morning, Maya closed the door of her Hampstead flat to the outside world, letting the blanket of home enfold her. The heath, overlooked from the window, was dark and empty. During the short drive back, she'd been unable to stop thinking about the new guy, Troy.

Wandering into the kitchen and opening a bottle of Cabernet, the reassuring glug-glug sound of wine making its way to the brim had an extra calming effect.

She pictured Troy knocking on the door. Solid fists pounding against the wood. Another sip of wine. Opening the door, Troy muscles his way in. Resisting him is futile; pushed to the floor, she is powerless.

Maya popped over to a drawer in her desk, took out a bag of grass and rolled a small joint.

Dress rips open. *You fucking slut*, he says, eyes roasting, hands tender as he squeezes her breasts. He whispers how much he wants to fuck her and that there's no stopping him, the rough textured skin of thick fingers inside her.

Taking another deep inhalation of the joint, she headed towards the bedroom. A vibrator, tucked in amongst socks and knickers, is removed from a drawer and switched on.

Troy's cock in her mouth as he tugs on her hair.

"You dirty, fucking bitch!" he tells her.

It doesn't take long to climax.

THREE

Daniel

Daniel didn't need a gardener. Garden Force Maintenance Limited came once a week, a reliable and efficient company. They screeched up in their logoed van, manically ran round like an old time-lapse *Keystone Cop* film reel, mowing, spraying, strimming, pruning, leaf blowing, then clambered back into their van and sped off to the next stately home. Garden Force were terminators at war with nature, killing slugs, snails, fungi, moles, weeds, everything that threatened the controlled order.

And then came the scrappy bit of paper in the postbox with words that brought a wry smile to Daniel's face, a rare occurrence of late. *Be the change you want to see* came over as rather droll, proposing a reverence for nature. Noticing the name, he was reminded that Graham Bentley had mentioned a chap in a caravan called Liam, the name instantaneously vanishing without trace, as things so easily did these days, until the unpolished flyer revived the incident, arousing curiosity.

The gym in the east wing overlooked the gates with Falindon Moor beyond. Daniel's face glistened with a sheen of sweat as he peered out, pace building on the treadmill.

For sixty-three, his physique was quite remarkable, but not as remarkable as it had been thirty years earlier—now the aches, the creaks, and the deteriorating eyesight, hearing and memory, quite the nuisance really.

With investment banking now in the past, except for the odd dabble at the weekend when he still took the FT, day-to-day time had become elongated, each bit hankering to be filled, yet in terms of life span, it had shrunk, heavily hurtling towards a black hole.

If time is precious and doing the things one enjoys is imperative, he was damned if he knew how.

A dilapidated van pulled up on the grass verge close to the gate. Pressing the stop button, the treadmill came to a standstill. Daniel wiped the sweat from his brow with a small towel.

"Darling, the gardener's at the gate," Meredith hollered from downstairs.

"Righty-o," Daniel responded, setting off to meet him.

When arriving at the gates and doing a three-sixty-degree spin on his heels, Liam was nowhere to be seen. He was sure Meredith had said that was where he'd be. Then from the side of the house, he appeared, breezing over, looking around, taking everything in. *Was it rude to wander around someone else's property willy-nilly?*

It was the first time he'd seen Liam in daylight. His outdoorsy lifestyle caught the eye: hair cropped closely to the skull, a face—despite youth—leathery and weathered, showing off piercing blue eyes.

"Wow. Nice place you got!" he said, reaching out a hand for Daniel to shake. "I lived in a mansion once, a squat, but not like this."

"Ahh. Yes, well, thank you for coming, Liam. I had wondered where you'd got to."

"We were evicted 'cos they wanted to turn it into a care home or something like that."

"Quite," said Daniel, pushed a little off balance by the lack of decorum. "Let me show you around."

"Yeah, great!"

Liam was rugged with no airs and graces. Maybe it was being from the North of England, detected in his accent—call a spade a spade and all that. A squatter too. Anarchists intrigued Daniel, particularly now with so many protesting against environmental stuff. The lack of formality was curious, even if somewhat unnerving.

"Shall we start by the pool?" said Daniel, setting off to the walled swimming pool. On their way across a gently sloping lawn, Daniel, unsure what to say, speeded up his pace. Long silences whilst in the company of others had a tendency to cause his ribcage to shrink.

They arrived at the rosebed bordering the pool.

Stepping towards a rose, his white sneakers demolishing clumps of earth, Daniel took a fresh leaf between thumb and forefinger. The fluorescent leaf had a jagged, red edge like blood-stained teeth; he pinched the centre as it clung to the rest of the plant. Daniel moved his pads back and forth as though pinching salt.

"Do you know about roses?" he asked.

"Well, I don't know all their different names, but I know how to prune them."

"Jolly good. I reckon we've seen the last frost, so this would be a good place to start. Do you have your own secateurs?"

"Hold on." Liam turned away, snorting, and spat on the ground a congealed wad of phlegm from the back of his throat. "Sorry about that. Yes, I have all my own tools."

The revolting, congealed waste sat there, uncivil, perched on a clod of dried earth like a boiled slug on a throne. This Liam chap was a bit of a lout, possibly not the right kind of person to employ with his lack of cultivation. What would he do next? Urinate on the azaleas?

"So, tell me, Liam, what's it like living on Bentley's farm? I saw your caravan yesterday. Is it not possible to find somewhere more suitable to live?" said Daniel, curbing his prejudice.

Liam tittered. "Why would I want to live anywhere else? I love it there."

"Interesting." Daniel frowned, trying to comprehend. "You *actually choose* to live in a caravan?"

"Yeah, why not? I'd hate to live in a house again, particularly in a town. What about you?"

"What about me what?"

"Do you like living here then?"

It was Daniel's turn to laugh—though it ended up being more of a smirk—at the absurdity of such a preposterous question. Yet, searching Liam's face, there was no irony; the question seemed earnest.

"Oh yeah, sorry, that must sound pretty stupid. But seriously, I'd hate living in a massive house, all the things that'd need doing. I mean, no offence, but I don't see the point in having such a big house."

"But what about water and electricity?"

"I have water. I have containers—I carry them in a wheelbarrow from the top of the farm."

"Wouldn't you prefer to be connected to the mains?"

"Nah! Too much comfort makes you numb. It's like a chemical cosh."

"I beg your pardon?"

"Like you're not quite present in the world, as though it's passing you by, like waiting for life to begin. I get water 'cos I need water. Even if it's slashing down with rain, I still need to push the barrow through the field no matter how boggy it is. Or I have to chop wood for the fire, otherwise I'll get cold. It makes you appreciate it more."

"Well, I must say, that is rather admirable, but it sounds like jolly hard work."

"Well, it's not like I'm making any sacrifice. I just prefer to keep it real."

Daniel smiled. *Keep it real* indeed. This Liam really was an oddity. Simple in his ways and conceivably not very bright, but he was affable. Actually, that was much too presumptuous, there was no cause to judge him before giving the poor chap a chance to prove himself. He had no right to think such petty thoughts. Petty thoughts were the canker of society, drivelling on, negating life.

Unlike Liam, whom it could be assumed was not particularly well educated, Daniel in his youth had been studious, attending Oxford, majoring in maths and economics—practical, level-headed subjects. Looking back, he now conceded he'd been a bit of a bore. An obedience to something that now eluded him meant a forfeiting of the swinging-sixties. It happened, just somewhere else, and he hadn't been invited, or if he had, he couldn't allow himself to go. It certainly wasn't happening in the Oxford he'd known.

It had often crossed his mind to pursue art and drama, but this particular rumination was quickly quashed as a silly, flamboyant self-indulgence, holding fast to the belief that dignity, manners, politeness and a sharp intellect were the foundation of good breeding, and the arts, self-exploration and feelings were a trifle namby-pamby. This tedious misdemeanour made life insufferable, for secreted at his core was another Daniel, cocooned away from the world.

Daniel pictured a monarch butterfly emerging from its chrysalis, immaculate, papery wings, like hands leaving prayer to feed from golden rays. No longer crawling from branch to branch, earthbound, but now heavenly. Free. *Be the change you want to see*—those words again. A Daniel who wasn't always seeking permission: a Daniel who went backpacking, smoking pot-filled hookahs in Marrakesh, living in free-love communes where everyone had rumpy-pumpy with each other, wearing homemade, colourful clothes and, as well as talking about how they were going to change the world, living the change they wanted to see.

There'd been such little change in life, on top of which was a blatant lack of friends, an aberration for someone who at one time had been quite gregarious. Living rurally whilst raising a family over the decades had taken him further and further away, drifting so far out that he'd forgotten how to get back. Even his chums from Oxford and boarding school, whom he thought to be fiercely loyal, no longer got in touch. The children were all grown up, living their lives: Gerald, the eldest, running an export and import business in Australia, rarely got in touch; Simon the investment banker, like Daniel had been, was incognito in London; and Maya, the youngest at thirty-two and childless, was an uncomfortable subject, with no one quite sure what she did or daring to enquire.

"So, Liam, tell me, how much do you charge?" said Daniel, quicksand cogitations aside.

"Fifteen quid an hour, and would it be alright to nip in the pool now and then?" said Liam, sparkly eyed, a wide, mischievous grin lifting his cheeks.

"Well, let's just stick with the fifteen pounds, shall we."

FOUR

Troy

Bare chested, Troy opened the wardrobe, which, judging by its cheap and cheerless quality, could be straight from a skip or maybe it had been there since the 1950s. The rest of the furniture was crammed in the small space: the same old shabby—no chic whatsoever. Mauling through the dingy rack of clobber, unfit for the Sally Army, he took hold of a checked shirt, catching sight of himself in the wardrobe door mirror.

And what a body! No stomach fat or flab, just pure muscle. A washboard six-pack. Pulling some poses, flexing his biceps, it was easy to admire the honed perfection of each bulge lined with vein and sinew. He tilted his head forward, looking up into his sultry eyes, flirting with himself. At certain angles, he could be a young Brad Pitt. A carbon copy of Adonis made possible by a workout a couple of hours each day.

The gym membership was pricey, so he'd bagged some weights off eBay, kept under the bed, the only free space left in the pokey shithole described as a studio flat on the estate agent website. For

Tottenham, it was overpriced, but the landlord was willing to take people on housing benefit, unlike most other places he'd seen, so it'd have to do for now.

Being Wednesday, the question arose as to whether to go back to that hippy-dippy dance thing again.

It wasn't that good, full of middle-class, arty-farty types, but Jezza suggested it'd be good to mix with new people, less toxic.

Jezza was part of his compulsory rehabilitation counselling, stipulated in the terms of his sentencing agreement on release from Pentonville.

The last stint was a bit of bird in Pentonville for ABH to this twat who'd got off with his ex. It was only a bit of a slap—nothing out of the ordinary—but men aren't allowed to be men anymore with the bleeding-heart brigade on your case all the time. It couldn't be helped. *It's natural to feel fucked off when someone else shags your bird, in it?*

Jezza was the bleeding-heart brigade type too, but he was an alright geezer. Good at listening. Shame about him having to have professional boundaries, otherwise they could've been mates, having a laugh down the pub an' all that, even though Jezza didn't laugh much.

Jezza was still an unknown quantity. Not on Facebook and his website didn't have his home address. How comes he got to hear all about Troy but not the other way round? Was he married? Did he have kids? Did he like chicken biryani?

Jezza had recommended the class as a means *to find an outlet for a more creative way to express feelings*. Whatever happened to community service, a bit of litter picking or scrubbing graffiti off council estate walls: that's how it used to be back in the day. Unlike counselling and the weekly anger management group, the hippy thing wasn't compulsory.

Last week at the hippy do-da, the horny-looking teacher had definitely glanced over a few times. A bit of alright she was n'all. No bra. Nips poking through the T-shirt for anyone to get a butchers, and what a knock-out pair. Love to get his hands on them. She was easy to find on Facefuck too. Sent a friend request, and the next day it was accepted; didn't mean that much though as she had about three thousand friends. Scrolling through her pictures, Troy nailed his attention to each image, stripping her naked. The fantasies weren't so much about fucking her, more a case of being held, her tits against his body, all snug and warm.

The rest of it was a joke. Full of weirdo, hippy types. Jezza must be having a laugh.

Pushing his arms into the sleeves of the faded shirt, he made his way to the fridge where he came face-to-face with Jesus, a magnetic, 3D, blue-eyed Jesus with long, golden locks. It was one of those pictures you could look at from one angle, Jesus praying, eyes closed, and from another, eyes open, a peaceful expression on his face.

He opened the fridge door, took out a carton of milk, giving it a cursory sniff, then knocked back half a litre, sticking the carton back in the fridge.

The power of Jesus was discovered in Pentonville. In the nick, there'd been a Bible—talk about boring! Bits here and there weren't bad but when you're banged up in a cell all day, it's like being a monk: loads of time to reflect on life; God becomes real, so there's no need to read about him, you tune in. Unlike most people. Funny that, how prison sets you free.

In England, though, Christians were all wankers, not like the yanks: they didn't fuck about. For instance, you wouldn't get a Brit—except maybe Anne Widdicombe—being honest about all the evil happening in the world. On *The Flaming Cross*, a Facefuck group, Troy had found his brethren, opening his eyes even wider to the amount of evil going on in the world. For example, it came as a revelation to find out that yoga, meditation and New Age tosh were all a form of satanism.

Devil worshippers were everywhere, cannily disguised. That's the thing about Satan, he's clever. Troy thought it best not mention the hippy dance thing to other people on The Flaming Cross group—didn't want to give the wrong impression.

Some people saw Jesus in a slice of toast or an oily puddle in the road; for Troy, he was everywhere, hearing him too in the marrow of his bones, and the bones of the universe, talking very loudly. This wasn't lunacy or hearing voices. They were signs. So, when Troy asked God whether he should go back to the hippy dance class and waited for an answer but nothing came, he took it as a no, but then switching on the TV, there it was: *Come Strictly*, the celebrity dance competition—God had spoken.

* * *

Arriving on time this week, the skinny guy with a smug face was on the door. The same one who'd been whingeing about the dolphins not having enough ocean to swim in, or some other bollox last week. The facilitator woman was with him, chatting in his ear. The skinny guy looked like he had a boner. A cockeyed smile on his mush.

"Hello again," said Troy, eyeing up the babe.

"Oh, hi," she responded and looked back towards the skinny guy.

"Mary, innit?" said Troy.

"Maya. Good to see you again."

"Nearly right then. Maya, Mary, tomato, potato. Let's call the whole thing off, or possibly not?" When on the pull, he was quite the cheeky chappy.

Maya smiled, and what a smile. Face beaming, right from her twinkly brown eyes to her dainty chin, so genuine, clearly from the heart. Knocked off guard, he felt like a fraud. Such a pure heart, like the Virgin Mary; it was in her eyes. A faint shimmering of light radiated around her. His ability to flirt pulverised, rising from the ruins, humility and devotion.

"Enjoy the evening," she said, heading over to her mixing desk, putting on her DJ headset.

Some Indian flute music fluttered from the speakers as Maya gave instructions in a calm, clear voice.

"I invite you to feel the soles of your feet connecting to the earth..." she said, followed by a long pause, as though this was somehow difficult to understand and people needed time to work out what she meant.

"Her gravity holding you so you can trust yourself to let go and allow your body to move in a way that brings you more into the present."

She sounded posh, not plummy posh like the Queen, huskier, more sensuous.

"There is no way to get it right, so give up trying. And there is no wrong way either, so give up worrying. Just trust that your body knows exactly what to do ... and don't forget to breathe."

Troy pictured bodies writhing on the floor, hands grasping throats, gasping for air because they'd forgotten how to breathe.

The instructions continued and, like last week, it was impossible to switch off the cynic. Everywhere in the hall people were doing all sorts of weird shit. Some were actually rolling on the floor, clearly acid casualties. He noticed everyone had bare feet, so he took off his shoes, keeping his socks on, slightly embarrassed by his big toe poking through a hole. Half the women looked like they were gagging for it, and some were dancing as though they had serious mental health issues or were demonically possessed.

"If it helps you connect more to your body, close your eyes, making sure you have space around you. If any feelings of shame or embarrassment come up, put them into your movement. No one is judging you."

Troy was judging everyone, including himself. He felt like a proper plonker.

As the evening went on, everyone was invited to find a partner. Each person speedily looking round and grabbing whoever was next to them, hoping they wouldn't be left on their tod.

When it came to skirt, rabbiting was a doddle, but without the words, it was fucking hard work. This was what put him off coming back, particularly the bit about having to maintain eye contact: it was agonising. He'd even discussed it in his counselling session with Jezza. Jezza pointed out that connecting to new people that weren't his usual crowd would be *a healthy step forward in his personal growth*. Yeah, right, as if.

Troy wobbled at the edge, like he did at night clubs, waiting for his fifth pint to kick in, but there was no booze here. Just lots of freaks.

A good night out used to be getting as rat-arsed with the lads, as much booze as they could get down their neck, going to a club on the pull and, if no luck, ending up in a brawl or throwing up outside the kebab shop on the way home.

Jezza was forever rattling on about intimacy, accusing Troy of having intimacy issues. It wasn't too difficult to admit his old life was a train wreck: pushing forty was a bit old for getting bladdered every weekend with a bunch of middle-aged blokes.

Since leaving prison, there'd been little desire to knock about with the usual crowd—mates had got in touch, but they were tossers.

It was time to get a grip. Turn over a new leaf as it were. Stay on the side of Jesus and God and the Virgin Mary.

But this new life at the hippy dance place was worse than being banged up, everyone speaking a different language, stuck up their own arses with mentholated words: *I invite you to... I'm grateful for... Namaste...* Yada, yada, yada. If only there was a pill to stop all the cynical spew, but there wasn't, persisting as it did like gremlins chipping away at the rock face of belonging. He just didn't fit in despite no one being particularly cold towards him or unfriendly. In fact, the group was quite decent, which oddly aroused even more suspicion. Jezza had said *getting close meant risking being abandoned.*

Most people had partnered up. Daring to look around, Troy was approached by the skinny, smug guy. Dancing with a man was too LGBT, especially a skinny eco-warrior—a smug-faced one. But skinny guy didn't hold back, initiating some sensual moves, his wormy hips dangerously close, a closet woofter eager to make eye contact, which Troy put equal measure into avoiding.

Then, halfway through *Set Fire to the Rain* by Adele, Smug Face rolled onto the floor around his feet. Troy jangled in the air, arms overhanging like petrified branches, careful not to step in the smug-faced puddle. This wasn't dancing. Dancing was something you did after ten pints with someone of the opposite sex whose cleavage suggested you might be in with a chance. It was taking forever for Maya to say *change partners*; on and on it went until, eventually, the torture was over and Smug Face found his feet, doing a ceremonial nod and prayer gesture which Troy reluctantly returned, convinced more than ever he was being indoctrinated into a dubious cult.

The evening eventually wound down and everyone sat in a circle consisting of pretty much the same motley bunch as the week before, all very New Agey. The New Age movement with its astrology and tarot cards was known for misleading people from the truth and away from Jesus. But it was worth it just to look at Maya, for in her, there was a different truth. Also, attending meant that Jezza would put in a good report to the probation officer, stating that Troy was on track to being a reformed man.

The group closed, holding hands and doing an Aum together.

* * *

Changing out of their psychedelic lycra leggings and harem pants from Nepal, the cult transformed back into normal people who looked like they might work in boring jobs and watch nature documentaries with a cup of twig tea. Troy approached Maya who was clearing away.

"Top-notch class tonight," he said, lying through his teeth. "Your teaching is kosher. Best I've ever seen."

"Wow! Thanks. Great you came back. Have you done this kind of thing before?"

"Bits here and there. Hopefully I'll come back next week, if the money's not too tight."

"You can always help out with the setting up and clearing away if money's an issue?"

"Yeah? That sounds good. Do you fancy a hand now?"

"Sure, that'd be great. Maybe you could help Ian with the speakers," said Maya, looking towards Smug Face.

Smug Face flashed Troy a benevolent smile and Troy sneered a lop-sided grin back.

"Let me give you a hand with that, mate," he said, taking the speaker from Smug Face, as though it were made of air.

FIVE

Daniel

Shuffling the mouse along the pad, Daniel tactically moved the white knight in preparation to capture his opponent's queen, the opponent being level eight on the computer.

Liam could be seen from the window in the distance toiling away. He'd proved to be a staunch worker, managing a stellar job in the garden over the last six or seven weeks. Putting his back into everything he did, never shirking. A real trooper.

Daniel looked forward to his visits.

This man who lived like a faun in the forest with barely any possessions was fascinating. His shirtless, tanned, lean torso arched against the sun, trowel in hand, methodically digging out each weed, tossing them into a wheelbarrow. Each time Liam made an appearance, there was an inexplicable magnetic pull towards him.

The black rook compromised his castle, leaving Daniel's king in a precarious position.

Putting the chess on hold, Daniel had the idea to bestow on Liam his finest Ceylon Silver Tip tea, loose leaf and sun-dried, sent over from an old chum who owned a tea plantation in Sri Lanka.

The tray laden with teapot, cups and saucers along with some digestives jangled as he moseyed across the lawn. Liam was wearing earphones, his back to him when he approached.

"Good morning," said Daniel in a cheery voice.

Liam flinched, startled from his weed-pulling trance.

"Oh, y'alright. How's it going?"

"I thought I'd bring you a cup of tea for refreshment. In India they drink tea to cool down. Would you care for some?"

"Cheers, yeah. Thanks."

"Shall we have it over there, in the shade?"

"Sure, yeah. That'd be great. Thanks Daniel."

Liam jabbed his trowel into the earth, thick gloves thrown to the ground. They wandered over to a garden table and chairs beneath a majestic cedar where Daniel placed the tray. It was becoming quite the norm now to bring out tea and biscuits and liaise for a natter. They weren't exactly friends but there was an impulse to know each other.

Since the children had left home, there was regret for the inadequate amount of time he'd spent with them when growing up. Even when back from boarding in the holidays, there was always somewhere else to be, something else to do rather than providing the attention they presumably craved, and in all likelihood learnt how to stifle.

Placing his finger through the handle, he carefully poured the tea through a silver strainer into the cup. The tinkling cascade of golden tea was one of those sounds that ought to be played through loudspeakers whenever the world forgot how to be civilised.

"So, Liam, I'm curious, tell me, what do you listen to on your headphones?"

"Well, just now, I was listening to Radio Three."

"Oh, how interesting, nothing like some classical music to herald the day," he said emphatically. "I didn't know you liked classical music, Liam. How wonderful."

Liam guffawed and squinted at Daniel. "Why wouldn't I listen to classical music?"

"Oh, I do apologise, I didn't mean to appear rude. You just don't strike me as someone who might listen to Radio Three. What were you listening to?"

"What's the difference between someone who listens to Radio Three and someone who doesn't?"

This was a tough question, placing Daniel in an awkward position. "You strike me more along the lines of popular music?"

"It was piano music by Chopin."

"How lovely, one of his nocturnes?"

"Not sure, it sounded a bit Eastern European." Liam folded his arms across his chest.

"He was Polish. His compositions are very romantic. Have you ever listened to Beethoven's piano sonatas?" Daniel enthused, eager to redeem himself.

"No, you're right, I'm more into modern music to be honest. There's too much snobbery around music. It bugs me how some people talk about art as though they had some kind of spiritual connection with it, yet the way they live is soulless. They should create some beauty in themselves first rather than grabbing it from everywhere else like vultures."

Liam had crossed his legs and his foot was tapping the air at a furious speed. "But I love music, all music: Jazz, Radiohead, Rhianna, classical, African, you name it." He dipped his biscuit into his tea. "Nice cup of tea!"

Daniel didn't mention where the tea had come from—this might be perceived as pushing his sensibilities up Liam's nose. They were poles apart on the class spectrum but why couldn't they just be two men getting to know each other? Daniel never quite knew how to chat freely with Liam, but he never quite knew how to chat with anyone these days. Generally, conversation had become a chore.

Learning certain social graces had enabled him to present himself in a way that was congenial but lacked authenticity. Whereas Liam wasn't playing the game: he spoke in plain English.

"So, are you intending to vote tomorrow, Liam?"

"Nah, not allowed. No fixed abode means I don't get to vote. How about you?"

"Oh yes, I'll be trotting along, though I'm sorry to hear you're not allowed to vote, that's despicable."

"I don't care to be honest. There isn't even a Green candidate, and all the rest are the same, though I might've voted Labour just to stop any chance of UKIP getting in. How about you, who you gonna vote for?"

Well, Labour certainly wouldn't get his vote, not that he needed to worry: Labour had never managed to get in locally. And the idea of voting Green, even if they did have a representative, was preposterous: he'd paid enough tax as it was, no, he was a true blue and always had been and couldn't see that ever changing.

"I'll be voting Conservative."

"Fair enough," said Liam, turning his head towards the house, disinterested. Daniel had expected a comeback, their respective differences potentially allowing for an interesting topic of conversation, intellectual chess as it were, except it would be level one. A pawn against a queen.

"Have you always been rich then?" asked Liam.

Yet another one of Liam's unpolished inquisitions, hurtling from nowhere, inimitable in its blunt and unrefined manner. Fair play for the nobleman to rest his hand on the shoulder of the serf but certainly not the other way round. Liam was his gardener and certainly not someone he would be sharing the details of his wealth with. That was far too intimate. Daniel's head began to swim in a mild soporific fug. This weird out-of-body experience was a coping mechanism, normally reserved for Meredith when, on extremely rare occasions, she suggested they might go to bed early for some awkwardly alluded to rumpy-pumpy.

"Now that, Liam, is a fiendishly personal question, don't you think?"

Liam's eyebrows arched, his head wobbling from side to side, seeming unsure of his misdemeanour.

"Personal question? Is it? In what way?"

"Liam, you really do ask the funniest things." Daniel retorted with barely the faintest sign of humour. "I think we'd better talk about the beds and other jobs that need doing today," Daniel asserted.

Boundaries needed to be upheld. Liam was rebuked. Daniel lifted his chin, pushing out his chest.

"Well, I was born on a council estate, so your world and my world are a million miles apart, that's why I asked. I can't imagine what it's like having your life. Yet we're both blokes, so in some ways, we know each other well. Don't you think?" said Liam, insubordinately.

He was right and it was peevish to be so stuffy. Besides, Daniel didn't mind talking about Liam.

"What did your father do for a living?" Daniel asked.

"I never knew my dad. He left when I was a baby."

"Oh, I'm so sorry to hear that, Liam."

"Well, judging by what my mum says, I'm probably better off without him anyway."

"And your mum, where does she live?"

"Barnsley."

"Ah Yorkshire. Beautiful countryside. Is that where you're from originally?"

"Yup. Can't say I miss it much. I've been down south since I was sixteen. I was glad to get away."

"Why is that?"

"Nothing there for me. Bit of a misspent youth, shall we say."

Daniel caught Liam's gaze and saw a cold bitterness he hadn't seen before. A raw nerve perhaps? "And your mother, do you see her much?"

"Not really," Liam replied, distracted. "What about your parents?"

Daniel gave his knee-jerk default response when talking about his father. "Oh, my father was a marvellous man—" Then, realising how insensitive this might sound to someone who'd just told you they never had a father, he opted to be more candid. "Actually, my father was rather a bully. If I'm brutally honest."

"Oh. In what way?"

Bother! Liam looked so trustworthy and genuinely compassionate. *Why not open up to someone once in your life*, he thought.

"Well, he took to a leather strap if I misbehaved and once struck me so hard across the head with the back of his hand that I was practically unconscious." Talk about a sticky wicket, the lid to Pandora's box had been blown off—what on earth was he doing? Panic and shame sped like wildfire throughout his body: he'd just betrayed his whole family, not to a psychoanalyst but to a gardener! Who knew who Liam might tell this to? Broken glass words swilling around his tonsils, unable to take back. Had he momentarily lost his mind? The territory layered in trip wire.

"That sounds awful. Your own dad doing that to you when you're just a little boy."

It was true, a young boy, eager to play, run, laugh, love and do what all children do. Without warning, pangs of grief tumbled in from all sides like obese clouds.

Turning his head away, desperate to hide emotions, Daniel galvanised his will into full force, pushing everything back down. Back into the stiff-upper-lipped casket called self, and to what end?

Eyes closing, he took a gulp of air, his life was two-thirds through—what was there to lose? He'd already lost the better half of his life to self-restraint.

"It was hardly wonderful. Sent to boarding school at eight. He and my mother told me how lucky I was to be there. I detested it."

"Why would anyone send their kids to boarding school? That's awful."

"We sent all our children off to boarding school."

"Oh." Liam looked confused. "How come when you hated it so much?"

Daniel had asked himself this same question a hundred times or more. Meredith had been keen to send them too. They'd agreed their own educations had shaped them into the people they were, seeing themselves as part of an elite class that took one's place with an elite education, but really it had meant growing up too soon.

"I do regret it now. Particularly seeing the effect it had on Maya. She's never really forgiven us. I'm not sure any of them have."

"Do you talk to them about it?"

"Not really, no. It's not the done thing."

Daniel talked for over an hour, telling Liam of his childhood, the need for a warmer father; oddly though, Liam didn't talk much about his own childhood, mainly listened. Daniel told of his father being sent off to boarding school at six and had referred to it as a strengthening of character and independence. He was obliged to call his father, Sir, who'd been a captain in the Navy during the war. He ended up in a care home when Alzheimer's struck him in old age. On visiting, his father would break down and sob when it came time to leave. This was a man who'd never shown any emotion other than a controlling, cold anger. There was a peculiar sense of schadenfreude seeing him cry.

* * *

That evening, each in their single bed, a bedside lamp between them, Meredith asked what he and the gardener had had so much to talk about. Meredith was certainly not of the persuasion that one should acquaint oneself with the menial domestic help. She'd be devastated to find out that he'd talked so personally but, even worse, divulged things he hadn't even proclaimed to his wife.

"Cricket. You know me, once I get going."

"For over an hour?"

"Yes, I rather enjoyed myself."

"With the gardener?"

"Oh darling, don't be so Victorian. This is the twenty-first century, things have moved on. Sometimes you're so stuffy." Daniel was surprising himself: it was normally himself who could be a bit pompous and elitist.

"Well, just so long as you don't start inviting him into the house, dear," she said as though referring to a stray mongrel dog.

"Can you hear yourself? What is it that so upsets you about him?"

"We barely know him! God only knows what he gets up to in that caravan. It's creepy. Why you ever employed him in the first place, I don't know. We have gardeners, we don't need another one. In fact, why did you employ him?"

"Because he's organic and we care about the environment, don't we, dear?"

It was true that all their shopping was ordered from Waitrose and would certainly be mostly organic; they recycled all their bottles and no longer used plastic bags. They were also planning to have some solar panels installed onto their holiday chateau in the Pyrenees. A clear sign they did their bit to lessen their heavily trodden carbon footprint.

Meredith's eyes narrowed, her lips protruding into a stubborn pout.

"Well, I just don't know. He looks at me in an odd way."

"How do you mean?"

"I don't know, but he gives me the creeps."

"He's just rather intense, dear, that's all, try not to take it personally."

She rolled over, turning her back to Daniel.

"Goodnight, dear."

"Goodnight, darling," said Daniel, turning off the bedside lamp.

Engulfed by the dark, he ruminated over the conversation with Liam; the thought of seeing him again excited him.

SIX

Maya

"So, what's the thing with you and Ian then?" asked Troy.

Maya was driving her electric Nissan with Troy in the passenger seat. He'd been helping out at the Conscious Movement evenings for a few weeks now. Alongside the fact that he didn't have a car or bike was a fiendish attraction prompting the offer of a lift each week back to his place in Tottenham.

"How do you mean?"

"He's always hanging around you." Troy's broad London accent had a gravelly roughness to it as if corroded from smoking wood chips.

"Is he? He just likes helping to set up. He's part of the crew. Like you."

Briefly taking her eyes off the road, she encountered a quizzical look on his face.

"Oh, I thought you and him was going out together?"

"What? Me and Ian?" Maya threw her head back, chuckling. "Oh my God, no!"

"You're all a bit touchy-feely when you's together. He's always got his little mitts on you."

"He's always got his little mitts on me? You are funny, Troy. Ian and I are friends but, lovers?" Maya snorted.

"I was going to say, you're way above his league. You're beautiful, smart too. You could have any man you wanted."

Regrettably, this brought too much joy. Beautiful was not a word that sprang to mind when describing herself; this wasn't modesty either. Too short would be more accurate, nose too big. In fact when it came to it, there was quite a long list of imperfections— annoying white cracks of cellulite on the thighs, feet too big, hair too fine, legs too short, voice too plummy. Patriarchy had certainly done its bit, hammering away at her self-esteem, not to mention its uncle, the great advertising industry, objectifying women, exploiting them to believe they're a commodity, only having value when young, sexy and attractive. And is one still young in their thirties? Even as an aware feminist, it was still easy to get caught in the sexist snare. But it was okay to enjoy compliments. Most men weren't good at dishing them out. They spent most of the time searching for them, talking about themselves, extolling ideas that amounted to nothing of any great significance or that benefited anyone. Troy was always telling her nice things about herself, and he listened even if he didn't agree.

Troy was unreservedly opinionated. Whether it was too many foreigners in England and thank God for UKIP, who he'd voted for, being gay was unnatural, how capital punishment should be brought back, how women shouldn't have abortions, how Muslims are terror-ists and don't belong here, and on and on, endless bigotry spewing from a grubby tabloid mouth. The words contradicting the eyes. Did he believe what he was saying?

It was wrong to like this guy, and yet she couldn't help herself. They would debate things and he would throw in his counter argument:

Yeah, but sticking your cock up another man's arse is not normal, it's made for pussy, just like God intended.

If someone rapes and murders a child, then why should they live? I'd kill them myself if I had the chance, an eye for an eye.

People have abortions these days like it's normal, but there's a living thing in there wanting to be born.

Muslims come here and can't even speak our language and they want to treat this country like their own, yet we're not allowed to say anything in case we're called racialist.

And then he'd say, *My mate Abdul's missus had an abortion, I went to the hospital with her 'cos they didn't do it right,* and his eyes would moisten and his voice would soften as he spoke about how painful it was for her. The man was one big complex contradiction.

* * *

She pulled up outside Troy's flat which was above a dry-cleaner's on Lordship Lane.

Troy got out of the car and, after closing the door, tapped on the window for Maya to wind down.

"Fancy coming up for a cuppa," he said.

"Ooh, not too sure about that, Troy, not sure I can trust you," Maya said, playfully.

"I've got some sap-song-ee-lang-lang."

"A sap-song what?"

"You know, one of them posh teas you like. Got a Hobnob, too?"

Maya laughed. "Well, who can resist a Hobnob."

Entering Troy's flat, Maya was pained by its size, barely bigger than her bathroom. A wardrobe and chest of drawers took up half the room, a sink and cooking area a quarter, the rest just enough to squeeze in a tiny table, a chair and a neatly made single bed—a double would have been impossible. A mixture of aftershave, damp and oven cleaner pinched the air. Everything ultra-tidy and clean. Empty magnolia walls in dire need of a repaint. If homes represent a person's inner world, it could be assumed Troy was severely depressed.

"Home sweet home," declared Troy, indicating the surrounding box with his arms.

Maya was underwhelmed but didn't want to offend and at the same time was utterly transparent when it came to betraying her integrity.

"Don't worry, you don't need to say anything. It's only temporary until I find my feet," said Troy, rescuing her.

"It's bijou," said Maya, wanting to be sensitive.

"Yeah, right. Bijou, haha. Love it."

In the light, Troy became even more handsome; it was odd how someone so good-looking could have such ugly views of the world. Premature lines fissured his face, possibly from a life that had been tough. He was like one of those terribly clichéd, square-jawed, ruggedly handsome men you see in shaver adverts. There was something awry about him being in such a threadbare flea-trap. How can someone with his cocky, alpha male, get-out-of-my-way energy end up here? Maybe he was an addict of some kind?

Troy took off his jacket and hung it on the back of the door and headed towards the kettle.

"So, do you fancy some then?" said Troy, giving Maya the once-over, though it was more like the hundredth-over. Troy made no attempt to hide his blatant ogling.

"Some what?"

"What do you think?" he said, waving a packet of PG Tips in the air.

"Oh, tea. Have you got anything herbal?"

"You mean something a bit fruity?" He came over and lightly shoved her shoulder with his hand, peering down at her breasts, his lip curling. "I bet you do, don't you?"

Something began to stir, and she wasn't sure if it was a good thing. The excitement and anticipation were misplaced. Troy was being a dick and it was unnerving and arousing, both at the same time.

Casually pushing Troy out of the way, she wandered over to the window that overlooked various shop fronts and a pelican crossing.

As much as she liked a full-blooded man, she didn't need a volatile lothario.

"Maybe a chamomile, something to help me wind down a bit."

"Why? You feeling tense?" Troy's face was one big, disconcerting leer.

Outside below, it was closing time for the pubs and groups of people staggering by, laughing and shouting. Beneath the whooshing sound of cars, the beeping green man signalling people to cross could be heard. A police siren screeched like a high-speed whirring whip in the distance. Maya wondered whether she'd be heard if she were to shout for help.

Troy came over and leant against the wall, his arm crossing her head like an iron girder from his shoulder to his palm, anchored against the magnolia. His body, a barrier between her and the door. His lack of spatial awareness unnerving. Leaning in to her, the hotness of his breath warmed her neck.

"So how comes you come up here then?"

His eyes pierced into her in a way that said don't fuck about.

"Excuse me, Troy, could you back off slightly?" Maya said, forcefully.

Troy's face softened and he backed away.

"Sorry, am I being a bit of a knob? I just thought you felt like I do."

"How do you mean?"

"Come on, you know what I mean. I fancy you like mad. You must know that."

Maya did know; it was mutual. The idea of a casual rollick in the sack was appetising. Juices flowed whenever he was around but only the wolfish ones. It could never be serious. Intellectually, spiritually and emotionally, he was a neanderthal, but that didn't stop her fantasising about being shagged rotten by him. His fearless, pushy arrogance incited all kinds of deranged fantasies. The more masculine he was, the more feminine she could be. At the same time, there was something menacing about him that provoked an extra vigilance.

"I liked you as soon as I got an eye full of you that first night at your thing. I sees you giving me the eye too—you can't deny it."

Troy had moved to the bed, sitting on the edge.

Feeling particularly horny, Maya wondered if she was ovulating. "I'm not up for penetrative sex but we could do other things."

"Come here then," said Troy, patting the bed with his beefy hand. He didn't mess about. Most men these days were sensitive and respectful of women. Troy was the opposite: loutish and abrupt.

Idling by the window some more, her thoughts ticked over. Maybe it's better to be careful with this man? It had only been three or four weeks and he hadn't given much away. She knew nothing about him.

"What you waiting for?" said Troy.

Maya's phone buzzed in her bag. She pulled it out. It was a text from Ian.

Great night tonight Maya. So many people. The atmosphere was humming. Well done. Sweet dreams xxx

"Who's that from?" Troy asked.

"An admirer."

"Oh, yeah. Who?"

"God, you don't hold back do you, Troy. None of your business."

"I bet it's from Smug Face, innit?"

"Who?"

"Ian, it's him innit?"

"Smug face?" Maya became agitated. Even if Ian was unassuming and feasibly vanilla, he was a friend. "Do you not like Ian then?"

"He's alright. Wouldn't trust him though, seems a bit shifty." Troy stood up and approached Maya. He raised his hand slowly and stroked her face, looking into her eyes. Maya hated the fact that she'd become so wet and turned on by this caveman. He leant in to kiss her on the mouth, and she allowed it, his tongue entering her mouth, his warm hand cupping her breast.

Her Guru, Swami Gandalih said, *Trust more the man who hides nothing—for his heart is all the truer when he shows love.* In some respects, Maya knew where she stood. There was no political correctness, no ethical snobbery; he was a sexist, racist bigot. He wasn't trying to be nice—there wasn't an ounce of charm.

Maya felt herself being lifted off the ground. She wrapped her legs around his trunk. Her back against the wall, Troy pulled up her T-shirt and began to suckle on her breast, sucking hard as though determined to elicit milk. Maya's hands cradled his head, nursing him, like a baby. Legs gripping his waist, she was carried to the bed and thrown down.

"Just to be clear, we're not having sex," Maya reiterated.

Pulling down her jeans, Troy didn't respond.

She pushed him back with her hand.

"Troy, did you hear me!"

He stopped and looked at her, a licentious hunger in his eye.

"Yeah, course I did. I was thinking of a bit of the old pearl diving."

"Okay." Maya allowed him to pull off her jeans along with her knickers, feeling self-conscious as Troy's tongue slid along her vulva lips. It had been a long day and she wondered if there were unpleasant odours down there. On top of this, she hadn't shaved her legs for a couple of days and worried she may be stubbly.

The soft weight of Troy's hand rested on her naval, his finger pads scratchy. The licks were surprisingly delicate. Maya's pleasure began to intensify as he lapped away, thereupon eventually finding her clit. Oh, my fucking God, this guy was a pro. Maya grabbed the side of the bed and bit down on her lower lip. She could not allow Troy's cock inside her, but all she wanted now was Troy's cock inside her.

The orgasm came amazingly quick—normally there'd have to be thirty minutes of foreplay along with the vibrator—but Troy's tongue seemed to know just the right amount of pressure, making her yoni purr.

A few orgasms later, Maya had had her fill.

"Phew, I think I've been to heaven and back," said Maya.

Troy resurfaced.

"Nice," he said.

"So, what about you?"

Troy was still dressed whereas Maya was almost naked.

"Play with your tits for me!" he ordered.

Maya remained languid, rubbing her breasts as Troy unzipped his fly and took out his cock to masturbate. It was gratifying to see how much pleasure he got from looking at her breasts and the amount of gusto he put into rubbing his cock. His face screwed up in concentration, then slackening, eyes rounding, breath held as cum shot up into the air like a little firework celebration.

Troy flopped on the bed beside Maya, relieved.

This new bit of rough was perfect for scratching an itch. There was no danger of getting overly attached to him. Ethically she should have resisted, Troy being one of her students, but she justified her indulgence by reminding herself that *he'd* asked her out and *not* the other way round. At least that's how she thought it happened. Besides, they were both adults and could look after themselves.

SEVEN

Meredith

Why hadn't Daniel just cancelled the gardener? Having him there was bothersome, silly obligations to make him tea purely because Daniel had suggested it. He wasn't *her* new friend; he was Daniel's for God's sake.

She poured the hot water on the tea bag, not bothering to string the label around the handle, and headed out into the garden.

Summer had at last arrived a couple of weeks before it was supposedly midsummer.

Wearing a belted, ivy-green, pleated tartan tweed skirt, blouse buttoned up to the throat with an olive-green, diamond-quilted, sleeveless jacket, she'd obviously overdressed for such blistering heat. And there he was, shirtless, typical council estate builder, body all sweaty and tanned like an Arab.

Walking towards him, her hips sprouted a mind of their own, resulting in less command over them. Attempting to eradicate the pendulating wobble, she stiffened up into a more upright stride.

Approaching him, the tea was plonked on the ground, milk orbiting the murky brown tannin. No biscuits.

He had that dissecting look in his eyes, collaging her thoughts into a jumbled mess of duality: haves, have-nots. Cultured, uncultured. Young, old. Ugly, beautiful.

Her body had aged, the weight of gravity pulling to the ground what was once firm and pert.

She'd been quite stunning once—full lips, high cheek bones—but a hardness had set in, annihilating the softness that completes beauty.

It was a struggle to find conviviality when nearing him.

"Mr Bloomberg is not around today, but he said he'd appreciate you turning over the compost and tidying the main greenhouse, if you would be so kind."

"Sure. No problem."

About to walk away, she hesitated. Turning, feigning a look of someone attempting to work out a puzzle, she approached again.

"I expect you'll miss your little chat with Mr Bloomberg today?"

"Yeah, probably. Daniel's a really nice guy."

Her refrigerated composure dropped a few more degrees. Who did he think he was using first-name terms for her husband?

"So, tell me, what do you and, erm, my husband talk about that is so fascinating?"

It was a pain to talk as if referring to a mutual friend, yet nonchalance was the name of this particular game, heaven forbid anyone saw the dark pit of envy hidden away.

"Lots of things. Everything, you know—life. This and that."

The gardener was looking directly into her eyes, searching for a weak spot. Well, it would take more than that to intimidate her. Meeting his gaze with a laser glare, he shuffled on his feet, pinned like an insect.

"Yeees!" she drawled, quickly looking Liam up and down with obvious distain. "This and that, hmmm. Well, enjoy the rest of your day." Proceeding towards the house, his eyes burnt into her back like branding irons. The lawn stretching for miles, every step determined to maintain a steady walk. An uncontrollable life force thrumming inside, dominating the hips again, forcing pelvic muscles to stiffen twofold.

Once in the house, Meredith resumed her usual march, unsure of where to go. Deciding on the drawing room, she sat down on the sofa, picking up the Tatler, flicking the pages with a restless agitation. Landing on an article describing in detail where Prince William and Kate like to holiday, she was reminded it had been months since they'd had some time away.

She would insist that herself and Daniel visit the château in the Pyrenees for a month. Flights would be immediately booked and a call to Edith, the *gardienne*, would be made to let her know when they'd be arriving.

The thought of the château lifted her spirits with fond memories of frequenting there whilst the children were away boarding. The marriage once held mystery, adventure, fun, sex, or did it? It was hard to tell, it had been so long—maybe it had always been like this. Life had become rather tedious. Time was speeding up, piling on the years. There was still a vague appetite for sex, but this thirst hadn't been quenched for years, at least not in any satisfactory way. The late menopause didn't help, it was true, but Daniel rarely showed any interest. Did he find her unattractive? A lot of time and energy had been put into staying in good shape. The low-carb diet assiduously committed to through the advice of Casandra, her dietician.

An hour in the gym each day preventing the waist from expanding like other women of a similar age. Swimming, long walks.

Sex was never mentioned.

Of late, she wanted to bring it up more and more—surely that's allowed in these modern times?—but Daniel could be a grumpy sausage.

The eight-year age difference probably didn't help. According to online medical experts, it's common for men to occasionally struggle to maintain an erection in their early sixties. But it was impossible to talk about it; Daniel would get all sniffy, saying he had more important things to think about.

These experts also pointed out a mélange of other ways to enjoy sexual intimacy. *A fat lot of good that does.*

Daniel had never been terribly adventurous in bed, but au contraire, he was Marquis de Sade when it came to porn. When browsing online for *pleated tartan skirts*, Meredith stumbled on a previous search for *tarts in skirts,* which was not something she'd be searching for. Daniel had perilously neglected to cover his tracks, not realising in this modern age all gadgets were linked: phones, laptops, main computers. Sleuth-like, Meredith traversed further along the trail, pulling up previous searches, discovering various fetish sites he'd clearly engaged with, such as *Looking up Skirts, Cocks in Frocks and Naughty Teachers.*

In a marriage, really, one ought to be able to bring these things up, but Daniel would be mortified. It's like when someone breaks wind at high tea, you just don't point these things out, even if it is only the two of you.

Was it silly seeing it as a betrayal or comparable to being sexually discarded? If he could get excited by looking up women's skirts like some pubescent teenage boy then why couldn't he get excited by the real thing?

As for men in dresses, the mind boggled.

Did Meredith have the real thing when it came to sex? She was most certainly not enthralled by kinky games, at least of the role-play variety—sure there'd been the odd fantasy that had managed to escape the prim centurions—but really, even French kissing was so faded-a-memory, she couldn't be one hundred percent sure it had actually happened.

She'd been a good wife, never any objection to go along with anything Daniel was keen on, which mainly amounted to the missionary position. It was all dreadfully common or garden.

She had, though—well, almost certainly, possibly—orgasmed a few times, or at least what she'd experienced sounded very similar to what she'd read about, but these things were hard to know for sure. Daniel was only her second lover, so there wasn't much to compare it with. Colin Hathaway had been the first; it was still painful to think about him—even after all this time, it evoked regret. Picturing him still prompted a tingle, even after all these years.

The women on the *Looking up Skirts* website had looked barely eighteen years old. Maybe this was the reason why Daniel lost interest: she'd become too old and ugly, past her sell-by date. Since menopause, she worked hard to keep her weight down, but hair had grown thinner, the odd wiry, black bristle had found its way onto the chin, instantly plucked, and down below, well let's just say lubrication now comes in a bottle.

It wasn't so much the sex that was missing but the company, having fun.

All this mulling over sex was a fool's errand, never led anywhere, just endless frustrating circles.

She stood up and walked towards the window. The gardener was heading towards the main greenhouse. Swaggering. She wished she were eighteen again, or rather eighteen and someone else, someone daring, wild, free to follow her passion rather than always doing what she believed to be proper.

At nineteen, she'd met Daniel who, in her parents' estimation, held all the right credentials: wealthy, connected.

Love? Was it still there? Had it ever been there? He'd never been brutal; he was articulate, sensitive, kind, always remembered their anniversary. Maybe love is a silly romantic fallacy for the hoi polloi— better to be shrewd.

With her best years behind her, what was left?

And that stupid gardener just kept irritating her, and she wasn't quite sure why.

EIGHT

Troy

Twisting the plastic knob, a meagre trickle of lukewarm water drizzled to a stop, and though somewhat cheesed off with its incompetence, Troy remained largely upbeat as he stepped from the shower, teeny puddles dripping from him onto the honeycomb, vinyl floor. A musty stench of mildew like an old drain permeated the bathroom, despite the copious amounts of bleach used to scrub everything. It was a closet with a sink, shower and toilet, no window for aeration. To fit in, you had to be a diminutive contortionist, miraculously squishing each part into whatever space there was. It was shared with three other tenants in the house.

Troy was sprucing himself up before heading out to see Jezza. Unlike the others—in the waiting area or leaving as he went in, dabbing their eyes, blowing their noses, hangdog, no-hope saddos—therapy wasn't something Troy needed. It was a scam, a nifty few months off his sentence; all he had to do was turn up. Job done.

Jezza listened, nodding in all the right places like one of them dogs you used to get in the back of cars, while Troy talked. The whole facade was idiot-proof.

The session was the only thing booked for the day.

Pushing a tube hard against the edge of the sink and slowly pulling it down to the nozzle, Troy squeezed out the last remnants of stripy gunk onto a toothbrush. Brushing his teeth, he played with various facial expressions in the mirror above the minuscule sink. The thoughtful face wasn't bad; that would be the one used when being interviewed on TV.

Bending down he put his mouth to the water from the tap, swirling it round, spitting it out. His mildly stained, oven-chip teeth were something of a let down, but one day he'd get them done like everyone has done in America.

"So, when did you first find Jesus, Troy?" he said in mock American accent, the toothbrush now a mic.

"Well, some people find his face on a vegetable, a carrot or a potato, or maybe a cornflake, but I found him here"—Troy rubbed his chest—"in my heart, when I was doing bird."

Good answer; people should get a load of this. A YouTube channel—a million, no, a billion subscribers. The world should know that Troy Ward has a direct line to God. It was mad how no one had recognised his unique, philosophical slant on life.

"Jesus came to me in my cell, I thought it was a dream but it were real. And yes, Jesus is white for all those silly fuckers who say he's black. He told me, 'Troy, you's done enough time, mate,' and that very same day, I got a jam roll for good behaviour."

The audience was cheering.

"Or should I say, *God* behaviour."

Troy laughed at his joke, along with the imaginary fans.

"The Holy Spirit nudged me and said, 'Wake up you silly cunt,' pardon my French, and he said, 'True love is God.'"

He thought about this last comment, playing with it out loud.

"God is love ... to serve God is love, love is God." He liked that one the best.

"Yes, love is God." His eyes welled up and he leant into his reflection. "And I love God."

Interviewing himself was good practice for when fame came along— which it would, one day.

Chatting to himself always ramped up when on a high, and since meeting Maya, he'd been on cloud nine, ten, eleven and still climbing.

Maya wasn't just any woman. She was Mary Magdalene. Not like a prossy, though it had been surprising how game she was when she'd come to the bedsit.

She could see his worth, made him feel different from how other women had in the past. She needed him, just like he needed her. It wasn't just her tits, it was something else that he couldn't work out. He wanted to be with her all the time; he could talk about anything with her even though she was a total, fucking hippy.

He enjoyed thinking about her, wondering where she was, who she was with, what she might be talking about, that kind of thing. Maybe *enjoy* was the wrong word—there wasn't much choice, it was a compulsion, that tumbling feeling of falling in love with someone and everything else disappears, and you have to check up on them to make sure they're not lying and stuff like that.

* * *

Jezza was sitting crossed-legged in his chair, gold-ringed index finger toying with the tip of his nose, pensive. Only ten minutes left until the end of the session. Troy had been doing most of the talking, mainly about his past. Beneath the poker-faced smile, Jezza looked run-down. It was hard to tell his age, but guessing, around sixty. He was your legit counsellor that'd cost an arm and a leg but saw pro bono clients with *Back on Track,* a charity for those just out of prison.

The office was plush: Persian rug, an old wooden desk, antiquey nick-nacks meticulously placed about the room.

"And how are things with you and Maya?" he asked.

Troy had been enthusing about Maya for a few weeks now, telling Jezza how well they'd been getting on. How she was really into him. But today Jezza kept on about Troy's childhood, detention centres, boring shit like that.

"Pukka mate. She's sound. I reckon I've landed on my feet with this one."

Jezza looked dubious; he always looked dubious—maybe it was just his face. He didn't have that many facial expressions: there was dubious, doubtful, guess-what-I'm-thinking and I'm-very-mildly-amused-though-not-amused-enough-to-actually-crack-a-smile.

"What is it you like about the relationship?"

There was no simple answer to this. He felt excited when with her, turned on by her body, he liked that she didn't always agree with everything he said like other girls had done in the past. She had a mind of her own. She was also the poshest bird he'd ever been with.

"Don't know. She's nice, you know what I mean."

"Last week we talked about the possibility of you disclosing to her your prison sentence and the reasons you'd ended up there. How did that go?"

Another toe-curling question. Only a dozy git would tell a bird about prison, unless he wanted dumping. It was a case of having to be on the ball with this guy: how much did he liaise with the probation service? Keeping schtum about being a naughty boy would avoid any bollox Jezza had about him breaking some agreement.

"Sound. She ain't bothered. She accepts me as I am."

"That's great you told her. How did it feel telling her?"

"Didn't bother me. I am what I am. I ain't ashamed of what I done."

Jezza adjusted his position in his seat and cleared his throat.

"I know we've talked about this, Troy, but what you did was enough to get you a prison sentence. The man was in hospital with some serious injuries and your ex-girlfriend had two broken ribs and severe bruising to her face."

"Yeah, but like I've told you last week, she's a lying cow and they couldn't prove I'd hit her."

"But there are other women who've accused you of stalking, threatening behaviour, and psychological and physical abuse."

"Jezza mate, listen..."

"Jeremy."

"Sure, mate. Listen, you me both know women and how they can be, they act like they want you to be all sensitive, but in reality, they all want a real man."

"A real man?"

"A man who can defend his woman, a man who knows how to handle himself, someone who has balls."

It was Troy now who felt like the one with knowledge. Jezza was not a real man, most likely a man under the thumb, a man who was more into books than shagging his wife. He wouldn't get what it meant to be a real man, but in the real world, if there was a nuclear war, who'd have the best chance of surviving: Jezza with his books and sceptical eyebrows or Troy who knew how to look after himself and was a muff magnet.

"So, when you were violent towards your ex-girlfriend and her new partner, was that you being a real man?"

"Alright, that was a bit of a fuck up I grant you."

It had to be said, Jezza could be an irritating shithead. Up until recently, he'd been on his side, but now Troy was realising the truth—he was like everyone else. No one was on Troy's side. Everyone was out to get him, except Maya.

"Has any anger surfaced over the last week, any violent feelings or thoughts when you were together?"

"I love Maya."

"You love Maya? You've fallen in love with her?"

"For real, she's perfect. I can't think of anything I don't like about her. And she likes me too."

"Has she told you this?"

"Course she has, what you thinking I'm making it up? Jezza mate..."

"Troy, would you please try using my name, Jeremy. Why do you insist on calling me Jezza?"

"Jezza, it's short for Jeremy, in it."

"Do you see us as friends?"

The veins on Troy's forehead began to pulsate—was Jezza taking the piss? Perhaps a hint of sarcasm in his tone? His whole life people had taken the piss out of him. Permanently in the bottom class at school, clothes frequently either too big or too small, this is how he'd learnt how to handle himself, like that Johnny Cash song about the dad who gave his son a girl's name to toughen him up.

Being hard was the ultimate crown, it demanded respect. But like a king, you couldn't trust anyone; everyone wants to bring you down, take your glory. There are never any proper friends, just sidekicks who do what they're told, afraid of what you'll do to them if they don't. And now he'd got rid of his so-called mates, no longer liking them, too much like looking in a mirror. Troy wanted to change, move on, be someone better. Jezza though, a friend?

"Why would I see us as mates? Just 'cos I call you Jezza? Nah mate, I can't imagine us being mates."

"But would you like to be friends?"

What was this geezer on about? Was it a trick question? Did he actually want to be mates or what? Sometimes Troy found it hard to work out what Jezza was actually asking him. He looked at the clock hoping the session would end soon.

"What, you want to knock about together or something?"

"How do you imagine that might be?" Jezza's face was neutral, yet he was seriously messing with Troy's head. "I wonder if what you'd really like is a friend you can trust, show your feelings to. You give off the impression that you don't care, but I wonder if deep down you do care but that you don't know how to connect with people. You mentioned earlier that your mother was violent."

"I never said she was violent, I said she hit me."

"She betrayed your trust."

"Jezza ... sorry, Jeremy mate, all children got hit when I was a kid."

"She also locked you in the cupboard."

"Yeah, but not all the time."

"You also mentioned that your stepdad was violent towards you. With all this, Troy, it's understandable that it would be difficult for you to trust. I think all this calling me Jezza and mate is a way of keeping me at a distance. You don't want to see me as I am but as a fantasy. A fantasy friend who you don't need to know in any real way."

Gripping the chair, Troy's breath became shallow, stomach a pit of maggots. He'd talked about stuff like this before with Jezza and would prefer to not talk about it again. His parents had done their best and he wasn't one for dissing them. This was all in the past and how would dragging it all up help? It'd be like someone from a concentration camp watching old newsreels of Auschwitz—what would be the point?

"What has Maya told you to give you the impression that she's keen to be in a relationship with you?"

"Told me that she's never met anyone quite like me, that, that erm, I'm buff ... I don't know, loads of things. What, you want me to count them?"

"I'm just aware, Troy, that you've sometimes in the past misinterpreted situations and this has caused you to act inappropriately towards women."

Feeling more and more backed up into a corner, the session had become gruelling. Jezza was on his case and giving him the third degree, talking about the old Troy from some stupid criminal records obtained from the probation service. He'd moved on now.

"Well, we had sex, so I don't see how that'd be misreading the situation. Unless it was her way of just saying hello when she stuck her minge around my cock."

Jezza took a deep breath through his teeth, grimacing.

"Okay, that's an interesting way of putting it." Jezza looked at the clock. "We've come to the end. Maybe we can talk more about the sex next time."

Hopefully not, you cunt!

* * *

Outside the therapy room, the air around Crouch End was muggy. The long day loomed ahead. No job meant plenty of time to kill. Money was a bit of an issue, but with his entrepreneurial knack, Troy was sorted. Recently he'd broken out into a lucrative business selling gadgets. A nice little earner indeed. It was amazing that people, particularly in areas like Crouch End, would wander around with a grand's worth of tech on them, but today was not a day for thieving, especially not in Crouch End—that'd be like pissing on his own shoes being there on a regular basis. Anyways, he had other plans.

He took a 210 bus over to Hampstead Heath. Still a bit wound up from the third degree.

Parliament Hill Fields was busy with picnickers, dog walkers, office workers eating their lunch, enjoying the sun.

Sitting on the grass, usual spot by the tennis courts, Troy took out some ham sandwiches and a flask from his rucksack. Tilting the flask over the cup, careful not to spill the tea, he pondered over what Jezza had said. *Turns out Jezza's a bit of a knobhead really, not an ally after all.* Truth be told, Jezza was one of those blokes that Troy couldn't stick, the kind who thought they were better than you because they went to university, own a house, have kids, not that he knew for sure any of these were true, not yet anyway, but ten grand says he's right.

What did Jezza know about passion? Fuck all!

Maya knew a good thing when she saw it. Troy wasn't one of those stiff geezers who thought they were it. He imagined kicking the shit out of Jezza. *See how clever he is then.*

He looked over to the flats nearby where Maya lived; going into his rucksack again, he pulled out some pocket binoculars. No one could tell he was looking into her flat—they would just think he was a birdwatcher, which he was, just not the feathery kind.

NINE

Liam

Mr and Mrs Fisher in their nineties still managed to drive a car generally well below the speed limit. Once, Mrs Fisher was driving so slowly along the main A-road near their home that a mile-long queue of traffic trailed behind them, which she was completely oblivious to. If there was ever congestion around Woking, Liam would think to himself, *Ah-ha, the Fishers have gone shopping.*

When using their toilet and seeing how fastidiously they maintained their three-bedroom house—everywhere immaculately neat and tidy—it was clear the house ran like a tight ship, regimented to the highest standard, meals at the same time each day, trips to the supermarket every Tuesday morning. Quite admirable really if you like that kind of thing.

Conventionality and order extended beyond the house; if there were a prize for the most soul-destroying, unimaginative garden, they'd win it, hands down. The plants were the generic kind, the top pick for supermarket car parks: choisya, laurels, hydrangeas, pyracantha. A stone effect bird bath stood in the centre of the perfectly squared lawn, edged with clear, straight lines. Three hours at the Fishers' was like a flogging.

The main task was to make sure everything was pristine: no weeds, tedious trimming of endless lawn edges. At the Fishers', death was in the air— not theirs, his: Liam's spirit could barely breathe with all this order and control. The universe stagnant, the spiralling cosmos a windowless box.

In order to break the clip-clip-clip monotony of the edging sheers, he took a break to do some weeding, eradicating wild revolutionaries amongst the unmerciful ordinariness.

On his knees in the darkened undergrowth between being stabbed to death by a pyracantha and the intense shoe polish fragrance of choisya, Liam teased out taproots with his trowel. Hesitancy, along with a vague sense of wrongdoing, was felt towards the dandelions, thistles and buttercups and all the other unwanted plants that had strayed into the wrong place, now tossed carelessly into a barrow like discarded solders into a grave.

Life was life, no matter what form it took.

Weeds, like the fox or crow, personified the gypsy, unwelcome by the villagers. He'd met the local Romanies, destroying any idealised view he'd previously had.

Upon selling a vintage caravan to one particular Romany, who wanted it for shows, he'd been invited onto the site where he chatted with the man and his family in their chalet fixed to a concrete foundation. Quite the honour for a gorger as they fiercely protected their world from the beady eye of social services and the moral masses brandishing their sanctimonious pitchforks.

The traveller women came over as oppressed, bossed around, trapped in arranged marriages. There was no romantic—if somewhat clichéd—passionate flamenco dancing beneath an endless sky to fiddles and guitars; the only flickering light came from a ninety-inch-wide plasma TV screen rather than any blazing fire. Gaudy ornaments, such as miniature *lifelike* gypsy caravans advertised on the back of a TV guide, sat on mantelpieces above electric fires, trying to recapture the nostalgic essence of old, ancestral ways. But since they'd been pretty much outlawed, only the blood remained, the rest was left by the wayside.

Alcohol and occasionally stronger drugs were used as self-medication for these disenfranchised foxes and crows, no longer allowed to roam freely. Liam saw himself more akin to the traditional Romany, except without the vardo wagon or hereditary line. Instead of seasonal crop picking it was weed pulling; maybe his roots lay in a previous incarnation.

Three hours of life unlived, self-respect reduced to a grovelling hand, he went to the door, letting Mrs Fisher know he'd finished for the day—putting the cash in his grubby palm, she commented in a plummy voice that he'd "worked like a black man," and then added, "Oh no, but they don't work, do they!" This was uncomfortable, certainly not as humorous as intended—far from it: it only served to expose her prejudice and parochial, little Englander view of the world.

Beneath the old lady's knitted apple-pie face lurked crabby, strained wires. She'd been brought up in British Colonial India in the 1920s and 30s, and though he partly wanted to forgive her because of her age, he had the mind to tell her how obscene and ignorant her comment was and that most black people probably worked harder in one week than she had in her whole life.

But nothing was said; he didn't laugh either, just gave her a blank look hoping it would speak volumes, but more likely she failed to pick up this nuanced, possibly too subtle, facial coding. A shot of cowardice and chagrin pricked Liam's conscience. He'd inadvertently colluded in her bigotry.

This ninety-something little old lady was strangely frightening and not to be answered back. Something about her was reminiscent of Margaret Thatcher's iron-ness whom Liam should have been too young to remember, but being born in a mining area, there were certain people you were not allowed to forget—the macabre image of Thatcher's effigy being burnt on Guy Fawkes night when he was a toddler would be forever imprinted on his brain.

Mrs Fisher was the epitome of the British Colonial Empire, the ruling class: her tone, her clipped way of speaking. But what really bothered Liam was it reminded him of when his mother told him how her parents had visited London in the mid-1970s and told her how there'd been signs on pub doors that said, 'NO BLACKS, NO IRISH AND NO DOGS'. How could people be so small-minded?

On the other hand, Mrs Fisher was always cordial and pleasant. Bringing him tea and cake, showing appreciation of his work. Even buying a small gift at Christmas. Could he forgive her racism? If she had her own way, she'd probably bring back slavery at the drop of a hat. As nice to him as she was, he was always glad to get away from that house.

He stuffed the crispy notes into his pocket, desperate to get back to life and the natural order of things that existed all around his caravan.

* * *

Pulling up to Bentley Farm, Liam got out of his van to open the gate. A faint smell of elderflower wafted on the air. Driving the beat-up, old van down the track through the field, young heifers danced aside, kicking up a sweet, dry dust from the scattered hay. He drove past Bentley's farmhouse, over the brow of the hill to the end of the track where he parked the LDV. No longer in the sight of the farmhouse, he walked through the privately owned woodland and into a clearing where the caravan resided. The cool, translucent canopy served to keep the caravan from becoming an oven in such a heat as the day was. It was funny to think Daniel owned all this. The only other people seen down there was Kevin Bentley taking a bunch of bank managers and such like, dressed up in deerstalkers and tweed, wandering around with rifles, searching for pheasants. A thousand quid they'd pay to shoot the slowest bird in the world, birds that could barely fly. Liam wanted to tell them he'd catch them one with his bare hands for a hundred quid—not that he would really, he'd rather shoot the bank managers; for that he'd pay a thousand quid, easily.

The caravan was a 1960s Royale, a stunning piece of twenty-two-foot retro vintage bought locally. It had a classic sixties shape, a curved, art deco, streamlined lanterned roof, allowing extra light. Entering, a bouquet of sawn wood mingled with smoke, herbs and spices allured the nostrils. Pretty much a shell when bought, no electric fittings—gas lighting was still being used in the 1960s. In four years, he'd devoted his heart and soul to refurbishing the inside. Everything was natural, recycled wood: beech floorboards picked up at a reclamation yard, planed down at the local sawmill and laid. A large slab of oak along with its bark, planed, sanded and waxed, became the table. He'd built a bed and cupboards and replaced all the panelling with larch. The fireplace was the original and still intact, around it recycled tiles found online that had come from an old Victorian bakery. A cast-iron chimney led up out of the roof. The door had a circular porthole with a stained-glass window depicting a bright yellow sun, its red rays rising over rolling hills. Even the cooker was from the sixties to keep with the retro style. Cheerful orange, yellows and sky blues lit up the space. With the original split-front windows, the caravan never lacked light during the day. Everything was kept clean and in order: his books and CDs all above his bed, the rugs shaken out every couple of days. Liam was houseproud and there was always some new tweak he was planning to add to his home.

Outside the caravan was a fire pit and a small veg patch. A quick walk away from the caravan was his compost loo, and round the back of the caravan was a shower: a large watering can pivoted on a hook, with twine on the nozzle which could be pulled to release the water.

Liam took a seat in a rickety, old wicker chair kept outside, admiring the view. The little owl, a frequent visitor, hopped onto a fence post nearby. Unlike most owls, these came out during the day. Liam watched it as it made its distinct, high-pitched yelps. Sitting there, he had a clear, warm feeling of appreciation. The richest man in the world. No computers, no TV, no YouTube, Facebook or Twitter. He wasn't bothered about being famous or wealthy like he had been in his youth. All that needing attention to feel like you exist.

He thought about those who live in Elephant and Castle, where he'd once spent a few weeks, and was sad for them not having what he had; he thought of those having to work in offices, being cooped up all day like battery chickens, watching the clock tick the years away. *Yes*, his thought echoed back, *I am the richest man in the world,* in that moment.

Elated so much by the surroundings, he didn't bother to go into the caravan but sat relishing the moment, amazed at how the simple things in life were often the most profound.

Sometimes on an evening he'd go for a walk and find a spot and lie flat on the ground, looking up, not caring how odd he might appear if someone were to see him. It was an impulse to connect his whole body to this beautiful, turquoise gravity ball, spinning and dancing around its local star that right now was falling towards the horizon in this strange, infinite mystery.

A young group of heifers wandered over, treading with both trepidation and curiosity. Remaining completely still in the wicker chair, they came closer. The slightest move and they'd be off. Their ears rotated like radars, listening attentively for danger, their noses keen for each minute particle of scent. After a few moments, they were up close, their raspy tongues and wet noses exploring this funny looking being. Liam allowed it to go on for a while, finding it amusing and oddly tantalising as he wondered about these strange, other beings. Then, lifting a hand to scratch his nose, they jolted and were off, jumping away from him, tearing back into the herd.

With no inclination to enter the caravan, Liam decided to wander down to the stream less than five minutes away. Once there, he plonked himself on the ground, his back against an alder, watching water chatting away, passing over stones, bearded moss gliding in the same direction. Above, midges hovered in a synchronised dance, appearing random and chaotic yet holding some geometrical form within the hazy swarm. The dappled shade above the stream cooled the air which Liam drank as though his lungs were cupped hands, tasting the sweetness and flavour of the woodland. Nearby, the dusk light threw a magical glow over everything, illuminating all the colours, a song thrush repeating its complex melody to all that would listen. Everything was in its place, in perfect unison. Liam took off his work boots and socks and carefully dipped his feet into the invigorating stream which both cooled him down and brought him more fully into his sensual body. As the rippled, golden water flowed over his feet, the drift of time became ever more conscious, like a dandelion seed eternally riding on the breeze.

TEN

Maya

Maya enjoyed her jollies. Being the centre of attention wasn't the only reason she relished holding court—though she couldn't deny this was part of it—simultaneously she enjoyed being of service. Hosting informal get-togethers was her forte. The swami had said, *The generous heart is always fed, but the greedy heart is in a state of perpetual hunger.* And it was true: the more she gave to others, the more she was nourished.

Her colourful posse of around a dozen Conscious Movement regulars had gathered for a soirée on top of Parliament Hill to watch the solstice sun set over London.

A jazzy array of Aztec and Indian blankets were strewn across the grass whilst randomly placed around was a banquet of various salads people had bought along: quinoa made golden with turmeric; roasted pumpkin, sesame and sunflower seeds in shoyu sauce; rocket drizzled in extra virgin olive oil and aged balsamic; raw red cabbage, carrot and beetroot; potato in dairy-free mayo; tomato with fresh oregano and thyme—from the deli there were kalamata olives, pots of humous, bread sticks, grapes, strawberries, guacamole, Moroccan couscous. Each person had brought their personal bottles of water with cartons of fruit juice to share.

After a year of exchanging personal stories, dancing their deepest truths, endeavouring to attain authentic camaraderie, the small alternative satsang interacted easily.

Troy, who hadn't arrived yet, wouldn't fit in, but rather than feeling jittery, it amused her. The monotony of life could be so mundane; sometimes things needed stirring up. She loved her little dance troupe, but it could all get a bit pious, each one trying to be more peaceful and Buddhist than the next.

Being spiritual was all well and good, but surely every aspect of life had a spiritual kernel, even bigoted, hardened men on the borderline spectrum who didn't mince their words.

Troy's no-nonsense approach to life was refreshing. He broke the rules, and Maya had spent her life obeying too many silly rules.

At boarding school, she'd learnt quickly that you never show anyone what you're feeling, as this was seen as the ultimate weakness. She knew now, as an adult, these rules were detrimental to her well-being, but they were so ingrained, she couldn't help herself. Troy was the antidote to this, a man who didn't think before he spoke, saying whatever came into his head. Everyone else was considered and extra careful before uttering anything, and it always made Maya distrust them a little. It was obvious, for example, that Ian was longing to have sex with her, but he would never in a million years mention this.

In the distance, towards the ponds, a silhouette was making its way up the hill. The clockwork, side-to-side swagger made Troy instantly recognisable. Maya gave him a wave to let him know where they were; he waved back with a slight raise of the hand.

Nearing the top of the hill, Troy came more into focus with his wrap-around shades, carrying a plastic Tesco's carrier bag. She wondered if she would kiss him. No one knew that she'd allowed Troy's uncultured tongue to spin in the vortex of her base chakra. She wasn't ashamed of him, she just didn't want him thinking they were now on the bus to coupledom. She opted to simply hug him, immediately feeling his hand on her bottom, giving a large squeeze.

His body oozed testosterone. Peering around, smiling at the group, he said hello to various faces.

Dipping his hands into the Tesco bag, he brought out some ham slices, Doritos and a four-pack of lager, adding them to the feast.

Buddhist guy with the unpronounceable name also arrived shortly after, carrying his djembe drum. He carefully placed his vegan sweet potato curry to the spread. Maya got up to welcome him with a hug; there was no bottom squeezing.

"Alright mate," Troy said to Buddhist guy, going over to pat him on the back. "How's it going? Gonna give us a tune then on the bongo?"

"Sure, later. Wow, this is super impressive, Maya, so much good food."

"Oh my God, I certainly didn't make it all. Everyone here brought something," Maya replied.

"Sorry, mate, what's your name again?" asked Troy.

"Candrasurya."

Maya was determined to get this right, it sounded like Sandra—Surreal—Candra—sir—ria. Yes, she had it ... maybe.

"Where's that from then?" asked Troy.

"It's Buddhist."

"Alright, so it's not your real name then?"

"Yes, it's my real name. I was ordained."

"What were you called before then?"

"Gavin."

Maya stifled a snigger. If only he still called himself Gavin, it would be so much easier to remember, even if not as exotic. Gavin helped himself to a paper plate, piling food onto it.

Ian wandered over to join their conversation.

"Hey, Candrasurya, how's it going, man?"

Of course, it was inevitable that Ian would be able to pronounce his name.

"His real name's Gavin," Troy joked.

"Troy, hi. How are you?" said Ian, as if he hadn't already noticed Troy. Troy who had referred to Ian as *Smug Face*.

"I'm good, mate, never better."

Both Troy and Ian had big smiles on their faces as if BFFs.

"I'm curious, Troy, what do you do for a living?" Ian asked, jumping straight in.

"Why, you looking for a job?" Troy threw back.

This catty face-off between them was dull. Sandra Surreal managed to escape by joining another conversation.

Ian took off his jacket and underneath was wearing a bright, blue Hawaiian shirt covered with red yachts.

"So do you work out, mate?" asked Troy, which was odd as Ian was definitely not someone who looked like he worked out. His arms were spindly and white like pipe cleaners.

The conversation was sad. Maya was all up for truth and honesty, but this was just pathetic. It was just cock wrestling. She leant back on her elbows, tuning out of their banter. Not far away she could hear the cooing of a pigeon settling down to roost in a gnarled, old oak.

Lulled into a trance by the soporific sound of the bird, she found herself with the peculiar sense that the people around her had been sucked into another dimension, where hidden characteristics were exposed to her eyes only. Ian was a whiny, scrawny kid, retreating into his head as though it were a safe house, away from the harsh judgements of a bullying world. Troy was terrified of everyone, puffing his chest out like a panicked chimp, making sure his monkey noises were the loudest. Sandra Surreal was on a stage, needing everyone to notice how special he was in his quiet, zen-like way.

Over the city in the distance, the sun transformed into a flaming tangerine, hovering over the gherkin, about to be juiced.

"Hey, Candrasur ... sur ... reel?" said Maya

"Candrasurya," he replied.

"Gavin," said Troy, becoming tiresome.

"Fancy playing your djembe? I need to dance as the sun goes down," asked Maya.

There was an almost unanimous cheer. Troy, who maybe hadn't heard, took one of his ham slices from the packet and put it in his mouth and finished off a can of lager.

Sandra Surreal started to slap some rhythmic patterns on the drum. He was good. The steady pulse of high and low tones rumbled across the ground, kicking everyone into action, animating and galvanising their limbs. It was magic seeing all the shadowy forms against the fiery sky. A heathen band of writhing torsos.

Maya approached Troy, who was the only person not moving. She reached out a hand, but he was like a pylon concreted into the ground, a zillion volts in his head. Maya let him be with his ham slices and moody stasis.

In the jumping and arm flinging jubilance, Ian shimmied over and took her by the hand, twirling her around, which she delighted in. They brushed up close together. She could taste his movement, and for all his so-called smugness, he was no shrinking violet when it came to boogying on down.

The clan began to weave in and out of each other until the sun had fully set and there was just a sky alight with oranges and red hues.

Troy remained pensive, looking down the hill, drinking his can of lager and finishing off the ham slices.

There weren't many things more enjoyable than the energy of the whole tribe in synchronised formation like an old Hollywood musical. Dancing is as old as the universe; everything is a dance. The moon dances around the earth, the earth around the sun, electrons, atoms, molecules are all part of a cosmic dance. Maya was like a whirling dervish in which dancing took her closer to God.

The tempo wound down, inciting bodies to flop onto the ground having honoured the god, Ra. Sated, Maya sat down. Next to her was Nadia. Nadia was beautiful in her gorgeous, black skin; she was the darkest woman Maya had ever seen. Her eyes were sparkly and raven, going on forever. Her body voluptuous and soft, made for cuddling. Nadia was the epitome of everything a woman should be. Nadia had recently joined the Conscious Movement cortege. They'd both chatted a few times at the Conscious Movement evening, and Nadia was always amicable. As they chatted, Maya mentioned she had some tension in her neck which prompted Nadia to offer a back rub. Removing her top, the warm night air kissed her breasts, a reminder of life's pleasures.

Nadia's fingers worked their way into clenched knots, loosening them like decaying teeth desperate to be pulled from an agonised jaw.

"Whoa, you got it, you hit just the right spot," said Maya.

"What have you been doing, girl, to get so tense in there?" Nadia said in her bouncy Caribbean accent.

"I don't know, lugging speakers? It's always tight in that bit."

Nadia's hands glided across Maya's shoulders like dolphins through water. The sponginess of her palms absorbed more than just the aches and pains, they touched a younger part, a part that wanted to nuzzle into Nadia's ample bosom and be told things like, *You're my precious little angel, I'm going to take care of you.*

"You need to relax more," said Nadia.

"I know. I need more sex."

Nadia burst into bubbling laughter.

Troy, who had gone quiet, was looking in the opposite direction. Even the back of his head made it obvious he was pissed off about something.

"You should try one of these, Troy. Ian gives very good massages."

"You're alright, I'm fine as I am," said Troy, not turning to look at Maya.

"Men are a bit funny when it comes to touching each other," said Ian.

"Yeah well, can't be too careful," said Troy.

"How do you mean?" Ian responded.

"Well, no offence mate, but I'm not gay."

"Does touching another man make you gay then?" said Ian.

"Don't know, mate, you tell me?"

"Even if I was gay, so what?"

"In the Bible, it says, *Do not have sex with a man as you do with a woman for it is detestable*," said Troy.

Troy had everyone's attention now.

"So, you think being gay is wrong?" asked Nadia.

"It's unnatural, yeah, but each to their own, though it's still a sin."

"And polygamy, is that a sin?" Maya threw in, redirecting the conversation.

"Yeah, polygamy is a sin too," said Troy.

"Actually, the Bible has quite a lot of polygamy in it," said Nadia.

"Oh, that'll suit me then," Maya replied, making them both laugh.

"Go on, Troy, have a massage. You look like it'll do you good," said Maya.

"I'm not gay, by the way. And if I was, you wouldn't be my type," said Ian.

"Oh, so what's your type then, Ian?" asked Nadia.

"A man who's sensitive and gentle," said Ian, unfazed.

"What, you saying I'm not sensitive enough for you then?" asked Troy.

"It's not the first thought that comes to mind," Ian replied.

"Are you having a massage or what?" said Maya.

"Fuck it, alright then, why not."

There was a cheer as Troy took off his shirt. There was even a jokey *ooh-la-la* from one of the women. Maya gasped as she was unexpectedly met in the last of the fading light by the sad, pained blue eyes of Jesus tattooed across Troy's chest. Scarlet blood dripping from a crown of thorns, a lone tear trickling from his eye, his face gaunt and hopeless. She concluded it was the Robert Powell Jesus from the seventies.

"Fuck, Troy, you kept that a bit of a secret, didn't you?" said Maya.

"Not really, just not in the habit of taking my clothes off in public, like you."

Everyone began to gather around to take a closer look.

"If you suck your stomach in, does he wink or anything like that?" said Ian.

"Silly cunt!"

"It's so well done, all the detail, he looks a bit like Bin Laden, don't you think?" said someone else.

"Are you giving him a massage or what, Ian?" prompted Maya.

Ian dug his fingers into Troy's shoulders. Nadia had finished on Maya, and Maya put her top back on. She took some grapes and leant back to watch Ian and Troy silhouetted against the city lights in the distance. Seeing a man touch another man fascinated her; she felt like David Attenborough coming across a rare breed of animal. Men, unlike women, rarely touched each other in a sensual way. As a child, her brothers only ever had fights, her dad, even now, still didn't do hugs, and even the men who came to her evenings when landed with another male danced like chickens on a hot plate.

Troy looked like he was receiving colonic irrigation rather than Ian's soft touch, and it was soft. Ian had given Maya some of her best shoulder rubs.

"Troy, try and relax a bit, maybe close your eyes. He's not going to hurt you, are you Ian? He's very gentle," Maya reassured.

Ian's body leant into Troy like a man drilling a pneumatic drill into solid rock, his thumbs kneading the taught, muscular armour-plating, searching for something pliable and soft.

"Breathe!" Maya suggested.

"Shut the fuck up, I'm enjoying this."

And he was, she could tell. His brow was easing into a smooth calm. Ian had also closed his eyes. What would happen if Ian worked his way down to Troy's cock and she was to go over and stick her tongue in Troy's mouth? Would he enjoy it?

Troy and Ian made love for another ten minutes in Maya's head, and even if they hadn't in reality, at least she may not have to hear the term *Smug Face* anymore.

"Cheers Ian," said Troy after they'd finished.

"You're very welcome, Troy," said Ian.

Her job was done: she'd served both of them.

* * *

By eleven, everyone started to leave, taking their Tupperware, blankets and drums.

Maya and Troy walked down the hill towards her flat. Troy had been there before but only to help with shifting the gear for her classes. Nothing had happened since the night at his bedsit.

Watching Troy over the course of the evening reinforced the knowledge that there was never going to be much of an intellectual rapport between them, which wasn't the worst thing in the world. There'd been lots of men who'd waxed lyrical about freedom, but they were always bound to their intellects.

In an odd way, Troy not joining in when everyone else let loose gave him kudos. He hadn't conformed—he'd been a moody git, not giving a shit about what anyone else thought. Sitting there eating his unethical ham slices and drinking his unruly cans of lager. And his outrageous tattoo was a real hoot for Maya. He was a strange alien underworld that a part of her sought to gravitate towards. They arrived at Highgate Road, a moment away from her flat. Her mind was made that she'd let him stay the night—after all, what was there to lose?

Turning towards the direction of her flat, from out of the night, a lone figure staggering along towards them shouted from across the road.

"Troy! Is that you mate?"

"Shit!" said Troy, just loud enough for Maya to hear.

The man crossed the empty road, zigzagging, attempting to walk a straight line.

"Troy, my man. Good to see you," he said, reaching out a hand graffitied in Indian ink dots, crosses and a tiny swastika.

"Gazza. Y'alright mate," said Troy, taking Gazza's hand firmly.

"Fucking 'ell you cunt, long time no see," said Gazza, slurring his words.

"Hi Gazza, I'm Maya," Maya said, introducing herself.

"Alright darlin'," he said, then turning to Troy, "Aye-aye," losing some balance as he turned to look at her. His eyes had that deadened look that addicts sometimes have when they've French kissed with the devil on some bad trip.

"Where've you been? Last I heard, yous was in Pentonville. How long's you been out this time, then?"

"Fucking hell, mate, keep it down, you're embarrassing me. You're pissed as a fart."

Maya was intrigued. Troy had been in prison. No surprises there. You'd have to be naïve to think otherwise. Maya was not naïve—a wild femininity allowed her to see the soul of a man.

"Come on, let's go," said Troy to Maya, pulling her away from Gazza.

"Nice mate, yeah, still a prize cunt then?"

Maya noticed the muscles in Troy's jaw tighten. He spun round and took hold of Gazza by his T-shirt, as if in a melodramatic soap opera. She almost shouted in a mock, loud East End accent. "Cam on babe, 'e ain't worf it!" But it wasn't funny because this wasn't a soap, it was real.

"Come on, Troy, he's drunk, let it go."

"What, worried I'm going to tell your bird what a nutter you are? He likes to hit women you know! How many ribs was it?"

Okay, so maybe the soul-locating system was in need of a service as she had missed this. Troy *likes to hit women*. He was a woman-beater on his way to her home, to stay the night.

Troy, letting go of Gazza's T-shirt, walked away, counting his breaths. After a few yards, he arrived at a lit-up plastic advertisement on a bus stop. His face screwed up like chewed gum, he pounded his fist into the glossy image. Somewhat ironically, the ad selling toothpaste displayed a smiling woman who would be toothless if she were real.

"Fuck!!" was all he said.

Maya didn't quite know what to do. Gazza stumbled off back across the road, a wandering apparition on his way to spook another mortal.

The swami had said, *We are all mirrors to each other's soul, there are no enemies, only shadows in which we hide.*

Maya had never been one of those sweet, little girls who liked ponies, dolls or glitter. She'd liked Doc Martens boots, short, cropped hair and devouring autobiographies of ex-junkie rock stars. As a teen, she'd been quite a force of nature—she knew what it was like to punch a bully in the face, grab a prefect by the hair in toilets, scream 'fascist bitch' in a teacher's face.

Prison might be there to reform people, but it failed to see that real freedom was inside and not outside the self, and that the inside incarceration was much harder to escape. And even if you did reform, we're so institutionalised that we just keep reoffending.

The puritanical judgement was raising its head and it spoke in a voice not dissimilar to her mother's.

She wasn't going to end up like that cold bitch. She was willing to see the heart of Troy. No one is born bad: bad people are wounded people.

Troy remained at the bus stop.

She walked over to him and put her hand on his shoulder.

* * *

Sex with Troy wasn't the kind of sex you wanted to tell your friends about: he did all the right things, but Gazza's eerie words kept haunting Maya. Even the ribbed condoms she pulled over Troy's cock were a pathetic cosmic reminder. *So how many ribs was it, Troy?* she wondered. She could have just asked him, but a part of her hadn't wanted to know, which was worrying. Three ribs maybe? Broken or bruised? Who was the *she*?

Had he punched her? Kicked her? Was it an accident? Had she fallen? People tend not to get locked up for accidents.

She'd ask him, when the time was right.

ELEVEN

Meredith

Meredith and Daniel ate together, watched TV together, went on holidays together, were always at home together, yet it could easily be said they were never genuinely together. There was an unspoken contract—a tacit prenup—in which they had agreed not to let the other be privy to anything indelicate, too intimate, their deepest dreams, their disappointments, their jealousies, their innermost hopes, and there was certainly no talk regarding copulation. It was all hermetically sealed within a psychic vault, akin to the kind you'd expect to find in an impossible heist movie.

But a bête noire was beginning to expose fine gossamer fissures across their reputable veneer, like crazing on old porcelain.

Everything had got a bit dry. Maybe it was the menopause—could menopause suck moisture from the air? Her skin felt prickly, as though wrapped in coarse wool. Life needed moisturising, a pamper. A week in the spa wouldn't do it. It needed to be something more substantial.

Daniel patted his mouth with a napkin, having just polished off some braised venison with rosemary. This was a favourite of his that Meredith cooked to a Michelin three-star quality. Even as a young debutante, she'd prided herself on being a dab hand in the kitchen. She topped up Daniel's glass with more Bordeaux, having watched him guzzle down the first with dinner.

"Darling, I've been feeling rather beastly and decided that I desperately need a break and I'm afraid I've booked us flights for Carcassonne next week. I know it's frightfully short notice, but I truly need to visit *Le Nid*." *Le Nid* or *The Nest* was their chateau in the French Pyrenees.

"What!" Daniel exclaimed, close to spurting his claret across the dining table.

Meredith repeated herself, almost verbatim—she'd been rehearsing the lines all day.

"I can't just leave everything like that. Why on earth didn't you ask me first?"

"I know, I know I should have, sausage. I'm very naughty—I did it on the spur of the moment without thinking. I suppose we don't have to go—I can cancel the flight. I am sorry, it was very inconsiderate of me."

"Dear, it's just... Darling, I... There's so much to do."

"Like what?"

Meredith knew this was nonsense. There was never anything to do. There'd be nothing to do at Le Nid either, but it was a change, they'd relax, and it was an opportunity to put some pizzazz back into their tired wedlock. Meredith had fond, nostalgic memories of the two of them at Le Nid. It was a place they'd gone to when young— free of their children and responsibility.

Daniel was easy to read; she could see him racking his brains, unable to come up with anything that urgently needed doing.

"I have lots of paperwork to do!"

"What kind of paperwork?"

"Well, I told Simon I'd look over some documents for him and..."

"Darling, couldn't you do that at Le Nid?"

"It's just very short notice. Why don't we go in a couple of months?"

"When you were young, you were so much more adventurous."

"That's because I *was* young!"

"But, sausage..." Daniel liked being called *sausage*. It softened his heart, making him more malleable, appealing to the young Daniel who enjoyed being babied. "It would be so lovely to spend some time together."

"But we're together now."

"Romantic time. Fun time."

Meredith was determined, and she knew how Daniel's stick-in-the-mud stance could be dislodged with her dogged perseverance and with the added help of more wine. They both knew he didn't stand much chance once she had decided on something. It was settled; the next week they would fly out to Le Nid.

TWELVE

Maya

The cool air circulated Maya's dress, setting it free from the clammy heat of the day as she rocked down Kingsland High Street on her bike.

She'd received a text from Nadia, the day after the soirée on the heath, inviting them both to her flat in Hackney for a *Vietnamese games evening* with a few others. It was an odd invitation as she and Troy were not an item. As a delicate attempt to assert that they were not a couple, she'd told Troy that she'd see him there.

Every nationality appeared to live in Dalston. Pedalling down Kingsland High Street, she saw a bushy bearded Hasidic Jew pushing a 1950s pram in his white shirt, Victorian black waistcoat and large furry hat. These days, most of the Jewish community had emigrated over to Stanford Hill. Dalston was now mainly Afro-Caribbean, and yet dallying along, Maya saw African women in brightly coloured headwraps and tight-fitting, shiny satin dresses showing off their ample curves, a gang of Muslim girls in hijabs giggling at an image being shared on a mobile phone. Outside Turkish cafés, men drank tiny cups of coffee, smoking hookahs. There were the Polish super-markets with names that had such strange letter formations they struck her as illegible. And then there were Halal butchers, Italian delis, Bengali minicabs and, of course, the ubiquitous Indian and Chinese takeaways. The whole world was here. It was the perfect place to meet for a *Vietnamese games evening*. But it was also a place of poverty—this wasn't Hampstead, this is where you lived if you were less affluent. Nevertheless, over the last few decades, there had been an influx of new immigrants, the young, media-savvy first-time buyer, the Hoxton overspill with their tweeds, ironic handlebar moustaches and retro eighties style.

The Rio was showing *Selma*, the Martin Luther King Jr movie, which had just come out. This was the point where she'd been instructed by Nadia to go a bit further and take a left through the Ridley Road Market. The smell of charcoal and fried onions hung in the air. The traders had all left as Maya stood high on her peddles, whisking through a wasteland of cardboard crates and KFC cartons, feverishly pecked at for leftover chicken bones by dishevelled-look-ing pigeons. She rang her bell, enjoying the sound of their flutter as she cycled through.

Nadia was a hybrid: working-class, traditional Christian Carib-bean mixed with middle-class, atheist Hoxton arthouse. She earned her living working for an IT company designing websites, and this was as much as Maya knew about her.

Arriving at the Victorian warehouse converted into flats, chain-ing her bike up to the railings outside, she climbed the steps to the entrance and pressed the buzzer. From the intercom came Nadia's warm, honeyed voice.

"Hey, girl. You made it. We're on the second floor."

Maya was buzzed in.

Waiting for Maya in the doorway to her flat, Nadia greeted her with a cosy embrace. The doughy softness of her considerable boobs was soothing, diminishing any apprehension.

She stepped into the hall to be greeted by a framed black and white poster of a black man who appeared to be from the turn of the nineteenth century, his smoky grey hair swept back as though he were at the prow of a ship, forging into a resistant wind, his eyes fiercely sad. Beneath him it read, *A slave is someone who sits down and waits for someone to free them—Frederick Douglas*. She'd never heard of Frederick Douglas before. Not even at school. She handed Nadia a bottle of red wine. Animated chatter fused with ambient music could be heard from beyond the door.

She was unsure what the night held in store. The text had said *Vietnamese games evening with drinks and snacks*. Maya hoped to God it wasn't Risk or Monopoly or even worse, Scrabble. She was pants at Scrabble, mainly because she found it so boring and couldn't quite find the motivation to shift her brain into the right gear. But she loved Vietnamese food.

Breezing into the living room, she spotted Ian, pensive as he sat cross-legged on the floor nodding, listening attentively to Asenka.

"Ian, wow, wasn't expecting to see you here, and Asenka."

They both smiled and stood to give hugs. A wave of jealousy swelled in Maya that she hadn't expected.

On the sofa were two unfamiliar faces; they stood to say hello. Both of them towered over her like American basketball players.

"Hi, I'm Floyd," said the taller of the two, wearing Harry Potter glasses, "and this is..."

"Martha," butted in his slimline companion.

Martha, also black, was more panther than human. Both had a cool, bookish air about them.

Maya had never been to a dinner party where fifty percent of the people were black. She was overly conscious of her white fragility. She wasn't sure whether to hug, shake hands or do a high five. The fact that there was some anxiety about this made her aware of how home-county she still really was—she'd always seen herself as quite urban-metro à la mode.

"Your place is lovely," said Maya, turning to Nadia.

"I know, I was so lucky to get it," said Nadia.

The enormous open-plan flat with its expansive windows let in the city skyline.

Troy hadn't yet arrived. Cycling there alone had been a useful way of signalling to Troy that they weren't a couple without having to bluntly state it.

It was unusual not to be the host or the master of ceremonies. Being a guest meant engaging with people from a diminutive place, rather than being the queen bee. It was harder to hide.

She was relieved when the doorbell rang.

"That'll be Troy," said Nadia. "Help yourself to food and drink, honey."

Nadia disappeared to let Troy in, and Maya wandered over to the table to pour herself a Merlot. The wine would help her relax. The food was decidedly un-Vietnamese. There were crisps, nuts, Pringles, olives with various dips and cheeses, but no fried rice cakes, lemongrass tofu or spring rolls.

"Did you have to cycle far?" said Martha.

"No, not at all. Hampstead."

"Oh nice. Is that where you live?"

"Yes."

"Cor, lucky you. Whereabouts?"

It wasn't that Martha was doing anything wrong, but Maya suddenly saw herself as spoilt rich girl. Maya had not had to work to buy her flat, it had been a gift from her parents—not even a birthday present, just a random gift of a home to have whilst she lived in London, though there was always an astute awareness of the investment element of any property they bought.

"Parliament Hill Fields?" Maya said with a rising inflection, as though they might not know where this was, yet knowing full well they would. Her voice went into upspeak when anxious, so she took another glug of wine.

"Man, I'd love to live there," said Floyd followed by some warm laughter.

Maya was about to say, *It's all a bit white-middle-class*, to put them at ease and let them know she was on their side, then thought better of it.

Nadia and Troy walked in, alleviating her anxieties.

Martha introduced herself to Troy, and Troy and Floyd greeted each other with a complex fist bump. Maya instantly elevated Troy to the higher echelons of urban credibility.

"Hey babe," he said to Maya, which threw her—they were definitely not at the babe stage, nor would they ever be.

"Hey," she said back.

The bullish contours of his frame protruded like balloons from beneath his T-shirt, stretched to the limit.

"Where do these go then?" he asked Nadia, holding out a four-pack of Special Brew.

Maya breathed more easily after Troy arrived, his temerity a welcome distraction from her misshapen, high-born guilt.

She'd never fully embraced her refined plummy accent, despite over the years attempting to conceal it behind a mockney twang — the H-dropping never came as naturally as she would have liked.

Being born of noble descent was more of an embarrassment than something welcomed. She enjoyed the rougher edges of the working class and their brazen, straightforward, no-thrills-attached ways, but black men were a rare phenomenon in her social circles.

There had been one black girl at school, but Maya had not known her.

Troy's can hissed open with a spurt. He sucked the froth, preventing it from spilling onto the floor.

"So, what games we playing then? Better not be Scrabble, I'm shit at Scrabble," said Troy.

This man had no sophistication. He was a lout shooting from the hip, but when he spoke, she was in altitude where the air was easier to breathe.

Nadia laughed. "Scrabble! You're kidding me, right?" she said.

"No, seriously, I'm shit at it," he reiterated.

"Troy, did you not read the text?" said Ian.

"Yeah, course I did, you knob!"

"It's not a board game," said Nadia. "It's a game called The *Into-Me-See* game."

The *Into-Me-See* game had been the buzzword around town for the last few months. Various people on the alternative personal growth scene had been raving about its life-changing effect. It had been created in a hippy community somewhere in the States and had found its way around the world via social media.

Maya had been invited to such an evening once before, but she'd managed to avoid it. It certainly hadn't been mentioned in the text.

"Blimey," said Maya. "That is so cool. Your text just said, *Vietnamese games evening, I* was a bit worried about Scrabble too."

"What's wrong with Scrabble?" said Floyd.

A clamour of disapproving jeers erupted.

"Vietnamese games evening?" said Nadia, confused.

Maya double-checked her phone, and there it was in clear Helvetica font: *Vietnamese games evening*. She showed it to Nadia.

"Oh no. Predictive text! It's meant to say *Into-me-see*, not *Vietnamese*," said Nadia.

Hello, Earth calling Nadia, how do you invite someone to a Vietnamese games evening but actually mean intense soul-bearing, skin-peeled-off-whilst-you're-still-alive evening!

And how can someone who makes such a colossal error with the invite hold a safe space?

"Are you two going to be okay with it?" asked Asenka.

Maya was rattled. Of course she was okay with it. She could have invented the game herself, for fuck's sake.

"Ooh, I think I'll survive," Maya responded, trying not to sneer.

"What about you, Troy?" Asenka asked.

"I dunno. What the fuck is it?"

"*Into-me-see* is a play on words for intimacy," said Martha. "It's a game where we all get intimate."

"You're 'aving a laugh! What, like spin the bottle?"

"Oh Troy, you've not heard of the Into-me-see game? You haven't lived, honey. You are in for a treat," said Nadia.

Maya poured herself some more Merlot. From what she'd heard, the game could be quite gruelling. It was more like an intense therapy group than recreation.

"It's a game where you show others who you really are deep down," said Asenka.

"Fuck me! I think I'd prefer Scrabble?"

"Yeah, I'm up for that," said Floyd, bouncing up and down on the sofa with a big grin on his face.

"Typical men can't deal with showing their hearts," said Martha.

"Excuse me, I'm a man and I'm definitely up for it," Ian protested.

"I wouldn't be too sure about that," said Troy.

"Ouch! Troy honey, put away the claws. It's a game of trust and vulnerability."

Why on earth did you invite Troy then? mused Maya.

"Don't worry, I recon Troy's a big softy underneath all his bravado," said Ian.

The banter continued and the wine slowly began blotting out Maya's anxiety.

Everyone was handed a piece of paper and told to write down a question for each person in the room. The question had to be one they imagined the person being asked would avoid asking themselves.

"For example," said Nadia, "you might imagine that I'm quite shy..."

"Nah, that I can't imagine," said Troy.

"Well, say I am. So, you might write down, *What do I need to do to be more socially confident?*"

"Get pissed," said Troy.

"You can answer however you like, but the idea is to be open," said Nadia.

Nadia handled Troy's subversive ways well. There was a constant chuckle in her voice, like nothing got to her.

"Let's start. Oh, and everything that's said stays in the room. Agreed?"

"It depends, if Ian says he's into some weird paedo shit."

"Troy, this is a sensitive game, honey, and the rules are we need to respect each other. Can you do that?"

The evening was already starting to be more fun for Maya. *Troy, rules? Pfft.*

Troy drew a zip across his mouth.

The scrutinising began, with eyes narrowed as they pondered the deluded blind spots each player held onto in order to avoid some feared annihilation.

Ian's brow knitted into cold concentration, his tongue peeping through his teeth as he jotted down his question, eyeballing Maya.

Each question was then folded up and given to the appropriate person, then jumbled up so no one knew who the question came from.

It was a stupid game. Why would anyone want to hang their dirty knickers on the line for everyone to glare at? As a boarder, years were spent learning that the worst thing to do was let your guard down. Suzy, the school counsellor and the Swami Gandalih were the only people she trusted; everyone else had a hidden agenda.

"So, who's going to go first?" asked Nadia.

"I'll go first," said Troy, rolling up his sleeves like a jumped-up knight about to prove how brave he was.

It brought back the time she'd been told what delightful fun she'd have at boarding school as she walked naïvely beneath the stone lintel into the dreary darkness. Her back straight and her heart steadfast until turning around and realising Mummy and Daddy were gone, then she crumbled.

Troy was instructed to pick up a folded piece of paper from his pile, without opening it, and to pass it to someone else to read to him so that handwriting couldn't be identified.

"Here you go, mate, do the honours," said Troy, passing his question to Floyd.

"Troy, why do you act so tough?" read Floyd.

Ian raised an eyebrow and was looking pleased with himself. It was an obvious question, but Maya had decided not to ask it. She had thought of asking, *Why do you hit women,* or *What actually happened to those ribs your friend mentioned?* But that would be unfair; maybe his inebriated friend, Gazza, had been talking twaddle. Maya had written down, *What was your relationship to your mother like?* That was a good way to find out more about someone.

All eyes were on Troy.

"And what am I meant to do now?" asked Troy.

"Answer the question," said Nadia.

"Why am I so tough?"

"Why do you need to act so tough?" said Ian.

"Isn't it a bit unfair, Troy going first if he's never played before?" asked Asenka.

"Troy, you can change your mind if you don't want to go first," offered Nadia.

"Yeah, maybe I'll go later, if that's alright," said Troy.

"Of course. Who do you choose to go next? The person who goes first gets to choose who goes next," asked Nadia.

"But he didn't have his go, he bottled out," said Floyd.

"Floyd, I choose Floyd," said Troy, laughing.

"Your tripping, man, I wanted to play Scrabble," said Floyd, holding up his arms as though warding off a lynch mob.

Nadia was giggling wildly. "There are no winners or losers. The only thing you lose is a bit of your ego," she said.

Guru Swami Gandalih had said that *the ego is like a soldier trying to protect us from pain, but instead, we become a prison with our pain pacing us up and down, festering, longing for the light. To escape the ego, we need to set the pain free. Let the soldier go home to his family and burn his uniform on a bonfire.*

Well, that's all very well and good, but what about the level of pain?

No one could comprehend how shit Maya had had it, how could they? Privileged, little white girl never had to worry about money, as though money was the antidote to all problems. She bet Nadia had a big, fat, cuddly, warm mamma, not a bony, pinched-faced one who saw you as a burden. Who's to say that a council estate is any worse than the estate she grew up on, along with being sent away at eight to board, strict rules of inane etiquette, parents who were emotionally inept and being brought up by a nannie, though thank God for the nannie—she might not have survived without the warmth of her nannie.

"It's just I'd prefer it if someone else went before me," said Floyd.

"Maybe Floyd should have his go later, too?" Asenka suggested.

Martha playfully punched him on the arm. "Floyd! It's not about being tortured."

Floyd sheepishly retreated into his shoulders like a tortoise.

"That's fine. Floyd, who do you want to pass it on to?" asked Nadia.

"I'm happy to start," said Ian. "I've got nothing to hide."

There was an all-round cheer, at which point Ian cocked his head a little higher, his chin jutted out that little bit more and a victorious glint entered his eye. *Who's acting tough now?*

Ian passed the paper to Martha on his left to read out.

"Ian, when was the last time you secretly felt competitive with someone?" asked Martha.

"Hmm, good question," said Ian, pondering the words. "I like it. Difficult though as I'm not really a competitive person."

There were a couple of barely audible groans from around the room.

This had been Maya's question because she knew Ian was probably the most competitive man there, only his competitiveness was more sophisticated. If Ian scored a point, he wouldn't jump up and down shouting *loser* to the opposition, he'd sympathise with them, rubbing their nose in how pathetic he felt they were. His sympathy had a toxicity to it.

"Maybe you're the least competitive person in the room, Ian," said Maya with more than a twist of irony. "Would you agree?"

"I can't help it, it's just not in my nature."

"Is that 'cos you're crap at everything?" Troy threw in.

"Troy, Troy, Troy. Stop it with the put-downs, otherwise the game doesn't work. It needs to feel safe," said Nadia.

"He can't help it, Nadia. Don't worry, it doesn't bother me," said the egoless Ian.

"Maybe you're more competitive than you realise but can't admit it, even to yourself?" Martha suggested.

"There's nothing wrong with being competitive, mate," said Floyd.

"I think it can be quite unhealthy. One man trying to put another man down can't be good," said Ian.

"Or woman," said Nadia.

"Well, I find women less competitive than men."

"Bollox," said Troy. "They're just better at hiding it."

"Not as good as Ian, though, he's got it down to a fine art," said Maya.

"Okay. Maybe leave it there. If Ian says he's not competitive then that's what we have to accept," said Nadia.

"Maybe you could ask me some questions," suggested Ian, in order to be helpful.

"Nah. Let's move on," said Asenka, yawning.

The game didn't seem to be going that well.

"Sorry," said Ian, wide-eyed, wrinkling his brow, teeth clenched in a not-guilty demeanour.

"So, who you going to select to go next?" asked Nadia.

Ian looked around the room, deliberating, but Maya knew who he'd choose. Ian's biggest delusion was that he was an enigma.

"Maya. Is that okay?" he asked, smiling with feigned consideration, as if genuinely checking it was okay with her, knowing she couldn't say no. How could Maya—the one who runs groups encouraging openness—not be okay with being open herself?

Looking at him, she saw a weasel as she picked up a folded question from the pile and handed it to Nadia. Warm Nadia, with the cushiony, warm bust and sunshiny, soft tones.

"Be gentle with me," she half joked.

"Oh, honey. Don't worry. No one's judging," reassured Nadia.

Maya looked around the room, and the faces around her did mostly appear sensitive. Except Ian's—she couldn't quite tell what it was, but there was something behind his eyes, something that betrayed the earnest way his bottom lip pouted as though he was reassuring a two-year-old.

"Maya, when was the last time someone broke your heart?" read Nadia.

The gauntlet had been thrown down. She polished off her wine, slamming her glass down on the table, a bit too forcefully. She was hamming things up, which was an indication she needed to slow down a bit on the wine.

The question perplexed her.

"I don't wish to sound like Ian, but my heart has never been broken," said Maya.

"What makes you think my heart has never been broken?" said Ian.

"I meant it's a crap answer, like yours."

"Has a lover never broken your heart?" asked Martha.

"Personally, I don't believe in all that romantic bullshit," said Maya. "Hearts are just organs that pump blood around the body."

"Have you never been in love?" asked Martha.

Maya squirmed inside. Not having had a long-term relationship at thirty-two was a touchy subject. Even her friendships tended to burn out quite quickly. And yet in her classes and workshops, she endlessly talked about intimacy, the heart, love, commitment and connection, but it was a case of teach what you need to know.

Maya was happier with more than one lover at a time, and most men found this impossible to deal with. Too many men were enslaved to the archaic idea that once they'd stuck their lingam into her yoni, they could assume ownership, but she wasn't the kind of woman to submit to the domestic servitude commonly seen in monogamy. She saw herself as a modern-day Simone de Beauvoir. She belonged to no one and nor did her heart, therefore it would never be broken.

She cherished her freedom over the false promises of love made by deluded, romantic, adolescent men and their *till-death-us-do-part* kind of happiness which included having sex with no one else. How can that be good for you? She wanted her partners to enjoy their sexuality, even if that meant with other women. She, too, wanted to enjoy her sexuality with more than one man. It was nature's way. You can't stick blinkers on your libido.

Had she ever been in love? She wasn't opposed to love, in fact life was all about love. Love is what gave life meaning. But the word *love* has been abused: people use it to justify all kinds of insanity—particularly control freaks.

She'd tried monogamy in a couple of relationships, but it was never too long before the men became possessive, telling her to wear a bra, accusing her of flirting with other men, asking why she hadn't texted when she disappeared for a couple of days.

Whereas she'd now been in a few poly relationships, and they suited her personality.

"I don't go for the whole monogamy thing, maybe that's why my heart's still in good order."

Troy flashed her a look, his face scrunched as though she'd just declared she was into bestiality.

"Why put all your eggs in one basket? Your heart's bound to get broken then, and all you're left with is scrambled eggs," she said, pleased with her metaphor.

"Maybe someone broke your heart in the past and you don't trust men anymore?" said Asenka. "Like when you were a kid?"

Asenka and Ian were quite the pair, equally nauseating.

"Are you suggesting my heart's closed?"

"No, no. Aw, I'm sorry Maya, I wasn't attacking you," said Asenka.

"What was your relationship with your dad like?" asked Ian.

The room was getting stuffy with a lack of air.

"I want to know more about the three-in-bed thing," said Floyd.

"Is there any more wine," asked Maya.

"Having open relationships must be tricky," said Martha.

Nadia topped up Maya's glass.

"How's that working for you, Troy," asked Ian.

Troy was quiet. His usual shenanigans were gone.

"Sorry, but why are you asking Troy?" said Maya. "We're not a couple."

Troy took a slug from his can of larger and gave Maya a long look.

"Are you okay, Troy, honey?" asked Nadia.

"Yup," said Troy.

"I'm just after a bit of fun. Nothing serious, that's why we're a good match. I mean, no offence, but you could never be my type."

The last sentence was clumsy and she regretted saying it, but after too much wine, Maya couldn't help blurting out her thoughts, like vomit when the gut's full of poison. He'd been like a bungee jump— exciting while it lasted but you wouldn't want to do it for long, and she should have been clear about this from the start.

Maya looked around for some support and understanding, but everyone appeared fidgety.

"Remind me why we played this game?" she asked.

Nadia touched Maya gently on her shoulder. "Maya, no one is judging you."

Troy stood up, pouring the last dregs of lager down his gullet. "Fuck this for a game of soldiers!" And without looking at anyone, marched out of the flat, slamming the door.

Everyone was quiet for a moment, absorbing the shock of his sudden take-off.

Asenka was the first to speak. "Maybe you should catch him up to see how he is?"

"Sure." Maya stood, her head spinning with the sudden ascent.

The hubbub of people out for their Saturday night fill had thickened, echoing along Kingsland High Street, intermingling with buses and cars. Searching the pavement for him, Troy was easy to spot with his erect triangular gait, storming ahead, always looking like he was ready for something.

Maya hadn't treated him with the respect he deserved.

She ran towards him.

"Troy!" she called.

He turned. His face like a fist.

"I'm sorry, Troy, I was a dick back there. I do like you, it's not you... Oh God, I'm sounding like a cliché now."

She wanted to make him laugh, for him to see how funny it all really was.

Looking into his eyes, she saw there were no lights on, no self-reflection. They were penetrating her but not seeing what was actually in front of them.

Without warning, Maya was gasping for air as Troy's meaty hand pounced to her windpipe like an arachnid.

"You dirty, fucking slut!"

Maya's head wanted to explode from the pressure of no air. His face distorted and twisted, full of hate.

And then, as though becoming conscious of what he was doing, he let go, regaining his Jekyll hands. He stepped back from her, his eyes wide with worry and regret.

Maya fell forward, gasping for air, momentarily frozen.

"I'm sorry, really sorry, fuck, fuck..."

A raging scream of words found their way from the pit of Maya's intestines.

"You fucking psycho!"

Troy began to approach, his shoulders slumped, trying to make himself smaller so she might trust him. Maya raised her palms.

"Back the fuck off, you nutter. Come near me and I swear I'll scream."

Not that this meant much as no one had bothered to stop to help her when she was being choked—instead, people had crossed the road.

He pleaded for mercy, but Maya wouldn't give it, now able to feel something else.

"You fucking psycho, get the fuck away from me."

"Maya, I'm sorry, I'm an idiot." Troy wrung his hands, pleading for forgiveness, his eyes full of terror. "I'm such a cunt! I'm really sorry. Honest to God, I'm so sorry."

"Get away from me, now!"

Troy backed away, slinking off into the night, escaping the scene of the crime.

The swami had said, *if you truly love someone, let them be free*, or was it Sting who said that? Whatever, Troy was now in the past, and good riddance.

THIRTEEN

Liam

It had been one of those long, drawn-out, shitty, cold English summer days. Liam's backside jiggled around on a white plastic garden chair, moulded in opposition to the contours of his bony arse. Chomping on a vegan pasty, too hungry to care that its innards resembled cat sick and mostly tasted of salt, he was glad to be warm and dry.

Since meeting Daniel, he'd been inspired to take *Lady Chatterley's Lover* out of Woking library to read in Squeaky Clean's laundrette. He was the only person in there—a lone fish in an empty tank, one of those people in an Edward Hopper painting.

The machine turned, slish-sloshing hypnotically behind him. Framed outside the window, a bad-taste postcard presented itself, the kind you buy for ironic humour, showing how grim a place is; Woking was a grey, pebbledash, 1980s office block.

The book was boring or maybe you had to be in the mood. And he wasn't in the mood. All that angst about class. It turns out working for the upper class wasn't that bad, things had moved on: it was 2014, not 1914. Liam couldn't give a toss whether he was working-class, underclass, middle-class, or classless and free: it was a waste of time getting caught up in it all. Even UKIP with their toady-looking leader having done horrifically well in the elections wasn't going to get him down. It was summer, and surely that was a good thing.

Opposite, sellotaped to a scabby, peeling wall, an ad showed a housewife in a wide-eyed, ecstatic trance, leaning forward, a translucent white shirt held towards the light. A young girl stood by, admiring her mother, partaking in her ecstasy. In the background, daddy has entered the picture, smiling, hands on hips, back from the office. *Happy Families Prefer Surf!* it read. Liam looked at the poster, titillated by the kitschy wife's neat and tidy bottom, sizzling as it subliminally jutted out. A reminder of how long it'd been since he'd had sex.

He took another bite from his pasty.

He'd pretty much been single the whole time he'd lived in Surrey. Granted, he met lots of single (widowed) women in his job, but they were seldom under the age of seventy-five.

Maybe he just wasn't a good catch.

Truth was, he should have got his shit together by now, only three years till the big three-o. Going with the flow was okay on one level—it was easy and stress free—but it was hard not to compare yourself with others who had proper jobs, lived in plush flats, had mortgages or lived in giant mansions with swimming pools, tennis courts and enough money to buy a small island.

Was that fair?

Not that he wanted a proper job, or a mortgage. Rat race pressure was all it was, but what if he got old and still lived like he did now? Even when squatting, there came the wake-up call that the other squatters had degrees and parents with money, trustafarians who could afford to be anarchists. He didn't even have a bank account: caravans in woods are classed as no-fixed-abode. His life savings existed in a biscuit tin under his bed. All he had was the *now,* and living like a Taoist monk was not suited for the way the world was heading. Things had to change, he could no longer afford to eat, sleep, shit on a loop until the grey stone came with his name on.

Funny thing was, he didn't feel like this in the woods, it was just when he was in the towns.

Commuters marched past the window, through the pedestrianised town centre in automated fashion, hankering to get out of their armour of greys and navy blues. Woking wouldn't be remembered for its buzzing, razzle-dazzle vibes, even if Paul Weller was from there and it had the first mosque ever to be built in the UK. When in town, he felt cut off from other people, as if there was something that separated him from everyone else.

There was a generic boringness to commuter towns. Maybe it was the newness, the uninspired architecture. Or the mutant, hybrid people working in the city, like ghouls returning only at night to haunt their family.

Maybe the aversion to towns was a genetic deficiency. Liam regularly obsessed about his DNA—he'd rather kill himself than end up like his mother. As for his father, well maybe he was him already: persona non grata, anonymous, estranged.

He dried and folded his clothes. Outside, the light was growing dim, transforming the laundrette window into a giant mirror. Passers-by walked through his ghost-like reflection. They could see him inside, but less and less, he could see them out there.

Leaving Squeaky Clean's, he headed back to the farm, his loneliness dissipating now that the throng of strangers was somewhere else.

* * *

Daniel

Huddled away in his study listening to Barber's *Adagio for Strings*, the imminent jaunt to Le Nid weighed heavily on Daniel's Mind.

They knew no one in the Carcassonne region, except Edith, the *gardienne* who looked after the house, and she was more domestic help than friend. This meant just the two of them, alone, without their comfortable routines which marriage depended upon for equilibrium. The dreaded walks together along the River Aude, conversing about matters that were best left alone as they served only to stir up contention. He anguished over getting closer to Meredith—dreading being sucked into her inner world.

A romantic holiday? More like torture. A quiet life without the complications of spousal sensitivities would be more to his taste. Submerged deep in the labyrinth of sewers in Daniel's mind hid a fear of female sexuality, in particular Meredith's sexuality. It had been this that provoked his knee-jerk reaction.

The CD came to an end, and Daniel lifted his tired body from the chair, deciding to get some air before it grew too dark.

Falindon Moor was his usual pastoral haunt. Trekking through the heather and gorse, the scattered trees danced to the eastern wind singing its song. The sky, resplendent blue like a dunnock's egg. A dampness entered the air as the horizon began to swallow the sun. He walked for about three miles, knowing this only because of the app on his phone. All these gadgets that had entered his life, he couldn't get used to them, everything had become complicated. This was meant to be an escape from tech, but Meredith was insistent that he walk a certain number of miles each week for his health, always reminding him of heart attacks, men his age and whatnot. There was no doubt he always walked the recommended daily amount. The phone was brought along for a quiet life, squashing the resentment that gnawed away in his belly, though equally, this could have more to do with an existential flailing: What had life amounted to? Even with all the money and status, something was missing. It was only in these moments, alone and walking, he connected to something. A world more real.

He walked more and more these days. Death and mortality always a few steps behind, accompanying him, threatening to catch up from the shadows, at which point Daniel would never exist again. Eternal nothingness. Dismay torrented through his bloodstream, sensing the first maggot pitted in his stomach, lying in wait for its feast.

It was late, rooks shouted in raucous unison, returning to rookeries edging the heath. The horizon held a glow.

Had he lived his life fully? What if he'd married someone else? Would he have been happier? Would that deep sense of aloneness still be there? And what of this unlikely camaraderie he had with Liam? Liam would probably say they *must have known each other in a past life,* or some other New Age nonsense, but Liam offered hope, which was gold to Daniel.

A mangy fox in the distance had left its den as a waxing moon began to rise. It eyed Daniel suspiciously and then slinked into the undergrowth. Stars began to appear. Orion's belt could be made out like the teeth of a skull, its arms becoming eyes. It was time to head back.

Stepping out into the country lane, away from morbidity, he stopped to let a vehicle pass. The glaring headlights blinded him as the vehicle slowed down. The distinctive rattling sound of the battered, old LDV van was instantly recognisable. Pulling over just in front of him, Liam wound down the window.

"What *you* doing out past your bedtime?" joked Liam.

"Well, what a surprise, Liam. I was just enjoying a lovely walk on the common."

"Do you want a lift? I'm heading past yours?"

"That would be marvellous, thank you."

Clanking along the road in the dark, the windscreen a huge, white rabbit hole, Liam asked Daniel if he'd been anywhere interesting. Daniel mentioned his walk, choosing to leave out the bit about death tagging along behind him, uninvited.

In turn, Daniel asked Liam about his evening and Liam told him he'd been to Squeaky Clean's to do his laundry. Not the most stimulating start to a conversation.

Ahead was The Highwayman, the local country pub. Daniel asked Liam if he fancied a drink. Liam instantly accepted.

Daniel wasn't particularly cocksure when it came to banter, and as they entered the pub, privately some apprehension had sprung as to what they might talk about.

Apart from their brief first meeting, this was the only other time the two had met beyond the electric gates of the Bloomberg estate.

Being midweek, the pub was fairly quiet, some might say dead. The landlord had a bewildered look on his face seeing the unlikely pair enter. Daniel was a regular and the barman greeted him as he went to the bar.

Carrying a pint of the local ale and a double Scotch, Daniel sat down and knocked back a large slug of the whisky, the alcohol suitably easing away a more bashful side. It wasn't long before the conversation gathered pace. Drinks were downed quickly and Daniel, who'd insisted on another, was back at the bar ordering the same again. On the third double Scotch, words that had rolled so freely off Daniel's tongue became ungainly, tired of their own cadence.

Liam sat across from him, T-shirt covered in grass stains, bare knee protruding from a rip in his jeans, the leather on the tip of his boots worn down revealing the steel beneath the toecap. Daniel could never be seen with a tear in his clothes. Never live in a caravan. Never drive around in a battered-up, old van. The man before him was one step away from being homeless, whereas Daniel was a million miles away, if not more. This lack of order and stability staring back, enjoying his ale and crisps, was enough to give Daniel vertigo. He found himself on the precipice of a chasm that had opened up inside. Liam clocked the grave look on his face.

"Do you know, Liam? I envy you. I have everything, yet I feel your life is richer than mine in many ways. I've travelled the world, I've had the best education money can buy, I've even owned a private jet, believe it or not, but I sometimes wonder if I've ever truly been happy. Does that sound strange to you?"

"Sure, I get to go places like Squeaky Clean's, who wouldn't envy that?"

"There is that too," Daniel said, amused.

"Sorry, that was probably a bit callous."

"No, no. It was funny, well done."

"So, why do you reckon you're unhappy?"

"Things are not so bad, I shouldn't complain."

"I think it's good to talk, that's what friends are for."

Daniel was taken aback. Maybe it was the alcohol. He knew Liam wasn't much of a drinker, but to use the word *friend* seemed oddly out of place in spite of it being an accurate description of what they were.

"It's only that I used to think things would get better, life would get easier, but it hasn't, it gets worse. Oh, my word, I'm so sorry, I really am being an utter bore. Please accept my apology. Let's change the subject. I've drunk too much."

"It's fine. Go on."

"No, really." Daniel looked at his watch. "We should probably get going."

"Can I tell you a little story?"

"Of course, please do."

"Ages ago, I used to know two brothers: one a lorry driver, the other a computer geek. The one into computers ended up rich, on top of which he was handsome and stylish. The lorry driver on the other hand was loud, overweight, not at all good-looking. I was always baffled at how the lorry driver always ended up with gorgeous, intelligent girlfriends, whilst his brother was a total flop with women. The lorry driver was seriously loud, like a Viking, yet this didn't put people off him, whereas his brother had no real friends despite continuously reading self-help books to try and improve himself. I could never work out why the overweight, uneducated, loud lorry driver was so successful with people and his wealthy, intelligent brother was such a disaster. I came to the conclusion that with the lorry driver, you got what you saw, he was genuine, and for this reason you trusted him. His brother never really spoke truthfully, constantly trying to say the right thing. He couldn't believe anyone would like him for who he was."

Daniel was puzzled as to why Liam had related this story to him.

"So, you're suggesting I may not be genuine?"

"No, I didn't mean that. I meant things don't always make life better, it's how you feel about yourself."

"I think you have a point though. My whole life has been spent trying to do the right thing, but this has been at the expense of denying my dreams. Do you know, when I was twenty, lots of people who went to university went backpacking across India or Africa. It was the *in thing* amongst the cool students and I so longed to go, but I knew my father would disapprove, so I never dared. The closest I ever got to the sixties' counterculture was listening to Donavon's 'Mr Tambourine Man.'"

"You mean Bob Dylan."

"Oh, do I? Yes then, of course, Bob Dylan."

"I thought you said you'd been to every continent?"

"I have—holidays or business trips where I stayed in hotels or rented villas. I was so envious of those who grew their hair long, lived in communes and smoked pot."

"Actually, I forgot to mention the dad."

"Whose dad?"

"The brothers', their dad was also a lorry driver but wanted his boys to be successful and not follow in his footsteps so was always insisting they did their homework. The one that became a lorry driver just wasn't that academic and didn't do well at all, but his dad still accepted him and they were kinda always *matey* together, whereas the one who became *successful* never really got on with his dad even though he did all the things his dad wanted him to. It was kind of a Cain and Abel scenario," said Liam.

"How do you know all this about them anyway? Were they good friends of yours?"

"Not really. I'm just nosey and ask questions, and people tend to open up to me 'cos I like listening."

"I feel sorry for the rather hapless brother. I wonder if he ever met anyone?"

"It does sound like you spent a lot of time doing what you didn't want to do to please your father," said Liam.

"And for what? He's dead now and I'm still trying to please him. Such a waste. I'm sixty-three years old, you know! That must seem ancient to you, but inside I still feel like I'm eighteen, but then I look in the mirror and am shocked to see a face all lined and ageing looking back. I see other people my age and think, my God, do I look like them?"

"Imagine how Mick Jagger must feel. You look amazing for your age, and you're fit and healthy."

"The point is you can't get your youth back. Once it's gone, it's gone. So, you've got to live your life fully. How old are you, Liam?"

"Twenty-seven."

"Twenty-seven. Twenty-seven. Oh, to be twenty-seven again. My daughter's thirty-two and my eldest son is thirty-six. I wasn't there for them. God, I so regret this."

"There's still time to make up for the things you haven't done. You could easily have another thirty years left."

"Time!" shouted the landlord ominously, ringing a bell.

A warmth in Liam's eyes reached out like a hand touching Daniel gently on the shoulder.

* * *

Skulking through the entrance hall, Daniel was unsure what it was he had to hide. It wasn't out of place to go to the pub after his walks, but this normally meant one double Scotch, rarely two and never three. His trepidation, not completely unfamiliar, became more amplified as he approached the sitting room where Meredith, he imagined, awaited his return.

This was somewhat reminiscent of childhood when disobedient towards his mother who then ordered him to his father's study, whereupon he'd be instructed to lie over his father's knee, where his pants would be pulled down to receive a good paddling.

So accustomed to his fear of Meredith, he never thought to question it—it was just how it was. But the Scotch tipple had equally stirred up a dissatisfaction, a need for change. Straightening himself upright, he entered the sitting room. Meredith had her back to him, the outline of her face a ghostly pale blue as it reflected the light from the TV screen.

A large portrait of Daniel's great-grandfather, Rupert Bloomberg, dominated the far wall, boasting a walrus moustache that sprang out like tusks on a boar—all the rage of the late 1800s. The flickering glow of the TV brought his eyes to life, angry and critical.

Meredith didn't turn to look at Daniel. Her body was corpse-like, not just in the way it didn't move, but a coldness seemed to emanate from her.

Daniel had been at ease when talking to Liam, and now with Meredith, he was riddled with a familiar tension. He resented needing an excuse to justify why he'd allowed himself to do something without her permission. The violation he'd committed was more than being spontaneous, the real crime was he'd gone to the pub with Liam and enjoyed himself, even if in a slightly melancholic way—and Meredith, for some reason unbeknownst to Daniel, deplored Liam.

If Liam's name was mentioned just in passing, her face would become taught, and though half-heartedly attempting to conceal her antipathy, Daniel was still lacerated from the spikiness that radiated out of her.

He had something with Liam that he didn't have with his wife. In fact, he tiptoed around her like a frightened little boy! How on earth had he not been aware of this before. How ridiculous. He was sixty-three years old, as if he had to tell himself again, scared of his own wife. He needed to assert himself, be a mensch!

"I think I'll go to bed and read," was about as much assertion as Daniel could muster.

"Hm."

"What?"

"I didn't say anything."

"Good night, then." Daniel was about to make his escape.

"Nice time at the pub?"

"Oh, you know."

"With the gardener, were you?"

"As it happens, yes. Why?"

"Oh, just wondered. Have you packed for Le Nid?"

"No, I'll do it tomorrow."

"Did you do your three miles?" Meredith said, referring to the app on Daniel's phone.

"Oh, I forgot to check it."

"Well, check it now, silly."

"I forgot to switch it off, so it's still counting."

"And?"

"So, it won't be accurate."

"Why not?"

"I came back in Liam's van," Daniel muttered. This was the cardinal sin.

"You came back in that filthy, rusty old banger! My God, Daniel, have you no shame?"

He was now naughty Daniel, and naughty people should feel ashamed. His body went into a hunch, a child in a headmaster's office at school. Big Daniel had floated off somewhere out into the stratosphere leaving little Daniel all alone to be reprimanded. Using all his willpower, he summoned his more grown-up self back into the room. *I've had enough of this!* he told himself, taking a deep breath.

"Actually, I enjoyed it! I had a splendid time at the pub. I rather welcome Liam's company despite him being our gardener, which, I might add, shouldn't make any difference whether he's a gardener or Lord Williamson's grandson. To be honest, I'm shocked by your conceit. I may even go to his caravan imminently and smoke some pot, maybe you could join us."

"Oh, stop being so contrary."

"What is it about him that gets up your nose?"

"The gardener does not bother me in the slightest. Why on earth would he! You're being ridiculous."

"Liam."

"What?"

"His name's Liam."

"Yes, I know what his name is, I hear it often enough."

"So, why don't you call him Liam?"

"Because he's the bloody gardener and not a friend!" Meredith's voice jumped up an octave.

"There's no law to say he can't be both?"

"I don't want him as a friend."

"Well, I want him to be my friend."

"Why?"

"Because I find him easy to talk to."

"Am I not easy to talk to?"

"You're my wife. It's completely different. It's nice to be able to talk to another man."

"You never talk to me," Meredith said, a twisted hurt stapled on her face.

"We've been married for, what—" Daniel did some quick mental arithmetic. "—thirty-six years. You run out of things to say. You've heard all my best anecdotes."

"Anecdotes? Is this what you do, share anecdotes?"

"Partly, yes."

"And what else?"

Meredith was clearly going for a full confession. Admitting to bearing his soul to Liam would expose more rubble from the crumbling foundation their relationship was built on and denying it continued the lie, and at this particular moment, the lie was Sisyphus's boulder forever being pushed up towards Hades with no end in sight. Enough was enough; he wanted rid of this deceptive burden.

"I talk about me."

A silence ensued, a soundless hurt, a recoiling of something that would later strike using all the stored-up acrimony.

She'd learnt how to be stoic. It didn't take a genius to work out why Meredith was the way she was. Her parents were a dreary pair who jabbered on endlessly about anything of little or no consequence. Strict C of E Christians. Her father was related to the seventeenth-century Earl of Hampshire. She'd grown up in Barrow Manor in Kent and, like Daniel, had spent her later childhood at boarding school.

"You talk about yourself to the gardener?"

"Liam."

"You do realise he could be a con artist!"

Daniel remembered the story Liam had told of the two brothers and the one who became wealthy and then started to trust no one. Meredith reminded him of this brother. A weariness came over him but also a sadness that the young, vivacious woman he married had become so bitter.

He no longer knew how to be close to her, if indeed they had ever been close; if they had, it was so faint a memory, Daniel failed to recollect it fully.

"I trust Liam implicitly. He's not a con artist, he's done nothing to suggest this whatsoever. I talk to him because he shows warmth, and I feel this is something I've not had much of. It's been a strange old day, but I feel both happy and mournful at the same time. I'm looking forward to our holiday. We could do with a change. I'm sorry you struggle with Liam. I'm going to bed now, good night."

Meredith adjusted the cushion on the settee. Daniel, though compliant, was at the same time defiant. They had four weeks ahead of them in Le Nid, which was worrying: the relationship was going to be either rejuvenated or annihilated.

"Good night!" Meredith said, sinking back into a ghostly apparition.

FOURTEEN

Troy

The sulphurous smell of bin trucks trawling the empty streets of Tottenham greeted Troy as he headed back to the bedsit.

He was totally wired from lack of sleep. After leaving the crime scene, he'd gone to Hampstead to sit on the heath and wait for the lights to go on in Maya's flat, but after two hours of freezing his tits off in the dark with still no sign, he gave up, heading back to his digs. She'd probably gone back to Nadia's telling them all what he'd done. To his credit, he had let go, hadn't punched her, caught himself in time.

His world had been smashed, his heart shanked. How could he do that when he totally loved her? It was impossible to get some kip, head going mental, spinning illogical thoughts like a wild dog on ketamine. There was no one else like her. He'd fucked up good and proper. He always fucked up in the end. He was a useless shit, just like everyone else.

He logged on to Facebook; not there either. Maybe she was fucking Ian? He imagined her enjoying Ian's cock inside her.

The sound of Sunday morning traffic began seeping into the room.

It was impossible to sleep with this kind of shit going on in his head.

A guy in prison once told him about some monkeys who never had fights because they had sex all the time, which supposedly calmed them down; maybe the same was true of wanking. He searched online to distract himself with porn. A few hours later, he was more awake than ever—so much for the wanking monkey theory. He decided to bang some weights, push himself to the max, obliterate an insidious, rattling brain with some adrenaline.

With spittle spattering through gritted teeth, Troy powerlifted eighty kilos on the bench-press, his face flushed, the colour of a radish. Soon sweat was gushing from every pore. Every strain of muscle, a victory against all the arse-licking phoneys that populated the planet.

Placing the weights on the floor and lobbing his sopping wet T-shirt across the room, he flopped onto to the bed, still agitated, unable to muzzle his rabid thinking.

There was a charcoaled smudge where windows used to be halfway up a tower block on the North Peckham Estate where he'd grown up. It had been burnt out in some drug wars; that's how he was on the inside: worthless. Always worthless. Never wanted. Always alone. Always the stupid one who no one took seriously.

As an adolescent, he'd had a penchant for BMWs, a real hot-wire pro, joy rides, the lot, but getting caught more than once, he had ended up in a juvie. At first, he got on sound with his key worker, a *good bond* she'd called it, but then she fucked off, retired and moved away without so much as a goodbye.

And recently, things had been going so well, too, moving to north London away from the old crowd. Enough time had been spent inside, he was determined to make it work for once. But the anger was on a roll to fucking things up. Grabbing her was a mistake. But hearing she was into putting it about was too much to handle. She was a slag, but it was love and that's why it hurt so bad.

It wasn't her fault—she needed saving. The dance stuff, the people she hung out with, it was a cult.

Still, it was wrong to do what he did.

Walking back to Tottenham, he'd tried phoning her—she hadn't answered. At least a hundred texts sent, messages left on her voice-mail pleading with her to speak with him, begging her to call back, apologising, insisting that he was getting help, that he loved her, swearing that his outburst was a one-off.

There was one reply, which simply read, *Stay away from me you deranged psycho, or I'll call the police!!!*

It was just anger, it would pass—it had with other birds. They always ended up forgiving him. The weird thing was, the more she pushed him away, the more he wanted her. The more she hated him, the more he respected her.

By 10.00 a.m. it was time to call her again. Maybe after a good night's sleep she'd had a chance to calm down, soften. But now her phone didn't even ring; instead, an automated voice said, *This number is temporarily out of service.* He tried it again, and again got the same message.

The bitch had blocked his fucking number.

Projectile plastic darted in every direction as he repeatedly slammed the mobile down onto the kitchen table until there was nothing left. Then picking a kitchen chair off the floor, he crashed it down with the full force of his might until it splintered into something that resembled how he felt inside. A guttural bellow ensued as though from a wild animal in pain. He hadn't finished: the wardrobe took at least twenty kicks, dislodging all the panels.

It crossed his mind to wait outside her flat again until she arrived back. He could convince her that they were meant to be together. He would wait for as long as it took because that's what you did when you loved someone: there were no limits.

Then another brainwave happened—*buy another phone*. She wouldn't recognise the number; he could woo her, if only he could get her to listen.

* * *

Tesco's was chocka with too many ugly people in there, as if shopping was a day out at the seaside. Families huddled together round trolleys pushed by heroic dads. John Lennon's song, *Imagine*, blared out through the supermarket tannoy, a theme tune to all the cartoon families blissful in their consumerism, but it sounded like one of those crap *Top of the Pops* albums from the seventies you find in charity shops that no one ever buys. *Imagine there's no heaven…* Yeah right, another devil-worshipping lefty.

He grabbed the cheapest pay-as-you-go mobile on offer and took it to the checkout. An old lady was taking forever counting out her money, as though no one had anything better to do than stand in a queue all day.

A round woman in front of Troy had a trolley piled high with shit, mainly biscuits and crisps; she was already bursting at the seams.

" 'Scuse me, d'you mind if I go in front of you? I only have this," he said, waving his mobile in her face.

She didn't crack a smile; disgruntled, she mumbled something and moved aside.

Everyone was getting inside him like tapeworms. He hated them all with their crappy lives.

The old bat at the till was waffling to the acned checkout boy about how lovely he was and that it's rare for people to be patient these days. Eventually she took her sad, droopy face off, back to her meaningless life.

Troy handed his phone to the kid behind the till.

"Have you had a nice day today?" said the boy, smiling and looking at Troy.

"What?"

"Have you done anything nice today?"

"Do I know you?" asked Troy.

"I don't think so. Do you live round here?"

Troy's blood had reached boiling point. "Can you shut the fuck up, I don't know you. Just give me my change, you spotty little cunt."

"How rude," said the fat woman with the cartload of carbs.

Troy wanted to punch her—his body would feel so much better if he could grind his knuckles into her nose. She was so ugly and fat. A security guard resembling an ex-con started walking over. Troy would have actually enjoyed a fight. The skinny cunt looked soft as shit with his uniform too big for him. Troy pictured himself battering him, making him beg for mercy but knew he'd only end up back inside, and right now he couldn't afford that—he was on a mission. He held his hands up in surrender and left the store.

* * *

Back at the bedsit—now a trashed hovel—he scoured the shrapnel sprayed across the threadbare carpet, relieved to find the sim card. He downloaded his contacts into his new phone and then replaced it with the new sim.

He tapped on Maya's name, stiffening as her phone began to ring.

"Hello, Maya here."

"Hi..."

Click.

"Hello, Maya? Are you there?"

Troy dialled again.

"The number you have dialled is no longer available."

With a rabid lob, the phone came apart against the wall.

"Shit. Cunt, cunt. Fuck, Fuck, fu—ck!"

His mind oscillated erratically like a fairground waltzer going one way and then the other without any rhythm.

Maya needed to know that he loved her, that he was sorry.

He wouldn't see Jezza until Tuesday, two whole days away.

The dance class was Wednesday. She couldn't stop him going there.

The anger management group was on a Thursday. Knowing he wasn't the only one who raged was helpful: Tommy, a seventy-five-year-old grandad, was there for giving his wife, who has dementia, a black eye. Nathan, twenty-four, had slapped his girlfriend in front of her kid. Tez, an alcoholic on the wagon, was generally wound up the whole time, like a pit bull with his head stuck in some railings, waiting to get loose. The other guys weren't that bad, they just shouted, they hadn't hit anyone.

At meetings, they'd take it in turns to say which bit of the week had been the most difficult when it came to handling their rage. Last week, Troy had talked about how he'd grabbed Gazza but had managed to reign his rage in. He got a lot of pats on the back for that. He enjoyed all these other men—and they were all men, no women, men struggling with their shit. There was a camaraderie, like in prison.

The group had a buddy system where you could call someone if you felt the anger was *escalating out of proportion*—this term was used a lot. Chas, the guy who ran the group, said *rage is recognised by its disproportion to the situation*. He described all the symptoms: *unable to think clearly, fear, wanting to attack*. Techniques had been suggested, like write your anger out, go for a walk, bash some cushions, but never try to win over or control the other person. In the groups, this all sounded very nice, but in the real world when Maya told him she was into screwing around, all the techniques vanished from Troy's brain, and all that was left was a murderous coldness.

The room was a bombsite; he needed to get a grip, but his head was incapable of chilling.

In desperation, Troy scrambled around on the floor in search of the new phone, and it turned out it was still usable. He tapped on Tommy's name.

"Alright Tommy, it's Troy."

"Troy, nice surprise, how you doing?"

"Maya, she's dumped me and I'm fucking losing it man, big time."

"Okay, what happened?"

Tommy's voice was homely, like warm custard or freshly baked bread. It was impossible to imagine someone with such a kind manner having anger issues. He was one of those people you just automatically felt safe around, like a favourite uncle or that one teacher at school who was on your side.

Mr Winterbottom, the English teacher, was Troy's favourite. He was the only one who never got on Troy's case, even the times he got into serious scraps. Mr Winterbottom would say, "Come see me after school," and Troy would turn up and there'd be a packet of Jaffa Cakes, and Mr Winterbottom would say, "So, how are things at home these days, Troy? Help yourself to a biscuit." And then he'd just listen and ask more questions about Troy's home life, nodding and saying things like, "Hmm, that sounds tough," or "A bright lad like you could do really well for yourself if you put your mind to it, you know." He often wondered what happened to Mr Winterbottom.

Tommy pretty much got to hear everything. Troy told him about the *Into-me-see* game, the poly-whasisname-shagging-about that Maya had mentioned, his storming out of Nadia's and then the fight, and now the blocked calls. He didn't mention putting his hands around any throats, worried that Tommy might judge.

It was better not to think about the heavy stuff: the broken ribs, the threats, the bruises. The truth was, it wasn't all him, there was a demon inside. A constant dual between good and evil.

Tommy reassured Troy that it was natural to feel hurt, reminding him hurt, jealousy, fear, frustration and shame were what often lay beneath anger. A tinder of warmth was blown into a flame with the idea that his rage had different bits to it, like a story, and for a moment he could watch the ferocity of his anger from a safe distance, like one of those tornado hunters he'd seen on TV.

"As Chas says, people with anger are supersensitive, they hurt easily. We just need to learn how to show other feelings. When was the last time you cried, Troy?"

When his mum had let him out of the cupboard, he'd been in there for hours, though time gets distorted when you're alone and scared in the dark. He'd been crying good and proper then. He must have been about seven or eight at the time, and when he was still crying, she slapped him hard and he had to go back in. That was the last time he cried.

"Dunno, Tommy, ages ago mate."

"Well, maybe that's what you need to do, learn to cry again."

"You sound like my counsellor, he's gagging for me to cry. I think it gives him a boner to see people cry. I just want to be happy, and right now I'm going mental."

"What do you think would help?"

"Getting her back."

"Troy, maybe it's hard for you to let her go but you need to let her choose, give her some space and focus on yourself."

"But I want her to know that I'm alright now, that I fucked up and I..."

"She knows all that, you've told her, now just let her have some time. Just watch a movie, see some friends, go for a walk. Just focus on you, not her."

Tommy was making sense. He was being the bit of Troy's brain that had gone walkabout. It was good to feel like he had a mate again.

* * *

When Troy had got released from the young offenders institute, his key worker visited him for the last time before driving off into the sunset. Sussing out the whereabouts of her pretty, little, rose-covered cottage in the sticks had been easy-peasy. The woods nearby were a great place to bivouac and eyeball her from afar as she walked her dog each day, always at the same time. There'd been endless talk of Harold her Great Dane when she used to visit. It was common knowledge amongst his peers that dogs love antifreeze and were indifferent to it being deadly poisonous. There was immense satisfaction watching her blub like a baby over Harold's body as it writhed on the ground, helplessly, until it died.

Part Two

FIFTEEN

Liam

The midday sun was intense, its heat weighted, making movement laborious and strained. Daniel had pointed out the jobs needing to be done whilst away in France, which pretty much amounted to constant weeding.

Liam had already decided on a swim. The radio had mentioned 36°C across southern England—swimming was a no brainer. His parched body ached to be quenched by the cool water.

The key was hidden in the rosebed, beneath a stone that fitted snugly over a secret pocket, near the oak door leading into the pool. He'd discovered it when putting manure down for the roses.

Lifting the stone, a shot of adrenalin kicked in, exhilaration spilling over. The key gave the impression it originated from when the pool was built in Victorian times. Daniel had gone into elaborate details about this when asked how old the pool was. The rusty device had the weight of something magical: an opener to a treasure chest, a secret garden or another world beset with unicorns and sorcery.

Pushing the solid door open, he stepped inside. Until then, he'd only ever seen glimpses through the small, arched, glassless windows. Inside was another world. The sun reflected off the water, sending luminous, flickering streaks of light across the walls. Floors tiled with arabesque geometric patterns. The pool, doubtlessly refurbished since the late 1800s, had retained its original essence along with the door and key.

Liam stripped off his clothes, trailing them over a sunlounger. Taking a deep breath, he dived naked into the cool water. Swimming down along the tiled floor of the pool, the sense of melting from the heat disappeared, bringing form back to his body along with an ecstatic rush of aliveness. There was nothing like being stark naked in a place you're not meant to be.

Hey Meredith, how do you like this!

His head emerged from the cool surface of the pool.

"Hey Meredith, I'm in your pool," he said aloud, laughing at his own audacity. He knew full well just how much this would piss her off! Meredith and her *I'm so fucking above you!*

Swimming in the Bloombergs' pool was not something they'd approve of.

Would Daniel, as friendly as he was, allow the use of their pool when on holiday? Liam knew he was transgressing an employer/employee boundary. It could be that coded deep in Daniel's DNA was a faint impression of the subordinate servant being whipped by the master—he was certain he'd seen it in Meredith's eyes.

Sure, Daniel's a nice guy, but what if the social rules and etiquette he so fondly clung to were disobeyed. Liam, on the other hand, wasn't doing anything wrong, though he *knew* he was doing something wrong in the eyes of the Bloombergs. The pool was empty, so why not? It wouldn't harm them or the pool. Plus, on such a hot day, diving into something cold was simply a given, even if puerile—he didn't care. It was necessary to release some insurgent frustration as well as cooling down.

Pushing himself out of the water onto the tiled decking, he pattered over to the diving board and dived into the water. Body missiling along, a trail of lime green pee following, adding to the relief of not worrying about anything, knowing like a fox, territory had been marked. Turning onto his back, eyes closed, each limb a cardinal point morphing his torso into the shape of a star, evaporating into timeless space, face kissed by the sun. Loose limbs, chest open, flaccid penis, all dreamy and whirling inside, he had become boundless in a liquid sky.

"Shit! I'm so sorry!" came a voice, abruptly jolting him out of his euphoria. His eyes quickly darted towards the door, catching a momentary glimpse of a woman leaving, closing the oak door behind her.

* * *

Liam got out of the pool, barely bothering to dry before throwing his clothes on. He struggled to breathe, racking his brains, trying to work out who'd laid eyes on him—starkers, taking liberties.

There was no reasonable justification for being in the pool. *Viva le revolution* bravado turned into feeble apologies and pathetic excuses, none of which came to mind with any clarity. A cleaner possibly? Maybe she wouldn't say anything. What if it was a friend of the Bloombergs? They were bound to tell Daniel and Meredith.

Biting down on a knuckle, breath compressing against the ribcage, he approached the door. It occurred that whoever it was could be waiting on the other side. *Chill-the-fuck-out, why the panic, for God's sake?* His mouth punctured, releasing a flurry of air against the wooden door. Cocking his head, on the count of three, he gently pushed the heavy door open with a hand, stepping through, relieved to see there was no one there.

The house across the lawn was about thirty metres away, and to get to the *Fort Knox* gates, he needed to walk past it. The idea was to escape without having to explain anything. *This was too embarrassing. Maybe she didn't get a good look at him? Fuck, what an idiot!*

Liam fancied himself as quite a laidback kind of guy, yet right now he was nauseous, his mind running riot. *Why so worried? What was there to be so scared of?* Sure, there'd been a slash in the pool, but no one would ever know. Sure, a boundary had been transgressed, but the worst that could happen would be to lose one customer: Daniel. Daniel who'd become a friend. Daniel whom he'd built up some trust with. Daniel who'd been warm and welcoming and appeared to like him.

Eclipsed was the bit that didn't want to lose his dad all over again. Breathe! Breathe! An aching dread reverberated within, a young boy lost with no one to call out to. *Just keep breathing!*

About to pass the house mid panic attack, a voice came. "Hello." He ignored it, and then there it was again. "Hi there!"

He turned to see the same woman from the pool in a T-shirt and leggings. "Hi," she said again.

"Hi," he replied, heart quickening, catching her eye.

"I'm so sorry about earlier. I was about to go for a swim and didn't expect anyone to be in there."

"Oh, yeah, sorry, I was just really hot and needed to cool down." *Fuck! Why did I say that!*

"I'm Maya. Are you Liam?"

How does she know my name, and how come she's acting so cool about it? Daniel had often mentioned his youngest daughter, Maya. This was the worst thing that could possibly happen.

"Erm, I do some gardening on Wednesdays."

"Yes, my father said you'd be here."

He cleared his throat, scratching his head, looking down, stuck for words. On her left foot was a toe ring and a bright yellow sun tattooed on her ankle.

"Are you here on holiday?" The tattooed ankle suggested it was okay be informal.

"Kind of, how about you? Do you live locally?"

"About a mile away, in some woodland."

"Literally in a wood? Like a bear?" she said playfully. Her breezy banter put Liam at ease.

She obviously didn't care that he'd been in the pool. Daniel's daughter was not how he imagined. Very attractive, mousy brown hair in a short French bob, alluring hazel-brown eyes. Not tall, a delicate look about her that betrayed a zeal in her eyes, as though her body held both the urges of feminine power whilst at the same time, a deep-seated fear of this. Braless too. A frisson of sexual arousal lapped over him. He wanted to look at her body more but knew better than to ogle.

There was an elfish quality in her open face, easy to look at. He found himself gawping like a kid.

"Ha, kinda! I've got a caravan in some woodland."

"Wow, that's exciting. You must love it there."

"This time of year, it's great."

"Must be cold in winter?" Maya grimaced, as though imagining the cold.

Probably just being polite. This was a thing posh people sometimes did: good at appearing interested but it was hard to tell how genuine they were—probably not that interested in hearing about a caravan. Liam was crap at small talk. He wanted to sound fascinating, to keep her there.

"It is, but worth it for the rest of the year. January and February can be a struggle, but the rest of the time it's great."

He'd said *great* twice now, how monotonous. His face was burning on the inside as he toiled frozen earth vocabulary for something interesting to say. She probably thought he was stupid.

Palming the back of her neck, Maya gave Liam the once-over, a tiny smile on her lips.

"Do you have a TV?"

"No. Have a radio, though."

"What about Wi-Fi?"

"There's no signal, not even for my mobile." Could he be any duller?

"Wow, you really are off-grid, aren't you. So, what do you do on an evening?"

A glint spun from her eyes—sod the holding back.

"I dance naked under the full moon with wolves and bears…"

That did it. Maya let out a shriek of laughter.

"…and pixies," he added.

"When's the next full moon then?"

Talk about brazen. Everything about her contradicted the surroundings—maybe the Bloombergs had adopted a local traveller's child.

"Why, are you interested then?" This was too risqué, after all, it was the Bloombergs' daughter, adopted or not. *What if she says yes, then what?*

"I am! I love dancing, not sure about the naked bit though."

Now what? Now what... Now what! There was no sharp response, nothing ultra-witty, not even a cheesy one-liner—he'd gone blank.

She stood there, perfectly unfazed, knee slightly bent, hand on hip, the other shelving her chin, index finger poised against her lips. Gorgeously intimidating. The terrifying thing was she appeared to be flirting. Cooly open, butterfly smile, all loose with abandon. In order to meet her, he had to trust it was really happening, get on the bus. He opted for the next thing that landed in his head.

"Well, you'd be welcome to visit any time. What you up to later?" *Inglorious but still brave,* he commended himself.

"Hmm, now let me see. Nope, nothing."

"Great. Great. Come over, that is, I mean ... if you ... erm want."

"How about eight?"

This was surreal. It'd been ages since anyone—let alone a woman—had visited his caravan.

"Yeah, great, I mean erm, brilliant." Liam wanted to get away before his fumbling words escalated into saying something profoundly stupid, causing her to change her mind.

"And the moon?"

"Erm, the moon?"

"Will it be full? I want to see this dance." Her eyes widened as she gesticulated a witchy finger dance, playing with him.

"Um, new moon I think," he said, unable to keep up with her idiosyncrasy.

"Oh, that's a shame, so I won't see the dance?"

Was she serious? Of course not.

"Oh yes," he laughed nervously, "the dance can be performed under any moon."

She laughed again, and even though what he'd said wasn't particularly funny, her laughter, unlike his, was bolstering.

"Can't wait, what's the address?"

They took out mobiles, exchanging numbers so Liam could text the address.

Exiting through the tyrannous gates to his van parked up on the grass verge, he was unsure whether she was a witch or fairy goddess. He did know, though, madness was in the air, the very thing he feared most with women.

* * *

Every man's home—he hated the term bachelor-pad—has forgotten corners, blind spots in which dust collects, escaping peripheral vision. The caravan wasn't messy, but it had been a while since it gleamed, and having a guest, especially an attractive one, he was all psyched up into cleaning and tidying, raring to show off his woodsy panache. Rugs were shaken out, bed made, cooker cleaned, floor washed, table polished, every corner meticulously scoured for dirt.

Coming to a pile of books and CDs, it crossed his mind to leave a couple out, as if unintentionally. Maybe Kafka's *Metamorphosis*, or Dostoevsky's *Crime and Punishment*, which he still hadn't got round to reading since buying it five years ago. A Daft Punk CD casually lying on top ... no, underneath, or side by side even? After careful consideration, he added a bottle of white Sauvignon and red Merlot bought in Woking, or in this case, ordered from a dimly lit café on some cobbled street in Prague. Catching himself, he wondered what the fuck he was up to? His pretensions a reminder of just how much he sought intellectual endorsement from others. Putting the books away, his pseudo installation was dismantled, replaced by the authenticity of knowing he was northern, working-class and still had the occasional fondness for mushy peas.

Time dragged. Constantly checking it every two minutes didn't make it go any faster. He was unable to keep still, tempted to drive to the farm entrance—the only place he could get a signal—and double-check she hadn't cancelled. *Was it a date? Jesus, just chill the fuck out, you idiot!* He went outside, took a heavy axe and set about splitting some logs.

* * *

Through the trees, a blue car could be seen in the distance, leisurely driving down the winding track, bypassing the main house, down past the cows and towards the oak woodland. Liam recognised the VW Polo from the Bloombergs' house: it was the spare car, probably for the kids to use when visiting. Maya got out of the car, a green, cottony summer dress quivering on a sigh of warm air. If she was wearing make-up, it wasn't obvious. Liam swallowed a mouthful of saliva.

After a slightly awkward greeting—no hugs or handshakes—they went inside the caravan for a tour, which since its deep clean, appeared more spacious and airier whilst simultaneously cosy and inviting, like a newly feathered nest, except more zen.

Maya enquired about various elements as though in a museum. What Liam lacked in verbosity he made up for in spirit, touching each object as he spoke, the grain of the wood, the lead of the stained glass, the age of the tiles, proud of its handcrafted simplicity. Maya listened intently, her twinkly eyes flitting around, every so often meeting his.

Noticing a pair of underpants he'd missed, sneaking out from beneath the bed, his foot discreetly tried to nudge them back under without success.

"Shall we sit outside?" he suggested, grabbing the bottles of wine.

It was a balmy evening with the sun low but not yet on the horizon, giving off a tranquil ambience.

Maya took up the offer of some wine, and they sat on a blanket in a glade just beyond the caravan. It was very strange, as though they'd known each other for much longer. Liam wondered if this was always the way for her. They chatted intimately, drinking, asking questions, letting the other in a little more when answering. Maya brought out a little bag of grass and rolled a joint. They'd already drunk a bottle of red between them. Liam wasn't keen on smoking dope, particularly with alcohol—too many bad memories, too much confusion. A grotesque thought of his mother charged into view, skinny as a roll-up, all tangled up in paranoia.

His fractured brain snapped together, declaring it wasn't in a mood for being cautious. He was on holiday in a wonderful place called Maya, where he'd never been.

The sun sank lower behind the tress. Elongated rope shadows stretched across the land. A couple of swallows chased each other in the distance against scorched hues of pinks and reds. A crescent moon surfacing. Vivid colours animating the scenery for one last performance before dying to the night. Creatures in the distance could be heard every now and then as they re-entered the nocturnal world that belonged to them. Wildness, with all its unpredictability, was on the prowl.

"What a gorgeous night. You're so lucky to live here, it's beautiful," said Maya.

"It is." Liam closed his eyes and relaxed into the surroundings.

A pause, outstretched, lingered, in which there was nothing to do other than just be. The scent of meadowsweet drifted on the night air. Each bathed in the shared moment. After a while, Liam resurfaced and glanced at her. In the semi-dark, he saw a mystical goddess. He thought how strange it was that this goddess was sitting before him in all her divine femininity. Like a cat sensing the touch of his admiration, the lids of her eyes lifted, unhurried; beneath, warm and dewy pools enticed him. Liam was on fire with desire. Maya smiled. Liam realised he was stoned.

"So, what do you do at night to pass time?" Maya asked.

"Dance naked under the stars with the wolves and bears, remember? I told you earlier."

Maya laughed. "Oh yes, so you did, how could I forget. Go on then, don't let me stop you!"

It was a playful game, and Liam was in check, uncertain how to move.

Maya rescued him. "We can dance together if you like. Clothes on, of course."

Liam wanted to meet Maya in her wildness despite fearing this luminous witch goddess.

His arms impulsively floated into the air like charmed snakes, exploring the space around him, his movement lighting up a big smile on Maya's face, and joining in, she moved her arms in accordance. They sensitively moved around each other, rising onto their feet, playing with the space as the setting sun silhouetted them into shadow puppets—both careful not to touch but close enough to feel the warmth emitted from the other's body. Playfully tempting the other more into the dance. Between them, a charge was building; they bent and swooped like swallows. All the time keeping eye contact. For an orchestra, they had the quiver of leaves from an aspen on the night wind, the owl calling to a mate, their naked feet on the ground, the sweet, moist air between them. Together they created flames with sparks disappearing into the blackness. Magic was taking place. There was an accidental touching as Liam's fingers brushed against her arm with a soft caress. As brief as it was, both experienced its pulsation.

Maya's form weaved around Liam with scintillating grace.

She was the one in control, the one with the power. Liam was in a world he'd been to occasionally, but he didn't feel in control, yet he trusted Maya to be a good mistress of ceremonies. As they moved, this primitive mating ritual grew more intense, the breath deepened and sex pheromones released.

Liam hadn't thought about a relationship in ages. He hadn't been looking for one either. Becky, his last partner, accused him of being guarded. The tipping point came just after an evening out to the cinema: leaving the romcom they entered the stark lights of the real world where Becky suggested, as tactfully as she could, that maybe sometimes he *might just get a tiny bit cagey?* He'd gone all argumentative and sulky when she'd tentatively brought up the idea of meeting his mum again whom she still hadn't met after two years. Liam had secrets, and the closer Becky got, the more guarded he became.

Liam knew he was guarded; he'd been working on it. Even read a couple of books about *attachment styles* in relationships, concluding that he was probably *avoidant* and Becky *anxious*. When she dumped him, he panicked, not realising just how painful ending would be: it was akin to having a limb torn off without anaesthetic. He'd been so sure Becky was the one and was in it for the long haul—moods, distancing, secrets, along with the rest.

Things had changed. It'd been over five years since the split. He'd be thirty in three years and had matured. The old him made him cringe. *How pathetic he'd been, like some stereotypical man who couldn't show his feelings!* That was someone else.

And now, here he was—*John Travolta with Uma Thurman*, dancing a strange twist in the dark.

The pas de deux spiralled into a serene finale as Liam and Maya alighted the earth, wondering where they'd just been.

"Oh, that was such fun!" said Maya.

"Incredible."

"My God, it's so dark now. How do you get around in the dark?"

"You just have to trust your instincts."

"Don't you have a torch?"

"There is that as well," he said, laughing, "but I like to walk in the dark sometimes. You have to be careful of cow shit or holes, but your eyes adjust after a while, plus we have a sliver of moon rising."

In the distance, a waxing crescent moon was floating up above the black trees.

"Shall we go for a midnight walk?" effused Maya, taking the initiative.

They agreed to walk and headed into the open fields beyond the wood, still mildly inebriated and stoned.

"So, how come you get on with my father so well?"

"I'm not sure... I guess we have some things in common."

"That's nice. And do you get on with my mother?"

"Not really spoken to her much."

"There's a surprise."

"How'd you mean?"

"She doesn't like anyone. She's an elitist snob!"

"Sounds like you don't get on?"

"She's unbearable. I'm only here because they're on holiday."

Liam was unsure whether to continue down this path. He didn't see it as appropriate to start telling her how much he detested her mother too.

Maya continued. "Don't be sucked in by their charm. That's what they do, charm. Say the right things but never express what they really think."

The mood had sunk; maybe Maya was coming down from the wine and dope and a more depressive side was starting to show.

They walked along in the faint moonlight, their silence punctuated by a screech of an owl every so often. When they arrived back at the caravan, Liam lit some candles and a small lamp that ran from a large battery and made some fennel tea for them both. Maya looked at his books. They talked some more before she decided it was time to leave. As she climbed into her car, she invited him to the house on the Saturday. Liam accepted the invitation.

SIXTEEN

Maya

Having taken a taxi from Woking train station, Maya arrived at her childhood home late Tuesday evening.

The stern, sombre monolith, gaunt from desertion, was in fact a welcome solace. Her parents being there would have waylaid a visit, particularly the thought of seeing her mother.

Troy's cut-throat rage had been a wake-up call. The only reason the police weren't contacted was on account of knowing he was in therapy, that the ugly monster witnessed was not the whole Troy. She, too, knew what it was like to fall from grace, but those dead eyes were not the kind of eyes she'd ever want to look into again.

Deciding to block his number was as simple as not wandering around Afghanistan in a miniskirt: it might go against all your values but when your life's at stake, what can you do. The way he ranted and pleaded on the voice messages, anyone would think a family home had been broken—how would they explain it to their non-existent kids. Total, fucking nut job. Even the clingiest men found some self-respect in the end. They'd hardly been seeing each other, with actual coitus just the once.

Nadia insisted that Maya stay over at theirs for a couple of nights whilst formulating a plan.

Knowing her parents would be in France for a few weeks made going to Falindon an obvious choice. Space to ground, figure out the next steps.

Calls to her parents were intermittent, the months between, a port in the storm, mustering enough strength to go back into battle. Out of duty rather than any kind of love. It should have been more regular but that would be masochism. They nearly always ended in an argument, her mother using that one trigger sentence guaranteed to get under the skin: *Maya, darling, you know you've always been tempestuous, ever since you were a child, that's why men find you difficult.* Her mother never had anything positive to say and had no time for personal growth. The path Maya was on was *a waste of time that ultimately would lead nowhere, darling.* After hanging up, there'd be a need to lie down or to scream into a cushion, bringing to mind the Ram Dass quote which went something like, *If you think you're enlightened, try visiting your parents for the weekend.*

The full rota of domestic help had been specified, not that she gave a shit: the cleaners came in on Mondays and Thursdays, Garden Force Maintenance were on a Tuesday and Liam the gardener was on Wednesdays. She was surprised when her father had said, "Liam, Marvellous chap, heart of gold. Make him a cup of tea if you're around." This was completely out of character, so much so that she was duped into bringing up Troy, even his violent act. Her father responded with a rare warmth and empathy.

He was one of those absent fathers, either hidden behind a newspaper, escaping on a business trip or just a general lack of interest. The need for his affection had never gone away. It would be fair to say he had become ever so slightly more responsive over the latter years, enquiring about her relationships, even consoling her, but these were minimal; the softening was welcomed, even if it was all a bit late.

On the Wednesday, she'd got out of bed around mid-morning and dressed for a pre-brunch jog. Stepping from the house into the globally warmed air was like entering a sweat lodge. Starting at an easy pace, she crossed the familiar landscape of Falindon Moor, pressing play on her mental DVD player, watching reruns of childhood memories.

For many years, there'd been countless hours happily reminiscing over time spent on the moor, family picnics, collecting feathers, stones, moss and leaves to take home, concocting magic potions. This delightful part of childhood never questioned for its accuracy. Such memories were sacred, sustaining life, but as the years went by, the realisation that it was most likely only a few times they'd picnicked on the moor, maybe once or twice she'd collected the magic objects, reality began to trickle in. Memory was funny like that, believing the good bits to be longer than they were, when in truth, the bad bits stretched to such a length, every day was like being buried alive, particularly when you were sent to Teresa of Avila's elite boarding school for girls at eight years old.

A stinging bewilderment never ceased to torment her over how she could have been sent to such a horrendous private school. A school that had changed little of its ethos since it was established in 1732.

In prep school, Jacqueline Wilson books had been relished, stories involving kids, foster kids, parents who were drug addicts, kids from broken homes. Boarding at Teresa of Avila's, Maya saw herself as one of those kids, except in her case having a family and money improved nothing.

As adolescence approached, her parents and brothers began to mean less and less; during some holidays, the thought of going home brought no joy at all. *What was the point in going home if at the end of it you go back to prison? Better to make prison your home, less painful.*

There was no breeze on the moor. Keeping pace, enjoying the push of her body through the green open space, Maya's T-shirt clung with perspiration. Tired memories without beginning, middle or end churned over to no avail.

The only adult worth her salt was Suzy. Up until then, there'd been no indication of real love, the sort that invites you in without asking you to take off your muddy boots or denying you the right to speak truthfully for fear of any discomfort evoked. Suzy was someone who didn't use the terms *incorrigible* and *wilful*, a regular put down at home.

Even the teachers at prep school expressed doubts over her behaviour, reducing her *stubborn refusal to do what had been asked of her* as *negative attention-seeking,* kick-starting a daily regime of Ritalin, until it clicked that they weren't the nice tablets she'd been told they were, henceforth adamantly refusing to take them. That's when Suzy came along.

The problem was that it was easy to keep tablets a secret—you simply stuck them in your pocket—but a shrink was a different story, and seeing a counsellor was not cool. It was like wearing a T-shirt that says *Mentally Unstable* in bold letters across the front. In the world of boarders, it went hand in hand with spiteful teasing. And girls could be seriously evil when they wanted to be.

The letter from the head at Teresa of Avila's, found on a visit home in the holidays, suggested the need for psychological support due to *a reluctance to fully partake in the school's ethos of community and mutual respect around courtesy and forbearance*—they could have simply put *we caught Maya smoking weed,* she speculated, but everything in Teresa of Avila's was long-winded, articulated in dog-whistle vernacular..

It was reasonable to think her parents viewed the counselling, not about making changes but conveniently saddling someone else with the responsibility for the emotional well-being of their daughter. They wouldn't have known how to even begin discussing anything emotional—conversations were either intellectual, practical or academic.

Oddly enough, Maya found herself enjoying the sessions with the counsellor who'd insisted on being called Suzy, not Miss, Mrs or Doctor—whatever her surname happened to be.

Suzy was in her late forties and Maya hazarded a guess that she'd probably done her own fair share of smoking weed in her youth in the counter-culture eighties, probably went to Greenham Common. Her appearance, far from prim—like Maya had envisioned—proved she hadn't succumbed to the drab and dusty dress code like the rest of the school staff. Her clothes were vibrant and quirky, sporting funky earrings to complement a strand of red hair, dyed just above the ears.

It was a new experience to be listened to so attentively. Having someone agreeing when talking about the stuffiness of the school, understanding how oppressive that must feel, how difficult it must be for a child so far away from home.

At first, Suzy's attempts to connect emotionally were rebuffed. Maya accused her of trying to break into her head like a voyeur, a new word she'd learnt, a pervert even. Thinking she was doubly clever for pointing out that *therapist* when split spelt *the-rapist*, it turned out Suzy was aware of this, and she herself thought it odd too.

But one week when accidentally letting slip in the usual cynical, aloof way that she *no longer cared about living anymore,* Suzy's eyes visibly welled, milky sustenance, warm and sweet, lifelined through space, nursing Maya in away she'd never experienced, pure and genuine.

Being small for her age was tough, but as Suzy pointed out, she was both sparrow and eagle, each one deserving space: one to spread wings and reach great heights, and the other to be held with an even greater sensitivity.

Maya had seen herself as a wild horse unwilling to surrender to the will of a whip, yet the lashes had become intolerable and the thought of giving in became more appealing. Suzy came just at the right moment, unperturbed by the snarling teenage cynicism, instead saying how touched she was by what was shared, how honoured she was to bear witness. Reassuring that everything spoken would never leave the room. Of course, Suzy's radar, constantly locating parts in need of care, was all coolly played down whilst secretly cherished.

When the agreed standard twelve sessions came to an end, Maya pleaded with her parents to keep paying for them, which they did for three years until leaving school for university. It took a year before the suicidal fantasies were mentioned again, but sessions were never missed.

Whilst traipsing across the bleak terrain, some self-worth was assembled and a way out of what had been a post-apocalyptic, emotionally barren wasteland was discovered.

The main emphasis tended to land on how there hadn't been a good attachment with her mother, how cold her mother was, and how she'd been abandoned by her mother. Her mother was the star of pretty much every session.

Pain shot across her calf muscles as she shot across the moor, joyful with a determination to continue. The heart accelerating. Out-breaths had become audible puffs blowing out candles, each dead flame another year gone until a new season pixelated across her mind.

A whole adolescence without boys, surely a perverted injustice—she'd longed to go inland, hunting, away from the turbulent sea of oestrogen.

And she did just that, finding boys at gigs, festivals, mostly stoners or narcissistic hippies who thought they were enlightened because they'd attended an ayahuasca ceremony in Brazil or eaten psilocybin, but they were boys, just boys. They'd start out strong and adventurous free spirits like herself, but then around the four-month mark, they'd get all needy, clipping her wings. Demanding. Childish. The last thing she wanted was to have sex with a child.

Leaving school, she chose to study psychology at university but found studying utterly boring and, much to the annoyance of her parents, dropped out in her second year, choosing to reject any further steps along the academic path.

Here emerged a bespoke education, tailored to her more metaphysical needs rather than one that squished her into—whatever the opposite of a TARDIS is—a box big on the outside but with less room than a straightjacket on the inside.

Firstly, she went to Goa in India where she took ecstasy, danced on the beaches to nineties rave music and found a guru.

Then travelling to California to train as a Conscious Movement practitioner.

The goal was to lose the self-loathing, twist the thing that felt ugly inside into something that people would want. That niggling sense of not being good enough had been at her heel forever; trying to kick it away was useless—the kick would be against her own shin. The swami had said, *Your critical voice is the unloved child in you which you find unacceptable. Find love for her and you will find peace.* Easier said than done.

Troy undoubtedly had been a silly mistake that in hindsight she should have been aware of. All the signs were glaringly obvious from the beginning. The way he looked at her should have made her skin crawl, but it hadn't. Why was she drawn to fucked-up men? Why couldn't she fancy Ian? Okay, well maybe that was obvious, but there were some good men out there, surely.

Being dangerous was an aphrodisiac. *Safe is boring.* Her whole life had been too safe. Not in a good way safe with a security that blanketed her in love and warmth, but prison safe, restrictive safe, safeguarded from sensuality, passion and free expression.

And as for ending up like her mother, this would be worse than having to eat sand for the rest of her life.

This woman, incapable of love with all its messy, complicated circuitry. Everything had to be nice, aesthetically perfect, no depth or meaning. Anything but real. For her mother, real was a cockroach, ugly and distasteful. Only the holographic opulence of the unreal was safe. Safe from all that pain that the solid, three-dimensional world holds.

Yet, Maya could feel her inside like a bad omen waiting to happen.

But what is real? Her legs were moving in time to her stream of consciousness. On a runner's high, her brain pumping out endorphins as her feet hit the ground.

Reality is a shawl that covers a bird cage! We only believe what we experience, her guru, the divine swami, had once told her.

She was *in a dream and it was time to wake up. Remove the shawl,* he'd said.

She wanted to be like the sadhu, rejecting worldly trappings and facing the pain of being alive to each moment. But being awake involved pain. There was comfort in illusion, like an addict chasing the next fix to escape the squalor of life. The pain of truth and aloneness, the pain of disillusionment, the pain of not being loved by the one you most hope to receive love from. Being alone was a pain too hard for Maya to bear, almost as terrifying as the pain that comes from being met in the deepest recesses of the heart. With Suzy, she'd sobbed. Not cried, not blubbered, not shed a few tears, she'd fucking sobbed hard. Her heart, each broken piece, a rivulet to the floor.

Real love threatens to awaken the grief that sleeps inside.

Was there a choice? Was it the mind that chose or the heart? Was there a difference between the two? Maya's heart was caged, and she longed for something more. Her whole life had been going from one relationship to another, hoping to free her heart, but freedom always ended up as just another trap. It was hard being free when your natural habitat was a gilded prison.

She landed back at the house, exhilarated, exhausted and overheated. She made a banana, apple and coconut milk smoothie and took herself down to the pool to cool off. Noticing the key was missing, she pushed the heavy oak door and was surprised to see a blissful starfish man floating naked in the water.

SEVENTEEN

Liam

Microscopic droplets of rain levitated on the air, shrouding the wood like smoke from dampened, burning leaves. Trees peeking through took on a spectral form, watching over Liam as he showered under a plastic watering can rigged up outside.

Showering naked in the wood had become the customary way of getting clean. In winter, hot water was added, making it more bearable.

This was followed with a twice-weekly shave, his beady eye tracking the razor in a small mirror hanging from a wooden post as he steadily manoeuvred downward strokes along the jowls, extra careful to avoid nicks. Beards looked rubbish on him. He'd tried to grow one a few times, but they always turned out wispy.

Maya had been squatting in his brain since first clapping eyes on her, his attempts to evict her through reading, working, cooking, going for long walks were all futile; there she remained, indelible, with those vivacious eyes and friendly breasts.

Masturbation was the last resort. It would take the edge off sexual desire; he didn't want to arrive at hers, tongue lolling out, trying to steal a sneaky peep of breasts etched against her top. Why were women's nipples such a turn-on?

It was to do with not having had sex for such a long time. Quite a lot of frustration had built up; a wank would calm things down. The thought of Maya being sexual immediately made him hard. Soapy hands began to rub his cock, but then, taking a deep breath, he forced himself to stop, deciding instead to savour the rousing energy. Galloping up, turned on would just have to be what it was, though denying the pleasure was a small torture. He went inside the caravan, jousting rod jutting forth.

Choosing the right clobber to don for this fair maiden was the next step.

Inside the caravan, time was taken swapping various items of clothing, attempting to capture a thrown-together look, hoping to give the impression that he wasn't desperate—being seen as needy was the most vulnerable part beneath his indifferent armour. In the end it was a simple black T-shirt with jeans, cut just right to flatter his physique, a dab of aftershave for the slightest hint of a musky cedarwood fragrance.

Outside, the mist had turned to drizzle.

Over to the veg patch, he picked a few yellow tomatoes from beneath a cloche. There was nothing better than the smell of a freshly picked tomatoes: it reminded him of everything that was good in the world. His uncle Mick had shown him how to nip out the suckers from the main stem when he was a kid to *stop the energy going into all the wrong places*, Mick had said. Maybe that's why he'd got into gardening—he'd spent a lot of time with Mick on that allotment. He picked some rocket to complement the tomatoes with its peppery taste.

A tree creeper scuttled up a nearby oak in agitated fashion, its curved beak quick to extract tiny life forms from the crevices of the bark.

* * *

Liam walked to the door, a fine spray of warm rain blowing against him.

Just be yourself, be natural. Don't try and impress her. Ask her about herself, what she's into. Just 'cos she invited you to dinner, doesn't mean she fancies you. He checked to make sure his fly was zipped up and rang the bell.

Maya came to the door smiling, wearing a sleeveless, thin, dark, cotton maxidress with an African print and side split. Her face open and radiant, she welcomed him into the house. This was the first time he'd been in the Bloombergs' house. In terms of how he imagined a typical aristocratic mansion, it struck him as smaller, but still impressive. Above, a crystal chandelier, through some magnetic pull, forced him to become more upright. An air of power, wealth and authority permeated the atmosphere like ancestral ghosts reluctant to move on.

Here he was, a guest in this great, big fuck-off house. Standing in front of the gorgeous daughter of the Bloombergs'. He almost pinched himself to make sure that he was really there.

Discombobulated like a child in a toy shop, he wanted to check out the oil paintings ascending the imperial staircase and then go into all the rooms and touch the smooth rosewood furniture, rummage in the drawers for trinkets or leaf through the books, making sure to breathe in the mossy scent emitting from the pages.

Ever since discovering junk shops, he found it impossible to pass one without nipping in for a browse, curious about where everything came from, how old it was, the romantic story it held. From the hall entrance, the Bloomberg house was like a giant curiosity shop.

Was he now in a special club? The whole time working at the Bloombergs', he'd never once been invited in and assumed this was to prevent any misunderstanding as to the role he fundamentally fulfilled—the gardener—which meant domestic servant, not friend.

Maya spotted Liam's dumbfounded expression.

"I know, obscene isn't it! Two people living here with all this space like a couple of Russian oligarchs."

"It's massive. I've seriously never been in such a big house." Even the squats didn't compare.

"Come on, let's go sit in the living room."

Maya led Liam through some double doors beneath one of the staircases into a vast room with two sofas and a chair around a coffee table situated in the centre of the room.

Liam sat on a sofa whilst Maya went and made a pot of tea. Liam's keenness to nosy around was quelled by the dullness of the living room. He'd expected something out of Harry Potter, but the furniture was modern and tastefully boring. Meredith must have a deep fondness for the colours grey and beige. The sofas were grey, the chairs were grey, the walls were grey, the carpet was beige, the curtains were beige, the cushions were beige. The drizzly sky outside had more colour. There was no character to the room, nothing homely, everything perfect like a photoshoot from *Hello* magazine: everything in the right place but there was a sterility to it all. It was the kind of room that if something ended up out of place, such as a crumb on the coffee table, it would almost certainly scream.

Maya arrived back and placing the tray on the table, joined him, leisurely sinking into the opposite end of the sofa. Her bare leg becoming exposed, lingering for a moment. Liam noticed, becoming excited, forcing himself not to look down. Maya smiled, closing the split back to seamless.

"Shall I put some music on?" she said, taking her phone from the table. "What kind of music do you like?"

"I don't mind."

Maya scrolled through her phone, searching for something to play.

"I'll put it on shuffle," she said, and from speakers came a soft, folky, melodic acoustic guitar accompanied by a man's tender voice that warmed the room.

"How did you do that?"

"What?"

"Make the music from your phone come out of the speakers?"

"Bluetooth."

"Blue what?"

Maya laughed. Liam was back in the Stone Age when it came to technology. He still had the simplest of mobiles, one he'd had for years.

The music playing was heartfelt and intimate. Liam sank into the sofa with a sip of tea.

Maya's vibrancy and lack of formality brought dimension and colour to the opaque, bland flatness that surrounded him. Talking with her was effortless, and judging by her manner, the feeling was mutual, each of them fully engaged with what the other had to say.

Liam asked Maya about people in the picture frames, particularly the stiff-looking man in the portrait above the fireplace.

"Oh God, please. Isn't it fucking awful!" Maya said. "That is Field Marshal Rupert Bloomberg, my great-great-grandfather who was an utter twat by all accounts."

Maya had a way of swearing that put Liam at ease due to it appearing so incongruent with her background.

Liam noticed on a console table at the side of the room a photo of a woman leaning into the wind on the prow of a ketch, hair sweeping back, revealing a face full of joie de vivre against an oceanic sky, eyes sparkling, the whole world belonging to her.

"Who's that then?"

"Dear Mammaah," Maya said in a droll voice, stretching the vowels to their limit with a dramatic sense of irony.

"Wow!" It was hard to believe the stony-faced woman who'd once brought him tea was this same person.

"She *was* free once."

"Free?"

"Before we ruined her life."

"How did you do that then?"

"*We* were born, silly. But God, don't let's go there."

Was this Maya's way of a subtle invitation? Did *don't go there*, really mean a*sk me more?*

"Yeah, you said you don't get on, how come?"

"Oh, my mother is all about herself, no one else. No one can get close to her. She lives her life in an ivory tower. Do *you* like her?" There was a lean pause. "Sorry, I'm putting you on the spot. You seriously don't have to answer that."

This question had already been put to him at the caravan. She'd either forgotten or was determined to find a compatriot to help confront the coldness of her mother. Probably wise to remain discreet: they still barely knew each other.

"I've hardly met her. I mainly chat with your dad."

"Again, I can't quite fathom you and my father sitting down together. Are you sure we're talking about the same person? Stiff, boring, always distracted?"

"Maybe he's changed. His past was pretty tough. He talks about you and your brothers and knows he wasn't the best dad."

"My father said that? It must be something about you."

"How'd you mean?"

"You must have some kind of gift. He never opens up. It's a family trait: keep everything hidden. *Everything's fine* is our family motto written within the family crest, didn't you know, darling?"

"Maybe it's 'cos I'm not family, or that I'm a bloke? He talks a bit about his childhood too."

"I really am faint now!" she said sarcastically. "My father talked about his childhood. Fucking hell, Liam, I'm starting to feel jealous!"

"I think he feels guilty about sending you lot off to boarding school." Liam wasn't sure whether it was wise to say this to Maya, but he wanted to help her see that Daniel wasn't all bad.

"A bit late for that."

"I talk to him too. I tell him about me, so maybe that's it."

"For fuck's sake, I tell him about me too, but he's just not interested." Maya pursed her lips as though trying to stop her resentment spilling forth. "Maybe he's secretly gay? I have wondered. You're a good-looking man, so you never know."

"Thanks, he's quite attractive himself."

"Oh no!" Maya shrieked.

"Maybe I should ask him out?"

"No, no, no! Stop it! That is too much. The image of you having sex with my father is just too fucking gross!"

Liam laughed, picturing the surreal image of Daniel and himself eloping. "How come you're so different?" he asked.

"Am I? Different to what?"

"To your folks? Are your brothers like you?"

"Oh God no! They're even worse than my parents. One's a merchant fucking banker and the other is just a twat!"

Maya picked up a tiny, ornate, antique-looking box, opened it and took out some grass and started to roll a joint.

"Oh, I hope you don't mind but it's a bit early in the day, so not for me, thanks," Liam said.

"Sure. You don't mind if I just go ahead and have one?"

"No, of course not," Liam said, feeling awkward, imagining the dope bringing in a distance between them.

Maya lit the joint and took a deep inhalation, holding the smoke in the back of her throat and then blowing it into the cavernous space around them.

"My guru says, *When you believe you are doing good and this good makes you think you are better than others, then you need to stop being good*. So, I've stopped being good."

"What, you have a guru?"

"So, are you being good, Liam?"

"How do you mean?"

"Well, not sharing this joint, is that you being good?"

Maya took another toke of the joint, again her dress fell open, revealing her thigh; she didn't retrieve it.

"I'm not being good. I just don't like being stoned this early in the day," said Liam, picturing his teenage, lost self, constantly wrecked. "How come you have a guru?"

"He's my spiritual teacher. I found him in India. That sounds so fucking weird, doesn't it?"

"What, having a guru?"

"No, *finding him,* as though *he* were lost when it's myself who was lost, so really he found me."

Liam could tell Maya was beginning to get a bit stoned, sensing they were about to be on different wavelengths.

"Okay, give me a go on that."

"I thought you didn't partake at such an ungodly hour?"

"When in Rome."

She passed Liam the joint, and as she did so, her fingertips momentarily touched the back of his hand, boosting the beat of his heart.

As the day wore on, they continued to talk, each tempted by the other to open and reveal more of themselves, though Liam was more comfortable with listening than talking. He'd always been a good listener. At school, being sensitive meant he'd got on better with girls. Other lads, though, would call him gay. It was just that he was more interested in what girls had to say, whereas boys, he mostly felt at odds with; calling other girls slags or sluts was just weird, and violent.

When asked about himself, it was different, though, he became nervous, worried about giving away the person beneath who'd been crushed by the world, the loser with the mad biddy. Kids have special radars: they can zone into prairie children like Liam who seek refuge in the wilderness.

Maya talked about her spiritual beliefs and Swami Gandalih, about her brothers, how unkind they were to her as a child and about her work as a Conscious Movement teacher. Liam listened, asking more questions; the more she talked, the more animated she became. Looking at her was like watching clouds change formation, each expression bringing about a new person he'd not seen before: a young girl, excited and exuberant from her stories; a diva filling the space with her magnetism; a pale creature, not too unlike himself, afraid to come down from the lofty heights of dreaming.

They'd both been talking for hours until words became desiccated, turning to dust, hanging in the air, leaving a lull in the conversation.

There was no attempt to fill the void with more words.

Each looked at the other across the lengthening pause. The room around Liam fell away.

Paradoxically, he was both anxious and relaxed in the same moment, with a gaze that neither was willing to give up.

Something inside became untethered, something he'd forgotten existed, flooding the veins.

Maya's eyes were so unbelievably beautiful. Did she want him?

He wanted her.

The tenderness of those black dilated pupils told him what he needed to know.

His hand, near to a life of its own, reached, gently touching her cheek. It was rare to make the first move—the invite had to be spelt out in large neon letters for him to get the message—he wasn't going to risk being rejected.

With slight apprehension, he leant towards her, making sure the whole time that she didn't suddenly pull a face, his lips eventually meeting hers. Maya's lips were soft, causing his body to sing. Libido kicking off heavy chains like a bear escaping a pit, stealing into the night. He pulled Maya closer, her breast meeting his chest. Tongues like adders danced Celtic knots, tasting each other. He unbuttoned the front of her dress, exposing a pale pink breast, the hardness beneath his denims pressed against her thigh. He was perplexed as the roughness of his callused hand contrasted against the softness of her skin, yet soon they were swimming in the warmth of her giving flesh.

"Shall we go upstairs?" Maya said, breathless, standing, leading him by the hand.

How was this happening? He was about to have sex with the Bloombergs' daughter whom he'd known less than a few days.

Their bodies swept by a carnal force scrambled up the stairs, the oil paintings now of no interest whatsoever.

Maya's body moved lightly with a fervour Liam had not seen in a woman before—all the previous women had either lacked this kind of rampant desire or kept it well hidden. Liam towed behind: *the master's daughter was about to fuck the peasant.*

Liam was caught up in her gale like an autumn leaf, swirling on the air. His masculine prowess subdued as an unwanted child wandered into the bedroom. His keenness and excitement overshadowed by a fear. Maya's assertion had knocked his confidence. All the words he'd enjoyed and had been equally glad to lose were now impossible to regain. Internally he'd become amorphous—without edges—sonar waves reaching out, gauging the world from the shadows.

Maya pulled him down onto the bed.

"Wow, you're so warm," said Maya, in contrast to her own cool skin. "As soon as I saw you, I wanted to fuck you."

Liam was surprised: even though he'd felt the same, he would never say this.

The gravitational pull of her body made him woozy, free-falling into the vast apertures of her tawny brown eyes.

"Shall we get undressed?" she said, grinning like a naughty child behind the bike shed. They were in her parents' bedroom, on a single bed, a lamp on a bedside table, and then another single bed.

Liam pulled his T-shirt over his head as Maya began to undo the remaining buttons down the front of her dress which she kicked off onto the floor along with her pants.

The room was unremarkable, except for Maya and the view across the moor that could be seen from the window.

Was it just paranoia or was there something odd about Maya being so available? What did she see in him? He hadn't had that many relationships, the longest being Becky for two years, but other than that, he'd been mainly single.

He'd forgotten how intimidated he could feel in the presence of a naked woman, his lack of experience contrasting with Maya's lack of constraint. Sexually, he was still a little boy, in awe of the female body, putting the seven wonders of the world to shame. Yet, on the outside, he was clearly a man, a man that Maya showed her unrestrained desire towards. Rolling around the small bed, her body gradually became a consecrated home. A place he could be safe, no more games, no more masks. The missing piece to his puzzle.

This weaving that took place invoked something primeval in Liam. Primordial data exuded from her pores as he began to know Maya through her unique scent.

In all humans, there lies an animal outside the realm of formalities, and Maya was a she-wolf.

Tasting the salty sweat of flesh on his tongue as it meandered across planes, her cool thighs, undulating ribs, areolas. Towered nipples brushing the end of his nose, cheek, eyelashes, her downy pelt entangled with his.

Sex was more than bodies, it was souls, spirits, dreams.

Maya hummed like a queen bee served by Liam the worker, not that it was labour, in fact Maya was happy to help him pleasure her, touching her own breasts, moving his hands to the right places. She was in control, and he was happy to serve.

"Shall I put a condom on?" he said, coming up for air.

"Let's just keep playing."

Her fingers entered his mouth, his vulva lips wet and soft, his clitoris tongue, his fleshy opening un-biting. Taking her fingers out she massaged that tiny spot that gave so much pleasure, edging, stopping to ride ecstatic waves clearly coursing through her body. Did she even need him?

Then she pulled him inside, two bodies, like hands washing away the grime and grit of a loveless life.

Meridian between heart and sex synapsed.

Eyes locked together, faces aghast with pleasure. Rising and falling. Unworldly, life-giving power deeply rooted in all living things, unleashed.

"Let me go on top," Maya insisted, breathless.

Liam climbed down as Maya slipped herself around him, rocking back and forth. Moaning as he eased a finger into her anus.

"Fuck, you need to slow down otherwise I'm going to cum," Liam said.

Maya's rocking decelerated.

Muscles and bone, now fluid, like untroubled waves lapping onto a shore. How can ordinary creatures shape-shift into such other-worldly beings? The material world fragmented, defying space and time. Boundaries disintegrated. Separation became intangible. Had psyches merged?

Maya's eyes rolled into the top of her head as though looking into the eyes of God.

"I'm going to cum, shall I pull out?"

"No, it's fine, I want to feel you cum inside me."

A squillion static fibres sprouted from every pore of Liam's body, each mycelium wrapping around her, plugging into something greater, and then it happened, there was no holding back, he exploded inside her.

Liam gave a little laugh out loud, feeling Maya's weight pressing down on him. Maya laughed too, collapsing into him. They lay still, eyes closed, surrendered, gratified. They lay like this for a while, in silence, submerged in the afterglow.

Gradually, Liam was forced to leave the tranquillity of his body, welded to Maya's: he needed a pee—Maya told him where the loo was.

Walking across the landing, he could hear Joni Mitchel wafting through the air. Maya's phone was still playing her playlist in the living room. Relieving himself, he felt more at peace than he had for years. He'd forgotten how good life could be until this moment. Joni lamented about wanting *a river to skate away on,* and there he was, enjoying being exactly where he was. Then halfway through Joni's melancholic tones, the music abruptly stopped and a man's voice came booming from the sitting room.

"Hello. Hello, are you there? Hello. It's me. Where are you?"

The voice had a strong, abrasive London accent like Ray Winston's.

Liam quickly grabbed a hand towel from a rail to hide his nakedness.

"Babe, are you there? It's me. Say something, will you. Can you hear me?" came Ray's call from downstairs.

"Oh, that stupid, fucking phone," shouted Maya.

Liam went out onto the landing and glimpsed Maya running at speed down the stairs into the sitting room.

"Come on babe, say..."

There was a click, and everything went silent.

"You okay?" Liam shouted down.

"Sure. My phone does that, it automatically answers calls when it's on the Bluetooth speaker. Pain in the arse," said Maya, leaving the living room and ascending the staircase, unconcerned about her nakedness.

Liam wanted to ask who the Ray Winston sound-alike was but knew it was none of his business, and Maya didn't offer, so he decided to let it remain a mystery.

EIGHTEEN

Daniel

Daniel took a tiny sip of espresso from a miniature cup, delicately placing it back on the saucer next to a plate on which a croissant lay. He was seated at the bistro table on the terrace, wearing Ray-Bans and a light beige Fedora hat. The terrace, which was shielded from the breeze, was already beginning to feel like a furnace in the August morning sun.

Meredith sauntered through the French doors onto the terrace. The panoramic view was spectacular, showing off the medieval village below with its river and soft rolling hills beyond, stretching far off into the distance where mountain peaks stood in a hazy blue.

"It's so lovely here," she said looking out, sheltering her eyes from the glaring light.

Le Nid was nestled into the side of a rocky slope, hence the name. From the distance, people would marvel at the work assumed to have been involved in its construction, with its apparent awkward position, but hidden away, a narrow lane twisted and turned, eventually making its way into the drive. The chateau wasn't particularly humble, hosting six bedrooms, a large living room and a dining area big enough for a banquet.

The house was generally empty throughout the winter months except for Edith, *la gardienne*, who looked after the place.

Throughout the summer months, it was frequented at various times by all the Bloombergs, with the exception of Gerald their eldest son who rarely came to Europe since moving to Australia.

Edith was now in her early sixties but had always been *la gardienne*, and in return, she had a separate flat within the house and got a reasonable fee despite having little to do when the Bloombergs weren't there. Edith dealt with all the bills as well as the maintenance. She'd grown up in the local village and didn't have children of her own. Edith would make sure the house was stocked with food, aired and spotless for when anyone arrived.

Daniel had travelled light, bringing just enough clothes for the four-week stay, making a pact with himself not to haul along the heaviness of his existential crisis. Coming to the decision that time would be better spent relaxing, walking in the hills, possibly even attempting to rekindle his marriage.

And this business with Liam, well, Meredith had been right to ask why he'd spoken openly to him and not her. Maybe he wasn't the best husband, and this could be his Ebenezer Scrooge moment in which he would open his heart to all those people he'd neglected over the years, starting with his wife. If she ventured to ask him what he was thinking, he resolved to be truthful. This had nothing to do with any existential crisis, which was now safely back home in Falindon—it was more to do with a slow-motion epiphany he was experiencing.

"Would you like an espresso, darling?" said Daniel, cheerily.

"Mm, yes, why not."

"Had any thoughts on what you might like to do today?"

"No, how about you?"

"I thought maybe we could pop into the village and eat out for lunch."

"Yes, that might be rather nice. I wonder how Maya's getting on?"

"Why don't you give her a tinkle."

"Yes, I think I will. I'll text her now," she said, disappearing back through the French doors.

Daniel picked up the FT which lay at the centre of the table, and which he made sure, wherever he went, to always have delivered without fail. Taking another sip from his espresso, he opened up the pink broadsheet and pulled out the arts and culture section, turning the pages, looking for something to match his cheery mood. In the centre there was an interview with Grayson Perry, and laissez-faire, he settled into reading.

He'd read about the Turner Prize winning potter before and became intrigued, even to the point of checking out various sites online—*Chicks with Dicks* or some such site—though the less said about that, the better. How one could don women's clothing without feeling utterly demeaned was beyond belief. The comedian Eddie Izzard was another one who wore dresses and whom he also found beguiling. Neither were what one would call pretty with their make-up, often garish, and their dresses prosaic or outlandish, yet these only made them more fascinating.

Grayson in the interview talked about men invariably being victims of their own masculinity, how they paradoxically could be courageous when it came to extreme conflict yet terrified when it came to displaying soft emotions.

Daniel was reminded of Liam and how his generation appeared softer, though Grayson himself was in his fifties and closer to Daniel in age.

Grayson continued, suggesting men were prohibited from being *sissies* for the fear of being seen as weak. This certainly rang true for Daniel: his father would never have tolerated Grayson Perry. He would often refer to effeminate men as *nancies*, not that Grayson was effeminate in his manner—another oddity—it was just that he wore women's clothes. Daniel was reminded of when he was a young man watching a film in which the absolutely marvellous actor John Hurt played Quentin Crisp, the iconic transvestite who grew up in post-war Britain. Discovering you're gay, being cast out of your family into a harsh heterosexual world where getting attacked by strangers was the norm, must surely have been too much for any man to bear, and yet to wear women's clothes on top of this was surely only adding fuel to the fire. It was funny how much things had moved on.

Grayson was clear about not being gay. He mentioned how wearing a dress had been an aphrodisiac with its sense of liberation. Daniel would never wear a dress, not in a million years. He crossed his legs and took a bite from his croissant. He had, though oddly enough, vaguely considered it. But now was not the time to query his identity, even with that existential question mark looming close by. Right now, he was tickety-boo, whoever that was. All that *who-am-I?* nonsense could stay in the cupboard, back in Falindon—he was going to enjoy his holiday.

He popped the paper back on the table and leant back in his chair, stroking the bristles on his chin. He hadn't shaved that morning; maybe he'd grow a beard.

From just beyond the French doors, he heard Meredith chatting to Maya on a video call. Her voice had a peculiar sound to it when speaking to Maya, shriller maybe—shouty without being raised. Colder yet sweeter.

"Hello, darling. How are you settling in?"

"Hello, Mother."

Eavesdropping, Daniel wondered why Maya never called Meredith *Mum*. The word refused to roll off her tongue. He'd called his mother *Mummy* until quite a late age. Mummy, unlike his mother, had a soft and cuddly sound to it.

"Good, thank you, and you? How's Le Nid?"

"Darling, Maya's here, come say hello," Meredith shouted to him. "We're having a lovely time. The weather is perfect."

"You're break—ing up," said Maya, her voice glitching mid-sentence.

Daniel joined Meredith, standing behind her at the laptop.

"Hello, dumpling. How lovely to see you," said Daniel, leaning into the camera, hands behind his back.

Maya's face spasmodically jumped from one frozen expression to another, her voice out of sync with her mouth. "Hi, Da— s— a— ba— —nection."

"Oh, how frightfully annoying. You keep freezing, can you hear me, darling?" said Meredith. The connection at Le Nid had always been poor due to the location.

"What was that? You've —zen. Ah that's better," said Maya.

"So, dumpling, are you enjoying being at home?" David cut in.

"Yes, —ing lot— an— —ing."

"Sorry, Dumpling, didn't quite catch that. Could you repeat yourself?"

"Sw— ng— mming!"

"Swimming, Daniel, she said she's been swimming."

"Wh— d— you s—?"

"Oh, darling, this is just an awful line, maybe we should try calling you again?"

"—king —ell!"

Behind Maya on the screen, entering from the hallway, Liam appeared in the doorway, naked. The image froze, capturing Maya's glee with Liam, flagrante delicto, eyes rounded, biting his bottom lip, turning to escape.

The next image to jolt across the screen was the impromptu appearance of Liam's bottom and the back of Maya's head with the sound of a hearty shriek.

"What the hell is he doing there?"

The image remained frozen on Maya's static smirk, eyes half-closed, a screenshot from hell.

"Hello?" Meredith had slammed the laptop shut, run to get the phone and called Maya on the landline.

Maya picked up the phone.

"Hello again, Mother."

"Don't you dare 'Hello Mother' me! Why is the gardener naked in the house!"

"He's just had a shower."

"Why is the gardener..."

"Liam! His name's Liam," said Maya.

"Get him out of our house this instant!"

"Don't be ridiculous, Mother, why would I do that?"

Daniel could see that Meredith was either going to faint, have a heart attack or spontaneously combust into flames. He cleared his throat.

"Maya," he said, trying to affect a stern tone. "You really ought to respect your mother's wishes and ask Liam to leave. He should not be in the house, particularly when he's naked."

"You are a disgusting harlot! You can leave too!" said Meredith.

"Darling, you need to calm down..." said Daniel.

"Calm down? Calm down? Our daughter has clearly had sex with that horrible, horrible yob..."

"Mother, why don't you like Liam?" Maya responded coolly, apparently savouring the anguish she has caused.

Meredith screamed, hanging up the phone.

"We need to leave at once!" Meredith decided.

"Darling, you're not thinking reasonably."

"The gardener is in our house having sex with our daughter and you want me to be *'reasonable'?* "

"You don't know that they're sleeping together."

Meredith scoffed loudly. "Oh no, of course not," she shouted sardonically. "No, Daniel, the gardener is clearly naked because Maya kindly offered to do his laundry! Are you mad! Of course they're having sex. It's Maya! Maya who sleeps with a new man—or woman for all we know—every week. Maya who would have sex with the postman and the milkman if she could. Maya who took an E for her sixteenth birthday party which she was only too happy to tell us. It's Maya, Daniel. Maya!"

"So, she sleeps with him, she's an adult."

"Can you hear yourself? How pathetic you sound! Daniel, your daughter is having sex with your new 'best friend' and all you can say is"—Meredith paraphrased Daniel, parodying a weak and feeble half-wit—" 'so what, she's an adult'! For God's sake, grow some testicles, you pathetic man!"

Daniel was feeling stupefied from shock. It was glaringly obvious that Liam and Maya were having sex, but he wasn't sure how to respond. He searched for a paternal, mafioso, possessive rage and fury, but he just couldn't find it. Was he hurt? Had a trust been betrayed? Maya had brought back boyfriends in the past, and it would be fair to say that Liam was an undeniable improvement. Indeed, considerably so when thinking of how she'd described the last one, who by all accounts was an utter maniac.

A year ago, he would have hit the ceiling, he would have wanted to kill Liam, but something had changed. He wasn't even sure if it was such a big deal. That's what people did in their twenties and thirties if they weren't married, have lots of sex, wasn't it?

He envied them for this. His bonking had never really reached any great heights—before Meredith, there'd been one other woman and she'd been very prudish about sex. And then Meredith got pregnant and that was that: he had no choice but to Marry her.

"That's what adults do, they have sex, and so long as it's consensual, then it's not against the law. She's a grown woman."

"Well, thank you for that profoundly well-thought-out insight into the intricacies of sexual mores, Daniel, that really does make everything okay now."

"You're not normally so upset when you hear Maya is sleeping with a new man?"

"Daniel, why are you being so blasé?" She mimicked him as smugly nonchalant. "'Oh, don't worry, we're all so liberal and bohemian now.'" Meredith screamed again. "I want to kill that insipid oik! I will kill him."

"Why?"

"Do you not care about your daughter?"

"Nothing has happened to her. As you said, Maya is promiscuous, the funny thing is Liam isn't."

"How the hell would you know that?"

"He told me. He's quite sensitive and gets hurt easily so doesn't sleep around."

"You talk to the gardener about your sex life?"

"His sex life, yes?"

"Have you spoken about our sex life?"

Daniel thought about this for slightly too long before saying, "No."

"You have, haven't you!" Meredith was beside herself. She took a small raku vase from the fireplace and threw it at Daniel whose aged reflexes still allowed him to nimbly dodge the Japanese missile, which shattered against the wall.

"No!" he reiterated. "I have not talked about our sex life. You need to pull yourself together."

"Daniel, you are a bloody liar."

"Even if I had, which I haven't—"

"Don't even go there. If you have, I will kill you."

"I haven't. We talked about Liam's relationships." Of course, Daniel was lying, but he just wasn't sure how much as he was having an amnesic block around the conversation. He had said something about his own libido not being like it used to be; this was what was great about his new friend, he could talk about things without feeling like he was on a cliff edge.

Daniel looked through the window towards the distant mountains, hoping that one of them might magically talk to him, imparting some infinite wisdom as to how to deal with the situation. Meredith had lost her bearings, her eyes wide with fear.

He wanted to offer empathy, but he was fearful of getting too close. With trepidation, he approached Meredith, putting his hand on her back, hoping to comfort her and bring her back to some kind of normality. This was a new level for her: she'd never thrown anything before other than jagged insults.

"Darling, do you think it might be wise to take a deep breath?"

Meredith gave a nod and closed her eyes, taking a deep inhalation, her chest rising.

"That's the spirit," said Daniel.

A tear pushed itself from the corner of her left eye and tumbled down to the corner of her mouth.

"Just try to let it all go, darling. Let's just have a jolly nice holiday?"

The tears continued, each one more potent than the last. Pretty soon they'd built up quite a momentum.

Daniel wasn't used to Meredith crying. He suspected it was something she'd learnt to crush from an early age, like he had. She let out a moan to accompany the tears. Pain etched throughout her face in broad strokes, all decorum scribbled out. She fell to her knees, her hands clasping her face as she spluttered into uncontrollable sobbing. Pent-up emotion flooding out of her.

"Darling, I think you should try to take another breath."

Daniel felt redundant. She was out of reach. His hand on her back, a heavy, useless weight. Meredith took another breath, and this time the out-breath became a howl. She'd transformed into a wild creature. Silver bullets and crucifixes lit up in Daniel's head as panic began to rise: this was not the Meredith he knew.

He desperately tried to soothe her, rapidly rubbing her back as she leant over, her sharp spine forming a curve. A mass of snot, tears and primal guttural cries, the old Meredith nowhere to be found.

It was impossible to think clearly, striving to mollify the whirlwind saturating the air swilling at his feet. Confused, knotted sounds that half resembled words fell from her mouth, too mangled to decipher. Crouched into a foetal ball, endlessly sobbing with the occasional coming up for air, Daniel still beside her, one hand on her back, the other gripping the back of his neck.

It was a relief to know that no one could hear her. A part of him wanted to slap her hard across the face, like men did in old black and white films, but men were different now, there were the Grayson Perrys and Liams, and emotions were a good thing, weren't they?

After an eternity, the catharsis dissipated into quiet sniffling.

"Daniel, take me to bed please, I'm tired," her voice limped.

Daniel helped Meredith to stand, leading her to the bedroom where she lay down. He sat on the edge of the bed until she fell asleep. On the bedside cabinet, he noticed his phone flashing, letting him know he had a text message: *I'm sorry Daniel to both you and Meredith. You weren't meant to find out like this. Liam.*

Daniel switched off his phone.

NINETEEN

Liam

Back in his clothes, Liam half expected to see Meredith as he entered the living room.

"Well, that was hilarious," said Maya.

Liam was unsure what to think, but one thing he wasn't feeling was the hilarity of what had happened.

"Did you see my mother's face when she saw you? It was priceless!"

How to respond was unclear. It had been two weeks since they'd consummated the relationship and stepped inside their new, romantic pleasure bubble. Lots of talking, lots of being silly and playful together, and lots of sex. He'd pretty much been living in the house the whole time, apart from going to do his gardens and one night when they slept in the caravan. But the incident with the video call was a step too far. Maya struck him as childish, and this was the first indication of becoming unmeshed and feeling irritated with the person whom a couple of hours previously he'd been making love with.

"Did you know they were going to call?"

"Yeah, Mother texted a few minutes before the call to let me know."

"Oh, might have been good to have told me?"

"They'll get over it. Don't you think it's funny?"

"Well, looks a bit disrespectful."

"Which bit?"

"Me in the house naked. Us having sex. Daniel being a sort of friend."

"So? What have you actually done wrong?"

"Nothing, but that's not how they'll see it."

"Who cares what they think!"

Liam was flummoxed by Maya's reluctance to see it from her parents' perspective. He was also perturbed at the harsh lack of sensitivity she was showing towards him without any apparent awareness.

How could he feel so close to someone one minute and then so distant the next?

"Well, I care, to be honest."

"Why?"

"Daniel trusted me. It looks like I'm taking the piss by being here."

"God, Liam, you're really caught up in seeking my father's approval, aren't you."

"No! Not at all. He's a friend and I value his friendship."

"Well, if he's a friend, why would he mind?"

"You're his daughter and that might be quite a big deal to him."

"I don't think he cares that much, to be honest. As I said, I think this is more about you needing his approval."

Hold on, thought Liam, *how come this is suddenly now about me?* He pursed his lips, sucked in a gallon of air, holding it in his chest, waiting, arms folded, brain swamped with angry attacking thoughts that mainly consisted of *fuck you!*

This was the first time he'd felt angry towards Maya. He'd deluded himself into thinking that he and she were beyond anger.

Take it easy, he told himself, letting loose a gush of wind like a punctured tyre. His heavy brow and cold stare remained in the room.

Maya continued. "I really get that you bonded with my dad and now he's seen your cock paraded around his bullshit living room and knows you've fucked his precious daughter, who, by the way, never felt precious around him. But so-fucking-what! It's a trip, Liam, and you need to get free of yourself."

"Oh, is that your guru speaking then?"

"Maybe, but even if it is, I don't care. We're all brainwashed by something. If you're going to be brainwashed, at least be brainwashed by someone who likes life and living! My parents are asleep."

"I think they're just people trying to work it out. Like we all are."

"I'd love to agree, but you give them too much credit. Anyway, some of us may have already worked it out!"

"What, like you?"

"Maybe!"

Liam thought about this and wondered, *Is Maya an enlightened being or a New Age narcissist?* She certainly inspired him, and he felt good being around her most of the time, and what she said was making sense. She did seem liberated.

"Maybe you're just angry at your parents and you're using me to get back at them?" he said.

"Is that what you think? Why, because I didn't panic when my mother said she wanted to do a video call? Because she saw you naked? Because she has archaic ideas about what makes someone a decent person? It's all bollox, Liam, and you know it. As soon as I start complying with their world, I'm dead."

"In what way?"

"Believing that being alive and free and expressive is somehow wrong, that is death, and that's what they believe. You need to let it go, Liam. Life's too short, seriously, let it go."

"Let what go?"

"My parents, all the beliefs you have about them and you. All that stuff you carry about who you are, none of it's real—take the blanket off the cage and see a world beyond. Stop being a peasant, it doesn't serve you. Be someone who serves *you*."

"I don't see myself as a peasant."

"Then why behave like one. Why see yourself as doing something wrong because you're in my parents' house. So, you're a gardener! Does that make you inferior? Just because my mother thinks it does, but I don't, and my father doesn't seem to. It's all bullshit and you need to let it go, that is if you want to move on."

"Move on to where?"

"Being who you truly are. An alive, sexy, passionate human being who has lots to offer the world."

It was true, he had bought into Meredith's shame. He could feel it every time he so much as looked at her. But it didn't end there—the shame ran deep into his core, going right back to conception. He imagined it sitting there, stagnating, tucking itself in between his organs. In his head, he pictured a steel shoe box implanted beneath his rib cage. He opened it and there it was, festering.

"I don't want to hurt you, Liam, far from it. I think you're great, I just wish you could believe that too."

Life awakened in his body, surfacing from hibernation, stretching after a long sleep, ready to face the world, ridding it of a cold death that had reigned so much power.

How could Maya know this about him? No one else knew this. Did she have special X-ray eyes that could read his soul?

"So how do I let it go, all that crap I carry?"

"That's wonderful, Liam."

"What?"

"That you're not being like a typical man and telling me to fuck off, that is so fucking beautiful. That you want to do it. It's not easy changing patterns we've carried throughout our lives, they get ingrained, and we keep playing the same loops over and over because they feel safe and familiar. I think you just asking how to do it is doing it. In fact, look, I can see it!"

Maya pointed a finger out of the window towards the sky.

"Good fucking riddance." She shouted and laughed. "Look, it's all your bullshit, drifting away."

Liam pictured the shame he'd been holding tied to the end of a helium balloon, floating up and disappearing into nowhere.

Maya went over, putting her arms around him. This woman was crazy, but he liked her craziness. He'd never felt this much love, and there was a new space in his body for this love to go which evoked such deep feelings—none of which he understood—but they were warm and sad and alive. His anger had evaporated as he glimpsed something new—a lightness of being that he hadn't experienced for a long time.

There was a buzz in his pocket as his mobile vibrated. He pulled it out and saw a text from Daniel: *Has Maya mentioned Troy?*

TWENTY

Troy

Stomping back to the hippy dance class had been a stupid idea. For starters, some minger, a total woo-woo with a feather in her hair, had replaced Maya. On top of that, everyone blanked him. It went without saying that they knew, he'd done something bang out of order.

He'd hung about until the end hoping to find out where she was, but everyone acted like they didn't know him, even Smug Face Ian, which hurt because the hippy crew had become a bit of a family in some ways, the kind of family he'd never had.

They talked about stuff his old mates would've laughed at, such as self-help books on relationships and sex and that. Well, to be fair, his old mates talked about sex too, but only who they'd done it with, where, when and how many times and what position, and the only stuff they read on sex was online, with graphic images. He'd never admit it, but a part of him wanted to be like the hippy crowd, but he fitted in like the Virgin Mary at a brothel, and he hated that.

It's not that anything was said—everyone was polite and friendly—but that was as far as it went, no one ever called or texted, and if he texted anyone, they'd be too busy, had other plans or ghosted him. It didn't stack up. Socially, everything was spinning down the toilet into a right, proper shit pile.

They were all wankers anyhow.

Even Jezza had turned him down for a pint, some spiel about boundaries. When it came down to it, it had become pretty obvious that Jezza didn't really give a fuck. Likewise, after mentioning the funny incident in the supermarket with the fat cow and all her biscuits and the spotty checkout kid, Jezza hadn't laughed. Just brooded from under an immense forehead. Clearly no sense of humour. Nor did anyone in the anger management group want to hang out. He was Johnny-no-mates.

Yes, there was the old crew, but he was past all that, bunch of dickheads going nowhere, things had changed. Though, this didn't stop the bedsit walls closing in, suffocating him, trapping him inside a dark, loveless hole.

The isolation prompted a deeper calling to Christ.

Even checking out some churches in the area, but the local church in Tottenham was full of geriatric blacks so didn't really fit in there.

The Flaming Cross group on the other hand were much more his thing, sharing Christian YouTube videos on the Facefuck group. These were the real McCoy, people who had experienced God's truth. Mostly in America. Proper education, learning about discipline, how to be a disciple of Christ.

So many videos. Each one leading to another teaser on the side, vaguely related but interesting enough to prompt a hit, and umpteen clicks later, he was detouring through the warrens of the dark net where a whole gamut of secret information, way more fascinating than the Anne Widdecombe Christianity, though he still liked Anne for her honesty and courage to speak the truth. Straight up, though, this was the dogs bollox. Enlightening, and then some.

It turned out a secret group of people ran the world. There was undeniable proof, like eyes on pyramids everywhere and stuff on the Rothchilds, a rich Jewish family that started banks or something like that. The world was controlled by Satanic paedophiles who drank the blood of children. This secret society included the Queen, whom Troy had always liked, and President Obama, though this was less surprising as he was a commie.

Finally, there was somewhere that spoke the truth—genuine people who saw the forces of good and evil happening right now in the world. People who were awake whilst the rest of the world had turned into zombies. A heroic surge of blood rushed through him as he connected the dots.

In the Bible, it states in John 14:6 that *no man cometh unto the Father, but by Jesus, everything else is evil.*

Satan masqueraded as an angel, a clever sod convincing people they were on a path to enlightenment when they were on the path to eternal hell.

This included New Age people who dabbled in the occult with yoga, tarot cards, Buddhism, meditation, hippy dance classes.

It was a lie to believe being good was the same as being a liberal; loving thy neighbour did not mean standing by whilst the devil did his work.

Maya's hanging up on him and blocking his number had been a stab in the eye, but he forgave her, for she knew not what she was doing. He had to get her face-to-face and save her, for she wasn't aware she was possessed and controlled by the devil.

Also buying new sim cards every day was getting expensive.

And as for all that bollox in the anger management group about *writing out your anger, meditating it away, calling your anger buddy,* a waste of fucking time.

Tommy, his anger buddy, had been all right at first but then began switching off his phone due to a few calls Troy made after midnight. The middle of the night was often the hardest. *Walking it off* hadn't worked. A few hundred miles had been clocked up by now, walking around the block, and as for *'releasing it on a cushion,* the cushions had died a thousand times from being punched, strangled and disembowelled whilst he screamed, "Die, you fucking bitch!" until the neighbour knocked on the door for fear someone was being murdered, and despite all the anger management techniques, the raging flames kept licking away inside, but now he knew the tongue belonged to Satan. *For anger does not bring about the righteous life that God desires.* (James 1:20)

Jezza was not capable of forgiveness. Telling Troy to stop focussing on Maya, saying his anger was about his mother, but even though she used a belt and buckle to teach him how to behave, she'd been pissed and wasn't thinking straight or the odd punch she got in the face from his dad if she got too lippy. Troy forgave them because the rest of the time they tried their best and loved him, even if they never said it, and the cupboard thing, well it wasn't all the time.

Jezza said he was forgiving the wrong people, accused him of being in denial, saying this prevented him from moving forward. According to Jezza, Troy could not fully own the reality of his childhood. All this inner-child stuff that Jezza went on about was a load of tosh. He even called Troy a bully and said that the people he bullied represented his inner child. What the fuck!

Troy had risen above anger. Ascended to a better place than Jezza, Ian, Maya, Tommy and even Anne Widdecombe.

It suddenly made sense why he was alone: people were scared of the truth. He told the anger group his revelations, and they were envious, deluded—like most of the human race—brainwashed. But unlike everyone else, he had something they didn't—a direct line to God. God listened, spoke back and understood like no one else. To have such a relationship with God was a blessing.

God said that Maya needed to witness his love, that they were meant for each other; he instinctively knew this in his heart and gut, yet he still had the feeling she was sleeping with some devil-worshipping cocksucker who needed obliterating! God totally got this.

TWENTY-ONE

Meredith

Sunlight flooded the room, disorientating Meredith with its glare. It hadn't yet dawned on her as to where she was. In a foetal coil on the bed, she surveyed the room, trying to discern her place in space and time, assessing faint shadows on the wall like a sundial.

It was safer lying like this, comforted by her primordial shape. Not wanting to move: she was sick of moving, of doing, of worrying, of trying, all of which amounted to nothing. To just *be* for a moment felt better, to bathe in the puddle of warmth. She inhaled the clean fragrance of the pillow. Even the slight dribble that had left her mouth while asleep could stay there. She'd had enough of being who she was and was having a break from herself.

A skylark busily chattered outside. Maybe everything was okay, and perhaps there was nothing to worry about. This new way of thinking had a fluidity to it.

Then the gardener, frozen naked on the laptop screen in her house, stole back into her mind.

More stark images from the morning followed: the video call, Maya's smug tones, and then, shuddering, the raku vase shattering against the wall. Where had that frightful rage come from?

She watched them like a train passing in the distance, a train she wasn't about to get on.

The walls around her now weren't the familiar walls she was used to. Those were monstrous, rarely allowing the zenith of the sun to rise above them. Now, the room had some air and light.

Colin Hathaway, her first love, fluttered into mind. His delicate face open to life.

If she'd have stayed with Colin, things would have been very different.

Unthinkable really.

His soft eyes. His shy smile. His sincerity. Those warm, enfolding arms.

How stupid she was to be thinking such silly thoughts. Like a teenager.

He was probably married now with kids.

When she introduced Colin to the family, her father had gone apoplectic with rage.

He can't even afford a car, were his words once Colin had left.

Colin had been her first and Daniel had been her last; there'd been no one in between.

Growing up had been a dreary existence. From the age of eight, only ever home in the holidays.

There was no sex education back then. She and the other boarders would snog their own arm in preparation for their first boyfriends.

Even thinking about sex felt dangerous. The house mistress, who the girls referred to as Nurse Ratchet, would punish you for not wearing your boater, so God knows what would happen if you were caught doing anything sexual.

Life thankfully renewed when going to Oxford to study history; the freshness of youth permitted exemption from the tyranny of her past. It was pure heaven: cafés, pubs, bicycles, cigarettes, no curfews and Colin.

Colin was one of those very few lower-class people to get into Oxford.

Reminiscing about Colin was more frequent these days. Normally, there was an automatic response to chase away the renegade thoughts, reminding herself she was married, and anyway, his lack of social standing would never have worked.

She lay there, allowing him to linger, hanging around the corner, a lover waiting, glancing at his watch, wondering where she was.

Following her dreams, he'd be a poet hunched over his typewriter, tapping out his heart-wrenching soul onto paper as she massaged his shoulders. And she'd be … the lover? … the muse? … the mistress?

What little she allowed herself. Even less back then; all those pot-smoking, bra-burning feminists of the early seventies left her cold.

But Colin liked to sail, visit places, socialise; he was a jovial sort, he knew how to let go and be silly. They'd laugh together at their iniquity. In those moments, she didn't give a hoot about looking the right way or saying the right thing: she was free.

But no one in her family accepted Colin. Family came first, and Daniel was seen as a perfect suitor for Meredith.

Adieu, Colin, mon amour.

The honeymoon period had been short-lived with Daniel when discovering she was pregnant with Gerald, their first child.

Marriage followed quickly, along with ending her studies so she could focus on being a wife and mother, neither of which felt like her raison d'être.

Daniel, despite his societal endorsement, was not the most adventurous person. It transpired that he was often too tired for fun, for sex, for talking. He did, though, meet the family's requirements—decent, handsome and, most importantly, well-connected. Sex may have possibly been good once; it was just now everything was a trifle dead and rather dull, and Daniel could be quite dour.

The hoi polloi had this scurrilous notion that people of her ilk were bonking all the time—the idea that aristocracy saw themselves above convention, frivolously hopping in and out of bed with each other in some bedroom farce was frankly quite ludicrous. It's what they read in the Telegraph, but the reality was far from this. Or maybe they were, maybe it was just her and Daniel who were a couple of dullards. A stark contrast to Maya's devil-may-care approach to sex, not wearing a bra, taking drugs and the rest.

A cloud was drifting by, framed in the window. Time had sped up. Where had all the years gone? It seemed like only yesterday that Maya was a child. She, too, wanted to feel attractive again. It had been an awfully long time since a personable man had bestowed upon her a second glance.

All this reminiscing was turning into maudlin.

It was their third week at Le Nid. Meredith resolved to direct her attention towards her relationship, put the gardener incident to bed for a while. She knew only too well what Maya was like—this was nothing new—ever since Maya had fought her way out of the womb, she'd put up with her chaotic ways. As a baby, she'd been the least passive out of all the children: endless crying, screaming during the night, creating scenes with uncontrollable anger tantrums as a toddler, reprimands from boarding school concerning her behaviour, counselling at fourteen for smoking pot.

Maya had never liked her; they'd never managed to bond. The boys had been easier; maybe boys *were* just easier. Maya had brought home Tim, an alcoholic heroin addict. Shaun, the lead singer of a band called *The Slashed Wrists*. Dave, pierced ears with plates like an Ethiopian tribesman and studded eyebrows, and this had just been the beginning. It was as though she sought out men who were the least compatible with the family. Maya was not going to ruin Meredith's holiday again. The gardener was just the latest Neanderthal in a long row who would be history soon enough.

Daniel had become frustrating too. His intensity was most disagreeable, morose even.

The old Daniel was easier. It had all begun when he'd started talking to that irritating gardener who'd somehow contaminated him with a ghastly self-indulgence. All this business of talking about one's feelings as though expressing feelings was somehow now de rigueur. She didn't want to talk about feelings, she wanted fun, to play, to keep things light, to have sex once in a blue moon for God's sake—like she'd had with Colin!

Meredith's menopause came late. Rather than leaving it in her mid-fifties, she was entering it. It was the same for her mother too: genetic supposedly. Since menopause, her libido had fired up, she'd purposefully held out against HRT despite the sporadic, sudden feeling of being fired inside like a kiln and sweating from places she didn't know existed. Through *the change*, everything had become dry, not only the obvious down below bits but the mouth, skin, eyes, as though the Gobi Desert had taken up residence in the body. The only redeeming feature was that the ovaries were no longer leaving eggs on the doorstep of her womb for the likes of Daniel to come and fertilise, not that there was much chance of that happening. And even if there was, Daniel with his doom and gloom was about as sexy as a boiled potato. Was it normal to be thinking of sex this much in your fifties? Maybe this was the downside of marrying an older man.

Meredith lay there for another hour, basking in her contemplation. Each musing like balm to her aching soul. Eventually lifting from the bed, she took herself onto the terrace. Daniel was in a wicker seat that overlooked the view, tranquilly snoring, his head lolling to the side, his fedora just managing to stay on. She went back inside to change out of her clothes into something more summery and lighter, but each item of clothing was drab. She wanted something sensuous, even risqué, but she owned nothing in those lines. It was time to go off-piste.

Whilst Daniel was taking his siesta, Meredith ordered a taxi to the Bagnères-de-Bigorre, twenty kilometres away, to buy herself a dress. Hopefully, it was big enough for a decent variety of clothes shops.

Hunting for a dress along the main market street, Meredith weaved her way through tourists and shoppers. The stalls sold mainly food, an unusual amount of tea towels and bric-a-brac.

Heat bounced off the tarmac, causing her blouse to become sticky beneath her cardigan. Like an amphibian, her drenched skin needed oxygen.

She came across a sandwich board advertising a boutique named *Le Chat Heureux,* listing items: *Jupes,* Cardigans, T-shirts, *Chemisiers.* An arrow pointed to a side street.

In the window display, a pair of mannequins pointed at Meredith with their white, plastic nipples through slinky dresses. Next to one of them, silk scarves, lacy, white stockings and braziers hung over an old, moth-eaten armchair. A tasselled, glowing lamp stood behind the other. A mirrored, shabby chic bedroom vanity sat in the middle of the window, underwear hanging from the drawers. The theme appeared to be slovenly, but the clothes were alluring.

An old-fashioned brass bell rang above the door as she entered.

The shop, crammed with racks of clothing, was tiny. Thankfully, she was the only customer. The shop assistant or possibly the proprietor, an attractive young lady, smiled at her as she walked in. Her left arm covered from wrist to shoulder in a bouquet of tattoos.

"Salute," said the girl.

"Bonjour," replied Meredith, heading for a rack of dresses.

Meredith was meticulous in her dress sense; usually choosing clothes would involve avoiding anything that was too revealing. The tiniest hint of cleavage was a no-no. It had to be practical, a good fit and made from good quality fabric and certainly not allowed to be shape-affirming.

It had been yonks since she'd searched for a dress that said *look at me*.

She caught sight of herself in a tall mirror, her face desperate and aged, her jowls beginning to sag, and she could make out some new lines on her neck.

Going there had been a stupid idea.

"Avez-vous besoin d'aide?" said the girl.

"Parlez-vous anglaise?"

Meredith had never mastered the French language quite as well as she would have liked.

"Oui, madame. Would you like some help?" said the girl, her smile annoyingly pretty.

Of course she was smiling, everything was on her side.

The girl was sporting a cropped bob, chin-length, and bangs to the brow, very French and very chic. Her hair reminded Meredith of Maya who had a similar style, only shorter.

The air carried the scent of white musk; maybe this was the wrong kind of shop—there wasn't a stitch of tweed in sight.

"I'm fine for now, thank you," said Meredith.

The difficulty was, Meredith really didn't have a clue when it came to *le élite à la mode*. Something had happened without her noticing: a dreariness had crept up on her and taken over.

She summoned up the courage to request the shop assistant's opinion and even disclosed that she wanted something a little bit daring—this was a humungous task. The shop assistant was a beautiful, young woman in her mid- to late twenties at the most, whose body had not been through the same ravages of a woman in her mid-fifties.

However, there was no hint of spite. She appeared only too happy to help; maybe it allowed her to practise her English?

The girl, biting on her index finger, squinted as she looked Meredith up and down.

Meredith wasn't sure where to put herself, her eyes shifting from side to side, avoiding contact as the girl surveyed her, her head cocked to the side. Was it pity Meredith saw in the girl's face or just indecisiveness?

She was probably thinking that the English can't help their collective fashion faux pas.

"You 'ave a beautiful figure, it would be good to show it, no?"

"Thank you, that's rather kind of you to say so, and yes, perhaps a little," said Meredith, feeling coy.

The girl whisked through various rails and passed over a multitude of items, some of which Meredith tried on.

It certainly wasn't Christian Dior, but it had to be said, the girl's choices were exquisite and she also possessed a genuine charm that made Meredith rather giddy. In fact, the girl really was a peach.

After trying on half the shop's merchandise, the girl handed her a creamy-coloured, sleeveless dress.

"Voila! I zink zis would be perfect for you," said the girl.

Meredith went into the changing room and came out to look at herself in the mirror.

Meredith's eyes flew open, scarcely recognising the dazzling woman reflected back. She touched her arm to make sure the mirror wasn't some kind of trick.

She exhaled and smiled inwardly, her elation concealed.

The dress was uninhibited, emblazoned with the full-frontal image of the gigantic reproductive parts of a lily flower—petals, stigma, stamens, anthers and all. The hemline just above the knee, it was bold and sassy and fitted her like a dream. Not too clinging but enough to show off her shape.

It also revealed more than a hint of cleavage, which the girl had insisted on, and Meredith, drunk on her pizzazz, was unable to refuse.

She hadn't shown this amount of cleavage for many years; in fact, she hadn't shown much of anything. What had happened to make her appearance so stuffy like a repressed 1950s librarian?

"You better be carefool, yoh 'usband when ee sees you may turn into Casanova," said the girl, beaming.

"I'm sure that won't be the case," and after a thoughtful pause, she continued, "let's say it's been a while."

"Pah, men!" exclaimed the girl, shrugging, "Zey do not know a good zing when zey see et."

"Hmm, yes, well, quite."

"Me, if am not appreciated, I go where I am. Zey soon weck up zen."

Meredith didn't quite know how to respond.

"Yes, well, how much do I owe you?"

"You know, you should look over 'ere," said the girl, walking to another rail.

Meredith joined her and was taken aback to see a rail of corsets, wet-look latex skirts, French maid outfits and other such things as one might find in Playboy.

"Oh dear, I think I may have given you the wrong idea," said Meredith, her face heating up.

The girl held up a red corset.

"I min, look at zis. 'Ow sexy it eez. Et pulls in zee stomach showing off zee waist, cushioned wired cups, lifting zee bosom, cre-etting zee perfect curves. Pure silk, go on touch et."

Meredith hesitated and then took the risk, cruising the tips of her fingers across the cherry red, floral, detailed lace.

This was scandalous—the thrill of owning such things was depraved. The girl, who had now manifested into a madam, was grooming her. Pull-up bras, see-through lace, reds and pinks, and as if that wasn't enough, the girl produced rubber skirts, tight, transparent tops, crotchless panties and Meredith feasted on each one with her eyes and fingers.

It was madness. Complete insanity to believe she could wear these, yet her stomach tingled, her heart raced, her eyes shone as she imagined trying them on. Of course, she certainly wouldn't be doing any of that.

"My word, do women actually purchase these?" Meredith said, holding up a fluffy dog collar.

"Yes, zey do," said the girl with a laugh, exposing a missing molar in the back of her mouth, which far from being a blemish only added to her off-beat style.

"Well, I'm sorry but they seem rather absurd to me."

Meredith tried hard to erase the mental image of herself as a sex slave in Daniel's dungeon.

"Zey ah fun. We need to pleh, uzzerwise life ez too serious, no?"

The word *play* prompted Colin to pop back into her mind; if it were Colin she was returning to, he'd understand the importance of play. Colin's dungeon would be fun, not dark and dingy like Daniel's.

Thank God the shop was empty; the odd customer had come in and Meredith had inconspicuously turned away until they departed.

Being somewhere where there were no familiar faces offered anonymity, allowing emancipation from a calcified persona. Here, she was free to be whoever she wanted to be.

Why not have some fun? Wasn't that why she'd gone there, to spice up her sex life?

The girl continued delving into her kinky cornucopia, dangling all kinds of wonder and mystique in front of Meredith's eyes: fur-lined handcuffs, leather masks, long satin gloves.

"Ere, try zese on," said the girl, handing the gloves to Meredith.

The girl's face held no mockery.

Well, a pair of gloves can't do any harm.

Meredith slid her lightly mottled hand into the glove, pulling it up over the elbow to just below her bicep, her fingers reaching the satin tips. She then did the same with the other glove. Rotating her outstretched arms in front of her, she saw a transformation. Her arms now belonged to someone else: a woman with power, a woman who knew her worth, not the power that wealth and status had given her, this was something softer, more feminine, more exotic. She put the gloved palms to her face, the glossy texture comforting. They had the musky aroma of the shop.

For the first time, she smiled at the girl: it was true, they were fun.

TWENTY-TWO

Liam

Over the last few days, the name Troy had been clanging around Liam's head, invoking the image of a Trojan warrior, sword drawn, hilt grasped tightly in fist, face framed by one of those helmets with a brush Mohican on top. Charging towards him, clenched jaw, cutlas eyes, coming to get his Helen back. Though, Liam knew Troy was a place and not a person, he couldn't help but cast Maya as Helen of Troy, most beautiful woman in the world, and Troy—whoever he was—as a jilted god. Admittedly, this was all ridiculous; still, he was curious as to who Troy was.

A large swathe of gardening work had been chopped back so that they could make the most of her *sabbatical,* as she referred to it, spending as much time with her as possible before she returned to London. A month was not long, and the more he got to hang out with her, the better.

They'd gone in his van to a nature reserve with a meadow that swept over a couple of acres.

The occasional wispy cloud took its time, lazily passing over. The land washed in sunlight as they walked through a gate. A chorus of bumblebees and grasshoppers hummed throughout the tall grass and wild flora.

The air perfumed with thyme and mint. Butterflies dallied on the breeze—common blue, brimstone, speckled wood, peacock—there was a vigour to parading his knowledge of nature in front of Maya. He'd never been to college or uni and didn't want her to think he was stupid. She always knew more about things than he did, and sometimes her posh accent could be condescending. Her background raised suspicions as to why she was with him.

Today, though, was a day that should have been left alone, everything in harmony, everything except the unrelenting matter at the back of his mind.

"So, who's Troy?" he said, trying to sound casual, kneeling to peer at the iridescent sheen of a shield bug.

"Troy?" Maya responded, a terse tang to her voice.

Liam's throat was dry; he coughed.

"Yeah, your dad said I should ask you about a Troy," he replied, vocal cords tightening.

Maya stopped still, folding her arms.

"What? Have you been talking to my father?"

"No, he texted me!"

"My father sent you a text? How utterly bizarre! And it said, '*Ask about Troy? Da, da, daar!*'" Maya mocked, imitating the sound of dramatic chords. She continued in her melodramatic teasing, putting the back of her hand to her forehead. "Oh no, he's mentioned Troy!"

Liam's jaw tightened, unsure how to respond to the mocking. Heavy silence hung in the air. He stood, and they continued to walk further through the meadow.

"To be honest, Liam, I'm not comfortable with you and my father texting each other about me. When did he text you?"

"A few days ago, after the naked thing."

"*The Naked Thing!*" Maya said in a deep voice from a Hollywood movie trailer. "You make it sound like a horror film. Did you text him back?"

"I sent one text apologising, and he replied, '*Ask Maya about Troy.*'"

"How come you didn't mention it?"

"I felt a bit like you, you know, about me and your dad texting. I didn't expect that back, and 'cos it was cryptic and weird, I wasn't sure what to do, so I just left it, but that felt odd too, so I thought I'd mention it now."

"What, three days later?"

"Hold on a minute, how come this is becoming all about me?" His pulse was doing a war dance on his temples, a torrent of adrenalin surging through his body.

"Well, it is odd that you didn't mention it."

"I'm mentioning it now!"

"So, what else do you and my father talk about?"

"Maya, I'm confused. It was *one* text, I just told you."

"Generally, do you talk about me?"

"Not much. I said before that he regrets not being there enough for you." Liam was wishing he'd kept his trap shut. "Look, forget it.

I should've said. And whoever Troy is, it's none of my business. So, I apologise, my bad."

"Troy's a guy I've been seeing recently."

"Sorry, I don't get you?"

"Troy's someone I've been seeing, but to be honest, it's over between us. He became a bit of a dick. What about you? Are you involved with anyone else?"

Was he mishearing or was this more of Maya's peculiar sense of humour? In her eyes, he caught something cold and steely and was reminded of Meredith.

"Am I seeing anyone else other than you?"

"Yes."

"Hmm, not quite sure how to answer that."

Liam looked back towards the gate, his throat contracting, trying to swallow something unsavoury.

"Okay, so I'll take it from that that you're not. Fair enough."

"Why would I be seeing someone else?"

A thin smile had slipped across Maya's face; her voice had become haughty.

"I'm poly. Polyamorous?"

"Oh, so what does that mean exactly?"

Liam began vigorously wafting his hand around his head to fend off a couple of small flies buzzing about his face.

"It means I'm not monogamous. I sometimes have relationships with more than one person at a time."

Liam took a deep breath and let out a long sigh. The natural world around teemed with life, random and chaotic. Everything selfish and out to get what it could.

"And this Troy, is he still around?"

"I decided, just before coming here, to end it with him. That's why I ended up at my parents' for a bit of space."

"It's funny you didn't mention this," said Liam.

"Why would I?"

Why would she? Her heart had frozen over. Not mentioning a text makes him a deceitful fraud, while her not mentioning an ex she might still be seeing makes him a reactionary bore!

The fly couple were joined by another fly, all three trying to land on Liam's face.

"Fuck's sake, fuck off will you," he said to the flies.

"I don't think they understand English."

"Fucking hell, Maya! Can you stop with the stupid, fucking jokes. Or is that part of your spiritual path: when someone gets hurt, take the piss out of them!"

"Why are you hurt? We've only just met."

"Oh, so sorry, I must sound really boring to you. I'm just not into polyamory."

The last three weeks had been heavenly. He'd been wondering when it would end, and here it was, the fly in the fucking ointment: poly-fucking-amory. Helen of fucking Troy. Queen of fucking Sheba. Stuck-up, fucking toff!!!

"So, does that mean you don't want to sleep together anymore?"

"I'm not sure—I'm just a bit taken aback."

"I should have mentioned it, sorry."

"I guess we haven't really talked about any expectations. As you say, we've only known each other a few weeks."

"I haven't got any expectations."

Liam winced, breaking eye contact. Suggesting that what they had together actually meant something to him now felt ludicrous.

"Yes, I get that! You know what, I'm going to head back to the caravan."

All hopes about his new relationship had been instantly pulverised in Maya's chipper. He had seriously considered that she might be the one: her confidence and lack of self-doubt were captivating, but all he could see now was snootiness looking down her nose from a high horse.

Once, a moth attracted to a glimmering light, and now Icarus tumbling to the ground.

The drive back to Falindon was eternal.

Liam concentrated on the road and didn't care about being some wild libertine, no matter how trendy it was. Deep down, he was old-fashioned when it came to love.

Polyamory, ménage à trois, kink or bicurious wasn't his thing. Still, it had been a while since seeing anyone, a reminder of all that had been missing.

A hand had found an opening, reaching in, but he'd held on too tight, unaware that a meteoric skimming over was only intended, and now he needed to retreat back into his exoskeletal shelter.

"Anyway, I live in London, and you live out here," Maya said, bridging the distance.

"I know. When do you go back?"

"Not sure. When my parents get here. I *really* won't want to hang around for much longer. So, probably just over a week. You can always come and visit?" she offered.

"Yeah, maybe." Liam just wanted to get back and be on his own. Maya could fuck off.

He'd been accused of being closed, distant, even cold in the past. It was too easy for him to find fault, but accepting Maya's quirks was a whole new ball game. Maya was the proverbial rabbit hole, he didn't know where he would land, but it had to be said, the journey had been magical. Colours more vivid. Emotions intensified. More tuned in to the minutiae of his inner world. His intuitive lens free of the usual grime.

He wondered if this was the way of women, and when he got closer to them, he vicariously experienced more of this for himself through some psychic osmosis. His feminine side granted a residential permit: free to roam transgender style.

Liam pulled up outside the Bloombergs'.

"Do you want to come in for a tea?"

"No thanks."

"Okay, I'll text you later."

"Sure," Liam said, knowing full well he couldn't receive messages in the caravan.

* * *

Maya

After leaving Liam's van, Maya entered the house. She pondered on how Guru Swami Gandalih might approach such a situation. The topic of polyamory had never come up with him. He was on a different plane; he was beyond getting attached to anyone or anything. Maya wanted to be like that too. Was that wrong?

It was only 5.00 p.m. After a few minutes, she looked at her phone, hoping to see a text from Liam, even though he'd barely just driven off.

She began texting:

Missing you, already. Too jokey—she deleted it.

I'm sorry, I'm a bitch, I know. Too pathetic—deleted.

Hi. It's not that I don't care about you. Boring—deleted.

Can we talk? Deleted.

I'll see you in 5 mins, we need to talk. She added a heart emoji and hit send.

Arriving at the edge of the wood, she saw Liam through the trees chopping some vegetables on a table outside.

It was odd to see him just getting on with things. She'd thought— no, hoped—that he'd be more devastated.

He looked up as she walked towards him, a puzzled expression on his face.

"Did you get my text?"

"There's no signal down here," he said, laying his knife on the chopping board.

"Oh, yeah, of course."

The air was much cooler beneath the shade of the trees. Patches of bright light sifting through the canopy variegated his homestead.

"I'm sorry. I was being insensitive earlier, I know. Do you mind if we talk?"

"I'm not into poly-whatsitsname. So not sure what there is to talk about."

"I get that. I'm just not into possessing you or you possessing me. Women were forced into monogamy because we had no power, but now we can choose."

"And I'm only human, I get jealous. I can't help it, I'm hard wired that way."

"I get jealous too, but I can't let my feelings control someone else. You're the only one I'm seeing right now. Why can't we just enjoy what we have. You've got to admit, it's pretty fucking amazing between us."

"You know, I'd love to say yes but my heart tells me I'm going to get hurt."

Heart? They hadn't talked about their hearts before. Surely it was too early to be talking about hearts.

"It can be just you and me until I go back to London, and even then, who knows."

"I get hurt too easily, sorry. I wish I didn't, but I do."

She could see it was true in the weary expression on his face, his moist eyes cast down to the ground, occasionally looking up to meet hers. He wasn't attacking her, calling her a bitch like Troy had, he was being honest, and she respected this. His plaintive intonations awakened a tenderness in her.

"I do really like you, I just can't do the exclusive thing. I'd end up resenting you."

"I've heard you, you don't do normal relationships, that's why I came back here, so that's that."

He was right, she even confused herself. She didn't know what she wanted. She wanted to convince him that it would be fun, that relationships didn't have to be bondage, that the nuclear family was a lie we've been sold, that love was everywhere and not just with one person, that freedom to choose was worth more than obligation and duty and commitment that sprang from fear, not love, but this was her being controlling, her striving, her presenting love in her own unique little box.

"You're right, you need to do what feels right for you. All I know is there's a lot of nonsense in the world that we buy into, and most of it doesn't make us any happier. We convince ourselves it does, but if we're honest, we know it's a lie. Whereas me and you, that makes me happy right now, and that's all that matters. Not doing something because you're scared of getting hurt can't be a good way to live. If I lived like that, I'd never leave the house."

Maya wondered whether she was bullshitting herself. It all sounded great in her head, like a motivational speaker—*feel the fear and do it anyway* and all that crap—but in the real world, which she claimed to be referring to, how much did she step out of her own comfort zone? When she thought of the word commitment, she associated it with asylums and crime rather than trust or working through difficulties. There'd been so few people to lean on in her life: Suzy her counsellor and a nanny that she'd had as a child and maybe that was it, and that was all a long time ago. It occurred to her that she, too, was also taking a risk.

"And besides, I'm not averse to going deeper with you," she added, donning her best flirtatious smile.

She walked closer to him as he hovered over his knife and vegetables.

"What are you making?"

"A curry."

"My favourite."

Liam clamped his bottom lip between his thumb and index finger. From beneath a weighted brow, his laser eyes bored into Maya's. Was he looking for some kind of guarantee that her heart was sincere? A mistrust flickered in his eyes—he was clearly still reeling from the shock of her polyamory blow.

"Are you going to live here in this wood, alone, hiding away from the world, until what? Maybe what you need is to get back into the world, and maybe I can be your chaperone."

His eyes continued to dig into her soul. It unnerved her, as though he could see right into her, seeing all the bullshit. All the insecurities that hid away underneath. The power had shifted. He was displaying a new side; maybe she needed him more than he needed her.

He picked up the knife and handed it to Maya, and just like that, said, "Okay, let's see how it goes. You chop some onions."

"Yes, boss," said Maya, taking the knife. A warm, fuzzy glow shimmered in her chest as the relationship was declared back on track, which subsequently was a surprise—up until that day, she'd had a take-it-or-leave-it approach.

She hadn't even noticed that her feet had left the ground until that moment when her soles gently touched the soil again.

Maybe it was this sett where Liam resided with all the rich odours of earthy seduction—the decaying logs, the shaded damp spots, the dung dragged under by beetles and worms, all a distinct contrast to the odourless neutrality of her parent's home—whatever it was, it reminded her that the feet were just as important as the wings.

Liam may not be the most garrulous chap, but when he did talk, it came straight from the heart, and this was something quite special.

It was funny that she was the one who was forever telling people to connect to their heart, to open their heart, to follow their heart, and now she was wondering where her heart had been all this time: somewhere with her feet maybe, lost in the ether?

They cooked the curry together, and of course earth-man Liam knew just how to cook the best curry.

* * *

After the food, after talking, after sex, after wine, they went to bed, curling up into each other like squirrels in their drey.

In the middle of what was a balmy night, Liam stirred Maya as he sneaked out for a pee. Through the window, she could see his naked body, illuminated by a full moon, glowing radiantly as he peed against some prehistoric-looking hogweed, around him, tall, silvery trees rose from a white mist shrouding the woodland.

Maya also got out of bed to pee.

"Thought I'd join you!" she said, jolting him out of his dreamy, nocturnal trance.

"Fuck, you scared the shit out of me."

"Well, I hope you covered it over."

Liam laughed.

Maya crouched down to pee beneath an oak. It was nice to have got used to peeing in front of him: it felt liberating. So uncivilised, she loved it. She stood up and took a deep breath, filling her lungs with the cool, moist air, closing her eyes.

She pussyfooted back towards the caravan, making sure not to tread on anything that might hurt the soles of her feet. Liam stepped in her way, and she put her arms around him. His cool, bare flesh was soft and inviting. Maya rested her head on his chest. She revelled in the fact that they were both naked beneath a starry sky, a couple of night creatures together like those in the distance marking their territory with hoots and howls.

She felt Liam's warm breath on the top of her head. He was a good man, kind and thoughtful; she was safe with him. Looking up into his eyes, he returned her gaze. The moonlight played tricks in the shadows. Liam looked older, his eyes ancient. There was a sovereignty about him: she was in good hands. They kept looking into each other. She wondered about this other being whose eyes she was gazing into, old and wise yet vulnerable like a child.

"I could stay like this forever," she said.

"Me too."

"It's so magical here."

"I know."

TWENTY-THREE

Daniel

After the frenzied video call and the sweeping up of raku shards, thankfully, Meredith had gone through a gradual metamorphosis which, surprisingly, was an unforeseen turnaround.

Following her hysterical outburst, Daniel accompanied Meredith to the bedroom to convalesce, fatigue having got the better of him, prompting a nap on the terrace. Upon waking, solace was taken in the fact that she was nowhere to be found. He couldn't be doing with much more of that kind of nonsense.

The banshee that had possessed her unnerved him. But the oddest thing happened: When she arrived back, it was as though the wife he'd been married to all these years was gone, along with the recent incarnate banshee. In her place was a flower momentarily free of the bud, or to be more precise, a rather thrilling giant lily.

A glorious lily. Bright yellow stamen traversing her breast and shoulder.

"My God, Darling. You look absolutely breathtaking," he'd said, not quite believing his eyes.

"Thank you, Daniel. I rather thought I was in need of a revamp."

Skin could be seen everywhere: arms, all the way up to the shoulder, legs traversing to just above the knee, and cleavage, lots of it, bountiful lily-white flesh to rival her dress. Meredith was certainly not one for flaunting her anatomy, except for her morning dip in the pool which tended to be alone, so was far from a flaunt. Yet, her body was toned from workouts in the gym, swimming and her regular jaunts across the heath; it would be fair to say the ephemeral loom had woven a splendid thread when it came to his wife's pulp. One could say her womanly frame was rather pleasant: still a hot totty indeed.

The dress made her succulent, appetising, or would it be fair to suggest that, indeed, the lure could have more to do with the exuberant amount of good humour she was casting his way. This was why Daniel had also been feeling, in part, disconcerted. Sudden changes and expressions of affection usually meant Meredith was after something. Not only did he see a lily, he also saw a Venus flytrap.

Along with her peculiar je ne sais quoi, there was a buoyancy, even a playfulness, triggering alarm bells. Would it be too far-fetched to consider she could be in the throes of a *petit* psychotic episode?

Better to remain vigilant, not be caught off guard in case something was requested he usually wouldn't be prepared to give, but what might that be? Like a secret agent in an espionage novel, he pondered being lured into honey traps down the shadowy alleys of Meredith's new dominion.

It was also important to bear in mind the resolution he'd made to be more generous of spirit, more open and truthful—his suspicion was not in good faith. He pledged to do his utmost to trust from here on, even if it meant being infiltrated by some sweet-smelling femme fatale.

* * *

As the week rolled on, Meredith continued to be delightful, each day showing off a new outfit she'd bought from a shop in Bagnères-de-Bigorre. Full of diminutives and small, tactile gestures whenever close—adjusting his collar, a touch on the arm as she spoke, a lean closer to smell his aftershave, having decided to shave, continually feeding compliments. It really was quite unnerving.

It all came to a head a couple of days before they were set to return back to Falindon.

The weather had been rather splendid up until around early evening when ominous shadows could be seen creeping across the valley below Le Nid.

Foreboding, leaden clouds rumbling in from the west predicted a stormy evening ahead. A chill had entered the air. Meredith suggested Daniel make the main room cosy by lighting a fire.

When she said, "A fire will be romantic. In fact, why not fetch a Dom Pérignon from the cellar?" it stood to reason seduction was in the air: all that sweet talk hadn't been for nothing.

He concluded she'd been setting the groundwork all week.

"There's that exquisite nineteen seventy-one you're often talking about. What a perfect way to spend the evening."

Daniel tried to push aside thoughts about honey traps and psychic combat, replacing them with the hefty price of the Dom Pérignon, which was in the region of six thousand pounds.

"Darling, that's being rather extravagant, don't you think."

"Sausage, we're on holiday."

Daniel begrudgingly fetched the champagne and got the fire going. The clouds had cast their shadow into the room. Meredith turned on the lamps. Thunder, drawing closer, echoed from across the valley. Meredith held several sheets of paper in her hand.

"It's all rather Gothic, isn't it," she said excitedly, "like Shelley and Byron."

"Yes, shall we see if there's any good films on the telly?"

"Well, sausage, I thought we could do something a bit more romantic than watching telly."

"Oh."

"I thought we could have some fun."

"Right?"

"I went online and came across a website on *Seven ways to spice up your love life.*" A flash of lightning filled the room. Daniel's stomach collapsed into a quivering mound.

"Oh?" A loud crack of thunder tore through the house.

"So, it has seven different suggestions we might want to try."

"Hmmm." Blood drained from his face.

"I printed it out. Would you like to hear the list?"

"Darling, when did you do all this?"

"Yesterday."

"I'm terribly sorry, darling, but I'm really not sure I'm in the mood this evening."

"Sausage, you're never in the mood, let's be honest!"

"Oh, for God's sake, let's not go there," he said, rolling his eyes, the strategy being to start an argument to distract. A form of counterintelligence.

"Sausage pie, why don't you just hear them. It's a bit of *fun*. We can watch telly any time, we do that pretty much most evenings."

A lightning flash lit up Meredith's face, a siren calling on a stormy night. Was the glint in her eye evil or benevolent?

"Is it some psychobabble mumbo jumbo?" Second ploy: belittle the idea, make her feel stupid and embarrassed so that she will no longer want to share it.

"It's *fun*, Daniel, *fun!* And we don't do enough things that are fun." Another crash of thunder.

"Darling, I sincerely do not know what has come over you. Are you sure you're feeling okay?" Third ploy: gaslight.

"Oh, don't be such a party poop. I'm going to read them out and you have to choose."

Putting on a pair of spectacles, she read from the printout.

"Right! *Number one: Dressing up...*"

"Well, that's out for a start."

"Why?"

"Dressing up. Preposterous. We don't have any costumes."

"Well, anyway, *Number two: Connecting from the heart.*"

Daniel shook his head, huffing with impatience. Meredith soldiered on.

"*Number three: Play time.*"

"Oh, this is ridiculous." Sweat gathered on his forehead.

"*Number four: Role play. Number five: Erotic massage. Number six: pillow talk.*"

Looking at his watch, Daniel folded his arms across his chest, his brow deeply furrowed.

"I also brought your Viagra. Why don't we start with me giving you a shoulder rub?"

Removing her specs and placing them on the table, she popped open the champagne, pouring out two glasses, handing one to Daniel.

A shoulder rub wouldn't hurt. All that scouting for danger had solidified his neck muscles into concrete pillars, holding up his crow's nest vantage point.

The fire crackled wildly. Thunder and lightning, judging by its intensity, now directly above Le Nid.

"Turn around."

Taking a sip of champagne, Daniel did as he was told.

Taught fingers worked their way into muscles, undoing knots, popping bubbles of tightness accumulated throughout the shoulders. Gently attacking the rods of steel formed in his neck, defensive cladding falling away, easing his mind.

Daniel's whole body purred with each stroke, a reminder of just how much he liked Meredith's shoulder massages. Why then such resistance? Was it the erectile dysfunction, the pressure to perform and feeling ashamed that his virility was out of his command, no longer brandishing him with the sacred arrow of Eros?

When they'd first had sex, Meredith would jokingly call his penis, *Peter*. "Oh, 'ello Peter, fancy seeing you 'ere," she'd say, parodying a cockney accent for comic effect. They both found this amusing as well as it being a covert code that opened them up to a more permissive side of themselves. Calling it *Peter* and speaking in a cockney accent somehow put them at ease. As the years passed by, she grew more serious. Her ancestral roots having caught up with her.

He'd never taken well to her mother, a dowdy, humourless, strict woman whom one could presume was incapable of warmth. Meredith, the eldest of four siblings, had always had to be the responsible one, yet here she was, this other Meredith who'd managed to escape. Prior to Daniel, there'd been only one other man whom she'd neglected to mention. He only knew this for a happening by chance to come across a photo of the two of them together. She'd claimed it had been only a fling, nothing serious, yet a nuance within her voice suggested otherwise.

Over the years as she grew more distant, he found himself acclimatising to the austere altitude, the coolness became safe and familiar, so as much as he enjoyed the liberated Meredith with all her breaking free, it wasn't familiar.

Daniel liked his routine: FT at the weekend, shower before coffee in the morning, lunch around one, whisky no earlier than six o'clock, slippers by the bed, lights out at eleven thirty. He knew where he was with routine. It was safe.

The thunder roared outside, a dragon trying to enter the castle.

"So, sausage. You have to choose one." She topped up his glass, placed the Viagra tablet on his tongue and he gulped it back.

"Read them out again."

"*Play time. Pillow talk. Oh, what are the others...*" Meredith looked around for her spectacles.

Daniel shuffled his body, trying to turn round.

"Don't you dare. Stay still, I have you just where I want you."

They were both beginning to soften from the release of oxytocin elicited through touch and good quality champagne.

"*Dressing up!*" Daniel quickly exclaimed.

"You said you hated the sound of that!"

"I do, I just remembered it, that's all."

"*Connecting from the heart,* that was the other."

"Is that all of them?"

"I think so. Oh no, wait, *erotic massage.*"

Daniel's mind drifted back to the *dressing up* option. Did Meredith have a secret bag of costumes? A Batman outfit? Maybe a Little-Bo-Peep dress, but who would wear that, him or her?

The image of himself wearing a Little-Bo-Peep dress evoked a frisson of excitement, stirring him to laugh out loud. Well, if Grayson Perry can do it, why not Daniel Bloomberg?

"What's so funny?"

"Dressing up."

"Why is that so funny?"

"Well, really. Dressing up?"

"Darling, me thinks you doth protest too much?" and then "I have bought a skirt, you know."

Meredith hurriedly looked towards the list.

"How about *pillow talk,*" she suggested

"Hold on a minute. What kind of skirt?"

"A short one."

"A short one?"

"A short latex skirt, yes."

"A latex skirt, where on earth..." If he chose to, Daniel could now humiliate Meredith by ridicule, but her hormonal juices were contagious. "Where did you get it?"

"I bought it in town the other day."

"In town?"

"Yes, Daniel, stop repeating everything I say. I feel rather awkward mentioning it."

If there was an element of papering over the cracks of her fragile sexuality, it wasn't for him to throw upon them a scathing glare.

"Sounds interesting."

"It has a zip all the way up the front! I could put it on if you'd like. It's rather *érotique*," she emphasised, with a French accent.

Daniel's breath deepened, loins inflamed with a tingly radiance at the thought of seeing Meredith in a latex skirt. The thought of looking up the skirt and unzipping it whet his appetite, but mixed in with all of this was an equal amount of shame.

Like most boys, interest in sex began around thirteen years old, only he was at boarding school. Not a great place to set out on such a tumultuous journey.

Firstly, there was fagging, where certain younger boys got chosen by older boys to be their servants. This involved everything from sexual subservience to shoe polishing. Being from good breeding, he had managed to escape this ordeal, but it still meant certain house parents, teachers, prefects and other pupils should be avoided at all costs. Tactfully, a low profile was kept, dodging their gaze, but it didn't exactly make for a comfortable environment for a burgeoning manhood.

Secondly was the incident in the toilet cubicle when overheard relieving himself over a topless Ethiopian tribeswomen pictured in a geography book borrowed from the library. He'd been teased for years about this, despite all the other boys clearly doing the same thing—it was *the* most borrowed book from the school library.

And thirdly, being an all-boys school, girls were an alien species. Thankfully, there was one female teacher, Mrs Brodeur, the French language teacher who sometimes wore a skirt in which you could almost see the beginning of her thigh when she sat down, if you were lucky. It was many a boy who dropped his pencil in Mrs Brodeur's lesson.

"Yes, well, I must admit, I do feel rather intrigued with the mentioning of this skirt, so ... erm ... shall we go with that then?"

Meredith gave a bashful smile and left the room. When she shuffled back in, Daniel couldn't believe his eyes. Yet another sloughing of skins as his wife returned black-mamba style in a latex skirt, so tight, it could have been poured on. Tugging the hem of the skirt towards the knee, an uncertainty rose up in her eyes, maybe wondering if she should crawl back inside the old Meredith.

Snapshots flickered across his inner brow, ones browsed over online, the secret ones, the ones after which he spent an hour looking at that always left him wanting to shower away that part of himself. He didn't want to use the word *porn*—that made it even more wrong. The images weren't hardcore, they were the kind of tosh schoolboys looked at, though not these days with their iPhones.

He was quite sure Meredith wasn't aware of his little habit.

For someone in her mid-fifties, Meredith had kept her figure well. *Peter* certainly thought so too and was quick to rise to the occasion.

Meredith sat down opposite Daniel. He wriggled in his seat, not quite knowing where to look—he knew where he jolly well wanted to look but wasn't sure whether he was allowed to.

Meredith leant over to pour herself some more champagne but didn't pour one for Daniel.

"I'm afraid, sausage, you're only allowed one glass for now, we need to make sure Peter doesn't leave before the party's started."

"Cor blimey, guvnor," Daniel said in his clichéd, hackneyed cockney accent.

"Aimez-vous?"

"Oui!"

TWENTY-FOUR

Maya

With her parents due to land back in the UK in the evening, Maya made the decision to take the train back to London after spending a day with them. Conscious Movement classes needed facilitating, and she was missing her tribe. She'd stayed in touch on Facebook, posting some pictures of herself with Liam at the caravan larking about.

There was a reluctance to say hello to her parents but would do so out of obligation rather than any desire to see them.

Liam had taken more days off gardening which it was doubtful he could afford, knowing his unprivileged circumstances. He'd said he wanted to spend as much time together as they could before she hit the road.

The skies were clear except for the odd speck of cloud off in the distance. Climate change was blasting the UK with record temperatures. Maya suggested that they drove to Hastings for the day for a brisk dip in the English Channel.

In the van, which they'd decided to take instead of the car, Maya asked Liam where his mum lived. She knew he'd been brought up by his mum and his auntie and uncle, that his dad had walked out when he was a baby and now didn't know where he was, but not much else had been forthcoming. Maya knew it was a touchy subject, but this only served to intrigue her even more.

"My mum lives in Barnsley."

"Oop north," said Maya, crudely approximating a northern accent.

"Aye lass, up north," Liam responded in a thick northern dialect. He didn't really need to imitate a northern accent as it was already there, though softened, probably from his many years in the south.

"So, does tha' get ta see 'er then?" she continued in her Python-esque caricature, attempting to disguise genuine curiosity.

"No, ah dunt, lass."

"Why's that then, lad?"

"'Cos ah dunt want ta." Liam reached for a CD to put on whilst he was driving. He put on a Van Morrison album. Maya suspected he'd prefer to close the subject down.

"Fair enough. Oh, I love this song, turn it up."

The song playing was *Into The Mystic*. As the chorus came in, they both sang along together, their voices full, laughing.

They continued singing along to the bits they knew, driving down country A-roads through small, picturesque villages of Sussex, heading towards Hastings.

As they drove south, the sky began to become slightly overcast but remained warm, the natural light and shadow beginning to change, suggesting autumn wasn't too far away but not so close to take away the summer vibe.

Hastings was a couple of hours' drive, and once they were there, they headed for the Old Town which felt like it hadn't changed since the 1950s or possibly earlier.

Maya had visited Hastings a few times, preferring that unlike Brighton it no longer had a tourist boom which meant fewer crowds, therefore more space, which was a significant factor in choosing where to head for the day.

The people here were more ordinary, and Maya loved ordinary people—their Primark clothes, fish and chip treats, bad haircuts, cigarettes, beer in the middle of the afternoon, reading newspapers with bad astrology, half-clad women and stories about ordinary people doing stupid things. They were funny and sweet in their uncomplicated ways. Maya was almost envious of their simplicity.

People watching was fun, but today she wanted to make the most of being by the sea, and it wasn't long before they headed straight for the shingled beach with their picnic and towels.

Walking beneath the cliffs, an ease entered her through the waves crashing on the shore with long, calming *shhhhhhh*-es as it withdrew back into itself, salty air alone enough to want to live there forever in that moment.

The sea felt like home. Up until recently, moving to the coast had been a fantasy that kept getting shattered by a fear of being too close to the infinite and away from people. Swami had said, *When you see yourself as part of everything, then you are God, but when you see yourself as separate, you become one who is seeking God. When you truly love God, you love yourself because you are of him.* Maya wasn't that comfortable with how her swami would often use the word *God*, but she put it down to his cultural background and him not having had a god shoved down his throat who was a white, patriarchal, oppressive, Victorian, grumpy-old-man God, whose creation could never live up to his expectations.

She was drawn to the infinite and the oneness of everything intellectually, but hated being alone, which was a bit of a paradoxical conundrum. She was okay at being one with other people, but struggled with being one with herself.

Liam picked up a pebble and skimmed it across the surface of the water with six consecutive bounces.

"Impressive," said Maya, picking up a small pebble to try it herself. She threw the stone, but it sank on the first hit.

"You need to find a really flat pebble and hold it like this." Liam demonstrated how to hold the pebble. Maya had another attempt with little improvement.

"Oh, no! How do you do it?" She enjoyed giving Liam the feeling of being impressive.

Liam again threw another pebble which slid across the surface like a Frisbee, bouncing around ten times.

"How did you learn how to do that?"

"Weirdly enough it was my mum who taught me."

"Did she! Oh, how sweet. How old were you?"

"About seven or eight or maybe nine, not sure. We went to Whitby for a holiday once and she skimmed a stone. I was amazed. It was one of those things that adults do, like whistling or clicking their fingers that to them comes so easy, but for me, as a little boy, was really impressive. We didn't have much money, my dad had fucked off and paid no maintenance. My mum had fuck-all support, so everything we did tended to involve things that were free, so she spent ages teaching me how to skim a stone during that week, and as you can see, it paid off."

Despite Liam making light of the situation, Maya felt a deep sadness as he spoke like she'd never felt with him before. She walked over to him and put her arms around him.

"Oh Liam."

Liam looked at her with a puzzled expression on his face, but he reciprocated with his arms, enfolding her.

They walked for a bit more, and they both noticed a middle-aged, naked man on the beach.

"My God, what would my mother say," joked Maya.

"This must be the nudist bit. I forgot about that."

"That's so cool, shall we go for a skinny dip?"

"Okay, let's find a decent spot to sit."

The beach was virtually empty with only three other people there: the naked man and an old couple walking their dog. They found somewhere to set up camp for the afternoon. They laid a blanket on the pebbly ground, weighed down with their bags. Liam was the first to strip off, dropping his clothes into a pile. Maya followed suit. Together, they padded carefully across the sharp shingly beach towards low foamy waves breaking on the shore. The sea was icy cold, yet most likely the warmest it would be, being late summer and England. They both went in to just above the ankles.

"It's fucking freezing," squealed Maya.

"Don't be such a wuss!" Liam said, remembering how she'd called him this a few times now.

"Go on then, you first!"

Liam waded in up to his thighs. "Once you're above your groin it gets easier."

Maya took a deep breath and dived in, leaving Liam standing, cupping his genitals. Her head emerged from the water like a seal pup, hair slicked back, eyes on fire.

"Who's the wuss now?" she trilled.

Liam screamed like a Viking warrior about to attack a village and plunged his head beneath the icy surface.

Once in, Maya's body acclimatised, and the day that had existed prior to that moment vanished through the portal of Neptune's salty kingdom. Swimming naked was so liberating.

Another victory towards making sure not to end up like her mother. Liam was the opposite of everything her mother stood for: the way his body moved was real; there was no bullshit, no etiquette designed to conceal undertones of a nihilistic contempt for being mammalian. Every icy bite to Maya's body was a reminder of passion, and this was her way of exorcising all that her mother had modelled around what having a body means. And what better place to vanquish stuffy Victorian conditioning than swimming naked with your gorgeous lover in the sea.

She saw herself as part of a younger counterculture generation intent on reviving the sixties by allowing their pubic hair to grow, doing naked yoga, wild swimming, tantra. People were taking their lives back from the commodification of their bodies: why was the body seen as something indecent, shameful or sexual, just for not being covered? It wasn't like it was a different body when clothed. The genitals most of the time were not being used sexually, so what was the problem. Both Maya and Liam had both questioned the collective insanity around this, particularly when it went to the extreme of having to debate such nonsense as whether women should be able to breastfeed in public.

The sea imbued the naked body with a sanity. The coldness was a short, sharp shock back to the here and now, to a life that existed for all animals but that humans had mainly numbed themselves to, a piercing of some synthetic membrane that kept humans so warm and dry they were in danger of turning into dust before their time had come.

Maya swam towards Liam. "This is so amazing, it was such a brilliant idea to come here."

Liam pushed himself through the water towards her, his aqueous face sprinkled in liquid glitter. Soft, loving tendrils exuded from him, weaving around her, penetrating her like acupuncture, making meridians numinous. With this symmetry, this love, came reluctance, a reservation, a mistrust. Her heart protector stood strong.

She wasn't ready to surrender, but would this always be the case? Liam was a decent guy, but she caught herself thinking about the fact that he lived in a caravan, he was a gardener, he had no ambition, he was a drifter. That wasn't long-term commitment material; these thoughts mockingly flew in the face of all she considered herself to be. She then justified them with telling herself she was polyamorous, but even here there was scepticism—would she honestly remain polyamorous if she met the right person?

She swam away in her ivory nakedness, now turquoise and rippled in sunlight. He swam after her and made a mischievous reach for Maya's foot. She responded with a light-hearted shriek and, like an impish mermaid, darted away—the chase was on. Liam continued to pursue her until he was almost upon her, and she spun around and up onto her back, kicking her legs, splashing him away with more shrieks of excitement. Liam laughed more as he sought to take her ankle like a playful seal after a mate.

Could a day be any better.

Back on the shore, they dried themselves and dressed to warm up. Maya had brought a picnic of olives, salad, humous and rosemary bread to share. They ate and chatted. She didn't want to bring up the future and her going back to London, but it was there, like a faulty fluorescent strip-light, flickering in the background.

She wanted to find out a bit more about Liam's family; the more guarded he became, the more curious she became.

"How often do you go up north then?" enquired Maya, out of the blue.

"Rarely."

"Once a year?"

"Less."

"Why's that?"

"No reason to go," Liam mumbled, just loud enough for Maya to catch.

"Don't you go see your mother?"

"How come you're so interested in my mum?" he said, his eyes flitting from side to side as though cornered and seeking the nearest exit.

"Because it's your mother and I'm interested in you."

"Are you?"

"Am I what?"

"Interested in me?"

"What a strange thing to ask. Why would I be here otherwise?"

"Bit of fun, maybe."

"Liam, what are you getting at?"

"Well, you'll be back in London in a couple of days."

"I know, it's going to be weird."

Liam turned away, looking out towards the sea, his shoulders rounded, the spark of the day gone, leaving behind a slumping half man, half child. "Okay, you want to know about my mum?" he said, keeping his face turned away.

"Only if you want to tell me?"

"When I was born, my dad was a waste of space and fucked off, so I have no recollection of him. As you know, my mum brought me up, but she wasn't that great, and so when I was a kid, I spent some time in foster care until my auntie and uncle helped out."

"Oh fuck! That's awful, Liam. How come your mum couldn't look after you?"

"She had problems," he said with a haunted look.

"Couldn't your dad help out?"

"According to my mum, no one knew where he was."

"That's horrid!"

"Well, who knows why he left."

"Do you still see your mum?"

"Not really."

"Does your mum know where you are?"

"No! I haven't been in touch with her for years."

A wave of shock coursed through her body, goosebumps shooting up across the skin.

"Wow, why's that?"

"She has issues."

"What kind of issues?"

"She's schizophrenic or bipolar, her diagnosis keeps changing. The doctors don't have a clue."

"God, that must have been really hard for you as a child. Did she ever meet anyone else after your dad left?"

"Occasionally some man would enter our lives but never for long. They'd pick up something wasn't quite right. Eventually she got on the right meds, but it wasn't perfect, she hid her illness from others but not from me."

"Was she cruel to you?"

"No, not really."

"What were your auntie and uncle like?"

"They were okay."

"So, are you in touch with them?"

"No."

"Why not?"

"I left at sixteen with the intention of never looking back. I hated my childhood, and I was bullied and crap at fighting, so people would just take the piss out my mum. They called her Mrs O'Loony, 'cos she's Irish and mad. I couldn't take friends home because my mum would say weird things to them that'd make them laugh."

"Did she love you?"

"Probably. It didn't stop the bullying, the piss taking or—"

Maya interrupted. "She must really miss you? You should contact her!"

"No, that is not going to happen."

"Why not?"

"Because! I don't want to!"

"But you have to! She's your mum!"

"Is that how you feel about your mum then?"

"I hate my fucking mother, she's a stuck-up, elitist snob, embedded in the Victorian era, but ... do I love her? Don't know? But she is my mother, and she did her best."

"She sent you to boarding school at eight, though, that can't have been much fun?"

"Yes, she's a bitch, but probably not as bad as her mother was to her. My grandmother was the ice queen. I could go away and never contact my mum, and the weird thing is she probably wouldn't mind that much and that's why I hate her, but your mum, I don't get the impression your mum was cold, or am I wrong?"

"No, she wasn't cold."

"And?"

"And what?"

"Am I missing something here, Liam, I still don't get why you haven't seen her for years! I totally get why you'd be angry with your father. So many men are twats like that, just leaving, it's inconceivable how a father could do that and not care, but your mum has mental health issues that she can't help and she didn't give you up, but it sounds like you've given her up!" Maya knew these were strong words, and she wasn't even sure why she was feeling so passionate about reuniting Liam with his mum.

"It's a bit late now."

"How do you mean?"

"Five years is a long time. That was the last time I got in touch with her."

"You have to see her, Liam, seriously! She must feel awful!"

"That's what I mean. I don't feel good about what I did. I just needed to get away, and the longer I kept out of touch, the easier it got not calling her."

Maya saw that Liam was still sixteen years old—the boy who left was still running. It all became vividly clear: his whole persona was that of a teenager, even his body had a youthfulness to it. He was still in his messy, teenage bedroom with *no entry* on the door, and not until he went back to face his mother would he be capable of being a man. She wasn't sure how this made sense other than she felt it intuitively and that somehow shaking Liam into some awareness around this was her way of expressing love.

"You must go back to see her. Now!"

"Why's it so important to you?"

"Because I like you, Liam, you mean a lot to me, and I just know you have to do this."

"Ok. Maybe, let me think about it."

This was the best answer she was likely to get but knew he'd said it just to get her off his back. Was it the typical male *anything for a quiet life* response? Was Liam one of those men? She could have pinned him down to a date, but she didn't want to be that woman, the co-dependent type, always trying to fix the man. Liam's life belonged to him, and she'd done her bit, the rest would go whichever way it went. Besides, what did she know about having a mother with mental health issues? On second thoughts...

The westerly drive back from Hastings went quickly. The setting sun created a spectacular panoramic sea of pinks and reds and turquoises that filled the arcing sky. Each colour mesmerising and bewitching. Maya and Liam looked on, enchanted, their faces tinted a shadowy red as they caught the last remnants of the day. Neither had the need to speak as they bathed in celestial awe. This wasn't a new silence, it had been developing over the last few weeks; it had grown more comfortable with less and less inclination to fill it due to an ease between them that had naturally sprung from an affinity. Maya hadn't felt this so strongly before. She'd always had an impulse to talk, to entertain and be interesting, and silences could make her uncomfortable, but with Liam, it felt peaceful or reflective or quiet and didn't illicit her free-floating anxiety.

Liam, she suspected, had always been comfortable with silence, he was that type of man. Maybe he was too comfortable, all that living alone in a wood without the internet or TV, just books and the radio. He sometimes appeared to be less comfortable with talking: it wasn't that he was monosyllabic, he just didn't seem to want to talk unless the conversation had depth and wasn't about him. He was intense and this fitted Maya, but she also liked to socialise, get stoned with friends, dance, in fact she'd really been missing the dancing.

Outside, the dark thickened into a mysterious broth. The twinkling of lights in the distance brought a loneliness with them. She wondered what it must be like to be a wild animal out there, having to hunt for food, danger all around, always danger.

Around 9.00 p.m. they arrived at the house and saw the lights were on.

"Looks like they're back from holiday," said Maya. "Do you fancy coming in?"

"I'd better get back."

"Don't be such a scaredy-cat!" she teased

"Your mum hates me."

"She's scared of you, you're too sexy for her." Maya laughed. "What can she do that's so terrible?"

"What about Daniel, your dad? He must hate me now, as well."

"Why would he hate you? If they hate you, let them, you don't have to become a member of their petty hatred bullshit."

"I just can't do it, sorry."

"Go on, I'll give you a blow job."

Liam laughed. "Now that is tempting, but don't you think it'd be better to sort things out with your mum first?"

"That'll never get sorted, so better to just go in and get it over and done with—short, sharp shock!"

"For me or for her."

Maya giggled, "Both of you, you need to be adults. I'll hold your hand!" Maya smiled sweetly and fluttered her eyelids playfully.

"Oh, fuck it, go on then."

TWENTY-FIVE

Meredith

The electric gates opened allowing the taxi to pull up in front of the house.

After their intrepid adventure into kink, Meredith had dared to enjoy two more evenings sojourning into sexual intimacy with her husband, and by all accounts, the pleasure had been mutual. One could say the holiday went rather well. A husk shed, but whether a snake or a butterfly emerged was still uncertain. Being back home would be the ultimate test: would she slither back into a tightly coiled self-restraint or would her manifestation be airy and colourful, ready to drink the light. The latter of course would be her first choice, but regrettably moods were a disposition, not pages torn from a memoir to be gaily tossed into the flames of yore. Still, she was feeling optimistic.

Meredith lifted the suitcase over the step into the house as Daniel paid the taxi driver behind her. The journey back had been laborious with queues and relentless traffic jams. To the left, the spare car sat; she deduced that Maya must be inside the house.

It would be reasonable to think the prospect of seeing one's daughter would induce a sense of delight, but rather it was nearer to shouldering a mink stole, its head still alive, snapping at the neck.

Endeavouring to shuffle away from her disdain, she plumbed her conscience for traits Maya held that she could be grateful for: her free spirit, her strong will, her independence, her individuality, her outspokenness... At this point she stopped as these aspects began to border on the things she hated—*no, hate was too strong a word*—grappled with.

Though the lights were on, the house was deathly silent, the way a derelict building has no sound, a Halloween pumpkin hollowed out.

Marching across the entry hall, her heals clacking on the tiles, she called out Maya's name, but there was no answer. On the demi-lune by the door, there was a note which read, '*Hi. Hope your journey went well, gone to Hastings, back this eve. M xx*'

She wandered into the sitting room which was relatively untidy in a way she wasn't accustomed to. Maya's laptop lay open on the coffee table along with a small pile of CDs, a wooden bangle with an Irish-looking pattern carved into it, feathery earrings, a couple of empty wine glasses, two books—*Tantratastic* and *The Ethical Slut*—a denim jacket strewn over a chair and a pair of sandals hap-hazardly adrift on the carpet, each one a carefree distance from the other. Brushing aside her daughter's debris and not falling into her usual pickle confirmed how frightfully well she was doing.

Daniel trailed into the room behind her, haggard from the journey.

"I'll get us some tea, shall I?" she said, pulling herself taller, demonstrating just how unperturbed she was.

"That would be lovely, dear," he replied with a sigh, plopping heavily onto the sofa.

At the edge of the kitchen island were three wine bottles from the cellar, all puffed out and proud of their emptiness. Next to them, what could only be described as cardboard cigarette ends spilling out from a saucer. The dishwasher door hung open: dishes unloaded. It didn't matter. It was fine. Even the tiny tomato ketchup puddle on the granite top was fine. *It was all fine.*

She could do this. She had it all under control. No, not control, there was nothing to control, that was the old Meredith. She'd sit with Maya, and they'd chat amicably about their holiday. The matter of the gardener having been in the house could wait. In fact, why mention it at all, she didn't need to know about any of that, she concluded, pouring hot water into a tea pot.

Meredith took the tea into the living room. Daniel had slumped deeper into the sofa. The TV was on as he flicked through the channels.

"Would you mind making some room for the tray?"

Daniel groaned, audible just enough for Meredith to hear. Sitting up, he made a pile of Maya's things on the edge of the table.

Meredith poured out the tea. Daniel went back to switching channels.

They settled into watching *The Secret Life of Rabbits*, a wildlife documentary.

Having the space to switch off after an arduous journey was just the tonic.

Neither spoke as they sipped their teas and stared at the big screen. Resting her head on Daniel's shoulder brought about a soporific ease.

'*Outside the burrow, the young vixen lurks patiently. Eventually she will dig her way in. The doe, sensing danger, is now in a state of alarm. Not able to take her young kits with her, she panics, her only option to eat her newborn kits...*'

The inimitable chugging of the gardener's van outside the gate cut through the narration on the TV.

Maya must be in that filthy old rust bucket. The audacity.

Daniel kept his eyes peeled to the fox on the screen.

It's all fine. He'll drop her off and then be gone and so nothing to worry about, Meredith thought to herself as the TV narration continued.

'*With kits eaten, the doe remains frozen, her heart thudding as she hears the vixen digging away. The vixen's sharp sense of smell tells her that her dinner is only a short dig away...*'

The engine idled as someone, most likely Maya, got out and opened the gates. *Why would she need to open the main gates?*

Meredith sat up, alert.

Gravel crunched beneath wheels as the light from the van crawled eerily across the ceiling, shadows sliding down the walls, momentarily rearranging the room.

Why on earth would the gardener need to pull up into the drive?

The front door opened. Daniel and Meredith got up from the sofa to go and greet Maya. Entering the reception hall, there she stood, along with the gardener.

The floor moved beneath Meredith's feet, a swirling sea of baroque tiles swishing around. Knees ready to give way, anticipating a slow, painful death.

She must pull herself together otherwise a panic attack could ensue, either that or she'd faint or drift off into a dissociated psychotic ether. The firm palm of Daniel's hand discreetly placed on her lower back gave her an anchor, pulling her back into her body.

"Hiya," said Maya.

The gardener was stood behind her, an urchin with his face pointing down towards his raggedy trainers.

Meredith's jaw twisted into stone. Maya, the proverbial cucumber doing what she did, entered like a whirlwind, throwing everything into chaos without a care for how it all landed.

"Liam?" said Daniel.

"Hi Daniel."

"Liam's stopping for a cup of tea before heading back to the caravan," said Maya.

Inside, Meredith screamed. *This is not happening, how dare she do this to me!*

"I'll um, er, put the kettle on, shall I?" stuttered Daniel, looking towards Meredith. *As useless as ever.*

Being left alone with Maya and Liam was not going to happen.

"I'll make the tea," clipped Meredith, trying to erase the high-pitched shrillness in her voice. She reeled off into the kitchen, concentrating on steadying herself. Daniel was left with the agitators, hovering.

"Shall we have tea in the sitting room?" he said pathetically, within earshot; Meredith tutted.

Fluttering around the kitchen on tattered wings, she wondered how to wake from the nightmare she had found herself in. *That slut! Whore! Harlot! How dare she, who does she think she is, with him, that oik! That vulgar, detestable dimwit!* pounded as an internal monologue.

Composure. *It's fine. It's all fine.*

A desire to fling the dead soldier wine bottles with all her might against the kitchen wall was a hair trigger away.

No, it was okay. She had got this.

Meredith entered with the tea tray, sitting down next to Daniel, Liam's eyes in her periphery: Was he watching her? Could he see how unravelled she'd become?

"So, how was your holiday?" asked Maya, as though the situation was a typical encounter whilst obviously being blatantly aware of the brazen anomalies.

"The holiday was marvellous," said Daniel.

The atmosphere crackled.

"What did you get up to?" probed Maya.

Meredith poured the tea, trying to control the tremble in her hand.

"Well, we had some delightful walks, the weather was exceptionally good most of the time, wasn't it darling?" said Daniel, *such a weak man.*

Meredith furtively flinched as she was dragged into the odious parlour game. She absentmindedly filled a cup too full for it to be lifted without spillage.

"Bother!" she said under her breath.

"Oh, not to worry," Daniel quickly interjected. "I'll get another cup."

"NO!" Meredith blurted, louder than she intended. "No, it's fine, I'll go get one." She rose to get another cup, but before she was fully upright, Maya was already on her feet and leaving.

"I'll get one, I need the loo anyway."

* * *

Liam

So much for Maya holding his hand. Liam was stranded together with Meredith and Daniel in the sitting room—he'd want more than a blow job for this charade. He couldn't play these sorts of games, they were out of his league; he wouldn't know where to start.

Rupert Bloomberg and his walrus tusks glowered at him from above the fireplace.

"I'm sorry about what happened when you were away," Liam offered.

Was it okay to be direct? He was learning a whole new set of rules, or at least trying to, but they were difficult to understand. With Meredith, everything was a cold war. Stealth weapons. Cyanide in the tea.

"Sugar!?" asked Meredith, holding a teaspoon.

"No thanks. It wasn't planned, I didn't even know Maya was chatting with you online."

"Milk?"

Meredith was somehow different, off kilter, it reminded him of his mother on one of her episodes. He almost felt sorry for her, but the razor-sharp dagger stare slashed away any empathy.

"Yes, just a bit, please. It was just..."

"Maybe now's not the time, Liam..." posited a panic-stricken Daniel.

His spectre face unable to hide the fear he had of his wife. Such an odd couple: Dracula's daughter and her meek servant. This wasn't the same Daniel he knew.

Daniel's eyes pleaded with Liam.

"Oh, sorry, I er..." Liam wasn't sure why he was sorry. The madness was contagious, he thought, as the obvious deception continued to masquerade itself as normality. No wonder Maya was so intent on busting people's games and not talking bullshit, the present evening being the exception. He took a sip of tea, trying not to slurp.

Where the hell had Maya gone.

* * *

Maya

Maya strolled into the room clutching a bottle of whisky and four glasses.

How funny they all looked.

It was like walking into a sitcom, each character forced into eating dog shit sandwiches or someone telling an offensive mother-in-law joke.

A real stonker had been let rip.

Poor Liam. Meredith's stony silence clamped him to his chair, ripping out his sweet, juicy tongue with her oppressive, taloned vibe.

Cow!

"I didn't massively fancy a tea. Anyone else want a glass?"

Daniel was the first to pipe up when seeing the whisky.

"Jolly good idea."

"Mother?

"Yes, a small one," she said, tersely.

"Liam?"

"A large one for me."

"Ooh, cheeky," said Maya.

A stifled chuckle escaped him, instantly frozen in the frigid air.

Glasses were drained quickly—a race to inebriation.

Maya appointed herself as the glass topper-upperer, like an Amazonian shaman handing out a sacred brew in an ayahuasca ceremony. Firewater to shred the illusionary veils that kept everyone separate, powerful enough to tackle bulletproof energy fields.

On the one hand, her soul sought truth and honesty, on the other, it relished the torture—the lack of directness being the latter—like a cat with a mouse, watching her parents squirm.

Sitting next to Liam, her hand slipped onto his lap, offering him support, albeit rubbing her mother's overbearing nose in their wild philandering.

Vengeance was sweet, sprung from a well of untold pain, a well too deep to fathom.

As the evening wore on and more whisky was consumed, tongues got looser.

"How's your dancey therapy do-dah thing going, Maya?" asked Daniel.

"You mean my Conscious Movement classes? It's not dance, it's being conscious to each moment, breaking free from our character armour, our conditioning, our scripts."

"Oh, I see. Sounds fascinating."

"I'm sorry to break the news, but this is not a film, Maya, it's real life," Meredith chipped in.

"You see, that's typical of you. Why not say something different?" Maya countered.

"It's just time you realised that this pseudo New Age philosophy is rather tiresome."

"Well, I think Maya has a point. It's true, occasionally life can seem unreal," said Daniel, taking a sip of whisky.

"Yes, well that's because she takes after you, you're both unhappy people."

"I'm very happy with my life. How about you, Mother, are you? What part are you playing in your movie? Frustrated housewife? Aloof aristocrat?"

"You don't know me at all. You think you know everyone, but you don't. It's you who's in a film. You should have gone to drama school, acting would have suited you. And what about animals? Baboons, are they playing roles too, or are they not real either?"

"Okay, I think, maybe we should change the subject. Liam, how have you been getting on with the garden?" Daniel interjected, index finger manically drumming against his crystal tumbler.

Liam's head turned from Meredith to Maya to Daniel.

"Erm..."

"So Maya, what ever happened to Troy?" Meredith asked, clearly confidentiality was not her father's strong point. Meredith turned toward Liam, her drilling eyes boring into her pupils.

"Nothing happened to him, he's still alive and well I expect, somewhere in London."

"Oh, so you broke up?" continued Meredith.

"Why do you ask? You've never shown any interest in him before."

"I'm curious about your relationships, darling, that's all."

"Oh Mother, what bollox, and you know it!"

"Do you have to be so uncivil, dear?"

"What is it you really want to know?"

Daniel shuffled in his chair. "Shall we change the subject?" he chipped in.

Maya went into shamanic whisky topper-upperer role, handing out more grain-fermented medicine.

"I'm curious, Maya, how do you perceive your future? Children? Marriage? Or do you intend to live off me and your father forever in your bohemian, make-believe, fantasy land?"

"Yes, I'll get married to a man I don't love but one that my parents will approve of, who will fit the right image and we'll have babies together, which I'll hand over to a nanny until they're old enough to go to boarding school. Does that sound good to you? Also, I do earn a living in case you hadn't noticed!"

"Earn a living. Ha! With your quack, hippy therapy? You really think that's making a living, do you!"

"Oh, poor Mother, you really are quite sad, aren't you. You think watching TV most evenings, having a house big enough for a small village to live in, holidaying in places where a coffee costs twenty pounds, you think that's having a life. I know people who are in their seventies who have more life, sexiness and spirit in their little finger than you do in your whole body."

"Oh, do you. Of course you do, darling. And this one? How long shall we give it?"

"Please don't drag Liam into your viper's nest."

"How many relationships have you had in the last five years—can you actually remember?" Meredith asked Maya.

"No, remind me."

"Each one worse than the next."

Leaning forward from the sofa, Liam placed an empty tumbler on the table, his features gathered up into a disenchanted knot as he scratched his scalp.

"Meredith, what have I done to annoy you so much?" said Liam.

"I beg your pardon!"

"Ever since I've known you, I've always felt you don't really like me."

"Have you, well I'm so sorry to hear that."

"So, do you like Liam, Mother?" came Maya, topping up the glasses.

Daniel's hands rose into the air, attempting to calm the proceedings.

"Why don't we all change the subject or just call it a day. It's getting late, and we've all had a bit too much whisky and saying things we'll probably regret in the morning."

"Oh, Daniel, for God's sake stop worrying, your friend here wonders if I like him."

Meredith was as pissed as a fart.

Drink suited her. Made her more genuine, less hidden.

She wasn't your slurring, fisty pisshead with windmill arms outside a nightcub, her technique was another form of GBH: Gruesome Bitter Humiliation. Maya had spent her whole life mastering how to block her mother's ninja psychic warfare. The living room was a dojo ring whenever the two of them were in it together.

"Well, if I'm really honest, I'd have to say, no! No, I do not like you one little bit. Never have and never will, nor do I like that you and my daughter are having sex, but Daniel likes you, Maya likes you, so what can I do? Hire an assassin?"

Perhaps there was even a sense of humour.

"What is it you don't like about me?"

Everyone turned towards Meredith, shocked but keen to hear her response. Her face blanched, eyes awash with fear, standing up, struggling to keep steady on her feet.

"I'm going to be sick!"

She zigzagged out of the room, Daniel quickly following. The sound of Meredith vomiting could be heard throughout the house. There were possibly tears too, quiet tears that she refused to let anyone else see, or maybe that was just Maya's imagination.

Maya leant over and kissed Liam on the mouth, her hand on his crotch, feeling the contours of his blood-filled lingam under the jeans.

"I'd better go."

"Don't be crazy, you can't drive, you've had too much to drink. Why don't you stay?"

TWENTY-SIX

Maya

Maya opened her eyes, unsure of the time. Closing them again, the slash of incandescent light that ran down the thick velvet curtains remained imprinted on her retina.

Images from the night before tumbled in—her mother getting off her tits, spitting out home truths. A subtle strength in Liam had also come to light. All the previous men had been cringingly obsequious around her parents. Liam was just Liam, there was no going out of his way to prove himself, which was *fucking beautiful*.

Still asleep, his face, soft, was easy-going on the pillow. Hermit-man, captured, loved-up, reintegrated back into his heart. The painful story too often scribbled across his face was gone, angsty lines all softened, melded back, leaving barely a trace.

Surely, that had to be a good thing. Living like a hermit is the kind of thing you do when you're depressed or old or a crab.

She'd served him well, she'd make a good guru, even if she said it herself. Job well done!

And all within the space of a few weeks, yet it felt like forever. The very first time she'd said hello, his face had seemed familiar, or was it his soul?

Letting go would be difficult. It always was. That was life.

Anyway, London wasn't that far, and besides, she was ready to leave: real life beckoned. This had been a holiday fling and her work and friends would be standing by for her reappearance. Troy would have got over her by now; having blocked his number various times, he would have got the message. There'd been no calls or texts over the last couple of weeks, thank fuck!

Liam could visit, but she would remain adamant about not wanting anything too complicated.

Liam opened his eyes and caught Maya admiring him. She smiled shyly.

"Good morning," said Liam, smiling back.

Maya snuggled her naked body into him. "Good morning, gorgeous."

His cock was also awake beneath the sheets, an aphrodisiac for her ovulating horniness; rolling onto him, she straddled herself for a hormonal morning smoothie.

* * *

Meredith

Meredith's coming back into consciousness involved a pillow over her head, attempting to keep the world out. Her head was the Black-wall Tunnel in rush hour: it was rare to drink so much. Daniel stood beside the bed, holding a cup of tea and some paracetamol. She made a grunting sound which when translated meant something between *Good morning* and *God Almighty*. After throwing up in the toilet a few times, Daniel had taken her to bed and tucked her in before joining her—deciding not to return to the scene of the crime. She couldn't quite recall what she'd said to Liam except something about an assassin.

Daniel hovered around the bed, dithering about what was anyone's guess.

"Shall I undraw the curtains, dear?"

"No. What time is it?" Meredith snapped, wearily.

"Nine twenty."

Meredith groaned again. She'd been doing so well. This setback had shriveled up her insides. Skin prickly like a cactus. Whisky had not been a good idea. Her mouth cardboard. She knocked back the paracetamol with tea, anointing her parched throat. All life depended upon fluids, even cacti. A swim in the pool would help regain her fledgling wings.

"Would you like anything else?" asked Daniel.

Before she could answer, intense, pleasurable moans from across the house raided the bedroom. Satisfied *ooohs* and taken-by-surprise *aaahs* took over the whole house, all of which distinctly belonged to Maya who patently wasn't holding back when it came to expressing pleasure whilst having sex. Clearly a deliberate attempt to sabotage her mother's equanimity or at least the remaining threads, now sheered.

Meredith glared at Daniel, her face a porcelain mask covered in cracks yet trying to remain smooth and unblemished by the reverberations of Maya's audible, orgasmic peaks. Without any words, in a zombielike trance, she sleepwalked from the house, still in her nighty, marching across the lawn. Far away was Daniel's voice telling her *it doesn't matter, darling,* to *ignore it, dear,* a phantom hand against her arm as he raced to keep up.

The door to the pool wasn't locked. Inside, a pair of cut-off denims lay lopsided on a chair to dry.

Diving in without any hesitation, her body glided beneath the surface, no sounds of moaning, no Daniel trying to rescue her, no gardener, just her sharklike body torpedoing through the water.

Swimming back and forth from one end of the pool to the other had a logic that thought alone could not find. If it were the sea, she would have swum in a continuous straight line until she could swim no more, allowing the ocean to have her. She'd had enough of dealing with herself; the water could swallow her and own her. Be done with the dryness, the humid closeness of this never-ending desert called life. Her torment was all-consuming, a plague of locusts taking every last piece of her until hollowed out, empty. She detested the amount of hatred that she carried. Her limbs crashed against the pool's surface, each blow a release of venom. Sucking in clean air and breathing out bile. After she'd exorcised enough of her demons, she stopped at the edge of the pool, gasping for air. Daniel approached her with a towel.

* * *

Liam

Liam and Maya lay sated on the bed facing each other, drenched in sacramental sweat, the duvet fallen to the floor.

The bedroom window opened onto the parched lawn, curtains still drawn, untroubled by the breezeless morning. Somewhere out there, Daniel was fretting, pleading for someone to slow down. Either he was talking to the weeds or Meredith.

"Fuck, we have good sex!" enthused Maya.

Liam nodded—there were no words. Chatting immediately after sex was impossible. It took a while to land, to hit the ground.

"How am I going to survive in London without you?" she continued.

Liam shrugged. He'd been alone for ever, up until recently.

"When you going?"

"Tomorrow."

Okay, that's that then! Fuck right off then and find someone else, isn't that what you do? "Oh," was all he could think to say.

"I know. We've had such fun, haven't we."

"What time?"

"My train's at eleven in the morning. We still have today though."

Liam turned onto his back, hands clasped behind his head, his attention focused on the wallpapered ceiling. He kept quiet, safer that way with his throat all choked up.

"You okay?" asked Maya.

He'd known what the deal was and had accepted it. Maya was a free agent about to take flight, regardless; it didn't stop him from feeling like he'd been dumped.

"How come you invited me in last night?"

"How do you mean?"

"Well, you knew it'd be awkward, so I'm wondering why you did it?"

"You didn't have to come."

"You were pretty keen."

"It's good for you to stand up to my mother's vampiric bullshit."

"Oh, so it was all for my benefit, thanks. Just odd that you invited me to meet your parents and now you're off to London and that's that."

"Liam, you already know my parents and there's some weird shit you have going on with my mother, but that aside, is this about me going to London?"

"I don't have a weird thing with your mother, it's her who has a weird thing with me."

"That's what I meant. I *am* going to London, but you can always visit, it's less than an hour on the train."

"I can't do polyamory."

"Well, right now, there is no one else. But I totally get it, I just can't do monogamy, I'd feel trapped. I think I have a fickle heart."

"Did you and Troy have an open relationship?"

"It wasn't a relationship—he got the wrong idea. Troy was a psycho, seriously."

"Sounds like he didn't see it that way. Does he know about me?"

"No, I haven't spoken to him. He kept texting, but I had to block his number until he got the message. He's in therapy and some kind of therapy group, and if he does anything, he'll be straight back to prison, so he wouldn't risk it."

"How do you mean *do something?* And *prison?*"

Lowering her gaze, Maya cautiously pushed the tip of her finger back and forth along the edge of her lower teeth.

"I mentioned he'd been in prison ... didn't I?"

"No, I think I'd remember that."

"It wasn't anything serious, so maybe I forgot. Liam, this is our last day together, let's make the most of it."

"Did you love him?"

The word *love* had escaped his mouth and stood frozen in the searchlight with nowhere else to hide.

"Maybe, I felt something for him, I don't know. What does that mean, anyway? It's just chemicals in the body."

"Oh well, fuck him then."

"Liam?"

"What?"

"What's going on?"

"Love is just chemicals?"

"Yes, oxytocin, serotonin, dopamine and endorphins, and no doubt other ones."

"This is such bullshit."

"In what way?"

"Love is not just a load of chemicals!"

"It is, sorry to disappoint you."

"Is that what your guru Gandalf tells you?"

"Swami Gandalih. No. It's a biological fact."

"Somehow you have just managed to reduce the most beautiful and sacred experience there is in life into something you can put in a petri dish. So, what would you say we've had going on between us, a few endorphins maybe and a bit of serotonin?"

Had he just inadvertently told Maya what he felt for her?

If there'd been any air left in the room, Liam would have taken delight in cramming himself into the tiniest speck of dust and being carried away through the window on thermals. The atmosphere was drained of all moisture and fit only for cold-blooded reptiles.

"I'm sorry, Liam, I didn't intend to hurt you. I've really enjoyed hanging out with you and having sex, but my life is in London with my tribe."

The words ricocheted around the room, each one eventually wounding him. Maya clearly didn't feel the same way he did.

There was a knock on the bedroom door, and Maya shouted, "Hang on," as she put on a dressing gown. She opened the door to see Meredith, dripping wet, still in her nightie, her face ghoulish, creases sketched in thick, black demonic lines, baring her perfect teeth in a snarl.

"Get out!"

"Wh..."

"OUT! NOW!!" shouted Meredith. "I've had enough of you both and I can't cope with you anymore."

Liam, impervious to this blistering blowtorch, beyond caring, rose from the bed naked and started dressing.

Meredith scoffed, averting her eyes, and as though addressing the empty space next to her, continued. "And you," her tone dropping a few degrees below zero. "You are not welcome here ever again. Do you really believe that my daughter could ever be serious about you? She is using you to get at me, you're just too stupid to see this!"

Liam in his jeans walked over to Meredith until he was an inch from her face, which was now pointing in his direction. Looking her into her eyes, he said, "Fuck you, Meredith. Fuck you! I have done nothing to you whatsoever. Why you hate me so much God only knows. Maybe it's because you hate yourself, your rigidness, your deadened heart, your empty, pointless life, some meaningless image you have of yourself. It's pathetic. I don't care if I'm not welcome here, why would I care? You have nothing to offer me or anyone, you're a taker. You don't see people, you see commodities and that is sad. Something really shit must have happened to you to be like you are, but that doesn't give you the right to shit all over me. So, fuck you!"

A substantial amount of this anger was really about Maya. He truly wasn't that bothered about Meredith's disrespect, he didn't need her to like him. Maybe this was why she hated him.

Liam put on his T-shirt and shoes and left. On the way out, he passed Daniel. He quickly glanced at him. "Sorry, Daniel." And left. Maya chased after Liam and caught him up.

"Well done, Liam, for saying that, she deserved it."

"Okay, thanks. I'll see you, Maya."

"Shall I come to the caravan now with you?"

"No. That's it. I can't do this. I want a proper relationship. You sleeping with another man would be too much, I couldn't bear it. I was hoping you might think differently. I've just really fallen for you. If I go any deeper, it'll be too painful, so... See you, Maya."

They hugged each other, neither wanting to break away, but he knew he had to. Walking away, he decided not to look back.

TWENTY-SEVEN

Liam

A pale, endless grey stretched beyond the perimeters of Falindon, droplets of rain squeezed from its sagging cloth, a huge, heavy void blanketing the earth. Birds huddled away, refusing to get their wings wet in such a pointless sky.

It was the first day of not seeing Maya or sleeping with her. She was gone. The only thing to do was machete through the dark foliage back to normality. The problem was normal now looked like hell; how could normal ever be okay? It was hard to believe that just over four weeks ago they'd never even met, and now Liam couldn't imagine how he'd survived without her.

His phone was in a coma: no texts, no calls, his broken heart willing it to snap back into consciousness.

Maybe she'd come through and see the error of her ways, come running back, realising he was the one. Nothing but a declaration of her love would suffice.

Maybe he should phone her, text her, get a train to London and move in with her, cried the cold-turkey deluge. Chase that one last hit of—as she put it—love chemicals. *No, it will get easier, eventually, it will, eventually, it just will ... eventually,* resounded the creaking platitudes, looped like a mantra, desperate to console his broken spirit. Yet, no matter how many times he said it to himself, he couldn't believe it. This was the worst part of breaking up, the inability to think or feel anything other than the loss.

On top of this, he tormented himself with fantasies about who she might be with, what man she might be talking to. Kissing. Licking. Fucking.

The day after she'd left, he went to Mr and Mrs Fisher's house. Keeping busy was the only option. The world muted through the ritual of gardening, drowning out internal rants with banal chatter from the radio, which was the plan, but all the songs played were about his relationship, and cutting the neat OCD edges of Mr and Mrs Fisher's lawn was even more soul-destroying than usual.

This particular job was the worst. On his knees, bowing down, doffing the metaphorical cap: yes sir, no sir, three bags full sir. Cutting the stupid, fucking lawn, pulling out stupid, fucking weeds, for what? The rich and their stupid, fucking control over everything. He hated everything. Why was he a stupid gardener? Maybe this was why Maya really didn't want to be with him: he just wasn't good enough. What kind of person spends their life gardening for people who have so much money they use it to wipe their arses, though truth was, Mr and Mrs Fisher weren't that rich.

Mrs Fisher tottered out, trying to avoid puddles, carrying a tray with tea and a slice of fruit cake. Handing over the tray, she asked him to weed around the hydrangea. Stupid, fucking hydrangeas and their lack of fragrance, papery flowers, useless to bees in search of succulence and sweetness, the epitome of suburbia, all lace curtains, synthetic, cushioned coffins.

The subservient dog, drenched in pain, took his treats for doing as he was told.

Over the last month, he'd been powerful and strong, life had meaning, each day an adventure, but this day—in the Fishers' garden—gardening was an insult to life itself. Dissatisfaction gnawed away. Was he willing to continue down this dreary path? Where was his self-respect?

Maya had used him; he'd been just a good fuck to her.

Persecutory thoughts hammered on.

Temptation to inflict pain on himself was huge. A distraction from the clatter.

A chiselled memory of his mother forcibly being dragged away from him as a child crowded his thoughts. In foster care, he'd researched online all the ways he might be able to cure her of the voices. A bizarre find was in ancient times, people had holes drilled into the top of their skulls to release the infernal yacking of evil spirits. A kind of medieval ECT. Right now, he wanted one of those holes in his head to let out all the bile, dripping down his face, washed away by endless rain.

Once again, Mrs Fisher appeared, and this time she called from the conservatory to avoid getting wet. Liam, bedraggled in his contemplations, wandered over.

The elderly matriarch smiled at him, synthetic teeth incongruent with her ancient face.

The new instructions were, after weeding around the hydrangea, to put a mixture of fertiliser with weed- and moss killer on the lawn. Liam told her he was an organic gardener, he didn't use weedkillers. No doubt comfortable addressing servants from her colonial days in India, Mrs Fisher pursed her lips, asserting that she needed a gardener who was willing to use weedkillers.

Liam agreed. She smiled sweetly and disappeared back indoors.

Liam took the large bag of toxic waste from the garage and, counting his steps and pegging out the lawn, carefully administered it.

After an hour or so, it was time to leave. He went to the door to collect his money. Mrs Fisher came with his forty-five pounds for three hours' work and commented on what a marvellous job he'd done, adding that she was relieved he'd agreed to use the weedkiller as she would hate to use 'one of those awful Eastern European gardeners'.

"So, how do you know they're awful?" replied Liam

"Liam, they don't even speak our language."

"I've met plenty who speak good English."

"Well, they're renowned for being lazy and they steal, hopefully now that UKIP have a huge following, we'll finally get a referendum on leaving the EU and say goodbye to them all."

Thankfully, this was highly unlikely. It was only people like the Fishers who voted for UKIP, and they'd all be dead soon.

"Do you know what, Mrs Fisher, with all due respect, actually most of them work harder than English people, hence the reason they get lots of work here. Been to any hospitals lately? Also, they're unlikely to steal as that would mean getting deported for one thing, but worse than that, they have to listen to the sort of racist crap that comes out of the mouths of people like you."

Liam waited for a response but there wasn't one. There was only a fearful look as though Liam had lost his mind and was about to murder her.

"So, I suggest, Mrs Fisher, you find yourself a Lithuanian non-organic gardener or possibly an Afro-Caribbean one so that you get to understand these people are far more hardworking than you have ever been because I won't be coming back."

And that was that, apart from the fact that Mrs Fisher in a few days would be reminded of him as she peered from the upstairs bedroom window and saw the words *WHITE TRASH* sprawled on her lawn in huge, newly fertilised, green letters where moss and weeds had once grown. He would've liked to have written something more profound and pithy but nothing else presented itself.

Despite feeling a surge of adrenalin from a momentary, virtuous, anarchistic revolt which helped take his mind off Maya, it wasn't long before she again took central stage: her loveliness, her kindness, her funniness, her beautifulness, her thoughtfulness, her everything-ness, it was agony—he desperately needed an escape. There was nothing left. No escape from the pain and self-loathing he'd spiralled into, a shitty life that would never amount to anything. Alone, with no one to help take the weight—everyone had wandered off. No friends, no family.

The wounded animal limped back to hide in his den, deciding that he would stay there until he either died or emerged, a Himalayan monk, free of all worldly attachments, or more precisely, his longing for Maya.

TWENTY-EIGHT

Maya

Mary J Blige's powerhouse vibrato arced iPhone to earpods, dejected warbles cooling down Maya's frazzled brain. Jiggling along, miniature dome droplets held fast to the window, resisting the train's velocity. Beyond the glass, the countryside passed by, cleansed by the much-needed downpour. Each moment bringing more distance from the cold-blooded feud she'd had with her mother. A twinge of gut excitement smouldered away, looking forward to hanging out with friends again, getting back to running Conscious Movement evenings, having some space.

The buzz of London imminent, the busyness, the anonymity, the cool funkiness, the multicultural, metrosexual vibe.

Liam was decent enough, but his neediness was stifling; still, it had been sad saying goodbye. That was all compartmentalised now, tucked away in the *I'll deal with it some other time* file, a boarding school trick.

The *cold-hearted mother* file, more like a virus attacking her system, was trickier to delete, like trying to cut through a titanium umbilical cord with a feather. How could someone with such a con-strained disposition give birth, let alone bring up three children? Not that she'd managed that either—this role had been given to Dorothy, or Nanny Dot as she was known. A suitable moniker as she'd been around since the year dot of each of the children's lives. A puddle of warmth oozed through veins as Maya reminisced and pictured her nanny's squat munchkin body.

Nannying each sprog up until boarding school, her Brummie bubbly personality, always playful, never short of a cuddle, always laughing at the smallest thing.

If only Nanny Dot had been Mummy Dot: this rumination had been quite the taboo and was quickly ascribed to Tilly, a tough and feisty doll, liking naughty words, always in trouble from bossy Barbie for doing bad things with Simon's Action Man.

Secretly, Maya believed she was Nanny Dot's favourite: she had to, it was all she had. She even received birthday cards at school for the first few years, but these faded out, though, without explanation. The first year in which no card came, Maya wept, *How could she?* to Suzy, her counsellor, who subsequently replaced Nanny Dot. A consolation.

Loving Nanny Dot took no effort, she just wished she could feel the same for Mummy Meredith.

Arriving home around 6.00 p.m., Maya unlocked the door, mildly struck by the stale smell of air, the rooms having had no ven-tilation for a month.

Opening a few windows, she then flopped onto the couch, wiped out from the journey. Checking her mobile, there were no texts from Liam, only a couple of texts from friends saying they were looking forward to hanging out but that they weren't free for a few days. Then a quick browse on Facebook: from Ian, a petition to save the bees; a picture of an old friend with her newborn baby, its face wrinkled and squashed like an old person, her friend, rosy, tired, relieved, a glint of worry lost in her eyes. Buddhist guy had changed his profile picture from one of himself looking like he was in deep conversation with a group of devotees to one of him meditating next to a busy main road with a cardboard sign saying, *How's it going so far?* Liam didn't have a Facebook account. Scrolling down the page, she wondered why she was on Facebook at all and logged out.

She turned the phone over and over in her hands, then put it away, out of reach.

Accept whatever is happening, observe it, then let it go, the swami would say, or maybe, *A path without a heart is a wasted journey.* A complete guide to the swami's pithy oracle had been digested over the years and memorised.

Regardless of being tired, stillness was the least favourite option: action always held the promise of something more potent.

Checking into her heart there was nothing. Blank, an empty vessel. The heart didn't seem to work unless it was with others. She was the Nietzschean falling tree in the forest, unable to exist without being seen. Was this vanity?

Too many questions, always too many questions—whirring, spinning cogs leading nowhere. Her heart, or was it the head, or even possibly the swami, said to switch off the chatter. De-crowd the mind.

She wandered into the kitchen. It was still early but not too early for a large glass of white wine. And chocolate.

Unwrapping a mega bar of fruit and nut and breaking off a size-able chunk, she stared blankly out of the window over Hampstead Heath, gorging herself as a way to find sanctuary from an unexpected sense of ennui.

The chocolate quickly became half a bar as the glass was topped up and a joint rolled. It wasn't addiction, it was hedonism, the path of least resistance and all that ... only, more and more, it involved either dope, alcohol or sex.

With Liam, there was a sense of belonging, a place where being was enough. Even Troy had commented on how she could never sit still, and it was true, particularly as she sat there looking out over the heath, fidgeting, a butterfly on a pin trying to become unstuck.

Eyes closed, she tuned into a perennial need to be free, but from what? Oh God, more questions.

Endless questions. If only the swami was there to answer them, save her from plummeting into the great abyss of solitude. The monster that drove her. A grotesque demon that dwelled in the basement, hidden away, unlovable and unwanted, a secret, an unwanted child longing to be found. A mother who'd been so cold throughout her life with a heart encased in granite. A father, intangible, a faint recollection just out of reach.

With Liam, when traversing the lean terrain of his body, a wild current had infused her entire nervous system from the tips of her fingers, landing in her heart.

What utter bullshit—she was just stoned, there was no Mr Right. It was that annoying, *one day my prince will come* fairy tale pulling her back in, just a story.

Thoughts flittered back and forth in search of reason, but trying to think her way out was useless.

The glass empty, again. The quiet of the room too loud.

Standing up, linking her iPhone to the speakers, she looked through a playlist and tapped on a slow Arabic song from Mali, a woman's emotive voice accompanied by the kora sang of sadness and loss, or at least that was what it sounded like.

Eyes closed, gently swaying to the melodic rhythm, inside a pain that needed expression. Dancing was her saviour: when moving, there was a connection to wisdom, a part that held a different truth, one that had escaped conditioning—dope sometimes allowed this too. When dancing, the freedom went further because she was more in her body and this brought her more into the world, back into the present moment.

Her body wept as it glided through the air, reaching into the void. The ancient weeping sound of the woman's voice resonating with the pull in her heart.

So where were the tears? Why the pretence that everything is okay?

Stop with the questions, just dance, you fool!

TWENTY-NINE

Daniel

Daniel had taken refuge in his study, sheltered from the intensity of Meredith's vortex sweeping through the house like a tornado. Sunk into a Chesterfield armchair—one his great-grandfather had occupied in Victorian times—he attempted to get back to himself, the drama all a bit much. The oak-panelled bunker was a place one could retreat to, a man shed, in a manner of speaking. Safe and secure, shielded from the cold, metallic sky that enveloped the house on this gloomy, damp day. Not reading anything, just sitting, thinking. Pondering would be too finer way of putting it; he was moping, mortified that Maya had left: they'd hardly even spoken. A tête-à-tête would have been rather pleasant, but with Liam being around and Meredith soaking up all the attention, it was not to be. Then again, they never really chatted, there was always some reason, but the truth was he didn't know what to say. It would seem his only daughter had sprung from an alien gene pool: vivacious, expressive and nonconformist were not family traits, her lineage more akin to Lilith with her refusal to be deferential towards Adam.

If Rupert Bloomberg had seen his son slumped in the same chair, doing the same *poor me*, he'd have bellowed, *Good God man, where's your grit? Pull yourself together before I give you a jolly good thrashing!*

Subservience had been indoctrinated along the Bloomberg lineage since time immemorial. His father had insisted Daniel call him sir; maybe this was why he prostrated himself before Meredith. Ironically, in business he was tough, ruthless even, but mustering the same clout in his personal life was a different kettle of fish. In all the years of marriage, never once shouting at Meredith, which could be viewed as gallant and noble, but the undertones of sarcasm, cynicism, mood, irritability, priggish arguments, intellectual superiority and moaning were anger in their own way, only pushed through a smaller hole. The problem was they never achieved the desired results: whining and being sardonic lacked the gravity of what he was trying to convey.

Since Maya and Liam had left, Meredith had sunk further into a melee and Daniel was clear about not rescuing her: the quagmire was her own making and all his sympathy had run dry. He wasn't open to talking and seeing the last remnants of his hard-earned equanimity more muddied by Meredith's strange, demonic possession. Discuss what anyway—where to get hold of polonium to bump Liam off so she could break free from her deranged, homicidal bubble?

If it wasn't enough her driving away the only compadre he'd managed to make in God knows how long, now she expected some consoling.

Meredith constantly presented an unsolvable riddle, a relational compass without cardinal points. He'd been twenty-seven when they'd met with a ridiculous amount of pressure from the parents to marry.

She was quite the filly, even if slightly dowdy, but the question of whether it was love or obligation sat uncomfortably at the back of his mind. It was a case of make do. Divorce was out of the question, of course.

There had to be more to life than this. Life had been so restricted and mapped out with little choice in the matter. Clinging onto a fantasy that life would somehow begin in the future, but now, there wasn't a load of future left. The recent nights of passion at Le Nid had pepped up his spirit with a taste for a wilder side he'd never dared to walk.

Was that it? A bit of holiday fun, and now the holiday was over, must crack on with tedium and dying slowly.

His mood was back; the existential crisis had been waiting for his return.

Death! That eternal void that gets us all in the end was debasing him: *You pathetic waste of life. Cling on as much as you like, soon you'll be torn away, like a babe from its mother's loving teat!*

All the hallmarks of that very first day at boarding school were there, sobbing, heartbroken, teased by the other boys for being a *blub,* their hearts already hermetically sealed.

Plus, the two-year stretch of nightly bedwetting, sneaking through darkened corridors bundled with piss-stained sheets, clean ones discreetly nabbed from the washroom.

Mastering the tricks of the trade didn't take long—denying emotions, toughening up, posturing a well-presented surface polished with manners and false dignity, eventually becoming a fully pledged member of the elite.

So, here he was, guarding his heart in despot fashion for fear of a coup d'état. Weakness never an option.

No one to help carry the weight.

Meanwhile, in a secret place down in the washroom, buried amongst the shame of sodden sheets, waited a pit of grief.

Fifty-five years without a single tear, alas, nor the taste of life's sweetness and joy.

On and on and on, the same old story, rigor mortised like the chair he was sat in.

He looked at a wastepaper bin and kicked it hard across the floor to the other side of the study. All those things never done for fear of getting it wrong and looking foolish.

Never standing up to his father raged through his mind.

Marching over to his desk, taking a pen, he jotted down a list of all the wild things he'd never done. Whatever came to mind would do:

Stole something (Though the offshore bank accounts were a kind of stealing.)

Acquired any tattoos

Smoked marijuana

Sunbathed naked

Slept around

Ridden a Harley-Davidson

Gone to a night club, got drunk and danced wildly

Had sex outdoors

Written a love poem

Hugged a man

Dressed up as a woman

Slept with a man

Hm, maybe the last two (or three) should be crossed off the list and burnt, destroying all evidence ... or maybe not!

Neurons danced like sparks amending all conventional thoughts downloaded to his brain. Writing the list was invigorating; with each new dare, along with their admittance, came a frisson. There was more:

Seen a lady of the night

Had an affair

Driven 140 mph down the motorway

The list was becoming humdrum, how about spicing it up.

Kill someone

Where in the blazes did that come from? he thought.

Who would he want to kill, his wife? How preposterous, of course he wouldn't. *Stuff and nonsense*, he thought, half tearing the paper as the pen dug in, rapidly deleting all proof of its existence.

And *see a lady of the night? Have an affair?*

Again, inconsequential thoughts not worth dwelling on—more furious scribbling.

As for *driving 140mph down a motorway,* how prosaic. Further swift elimination.

The rest of the list was intriguing, though there was a question mark next to *sleep with another man* and *dress up as a woman*, the latter having a curious excitement to it. He pictured Grayson Perry wearing garish colours, pink ribbons in his hair and an Alice in Wonderland pantomime dress. Not the kind of clothes Daniel had in mind.

He poised the pen ready to render the words illegible when it occurred to him how he'd once tried on his mother's high-heeled shoes and skirt. She found this an absolute riot, laughing uproariously. His father in the adjoining room must have heard, for he came running in to find out what all the joviality was about. Seeing his son, he flew into one of his rages, issuing an unmerciful spanking.

The injustice had stung substantially more than the physical pain.

Daniel was rarely a man of vulgar words, but his father was a cunt. A cold cunt who didn't have an ounce of love in his whole body.

"Darling," his mother had cried, "he's only playing."

"The boy's a damned pansy," were his father's only words as he left the room.

Where had that memory been until now? Lost in a Moroccan street market, running down narrow lanes, fearful of being caught and dragged back home.

Daniel was now the tyrant, not to others, but to himself. Forbidding a fair share of life.

Such a sad loss to be stood at the threshold of his autumn years, and from this vista, to look back at such an impoverished landscape. Yes. There'd been yachts, private planes, travelling the globe, a life many would envy, but it hadn't felt rich, it had felt dead. It would be impossible for others to understand, but being rich was horrendously boring. Never having to work, hounded by sycophants and gold diggers.

He wanted to grab life before it ran out.

He went back to the *Sleep with another man*. There'd been no sexual attraction towards men, so why the inordinate amount of fear and anxiety about it? Occasionally, a supremely handsome man might cause a slight scorching to the cheeks, but this was different—it wasn't sex he wanted, it was a desire for something closer, touch maybe, but that was it. Why had he not experimented more?

Who'd want my decrepit old body now anyway, he thought, scrawling over the words.

The rest of the list remained challenging enough for it still to have an edge, an edge he was willing to go to, and who knows, even jump off.

Taking some scissors from the drawer of his desk, he carefully cut each *missed opportunity* from the list, folded it, and placed it in a tiny pile. Shuffling the pile, he would randomly pick one and do whatever the lottery threw his way, no turning back. A world opened up where anything could happen. All options on the table. Writer, director and star of his own movie: an Arabian blind seer, his dowsing fingers wavering over the pieces of folded paper, hovering carefully. Pincer claws dipped down towards the prize, snapping in the *grab life before it's too late* amusement park. Opening his eyes, unfolding the paper, he read, *Dress up as a woman for 24 hrs.* A feverish laughter shook through his body.

* * *

It wasn't long before Daniel regretted the dress idea. Both *Stealing something* or *Smoking marijuana* would have been preferable. Firstly, there was no actual dress *to* wear, secondly, *stealing* or *smoking marijuana* could be done without anyone being the wiser. Donning a dress for twenty-four hours would be near impossible to hide from Meredith. Twenty-four hours was a silly amount of time—no one wears clothes for that long unless they sleep in them.

Naturally, it was plausible to not wear a dress at all, continue as if nothing had been written down, but that would be rubbing extra salt into his gaping existential wound, hammering more nails into the coffin of an already dead life. No, the only rule of this ad-hoc game was to commit to whatever was drawn from the lucky dip. There was no point in entertaining ideas of freedom if you weren't willing to give freedom at least a chance. Anyway, no one would see him except Meredith, and she certainly wouldn't be blathering about her husband being partial to frocks, and if she did, realistically what would be lost? Prestige? Reputation? Dignity? Those tyrannical dictators ruling over the totalitarian state of his life—a life lost from lack of risk. No, the old establishment was obsolete. There was nothing left to lose.

It would absolutely need to be done properly, not in a half-hearted way—this had been his whole life. It was time to take the reins, to forcefully hurl choice into the face of fate. Why live this fleeting lifetime in fear when there could be so much more to be had from each day?

Daniel hadn't managed to get a good night's sleep. Lying in bed, contemplating himself in various dresses had reeled through his mind with the shocked expression of Meredith's face superimposed over the top of each image. What if she went ballistic? Meredith had been asleep in her bed on the other side of the unlit lamp that stood between them. He'd thought it better not to mention anything about the dress whilst she was still brooding over the conflict with Maya and Liam.

As the morning dawned, the bravado had fallen further away. Looking in the mirror to shave, a saggy, geriatric face stared back. A face that no longer smiled, eyes disconnected, the reflection estranged. Attempting to meet his gaze, the face in the mirror melded into his father's—cold, critical, mean and void of love. Daniel hissed, "I hate you." The shadowy mask remained cold, untouched.

Determined to carry out his dare, he lifted his chin, locking eyes with his father's relic and spitting through gritted teeth. "Today I'm going to wear a dress, let's see how you like that, sir... Cunt!" The dreamlike oppressor blurred, fading into someone less familiar, friendlier, compassionate, an old friend getting back in touch.

He dressed, had breakfast and set off to Twickenham, just on the edge of London, a place he could remain anonymous.

A large, impersonal clothes store in a shopping mall was preferable to a boutique with assistants hovering around, offering help. Being midweek, the store was quiet. The women's section was on a separate floor to the men's.

Wiping away a bead of sweat rolling down the nape of his neck, he hoped others would assume the dress was a gift for his wife.

Tentatively, he approached an array of dresses hung from walls and racks or folded in small piles without the foggiest on how dress sizes worked. The only thing to do was to try some on, which meant getting to a changing room back on the men's floor and engaging with the changing room attendant who monitored the number of items taken in. It would be obvious the dress was for Daniel. His heart thumped like pistons against his chest, blood rushing in his ear. A drop of cool sweat meandered from his armpit over his ribcage.

Starting at the end, he began to part each dress from the last, each new fabric supermodel coasting along the catwalk rail, revealing itself. An assortment of vibrant colours, patterns, chichi, little black numbers, thrills, lace, short, tight, long, sexy, simple, virginal, passionate, conservative, boho, cheap, classy, it was a feast for the eyes compared to the men's section where shopping for clothes was a laborious chore. The dress would need to be one he could revere, determined not to resemble one of those men in loutish, drunken stag parties parading city centres on a Saturday night like crude, pantomime prostitutes flaunting enormous balloon breasts. His dress would be thoughtful. Who was the woman cloistered away? Was she a wallflower? Prudish librarian? Concubine? Whole new identities opened up before him.

To delay the agony of having to choose one—which was impossible—he closed his eyes, his hands gracefully scouring the air. Fluttering down, delicately traipsing the textures, his fingertips seeking subjugation, each cloth intoned melodic waves through the apertures of his fingertips until his hands landed gracefully on what would become the new Daniel, or should it be *Danielle?* A low-cut, sleeveless, sequinned, turquoise sparkly thing, adorable and terrifying all at once, shone before him. The gods had spoken. It was not what he'd had in mind—being clad with such ostentatious immodesty was unthinkable. Demure would be closer to home, possibly a twinset and pearls, but this indeed was a bold statement. Taking a deep breath, he grabbed the dress and slinked up the escalator, head bowed down, to the men's section.

Daniel approached the changing room attendant, a handsome young man, possibly an out-of-work model with chiselled features and square jaw. Showing him his one item, the attendant handed him a token.

"Enjoy," said the attendant, smirking.

A shrunken Daniel wandered to the changing cubicle, the unbridled garment dangling over his arm.

Until recently, he'd never questioned who he was, where he was going and why he was here; now he thought, *If I put this dress on, it changes all of that.* Pulling the T-shirt over his head, undoing his belt, trousers flopping down to his ankles, he stepped out of the grey shackles. Climbing into the dress, his long strip-light body glowed inwardly, morphing into a lava lamp, bubbles of air rising towards the heavens.

The snug dress ended halfway up the thigh, the upper part décolleté, exposing a troupe of wiry, silver hairs camped across his sternum. Tiny sequins arbitrarily winking. With a slackened jaw, brow softened, pupils celestial, he took in the deep turquoise, oceanic mystery, his old identity momentarily redundant, and in its wake, a woman of shimmering light. Daniel nervously touched his chest where his breasts might be, tentatively touching the cheeks of his derriere, the way he might touch a woman's, his body receiving the touch like a woman might receive it from a lover.

This thrill of his own touch was exhilarating. Hips, arms, legs, wrists all joined up, instinctively wanting to move differently, a whole new vocabulary of mobility within his reach, the space lighter, less dense.

It was surprising just how relaxed and unruffled he felt with this freedom he didn't even know existed. He was alive in the dress, feminine. Being a man all the time could be very stifling. He could even sense a vagina in place of his penis, envisioning the cavity, wanting to go there and sit within in its damp, soft, mossy walls. Being a woman was so much easier, and then erasing all trace of it from his mind, he quickly took off the dress, changed, paid at the checkout and took his dirty secret home.

Driving back to Falindon, Daniel wondered how Meredith would respond: it would be unfair to spring this on her after she'd been through so much with Maya but also wondered if this was the type of thinking that stopped him doing anything. It was just a dress. Scottish people wore kilts, the Japanese wore sarongs, the Romans wore togas. All this fear was ridiculous. Daniel had always been Daniel without actually knowing who Daniel was, but wasn't that true for everyone? Each of us performing our bit in this travesty called life. This was all part of the intimacy Meredith had been wanting with him. Well, indeed, she'd certainly meet more of him today—there was little doubt about that.

THIRTY

Meredith

A stain was left from caustic words, refusing to trickle off the proverbial duck's back. Words that percolated through a seamless capsule, biting into thin, tissuey skin.

Being called *rigid* and told her heart was *dead* exposed a raw nerve, proving she was flimsy. She certainly was not a so-called *taker*, she was adamant, holding to it with a firm fist, anchoring her to the last remnants of any self-preserving ego still intact.

Daniel, as usual, had crept away to hide in his study, avoiding her. This morning he'd gone off in the car, furtively announcing that he needed to go somewhere to get something. Meredith would prove she wasn't rigid, that her heart was not dead and her life did have meaning, though the answer to how this might be achieved hadn't quite yet arrived.

Balanced on the edge of the sofa, teeth chewing on her lower lip, the day ahead needed to be figured out. A young woman with brown eyes like pools and flawless skin vacantly looked out from the cover of this month's Tatler. Like thought bubbles around her head, the magazine offered articles on yachts, fashion and fifty ways to deal with boredom. Picking it up for a flick through, she discovered a book, clearly belonging to Maya hidden away underneath it, it was not one she or Daniel would ever purchase.

Resenting the book, her eyes narrowed, scowling at the title: *Tantratastic*. A picture of a naked woman with pert breasts sat with her legs wrapped around a naked man. A vibrator would have been less vulgar. Had Maya no shame? Skimming through the book, tutting at the drawings, graphic in their display of genitalia, Meredith found herself not wanting to put the book down.

Not that she was a prude—prudes don't buy kinky skirts—but seeing the book exposed how much more liberated and sexually evolved Maya was. Reading bits here and there, it became clear she'd been under the misconception that tantra was exclusively about sexual positions for contortionists and how to be good at performing them, muddling it up with the Kama Sutra and porn, but reading on, the emphasis was more on the heart and connecting and not much different from the *Seven ways to spice up your love life* she'd found online for her erotic evening with Daniel.

Le Nid, less than a week ago, seemed like another lifetime. *Tantratastic* spoke about the harmonising balance between yin and yang, how masculine and feminine energies complement each other. The book spoke of surrendering to the heart, letting others in, being open. Some of the chapters involved dressing up in sensual clothing, exploring your yoni (vagina) and lingam (penis), massages, eye gazing et al. Reminded of the journey she and Daniel had embarked on in the Pyrenees, she vowed it was time to get back on the trail. She ploughed through the book, choosing where to start.

A *cleansing bath to awaken the body* couldn't be too difficult. Most of the things on the list for this exercise weren't in her possession, such as candles, essential oils, rose petals or bubble baths, but she did have aromatic-scented bath salts that she received as a

Christmas gift from her son, Simon, and a laptop for music. She stepped into the water. Bamboo flute music played on the laptop. The object was *to relax and pamper* herself. Meredith was more of a shower person. Having such a busy mind, she'd never got the hang of relaxing in baths. Closing her eyes, her body submerged into the warm, aromatic-scented water which felt no different from normal water. The bamboo flute music dawdled on in a faint echoey kind of way. She tried to picture herself in the Himalayas or Peru or wherever the flute music was meant to be from. On YouTube, she'd typed *Tantra relaxing music* in the search box. Mozart or Duran Duran might have been more to her taste. *It's fine,* she told herself, wondering how long it had been now. Maybe there was something she wasn't doing right because nothing much was happening. What was in fact ten minutes had felt more like half an hour. Was the slowing down of time part of it? Ten minutes would have to be enough. She got out of the bath and went into the next part of the exercise which took place in the bedroom.

Meredith had texted Daniel to let him know she needed some privacy and that he wasn't to disturb her. To make doubly sure she wouldn't be disturbed, she stuck a note to the door insisting that when he returned, not to enter. It was important that *the space was contained and safe,* the book instructed. The bedroom curtains were drawn, not that there were any neighbours to see in. It was one of those things one did—nudity was reserved for the bathroom and beneath the quilt. Lamps were turned on for a *low, ambient light,* following the guidelines from the book. Parked on the floor in a bath towel, facing an oval mirror taken from one of the guest bedrooms, she *placed a hand over* her *heart area* and breathed into her *heart chakra, picturing it opening up like a flower to the rays of love and self-compassion.* Then plonking a hand over her genital area, she attempted to *visualise the love from* her *heart flowing down to* her *yoni.* Continuing to follow the instructions, the towel was removed, legs opened wide and there it was, a vulva, in all its glorious detail, staring back at her. *It is odd to have never looked at your own vulva,* Meredith thought. The word vulva sounded like a soft, purring, exotic machine. Genitals had always been referred to as "down there". She wasn't seeing the petals described in *Tantratastic* she'd been hoping for. The other hand placed on her sternum, trying to make contact with an imprisoned heart, was failing miserably. Her bush was thinning and looked in need of some spring foliage. A few renegade grey pubic hairs sprouted wildly around her labia. She'd expected it to be different, the size, shape and colour all looked wrong. The labial lips were big and ugly. Her mother had always referred to female genitals as "simply horrid" and she'd been right.

Meredith grabbed the laptop, looking online for images of vaginas which were surprisingly easy to find; her vulva just did not compare. The vulvas online were neater and more contained whereas this one appeared chaotic and messy, like an alien that had attached to her body. The book suggested that she *feel for the clitoris* which was described as equivalent *to a female phallus with superpowers due to the amount of nerve endings.* The author, Ruby Moon, invited the reader to *take a loving look at this temple of pleasure.* Meredith had what was termed as a *hooded clit,* more hidden; the book talked about how many women have been *shamed around their genitals and how important it is to see them as luscious orchids, helping them to reclaim* their *sexual power and find* their *goddess energy.* Parting her labial lips further until they were the shape of the heart symbol, shame transmuted into curiosity and fascination. The book assured her that her vulva wasn't deformed, ugly or shameful.

Not once had Daniel complained, but rarely had they gone beyond the missionary position; consequently this meant no oral sex. A vague memory of an attempt at cunnilingus popped out of the shadows—she'd been disagreeable, maybe it had something to do with trust, being overly submissive, preferring to stay in control. Daniel had given the impression he was only too happy to give up and go back to the missionary position. She herself had attempted fellatio once, but this had been when they'd been quite inebriated and his erection had become flaccid. The wildest time had been at Le Nid with the skirt but with the emphasis having been on Daniel's penchant for voyeurism. Something was missing, possibly the very thing her palmed hand was trying to meet through the bars of her rib cage. Foreplay had never been part of their sex life either.

Colin Hathaway was a different story, his stallion demeanour, powerful and authoritative, no twiddling thumbs with him: he knew what he wanted and went for it. His desire was simple: to take her, and she wanted to be taken. The imprint of his touch all those years ago reverberated through her body, tingling, a reminder of how hot and horny she was capable of feeling, when allowed to. Dwelling on the rise of warm, lapping tides, the tingling expanded, her fingers gently dancing in the temple of pleasure.

Sensations intensified. An instinctive move was made onto the bed, lying face down, hand still between legs, body weight adding to the pleasure. She could see Colin with his young, toned nineteen-year-old body, the confidence as he swaggered around her parents' garage, looking at her with his sultry brown eyes, wanting to possess her, his hands under her dress, on her thighs, his fingers between the cheeks of her bottom. Riding her hand, she pictured him pushing her roughly against the garage wall, ripping open her prim buttoned-up blouse, exposing her breasts, licking and sucking whilst his fingers entered her sapping, wanton vagina, hungry for his cock, pinning her to the wall with her tongue in his mouth. Meredith howled with pleasure as every nerve ending in her *superpower clit* was met, Colin putting his cock deep inside her, and just as she climaxed, Colin's face became that of the gardener's. Her Aladdin's lamp when rubbed had produced Liam, compelling her to swiftly abandon her rapture.

In that same moment, Daniel's car could be heard entering through the gates. Flustered and bewildered yet eminently more relaxed—aside from her epiphany being hijacked by her adversary—

she quickly found her feet, convincing herself it had been a trick of light, that it was Colin whom her mind had conjured up, wondering also if this could be classed as a form of marital infidelity. She was not someone who masturbated often. There was always too much shame and guilt to follow.

The front door opened followed by Daniel running up the stairs into the bathroom. Meredith dressed and swiftly returned the mirror back to the guest bedroom. Whilst there, she caught the sound of Daniel trotting downstairs to the kitchen. A few moments later she followed him down to the kitchen, and as she entered, there he was, casually making a cheese sandwich in a short, sparkly, sequinned, turquoise dress. Meredith's eyes widened in astonishment.

"What on earth!" she said, jaw slackened.

"Where's the pickle, darling?"

"Daniel?"

"Yes?"

"Why are you wearing a dress?"

"I felt like a change. Do you like it?"

Meredith was as dumfounded by Daniel's apparent sangfroid as she was by the star-spangled dress barely covering him.

Daniel went over to the fridge and bent down, exposing his hairy bottom.

"Ah, there it is," he said, retrieving the pickle from the lower shelf.

At this point, there was no holding back. Meredith howled in uncontrollable laughter, the anomaly of Daniel's skinny, white, hairy bottom peeping out from a sequinned, sparkly, tight dress, brushing such irregularity aside with his laissez-faire demeanour intoxicatingly absurd.

"Do you think turquoise suits me?" he added, cheerily.

Meredith, unable to get words out, doubled over, clutching her middle, braying like a donkey, tears streaming down her cheeks.

Daniel finished making his sandwich and asked if she'd like a cup of tea.

"Tea," she said, as though this was the funniest thing she'd heard in her entire life. "A cup of tea." She thumped the counter, trying to regain her composure but she had no control. Daniel, this man whom she had known for thirty-odd years as being a typically upper-class male, with all the etiquette, decorum and social trappings, here he was, Priscilla, Queen of Falindon, offering her a cup of tea.

Daniel beamed with delight as he tucked into his cheese and pickle sandwich. Meredith hadn't laughed this much for a long time, if in fact ever, and through this alone the dress became a welcome reprieve from the recent escapade with the Bonnie and Clyde duplicates, Maya and Liam.

"You look different, darling, have you been out for a walk? You look windswept," said Daniel, pouring water into a teapot.

Meredith, much calmer, felt the beginnings of a mild blush.

"I look different? Daniel, why are you wearing that dress?"

"As I said, I wanted to do something different. I've always fancied wearing a dress, and so I thought I'd give it a go. Just for twenty-four hours."

"Why would you want to wear a dress?"

"I really don't know, but it actually feels quite nice."

Meredith was thrown, unsure how to respond. She kept looking, wondering if she were in a dream: the shear outlandishness of the dress was overwhelming in itself, but Daniel behaving as though it was just another normal day made everything even more discombobulating. She ought to be annoyed but couldn't connect to any anger. Was Daniel gay and coming out of the closet or transsexual, the next step realignment surgery?

"Are you gay, Daniel?"

"Gay? Me?" Daniel laughed. "No, certainly not! It's just a dress. I wanted to try wearing one, that's all. A bit of fun, something different."

"Because if you are gay, you can always tell me, you know?"

Daniel explained about the folded bits of paper, and she listened with warmth and compassion. The peculiar thing was she liked the new Daniel.

This idiosyncratic position was a welcome break from the wearisome patterns that had become entrenched. It enabled a fresh understanding of Daniel. Even if it had arrived late in the day, it wasn't *too* late—it was a case of it's now or never. Sitting, drinking tea, words bounced between them, a meeting of minds; it was exhilarating. Daniel asked why had she needed privacy? Meredith was open about the *Tantratastic* book but didn't reveal the actual exercise.

The gardener's face unannounced, a fiery ember aglow in her pants, kept flickering in and out. At one point winking, making Meredith wish she could somehow lobotomise this bit of her brain. Was she attracted to the gardener? A thought too terrifying to contemplate. Her brain had a bug, causing normal thought processes to produce viral images of the gardener. If Meredith wasn't a rational person, she could believe that her antenna was picking up his psyche via radio waves, causing a glitch in her system. If only she could reboot her mind and be rid of this particularly annoying virus.

THIRTY-ONE

Pandita

Pandita stooped over the ironing board, removing the creases from a burnt ochre throw. Within a whisper, the swami slouched in his comfy chair, chomping away at a bowl of spicy-nut crackers resting on the arm next to the remote control. Each crunch a gnat spiking her brain. A quiz show host yelled in a booming voice from the giant deluxe plasma screen that hung from the wall, framed in plastic gold ornate surround—Pandita had ordered it online for the swami.

It was mid-morning. She'd been busy since 6.00 AM. The swami had only just left the bedroom. He'd gone from the TV in the bedroom to the TV in the living room. Some days he'd stay in bed all day watching trashy American TV, eating laddus, barfis and modaks, his gluttony concealed behind the closed wooden shutters of the temple. Piling on the weight since they'd first met and being diminutive in stature, it hadn't enhanced his image. When she suggested he lose some weight, he'd protest that his snack habit was hard to break.

On top of admin, ironing, cleaning and cooking, Pandita put up with the swami's competitive grumblings regarding rival spiritual teachers, indignation hiding his envy of those who had now gained celebrity status, the barometer being the number of subscribers each had on their YouTube channels. Droning on about the pressures of being a spiritual leader had become a regular occurrence.

"Pandita, hurry up with my throw will you and get me my garland, I am about to do my video calls."

Pandita prickled, it grated on her the way she was spoken to. Once upon a time he'd been so soft, his affectionate eyes, his considerate tone, his light touch, his willingness to listen, now these were reserved only for his devotees. She'd been a devotee once, young and longing for something she could only describe as a desire to escape. He'd persuaded her that in order to truly show her deepest devotion she should surrender her body to him, and this sacred union would bring her closer to enlightenment. Once he'd had her body, which had been fairly quick and unsatisfactory for Pandita, he'd told her she would most definitely reap karmic rewards, but now many years later, Pandita felt they must have got lost in the cosmic post somewhere because she was still waiting and didn't feel enlightened yet and had her doubts about the swami being enlightened: he was stressed all the time, everything had to appear perfect to the outside world. Even his long, white Santa Claus beard, which she shampooed, conditioned, and blow-dried for just the right amount of ethereal fluffiness. He'd become adept at being able to fall instantly back into calm and serene, laughing with an air of knowingness, enlightening witticisms, profound silences, he'd mastered the aesthetics of being a spiritual teacher. Not too knowing and not too humble, just the right amount of sagacious humility. She saw through it all. No one knew him like she did.

Pandita handed the swami his hessian shawl which he carefully threw over his left shoulder. He looked in the mirror, admiring himself; he certainly resembled an enlightened teacher, even if he could do with losing a few stone. He even gave himself a little smile of reassurance.

Pandita watched him as he waddled off into the temple, wondering what was next on her list of things to do.

* * *

Guru Swami Gandalih

Swami Gandalih sat lotus position on his cushions placed on a miniature stage. Behind him, a mural depicted the Himalayas. He switched on the laptop.

It was a Monday, and on Mondays he held video call satsangs for devotees with spiritual dilemmas seeking spiritual truth. Looking at his list, the first person scheduled in was a Maya Bloomberg. It didn't ring a bell, but his memory was not as it used to be.

His dark, chocolate brown eyes twinkled. He calmly gazed at the screen—five, four, three, two, one, action: he was on.

Maya Bloomberg's face was immediately recognisable. She was one of his wealthy devotees. This woman had been there from early on when the temple was a rudimentary structure consisting of bare breeze blocks and lots of rugs and plastered walls painted in bright reds, yellow, blues and gold, and she, among others of a similar ilk, had been able to financially support work on a newly improved ashram that would serve the cause to change the world into a better place.

As the years passed by, the swami had become more popular. Over the last few years, a select few of his followers from the US had been eager to get him the attention they felt he warranted by posting his talks on YouTube, Pinterest, Instagram, Twitter and about a hundred other sites. He now had approximately seven hundred and fifty thousand followers worldwide and growing, with more and more of his devotees being the preferred middle-class westerners eager to sit at his lotus-petaled feet. A satsang with the swami came to ten pounds per minute, which all went to the ashram's good cause, and perhaps a few more spicy-nut crackers.

The swami closed his eyes and did a prayer greeting.

"Namaste."

"Namaste," returned Maya.

Maya Bloomberg was mouth-watering; how could he forget this moon-lit desert flower.

Countless people passed through his temple, many of whom were whinging, insipid, spoilt westerners on a ganja-smoking hippy trail, who thought by travelling to India on their trust fund and seeking out a swami, they'd become enlightened despite their dire lack of any life experience. It would take more than a few allegorical anecdotes to wake these people up. But he remembered his conversations with Maya. She had something a bit different—her spirit was striking, she was alive, she wasn't afraid to say what was on her mind, and he liked this, maybe because he could no longer do this: the more exalted he became, the more godlike he had to appear. Only Pandita and a few others saw the earthbound Swami Gandalih. He was like the Queen of England or the pope, always having to rise above normal bodily functions. The swami was imprisoned by his holiness and often longed to be an ordinary, everyday person with a simple job (well-paid of course). Some days, he felt like a master of deception rather than an enlightened being.

"Thank you for seeing me," said Maya.

"It is always a pleasure, and how can I offer my service to you today?"

"I'd like to find out whether I'm in love."

If the swami had been from London, he'd have said, *Oh no, not that ol' chestnut!* but he was from Calcutta, so instead he said, "Love is easy, it is relationships that are difficult. I think it is your relationship that you talk about, yes?"

"Yes, I've met a man and am not sure if he's the one. Part of me wants to cling to him and possess him, which feels like giving up my freedom."

"What is it you like about this man?"

"His heart, he is true to his heart, he is genuine."

"Hmm, sounds like a good man, but you want to know if you love him?"

"Yes!"

"If the answer to this question is *yes,* you definitely do love him, so what?"

Maya closed her eyes, put her hand over her heart chakra and felt into the question. "Oh my God! It terrifies me."

"If the answer to this question is *no,* you definitely do *not* love him, so what?"

Again, she checked in with herself, contemplating her heart and allowing an answer to surface.

"I am safe, I can leave him."

"What is it that makes love so fearful for you?"

Still with her eyes closed and contemplating. "Entrapment, losing myself, not being free to do what I want, when I want, with who I want."

The swami noticed that Maya had the most wonderful pair of breasts and was reminded of the time he'd asked his guru if it was okay to look at women's breasts. His guru had said, *The woman's body will evoke all kinds of distractions that take you away from your spiritual path, so it is better to bring your attention back to the pure heart.* Swami Gandalih was about seventeen at the time and was already struggling with some guilt he felt during compulsive bouts of masturbation over fantasies he had about his guru's wife who was always very tender towards him. From that day on, he tried to divert his attention away from women's breasts, but Maya's breasts were supremely perfect and surely made of pure divine transcendental light. Maya opened her eyes and, with a frown, eyed the swami whose gaze had momentarily been diverted. The swami promptly awoke from his trance and put all his energy into not looking at Maya's breasts and meditated on the conundrum at hand.

"How would it be to have freedom and love at the same time?"

Maya closed her eyes, entering again into an intuitive and contemplative space.

"I'm a bird, an osprey, soaring high above mountains and forests. Around me, a blue endless sky. Below me, pinewood steppes disappearing into forever. My lungs fill with fragrant air."

"Are you alone?"

"The tip of my wing is touching another wing, an osprey like me, free in infinite astral twilight."

"A soulmate perhaps?"

"Yes."

After a moment, she opened her eyes. The swami could see the dreaminess in Maya's eyes, reflecting a distant, otherworldly place. He could see she'd felt moved by an overwhelming sense of joy. There'd been a time when this place had existed in him, but now he'd given up trying to get there after many years of disappointment, the giving up may have been the closest he'd got to arriving; it may not be as romantic but there was a sort of contentment.

"Does it frighten you to yield to your heart?"

"The heart is fickle."

"How is the heart fickle?"

"When I give my heart to men, they get the idea that they own me, and then my freedom is gone and my heart is no longer in it."

"Your heart is wise not fickle. What makes you think you might be in love?"

"My heart feels so open when I'm with him, and it's wonderful but also painful. I feel a happiness that I don't normally feel. I always think about him when he's not there. He makes me feel special. I'm at peace when we cuddle up together, we have fun together and we talk and talk about everything and it's always deep, and I feel like he knows who I really am underneath and accepts it."

It had been a long time since the swami had felt these things with Pandita. He'd become so grumpy over the last couple of years that it was possible that he'd never felt that close to anyone. His followers with their devotion was the only love he allowed in, but they didn't really know him, and with Pandita, he couldn't help but keep a wall around himself when she got too close.

"Many years ago, when I was a small boy, I was playing on the streets of Calcutta and there was a large bridge nearby. Under the bridge, I saw many pigeons attacking a small bird. I ran under the bridge to rescue this bird—it was an escaped, tiny, little thing called a zebra finch. It was terrified of me, but I held it firmly in my hand. I took it home and found a cage for it. The bird all day longed to escape, it had no company and was highly anxious. If I set the bird free, it would die in the wild, uncaged world, for it only new how to live in a cage, but escaping the cage had now given it a taste for freedom, yet this freedom was impossible for it to survive in. Sometimes we need to find happiness in the cage, we need to accept the

restrictions that a relationship may bring because freedom is an illusion. In the West, everyone is sold this idea of freedom, but it is like
Coca-Cola, just lots of sugar and food colouring, not happiness. If
the man you are with is as good and as honest as your heart tells you,
if he is honourable and not violent, if he loves you and you love him,
the challenge for you is to enter the cage, not escape the cage. We
leave one cage only to find ourselves in a bigger cage. Enter the cage
and find peace there and don't leave, unless of course, the pigeons get
in, which they always do in the end, and this is called *death,* when we
all are truly forced to leave the cage."

"But isn't that like living in fear?"

"It is the cage you fear and the illusion of freedom is what keeps
you imprisoned, for you see it as something outside yourself. You
are the cage. You have found someone who has opened the door to
your cage and now you are free, but you are not leaving the cage, it
is the cage that is leaving you." The swami was struggling to keep up
with his mixed metaphors and his thoughts were getting jumbled.
He gently closed his eyes for some pranic cosmic space.

Maya's ten minutes were up. The swami had another person
waiting, a Jed from LA. They ended their personal satsang and
namaste'd each other goodbye.

THIRTY-TWO

Troy

Tottenham Hale from the window was not a pretty sight. The wet pavement, a mute reflection of its grimness, made it twice as bleak.

The bedsit walls, reeking of mould, had become despondent witnesses to Troy's conquests over the past few weeks. Following the discovery of proper Christians online, he'd jacked in his anger management group, taking advice from his new *Flaming Cross* friends who'd insisted the anger lot weren't Christian, thus were heretics. Needless to say, he'd dropped the hippy dance thing too in the view that it was better to only hang out with true Christians, unless, of course, trying to save a non-Christian heathen.

The bedsit was grottier than his prison cell, particularly now that half the furniture had been broken from the outbursts of rage.

Being unshackled from Her Majesty's chicken coop was never easy—for starters, there was the lack of money: living on JSA alone was incentive enough to keep on thieving. Then there was the endless amount of free time to do whatever you wanted—no more 8.00 a.m.

five-minute showers, TV off at 7.30 p.m. with all the clockwork routine trundling along in between.

Even now, when allowed to cut sausages with a sharp knife, wear whatever he wanted, chew gum or talk about God—mentioning God in prison provoked an immediate zoning out from other inmates, and the ones at the top of the food chain would simply tell him to *shut the fuck up*—there was something he missed about being in the clink. The screws weren't that bad either. Liberty street was way harder—no friends to hang out with, no money, bills to pay, food to buy and the rest.

Tottenham was a shithole. Nowhere to go. Impossible to meet people. When it pissed it down, it wasn't a big deal inside as going out was not an option, and there'd always be someone to have a natter with. The irony of all that time ticking off days till freedom, and now that it was here, it was a case of another day gone with fuck all to do. Trapped inside a crappy bedsit.

When would it just stop fucking raining!

The online Christian forums had been a godsend, literally.

The *shoosh* of cars on the wet tarmac intermittently broke the silence.

Where the fuck was Maya? How come she was still playing hard to get? She was impossible to track down. Not once had she mentioned anything about her parents. Did she even have any? He hadn't asked much about her life; it had to be said, she could be a bit boring to listen to. It'd been well over a month since they'd spoken and she'd hung up on him; a lot had happened, he'd changed, getting closer to God and that, but it was still a struggle. He gave up spying on her flat after three weeks: the novelty of staring through binoculars at a darkened, empty window night after night wore off.

Jezza had suggested numerous times that he join a support group for ex-prisoners. Jezza, with his house in Crouch End, his certificates on the wall, his two daughters who were already more educated at twelve years old than Troy would ever be. Jezza didn't have a clue when it came to the real world.

He had made one half-decent suggestion in their last session though: *Why not open up an account on Facebook and search for an online ex-prisoners' support group there.* The group idea was a lot of bollox, but opening a new Facefuck account, now that was genius. Why he hadn't thought of this before was crazy. Of course, Maya had unfriended him, but what if he changed his name? Used a pseudonym. Which was when Jesus came to him—there were lots of Spanish people called Jesus, so why not?

He then Googled the Spanish translation for *saves* which was *ahorra*: Jesus Ahorra. He created an email address for Jesus, searched online for handsome Latino men, found one, copied the photo and used it to create a new Facebook account, sending a friend request to Maya. Easy-fucking-peasy.

That evening, he had a session with Jezza.

"So, how's your week been?"

"Shit."

Jezza remained silent. He did this a lot, like he had a personality disorder. He could've said, *Oh, sorry to hear that, Troy*, but no, nothing. Troy held still, determined not to speak, but the silence dragged on.

"...yeah, having no money isn't easy, you should try it sometime."

Still the fucking silence. Of course, he didn't answer because Jezza had money. Troy had seen what Jezza owned. He knew more about Jezza than Jezza knew about him.

"And did you find any support groups on Facebook?"

"Nah, not yet."

Troy endured more silence, desperate to hold his ground, his foot frantically bobbing up and down.

"And have you applied for any jobs?" Jezza eventually asked.

This same question came every week, and Troy answered with the same bullshit every week.

"Yeah, fuck all."

It would be unlikely that Jezza would look favourably on his achievements: knabbing a laptop, and an iPad, which he got three hundred quid for. Trendy cafés were perfect for that: sit at a window seat, open the laptop next to someone on their laptop, ask them to watch your stuff while you nip to the loo, and one in ten chance, when you come back, they'll ask you to do the same, and Bob's your uncle, out the door with an extra laptop and maybe an extra gadget thrown in for good luck. Better odds than a scratch card. The goodies then go to a geezer who knows what to do so they can't be traced and resells them. Only rule is, never go back to the same place. Not the best career but it was enough to get by until properly back on his feet.

Jezza peered down at Troy's rapidly bouncing foot.

"I wonder what your foot is saying?"

"My foot?"

"Yes, it looks agitated. I wonder if you're feeling angry?"

"*Let not the sun go down on your wrath.*"

"Sorry, I don't follow."

"It's from the Bible, wrath, anger, it's a deadly sin. I don't do anger."

"Troy, forgive me, but you often appear to be quite angry."

"Did you know Buddhism is evil?" Troy said, spotting a Buddha on the windowsill.

Jezza's eyes became rounded, arching his eyebrows. "Say more."

"Buddhists believe in nothing and meditate on nothing, which is evil?"

"Maybe you're referring to non-attachment?"

"It's a religion, innit?"

"Buddhism is more of a philosophy in which the Buddha advocated ridding the self of desire, but it's quite complex."

"So, you ain't into desire then?"

"We're not really here to talk about me."

"Bet you've got a nice motor though, eh?"

Jezza had a decent motor for sure, Troy'd seen it. A VW Arteon, only a couple of years old, worth at least £20K. This was on top of his vintage Morris Minor that was in mint condition.

"I can't help but think, Troy, if a part of you has a fantasy about how our lives might compare. Maybe you see me as having an easy life in comparison to yours?"

"The only person I compare myself to is Jesus."

"Hmm."

"Hmm," countered Troy.

"Christianity has some tenets similar to Buddhism, for example *reap what you sow* could be seen as karma. What are you sowing, Troy, and what do you hope to reap?"

Troy was no longer listening: he had no respect for a man who knew nothing.

"You think you're so much better than me, don't you. You wouldn't last five minutes in prison, you'd be everyone's bitch, your arse would be like the Channel Tunnel."

Jezza crossed his legs, looking at the door and then the clock.

"You know what, I've had enough, Jezza mate."

Troy stood up and left.

There was no point in seeing Jezza. He didn't even need therapy. Therapy was for fuck-ups who couldn't deal with life.

Outside Jezza's office, the remaining light was falling away.

He quickly found himself back in the high street, irritated with ducking in and out of brollies the size of garden parasols and their episodic eye-skewing prongs. Impatient, he stepped away from the pavement into a fried chicken takeaway.

Bet Jezza's feeling shit now! thought Troy, another conquest under his belt.

Whilst waiting for a bucket of chicken wings, he took out his phone, eager to check Facefuck to see if Maya had accepted his (Jesus Ahorra's) friend request. The request had been accepted, prompting him to go to her page. Scrolling down, there were petitions against the imminent end to life on earth, cute, cuddly animal videos, tons of hippy shit about love, and lots of communist bollox, and then he almost had a heart attack, his brain not able to compute what his eyes were relaying, his breath shallowing, heart piling into his ribs at great speed, thoughts splintering into poisoned shards, words turning to anagrams.

"No! NO! NOOO!"

"You alright, mate?" said the man behind the counter, holding a bucket of chicken wings.

Troy left the shop without the food, ignoring the man shouting out to be paid. The rain still bucketing down.

On the screen, Maya had her arms around some young buck outside a grotty-looking caravan, *My gorgeous new friend, Liam* written above.

A grenade had been shoved into Troy's hand, and it had just gone off. Hair slicked to his scalp, oblivious to the rain, he stood, shellshocked, staring at a happy-looking Maya. The cunt next to Troy's girlfriend was barely out of nappies.

Maya and Cunt Face peering out from the phone, straight into his eyes, laughing, brought about an incomprehensible kind of hatred, darker. Murderous rage pulsed from his forehead. The fucking bitch and that stupid cunt were laughing at him!

Below the picture were eighty-seven *likes,* most of them in the heart variety.

Then the gushing comments:

"Hello gorgeous." *Starbright*

"You make a lovely pair." *Howard Mills*

"What a lovely pic, babe." *Ian Wright*

"Wow, where are you? It looks lush." *Holly Molly*

"Falindon, I'm stopping at my folks' whilst they're away. You should visit us." *Maya Bloomberg*

"You dirty, fucking whore!!!!!" *Jesus Ahorra*, was the last comment.

Troy immediately Googled *Bloombergs living in Falindon*, and there it was, the Bloomberg mansion with a family photo of Daniel and Meredith Bloomberg, their kids, including a young Maya in front of them, and behind them on the wall, a painting of some silly toff bearing a bushy rat from each nostril.

Neurones spat sparks like a catherine wheel, swirling manically inside his brain, a crazed hamster on a wheel, pumped up with a cocktail of cortisol and adrenalin, wiring him in a way acid and amphetamine sulphate might, with no space for rationality or reason.

The way Maya had deceived him so viciously was unforgivable. She was not getting away with this, nor was the runt she had her arm around. *And the devil who deceived them was thrown into a lake of fire and brimstone* (Revelation 20:10).

It took five minutes to walk to Jezza's house. Jezza would still be at his office. Troy knew this because a few weeks previous, he'd waited for Jezza in order to follow him so as to find out where he lived. It had been a long wait, as his next patient, a depressed-looking middle-aged woman, had been sitting in the waiting area after Troy left each week.

All the lights were on with the curtains drawn at Jezza's. Troy pictured the wife and kids doing things that those type of people did: the kids would be having piano lessons, or maybe doing their homework before going to bed, whilst the wife would be... He couldn't imagine what she'd be doing, planning a new extension? These people were forever spending money on their posh houses.

The monsoon streets were empty. Finding a brick from a pile destined for someone's new extension, he wrapped it in his jacket and, with one brutal blow, smashed the tiny triangular window of the Morris Minor, quickly walking off. A couple of minutes later after observing from the other end of the street and seeing that no one had noticed, he went back, reached in, unlocked the door, picked the cheap bike lock on the steering wheel, and then hot-wired the 1950s car into action. These old cars were a doddle without fobs, trackers or alarms.

According to Google Maps, the Bloomberg mansion was ninety minutes away.

Retribution would be served diligently. The white lines passed hypnotically beneath the car, rain pelting in from the broken window. Every time Troy pictured the image she'd shared on Facefuck, the steering wheel got another punch.

"Fuck. Fuck! Fuck you bitch! Fucking bitch," he screamed, hammering the steering wheel some more.

He'd gone beyond anger management: this was white-hot blind rage, and in remote sub-zero deep space was a calculating control freak, and beneath that was a sharp belt buckle nunchuck.

As a city person and more than occasional jailbird, Troy hadn't ever really seen stars properly. Not that Falindon was a great place to observe the Milky Way, but climbing out of the car, the impressive drawing back of cloudy drapes was clearly a sign from God.

The tall gates to the Bloomberg mansion reminded him of prison. He'd known Maya was well-to-do, but never thought she could be this posh, proper royal posh.

The lights on the house were all out. Rather than ring the intercom, it made more sense to scramble over the gate. Instantly, he was illuminated by security search lights as he stormed up to the main door.

Ringing the bell, a light shone from over the top of the door inside. It wasn't long before a man appeared at the door wearing a dressing gown, through the gaps tiny specks of light twinkled.

"Where's Maya?"

"I beg your pardon."

"Where's Maya?" Troy shouted, loud enough for a slight echo to bounce back.

"Well, she's not here and I don't know…"

"Where is she then?" he screamed.

The man stood back, eyes widening, blinking ferociously, his ashen forehead scrunched up like a badly written poem.

"Why do you want to see her?"

"She's my girlfriend!"

"Oh, I see, you must be Troy?" he said, anxiously peering over his shoulder into the house. At which point, trotting down the stairs, came a woman. They were the people in the photo he'd seen online, only older.

"What on earth is going on?" she said.

"Where's Maya?" repeated Troy.

The woman shouldered the man out of the way. It was clear to see who wore the trousers in this house, her presence filling up the door frame. Unlike the man, her face remained composed and in control. Troy could not make direct eye contact with this woman, his bluster exposed for what it was: fear.

"Are you looking for her new boyfriend, Liam? He lives in a caravan on the Bentley farm," the women said calmly. Had Troy detected a hint of affection?

"Where's that?"

She was actually incredibly helpful, telling him the name of the road Bentley's farm was on. Supposedly the runt was in the wood at the bottom. Troy immediately bolted back over the gate and was gone.

First thing he did was drive to the nearest petrol station where he bought a jerrycan, filling it to the brim with petrol. It must have been heading towards the witching hour when he finally arrived at Bentley Farm.

Parking his car outside the gate, he took the canister of petrol out of the boot. On the other side of the gate, just inside the farm, was a beaten-up old van. Maya's mother had mentioned this, saying if that was there, he'd be in the caravan. He set off on foot across the field towards the distant woodland, careful not to make too much noise. The field was pitch black, the ground a swamp, in some places the muddy, cold water went well above his ankle. It was tempting to use the torch on his mobile but resisted, knowing it could give him away. An owl screeched nearby, all creepy, like a spooky horror movie in which Troy, an exorcist, was on his way to chase Lucifer from the earth or drive a stake through the heart of Dracula.

As he drew closer, entering the woodland, eyes adjusted to the dark. It wasn't long before he spotted the caravan. Above the door was a bleached skull, the devil's head, horns and all. Proof that God would approve of this mission.

Carefully undoing the lid of the jerrycan, tiptoeing around the caravan, petrol was poured all over the wood pile, over the step up to the door and anything that looked flammable, in particular over and around the tall gas bottle. Noticing a broom, as quietly as he could, he took it and placed the brush end under the door handle to prevent the door from being opened. Kneeling down, he asked God to forgive the runt and Maya for their sins. He took out his lighter and set fire to the caravan, watching flames rising to the arms of gnarled, old trees, useless in their protection. After a few minutes, the gas bottle exploded with an almighty bang, taking no survivors. Knowing this permitted a sense of calm, his face lit up in flammable serenity, wondrous at the power of infernos.

Troy didn't try to run, nor did he resist arrest. Only cowards run away, not heroes. To have slain a Rasputin gigolo that had mesmerised his sweetheart with pagan magic was something to be proud of. The sound of squelching feet rose above the crackling flames. Turning, a small number of what looked like bright yellow bell peppers dancing above the spongy fields approached. Flashlights swaying like lanterns in the dark. Solid bars of lights wavering, drawing closer. Benevolence lifted the corners of his mouth, all rage transmuted into Christ's energy, cleansing the earth of evil, a saviour to the pure innocence of the fair sex.

The blue lights of fire engines and police cars, unable to traverse the rain-sodden fields, flashed in the distance. The baptism was over with no one left to save.

Arms handcuffed behind his back, Troy, when asked if anyone was in the caravan, replied, "Satan!"

The rozzer scribbled this in his notepad.

"And did you see this, erm, Satan."

"Satan wears many cloaks, but mine eyes are conduits for Jesus who helps those who are blind to see more clearly. I have been blind but tonight I saw the light, and yes, I saw Satan."

"In the caravan?"

"In the flames, where he belongs, my mission accomplished."

"And was there anyone else in the caravan?"

Was there anyone else in the caravan? thought Troy, in front of him, a pig asking about a fire. He felt tired and weary. *Why was the pig there?*

With ping pong ball eyes, Troy searched the pig's face, his stomach lurching. What fire? What had he done? A woman from not too far away screamed the name, "Liam," crying and shouting, "No, No, what has happened!" It was Maya's voice, his Maya.

"Maya," Troy said to the rozzer. "It's Maya, at last, I need to see Maya."

In a bid to move towards her, he was restrained and responded with brute force, his cuffed hands eager to continue his mission, another pig stepping forward with paralysing effect.

In the distance, he watched her blackened silhouette, held back by two other darkened figures.

"Maya! Maya! I'm here!" he shouted towards her.

"You crazy, fucking idiot! What have you done!" she screamed back.

"I love you, Maya."

"You fucking moron, you utter, fucking idiot!" The shapes converged into a splash of ink, moving further into the dark, strobed like sapphires as they neared the multitude of emergency vehicles. Everywhere people were running, carrying things. Spotlights had been placed and lit within a cordoned-off area around the caravan. People in white jumpsuits wandered carefully around like glow-worms, cameras flashing. Troy was led away.

THIRTY-THREE

Meredith

Meredith's feet allied to a grey lino floor. Thoughts tumbled down free fall, crash-landing into a great pileup of regrets. Fixating on each step was all she could do to prevent keeling over. Led into the small interview room, the police constable, a grey-haired, portly man looking to be in his late fifties, told her to take a seat. The PC's face was kindly and sincere with thoughtful consideration written across his brow. The tone of his voice had a reassuring, soothing quality to it.

"First off, Mrs Bloomberg, would you like a cup of tea?"

Meredith didn't respond. The constable mimicked to his colleague the customary British teacup tilting gesture anyway.

Her body had caved in, eyes watery and brimming with remorse, staring blankly into space, sat across a desk from the PC. Barely able to believe what had happened.

"Okay, Mrs Bloomberg, I'm afraid I need to ask you some questions around what happened tonight regarding a Liam Mahoney, a Troy Ward and a caravan being set alight."

The policeman switched on the machine that sat at the side of the desk.

"This interview is being video recorded, and I need to inform you that what you say may be used in court as evidence if such needs arise. I'm PC Stuart Salmon, one-five-nine-two, here at Woking Police Station at twelve forty-five a.m. on the twenty-seventh of August Twenty-forteen. Could you please start by stating your full name and date of birth?"

"Meredith Bloomberg. Twenty-first of September, nineteen-ft-fty-nine."

Meredith was diffused vapour, rising without substance.

After her rights had been read, along with other official police procedures, she described her account of events.

"I was at home in bed, it was late, there was a banging on the door and my husband went down. He opened the door and there was this man. He kept shouting, 'Where's Maya?' repeating himself, like a madman. My husband said she wasn't there and told him to go away."

The other PC came back with the tea, placed it next to Meredith and sat at a far wall away from them.

"And did he?"

"Did he what?"

"Did he go away?"

"No, so I went down. I saw his face, he had the most frightening stare, the man was possessed."

"And what did you do then?"

Meredith picked up the cup of tea, herself a tiny creature at the bottom, peering towards the brim, a huge gaping mouth of guilt about to drink her.

"I told him to leave."

"And how did he respond to this?"

"He just kept ranting, 'Where's Maya.' It really was quite scary, but then eventually he left."

"Was anything else said?"

"It's all a bit fuzzy."

"And do you have any idea what made him go to the caravan?"

There was a long silence.

"I told him to go there."

"So, you told Mr Troy Ward to go to the caravan, is that correct?"

"Yes."

"And could you please give your reason for doing this?"

However it was put, it looked ugly. It was ugly, nothing could alter this. She knew she was capable of hatred but not to the point of sending in an assassin, her famous last words to Liam. The only redemption would be to come clean, atone herself.

"God only knows why he came into our lives" she said, half talking to another world where she imagined he might be. "He should have just stayed away. I detested him so much, I'm sorry, I don't know why, I just did."

"Was it to do with him being in a relationship with your daughter, Maya?"

"I never liked him, even when he was just the gardener."

"He was your gardener?"

"Up until a few days ago, when I fired him."

PC Salmon scratched his head.

"Can I ask why you fired him?"

"I don't know. I've been all over the place lately."

"Oh, in what way?"

The interview room was sterile, like you see in the movies—bare walls, strip light above—except the policewoman by the door, the table between her and PC Salmon, the video camera, they were all very real.

A tea stain on the floor in the shape of an island grabbed her attention. She wanted to set sail there, with Colin, far away from everything.

She'd killed Liam out of some spiteful splinter in her soul that she couldn't pluck free.

"It was me who killed Liam!"

The PC's face remained placid, understanding, free of judgement, quite reassuring.

"Are you saying, Mrs Bloomberg, that you set fire to the caravan?"

"No, I told Troy where he was, and I shouldn't have. I should have just called the police whilst my husband was at the door, but I had to go out there and tell him where Liam was because I knew he'd do something."

"How did you know he'd do something?"

"His eyes, he had murderous eyes."

The room was stuffy, no windows, no air.

"So, you're saying, you told Troy Ward where Liam Mahoney was because you wanted harm to come to Mr Mahoney?"

This sounded too straightforward and not quite right.

"A beating, yes, not killing. I don't know, it all happened so quick."

"But you thought Troy Ward may have been a murderer?"

"Well, no, yes, I mean he had the eyes of a murderer, but I didn't think he was a murderer. Do I need a solicitor? Am I a suspect here?"

"Why did you want him beaten up, Mrs Bloomberg?"

Meredith had dug herself into a hole she was now scrabbling to get out of. Rather than atone, which offered with it some saintliness, she now felt like an evil black widow spider trapped under a glass, about to get stood on.

"I felt taunted by him."

"In what way?"

"It was everything! The way he strutted about the garden like some peacock flaunting himself, the way my husband finds him so interesting, the way he was rubbed in my face by my daughter and the way he reminded me of Colin!"

"Colin? Who's Colin?"

"He was my first boyfriend."

"Was he a gardener?"

"What? Of course not, no. I was in love with him, so in love, but he was raffish. My father said he wasn't good enough for me, *too common* were his words. My parents could be rather supercilious on occasion, anyway, they introduced me to Daniel who came highly recommended. When I first saw him, I felt like weeping. I found him tiresome. Colin and I got up to all sorts of fun, constantly laughing. My life began when I met him and ended when I married Daniel."

PC Salmon shuffled uncomfortably in his chair. He looked at the clock on the wall.

"So, let me try and get this straight, the reason you sent Troy Ward to the caravan was because Liam Mahoney reminded you of an ex-boyfriend who your parents didn't take to?"

Hearing it like that sounded so simple, and it was that simple, but hearing it from someone else and not in one's head, changed it. A boulder rolled away, one she hadn't noticed until it was no longer there, tumbling into the distance, in its place nothing, wonderful, light-filled nothing. PC Salmon through his listening had become a priest, witness to Meredith's confession, giving her absolution. She was finally free.

"Will I go to prison?"

"Mrs Bloomberg, you've done nothing intentional to break the law. Troy Ward is likely to be the only person going to prison."

Meredith signed her statement and left the police station. Walking to the car, her skin welcomed the cool air. All those years living a lacklustre life, a life that was a lie. Truth sacrificed for safety. Appearing to be in order, aesthetically perfect to those on the outside, particularly those, who like her, had chosen death over living. Liam was alive, but not anymore. The salty tears were warm and kind to her cheek, reminding her of humanity and connectedness. It wasn't sex that was missing in her life, it was connection to a fellow human being. Daniel was a decent man, she had no intention of leaving him, but it was time he knew who she was—the lie had to end.

* * *

Maya

Immediately after her father called, Maya jumped in the car to head for Falindon. A knot in her stomach had already taken hold after seeing the vile comment on Facebook from Jesus Ahorra, obviously Troy, but now panic shot through her body, ramped up tenfold.

He was capable of anything, and the truth was out: he was a murderer.

Seeing the caravan burning, knowing Liam must have been inside and then hearing Troy's voice before she was dragged away by the police, her crumpled body let out a wail of devastating rage and sorrow.

A barrage of *if onlys*—if only she'd never trusted Troy. If only she'd tried harder. If only she hadn't accepted the phoney friend request. If only she'd gone to the police the night she'd left Troy. If only Liam knew how much she cared—each regret, a blunt instrument, bludgeoning her.

PC Salmon informed Maya that he'd spoken with her mother and that he'd be speaking to Mr Bloomberg later. They got straight to the nitty-gritty

"As you know, Ms Bloomberg, we've apprehended the suspect, Troy Ward. But I'm afraid we need to ask you a few questions. The suspect says you and he are in a relationship."

"Fuck's sake, he's mad. We saw each other very briefly. I left him over a month ago when he attempted to strangle me. But what about Liam, is there any news about him."

"It's not looking good. We can't confirm anything until we have a report back from forensics. In your estimation, how likely was he to be in the caravan when it was set alight?"

"He never went anywhere, except walks, but not in the dark. What did that evil psycho say?"

"I'm afraid we are not allowed to disclose that information."

"Did he say Liam was in the caravan or not for Christ's sake! He was my boyfriend! I need to know?"

"I'm aware this is a very sensitive matter and... Would you like a cup of tea?"

"No, I want to know if Liam is alive or not!"

"I regret to say that it does appear that the victim was seen inside the caravan, in which case he will not have survived!"

"Can't you track his mobile?"

"We can't trace a signal, which may be due to it being in the caravan and destroyed by the fire. Was it unusual for Liam to go places without his van?"

"I don't know."

No one worth caring about had died before. There'd been a couple of grandparents on her father's side, but they were pretty horrible anyway. And there was Amy Winehouse, and that was sad, but she wasn't a friend. The only real person was Liam. She could still taste the soft crease of his lips. The songs they sang together in the van still fresh and alive. The dancing in the dark, without music, no man had ever done that. Every moment was special and then reduced to a hormonal compound, another *if only*. They'd pretty much lived together the whole time, something she was incapable of doing. Life was mean. No matter how things were scrabbled, the universe was just all random chaos. The dream was over.

"We found out his surname, Mahoney, from the registration, but the time being now"—PC Salmon looked at the clock on the wall—"just after one thirty-four AM, we're struggling to find out where his next of kin might be, and until forensics finish on the caravan, there's not much we can do."

"He had no family that he was close to."

PC Salmon's eyes were kind. Warm, salty tears fell from her shredded heart. PC Salmon reached for some tissues in a drawer.

* * *

Daniel

What on earth had possessed Meredith to be so reckless—playing it down as a bit of fun, insisting no harm would come of it—it didn't take a genius to see Troy was unhinged. And yet the blame was not solely on her shoulders, he knew Troys was dangerous but had said nothing. Was he a coward for wanting no more arguments?

"Oh, for God's sake Meredith, be quiet with your deluded infatuation with the poor man," Daniel had said, storming off, calling Liam and leaving a message, then the police and finally his daughter.

The police operator was utterly incompetent, spending forever taking down times, dates of birth, names, reasons for suspicion, which as far as they were concerned, *looking unhinged and shouting* weren't enough to warrant any action.

Thirty minutes later, sirens were heard. Daniel knew exactly where they were headed. Bounding out in his dressing gown, he climbed in the car and drove straight to Liam's.

The narrow lane was cordoned off with waspy, fluorescent ribbons stretching from tree to tree, in front, a sign directing cars via a different route. Daniel parked on the verge. Wandering down the lane, the pungent reek of burning tyres drifted heavily in the air. As he got closer to the kerfuffle, shadows rhythmically shifted back and forth with unworldly knowingness as eerie blues and oranges tinged the hedgerow in the morbid disco. Uniformed men stood around, chatting, without urgency. Seeing as he was a friend of the victim and therefore useful to police inquiries, Daniel was let through.

Over the farm gate, a fire engine sat heavy and useless. Down below the fields, tree tops flickering with a golden glow could be just made out. An unbearable ache filled his heart. He never did get to sit in the caravan and smoke pot with Liam, see him in his own habitat, be the friend he wanted to be.

* * *

Daniel had scanned every poster, mostly just images with pithy slogans and numbers to call: hoodies in alleyways, a depressed-looking middle-aged woman, a number for domestic violence, the Samaritans, legal aid, hotlines for drug addiction and car theft. Up until Troy climbing over the gate, this world was always outside his periphery. He was safe, fortified by fences, alarms, status and position.

The station was quiet except for the murmur of Maya's voice from down the corridor. When she came out of the interview room, her face was downcast, somewhere else, a policewoman's arm around her, the fire in her that was so familiar had died. Greeting her, she looked up, face blotchy and drained, vacant, she said nothing. He wanted to hold her, reassure her, be the father he'd never been.

Daniel was called in to be interviewed. He didn't bother attempting to close his dressing gown to hide his sparkly dress as he walked into the small, dingy room, the seat still warm from where Maya had sat.

The policeman was a rotund chap, likeable enough to put Danial at ease. After the preliminaries, a more amicable tone was taken.

"Maybe you could start, Mr Bloomberg, by telling me how you knew Liam?"

"He was the gardener, a friend, of sorts."

"Of sorts?"

"My wife took issue."

"Why was that?"

"I don't know. Such a decent fellow. As you may have gathered, I'm a very wealthy man, Liam lived hand-to-mouth, but I trusted him implicitly. I can't believe he's gone. Why would anyone..." Daniel took a deep nasal breath. Fiddling with a sequin on his dress, his lower jaw pushed out, he closed his eyes, unable to make eye contact.

"I'm sorry we have to ask these questions, sir. I'm aware it's a difficult time for you, but could you tell me why Mr Ward was heading to the caravan?"

"My wife told him where he lived, we didn't think he'd burn it down."

"Yet, you called the police."

"He was clearly not well, she wanted rid of him."

"Rid of him?"

"Troy or Mr Ward, whatever his name is, we were scared. The man was off his rocker."

"What was your daughter's involvement with Liam?"

"They were seeing each other."

"And you didn't mind?"

"They were suited. Maya has never been able to find a decent man."

"So, you didn't mind your daughter going out with a man who lived in a caravan?"

"Isn't that what I just said? I trusted him. I didn't care that he had no money, I just want my daughter to be happy, something money can't buy."

"Well, it's helped me out over the years. Anyway, your wife, how did she feel about Liam?"

"You'd have to ask her."

"Did Liam have any friends nearby?"

"As far as I know, he had no friends in the area, he was a lone wolf." Daniel ruminated on this for a moment. "Maybe he was quite lonely."

"Did you attempt to call Liam, to warn him?"

"Of course, this was the first thing I did, but his mobile doesn't have a signal at the caravan, so all I could do was leave a message."

* * *

PC Salmon

Nothing of any great importance was gleaned from the Bloomberg interviews. The obvious motivation for arson was a simple case of jealous ex-lover seeking revenge. He'd seen it all before: men assaulting wives because they'd looked at other men, wives smashing car windscreens or breaking off wing mirrors because husbands had been unfaithful, exes posting naked pictures of their ex online to be cruel, and now possibly murder. PC Salmon sometimes wondered why people bothered having relationships at all.

THIRTY-FOUR

Siobhan (Liam's mum)

The grey-blue smoke gave the air the quality of Tom O'Keen's tap room back in Letterkenny where Siobhan would go on a Friday evening to collect her daddy. Her mammy would send her there because once he was on his third pint of the black stuff, there was no stopping him. It was actually a nice memory—the men were always kinder after they'd had a few, buying her crisps and lemonade, telling her what a fine-looking lass she was. Back then, you could smoke anywhere. Not like now. Everything had changed.

A slender arm of ash dangled from the waif-like ciggie, grey sediment fingers clinging on for dear life, waiting to be stood on. She stubbed it out, grinding it into the ashtray, then rolled another.

Not that she wanted to go back, no, there was little desire for that.

Igniting the new, crooked rollie, she dragged the smoke deep into her lungs and watched it leaving her mouth, adding to the haze of translucent slate that hovered around the room.

Tobacco cost a bomb now. She had to ration how many she had before having to attack the ashtray for dog-ends.

You smoke too much! It doesn't become a woman to smoke so much. Men'll see yer as a lackey's daughter.

Siobhan ignored him.

No self-respecting woman would live like you do! he barked.

It had been around thirty years since she'd left Ireland with Paddy.

Back home, Paddy had been a catch with his Yamaha 250, bags of weed and ridiculous good looks, a rock star even—his talent of raven locks that ran down to his arse crack, emerald eyes and rugged, manly features to boot.

Wrapping her arms around him like fly tape as she sat on the back of his bike, hurtling down country lanes, crossing the border to Derry where he dealt a bit of draw at *The Crypt*—a bikers metal dive. What did a twenty-five-year-old grown man see in her? He was the embodiment of uber-cool.

Such a craic—going into school off her tits on an early morning bong. Almost tripping. The nuns oblivious. The other kids in school didn't have a clue what dope was back then. They all know what it is now.

Yer man had been malleable enough in those early days, but then came the speed habit and he got all twitchy, with lizard eyes always on the move, treading on toes, crossing boundary lines, shitting on other people's turf, names that shouldn't be mentioned during the troubles echoing down corridors on the concrete estate in sinister tones, catching his ear.

Those time-bleached memories had grown faint, almost transparent. She relit her roll-up.

Such a young and foolish girl, full of hope and THC.

A sliver of orange light from the lampposts outside had been missed on the window. She covered it with newspaper, Sellotaping it firmly down.

That's not going to help, you silly cow!

She was determined to pay him no mind.

The buzz of wild optimism still lingered in her gut, the euphoria as she leant over the side of the ferry, bidding the shamrock shore farewell. And then bitter disappointment after her first week in Barnsley. Picket lines, men in donkey jackets everywhere. Thatcher's Britain.

Maureen and Mick were nice though.

Maureen not quite an aunt. She was Siobhan's mother's sister's husband's sister—whatever that was—they weren't blood related, but they were the next best thing.

It was hard to recall any time with Paddy that didn't involve smoking weed with the odd bit of acid now and then.

She could picture him now, sprawled across the couch, feet on the poof, light reflecting off button badges displaying band names, German iron crosses and pentangles that covered his cut-off denim—all he needed was some tinsel to finish the job. Across his lap, an album sleeve table to skin up another joint. The jacket only coming off when he went to bed.

AC/DC, Led Zep and Black Sabbath, belting out gobshite about *fairies in boots*. Paddy pontificating on the meaning of it all, the symbolism in the song. The fecker was away with the fairies if he honestly believed the songs had any deep meaning.

And the drinking, a total waster, and by proxy, so was she.

Such a wasted life!

Getting pregnant was a kind of godsend—even if it was like a juggernaut crashing through the walls at full speed—it woke her up.

Only nineteen.

A quiet buzzing sound from outside entered the room—better to ignore it, looking outside wouldn't help. She switched on the TV.

Giving up dope was a doddle.

Paddy's coolness began to appear immature. She wanted to hit herself for being so stupid.

All the worrying, lying awake at night wondering whether to have an abortion, the crucifying guilt.

He'd see his baby and change, that's what happened with men. She was such a bint.

"Marriage is shite, a bit of paper can't replace love," he'd said, the closest Paddy ever came to declaring any love for her. Then, her *child would not carry his name,* she'd told him. That was fine with him.

Having a child out of wedlock brought shame to the family. Soulless birthday and Christmas cards became the only contact with her parents.

The buzzing noise outside grew louder, a camera searching, maybe a drone? She sucked hard on the roll-up, trying to reignite it, the air bringing an amber glow. The TV babbled on without any attention being paid to it.

On the third of May 1987, Liam Eoin Mahoney was born, and he belonged to Siobhan.

Paddy did change; he became the other child in the house, more demanding and tantrummy, without the redeeming qualities: cuddliness, cuteness, endless unconditional love. He drank more, became angrier, ranted about his dissatisfaction with everything, and wondered why Siobhan kept the baby in the first place: he'd never wanted one. It was at this point that she threw him out. Liam was six months old.

Paddy attempted to come back, always when pissed, never showing any real interest in her or Liam, then he moved away with no forwarding address. Rumour had it he'd met another woman foolish enough to get on the back of his bike, that they rode off into the sunset, which was somewhere on a housing estate in Doncaster. He made no attempt to contact Siobhan; as far as she was concerned, the feeling was mutual.

Siobhan demanded maintenance, but Paddy claimed he didn't have enough to feed himself let alone anyone else, and there wasn't much chance of him ever getting a legitimate job where there'd be proof of earnings, yet he always managed to find money for his motorbikes, CDs and booze from dealing bags of weed here and there. Siobhan reached a point where she couldn't care less whether he was dead or alive.

Because Siobhan was so young and Paddy had always struck Mick and Maureen as being *a bit shifty*, they'd taken Siobhan under their wing, and when Liam had come along, they proudly became his godparents, seeing as they were never blessed with children of their own, which hadn't been for want of trying.

With Paddy gone, Siobhan had hoped that everything was about to get better. But words started to distort, twisting into something else with different meanings. It was around that time *he* came into her life.

Just look at how ugly and stupid you are, was the first thing he told her.

You're a stupid, fucking whore, why don't you kill yourself. No one will miss you.

He was assertive—no messing around. She was a *useless waste of shitty space,* and she should just *slash her wrists. He* started visiting on a regular basis. Telling *him* to go away had no effect, *he* was persistent, always getting what *he* wanted. It was impossible to get away, like marriage to a kidnapper.

She kept *him* secret—people were untrustworthy. *He* said there were cameras hidden in lampposts—that she was being watched by a secret society recording her thoughts intercepted through an antenna lodged inside the brain, waves of personal data running through the metasphere.

Liam never stopped crying, a cry at such a pitch it could only be deciphered by the secret society.

He said her baby was bad and that she *should kill it*.

Siobhan constantly tried to shut *him* up by turning up the music or talking over *him*; *he'd* never told her to kill Liam before.

One afternoon with Mick and Maureen, it slipped out. As suspected, they were not on her side, insisting she go to the doctor's, who was probably in on it. Trust had been broken.

She started drawing the curtains during the day so that cameras couldn't see in. *He* was ranting half the time, *kill the baby!* Then came the knock on the door. It was the secret society and they dragged her from her house: baby Liam's scream like echolocation had travelled through solid space, its vibrations reaching the secret society with frequency codes.

A woman picked Liam up and held him close to her chest.

Liam was a year old when first taken into foster care; Paddy refused to get involved. Maureen and Mick tried desperately to be guardians, but the legal system made it difficult. Eventually, Siobhan got the diagnosis—schizophrenia—and was put on *monster-killing meds*, as she liked to call them, which tended to work for so long but then every so often she'd end up back in hospital. It wasn't until after a long battle and much effort from Maureen and Mick, and with the consent of Siobhan, that Liam was allowed to stay with them when not with her. They'd finally got their baby, and this was how it was until he left home, randomly jumping from one place to another.

* * *

Liam

The train pulled in just before midnight. The five-hour journey had been enough to get through a large chunk of *Lady Chatterley's Lover*, a convenient diversion from the stubborn brood over Maya. Chewing over the obvious parallels between his life and those of the main characters, differences in class, him like the gamekeeper and Maya like Connie, the upper-class, free-spirited female protagonist. Class hadn't been an issue. Then again, the amount of wealth she came from sometimes got to him and he wasn't clever or well-spoken like her, which did make him wonder what she saw in him.

Stepping off the train with his bike and small backpack, he'd arrived home. No matter how much he hated Barnsley, it was home, always would be—it was in the blood, had never really left. Yet he buckled inside at the loudness of northern voices, afraid to speak up, come back in equal measure, too reserved for the instant coarse friendliness, his windpipe full of stones; it was harsh, and though he was of the same blood, his northernness was faulty, insubstantial, pathetic. The polite middle classes suited him better. He'd become a snob. A traitor to his tribe. The accents, people being straightforward, the instant friendliness epitomised normal—he'd just forgotten—yet this had been the background noise to his life, like the consistent hum of a fridge, gone unnoticed, maybe it had been unplugged, but here it was, humming again with all its blunt vowels.

He was home, cycling along the cool, empty streets to his mother's in the early hours of morning, past red brick terraces and yellow streetlights. He'd tried phoning the day before to let her know he was coming, but the line was dead. He'd called Mick and Maureen a few days earlier; they seemed to think she was okay, though being old and arthritic, they never went round there anymore—he just prayed she was still alive.

The image of his mum dead on the floor in her flat swished around his head, putting him on edge.

He pressed the buzzer at the entrance of Harewood Towers, a seven-storey block—she was on the fourth floor.

"Hello?" came a tinny voice through the miniature, round speaker. The camera had been sprayed over.

"Hi Mum, it's me, Liam."

"Oh my God!"

The door made a clicking sound. Liam pushed it open and headed to the elevator with his bike, relieved she was alive.

Heavy, creaking steel wires and grizzled, tired cogs grumbled as the lift descended. The bike, pushed up onto its hind wheel, was wheeled into the confined space, suffused with the astringent stench of urine. Scrawled across the chrome metal wall in childlike marker pen, *Ebony sucks cocks*, a balloon penis spurting forth huge droplets of cum into the air. Not exactly Banksy, or the sort of graffiti art The Guardian would put in its arts review—still, poetic in its own right.

His mum waited at the door, wearing a polyester dressing gown, the same one she'd had when he'd last seen her.

"Hi Mum."

"Liam! Liam, oh my God!"

The all-consuming ache in his belly had become unbearable, his only option was to gain some distance from Falindon. Maya's probing about his mother had skewered his brain, and now here he was, trying to figure something out, looking for comfort in an estranged landscape.

Seeing her vigilant eyes darting around, worried, was the reason he never mentioned his mum: the shame he felt was too much. Not contacting her had been cruel, but with no friends for support, everything up until sixteen had been torture. Staying with Mick and Maureen was haphazard, happening only when his mum *was having a rest*, the euphemistic term for *the bin*. They did their best, but being lashed out at didn't make it easy: he was emotionally all over the place, with violent outbursts and later discovering skunk and alcohol to quench the pain. Getting out had saved him. His main fear was ending up like her. Online it had said that you're thirteen times more likely to suffer from schizophrenia if one of your parents also has it.

His mum was older but still quite a looker in her mid-forties.

In the tradition of all mothers when greeting their son's return from far away, she asked, "Have you eaten?"

The lilt of her strong Irish accent that she'd retained made Liam want to weep, in fact everything about her made him tearful— maybe this was a reason for disappearing. It terrified him how this heart could be so open around her, this fragile, wild creature, lit up, out in the open, down at the bottom of the food chain, startle-eyed and anxious.

Liam wasn't hungry, there was too much going on. He explained he'd split up with someone, then corrected himself—it had only been a month, and to split, the unification should be consensual, and though he'd experienced an affinity, he couldn't be sure it was mutual.

Liam asked how she'd been. It was all a bit awkward: you don't just turn up after five years without any contact and act like you've only spoken a couple of weeks ago.

"Why didn't you call me?"

It went without saying this question would be put to him. On the train, efforts had been made to come up with a response that would sound reasonable, but there wasn't one. How could there be? The situation was left so long the thought of calling got harder and harder. A disenchanted fog engulfed him, made up of guilt and shame.

"Do you have any idea just how worried I've been? You could've been dead, Liam. I called everyone who knows you, and no one had a clue where you were. I even called the police, but they just said that this kind of thing happens and you're an adult and there's not a lot they could do. Thank the Lord I heard from someone who said they'd seen you at some festival or other, so I knew at least you weren't dead. How could you do that to me, your own mother? Your own mother, Liam. Why would you do that?"

Liam couldn't find any words, his throat contracted and dry. He looked away from her drooping face, fixing his gaze on patterns in the carpet, his brain overloaded, incapable of thinking straight.

"I don't have any excuses!" came his choked voice.

"Do you hate me?"

"No, of course not."

"So why?"

"I don't know."

"It nearly destroyed me for good, Liam. A few months after you disappeared, I ended up having another episode and having to go to the hospital for two months. Then I thought maybe you'd gone looking for your father, so I got in touch with him, but he was as useless as he's always been."

"I thought you didn't know where he was?"

"I didn't, but I contacted some of his old friends through Facebook and that's how I found him."

"You're friends with him on Facebook?"

"No, of course not, as if! I got his phone number and called him."

There were a couple of old photos in which his father could have been around the same age Liam was now, but a long curtain of hair made him difficult to read, though a stark dullness in his eyes couldn't be missed. In his arms, a gummy Liam, a smile filling up his face. The incongruity was painfully poetic in an Eminem sort of way. It would be strange meeting him, awkward, but maybe he was a decent guy now with things in common. Only a fleeting thought, stupid even, his heart feeling the gravity of the present.

Liam and his mum sat in the pokey living room. The TV on, smiley presenter charming a Hollywood star. Piles of newspapers filled half the room, unwashed plates and cups everywhere. On a smoke glass coffee table was an apothecary of meds, all standing guard in their bottles of various shapes and sizes. His mum lit up the ragged end of a rollie and took a deep inhalation, holding the smoke in the back of her throat before exhaling.

"Want one?"

"I've given up."

"Oh, well done, Liam. So, something good came out of not seeing me for God knows how many years."

They were straight into it—the familiar guilt, shame, self-loathing. Of course, he had good reason to hate himself: there she was, vulnerable and fragile, and here he was, cold, distant, guarded. He'd gone from one pain to another. Each one an Alcatraz. It was suffocating.

"Actually, I will have one of those."

Siobhan passed the tobacco and papers, a slight touch between hands that carried a distinctive tension held between mother and son. If they'd have been monkeys, they'd be picking and chewing on each other's fleas, but being human, they sucked on cigarettes and tried to work out what to say.

Was it a mistake to go there? He couldn't see any shift in their synergy. It had been so long, yet it could've been yesterday.

"Do you want a cup of tea?"

"What was it like talking to my dad?"

"Waste of bloody time."

"Did he ask about me?"

"Liam, what do you think. Yer man's an utter waste of space."

"Go on then, I'll have a cup of tea. Shall I make it?"

The air was hardening like a sea of cement.

"No, I'll make a pot."

She went into the kitchen. Liam took out his mobile phone which was dead. It was better that way, better than constantly checking for messages from Maya. Not that it made much difference—there she was running wildly in his head, bubbling with laughter, her scent freeing up the air, the funny way her profanity banged on his ear like a jazzy harp, her directness forging solid foundations. All of it a safety that was now out of reach.

The phone charger wasn't in his bag. Looking around the room, not much had changed—maybe more newspapers, a deeper beige in the nicotine-stained walls. The TV chattered inanely.

He pictured himself driving one of those machines with a wrecking ball, smashing through the walls, destroying this whole bit of his life. There was no one to turn to. Maya would know what to do, she'd just say it straight: do this or do that.

The odd imperceptible mutterings of his mother talking to herself drifted from the kitchen, reminiscent of his teenage years.

Adolescent hormones re-spawned, rushing through the body as he listened. As a child, he'd ask her who she was talking to. She'd deny she'd been talking at all, except on one occasion, she'd said she was having conversations with God as he was the only one who could truly hear her. This had always stuck in his memory, seeing his mother gifted with having direct contact with the divine and ending as seeing her as needing help.

She placed the tea-laden tray on the table and sat down again.

"So how long am I blessed with your company?" Her annoyance was not over, nor would it be for quite some time. What he'd done was unforgivable, they both knew this.

"I'm not sure, I haven't thought about it much. I just decided on the spur of the moment."

"So, how come you cut off from all your friends too? No one had any idea where you might be."

"Everyone I knew was into getting wasted, I didn't like those people anymore. Half of them became smackheads."

"So, where've you been?"

"In a caravan in Surrey. I've got work there as a gardener."

"Well, that's good news that you have a job."

She poured the tea, her hand trembling from the meds.

"I am really sorry, Mum, I should've called, I know. It wasn't like I didn't think about it."

"Oh, well now, Liam. So long as you thought about it, eh!" she retorted with bitter sarcasm.

She rolled another cigarette, licking the paper carefully, and lit it from her previous one before stubbing it out in the ashtray. As the night wore on, Liam got to hear about the neighbours in the flats where she lived: the one below who played her music too loud; the couple above who she could hear *at it,* every night; Dennis, the old man who'd just had a hip operation, with the lovely Jack Russell.

Liam discovered the phone had been disconnected for not paying the bills. A pile of letters threatened to cut her benefits too. Despite being diagnosed as mentally ill with paranoia personality disorder, social anxiety, audio hallucinations and infrequent psychotic episodes, she was still considered eligible for work. Next to the ashtray on the table, a letter from the crisis team enquired about her well-being. She told Liam she hadn't responded, afraid of getting sectioned, yet they were the ones who could get the disability allowance back in order. From what Liam remembered, the crisis team were decent people. Like real human beings. They'd come in, normally just one person, stick the kettle on and check with him how things were and then ask if they could chat with his mum a while. Sectioning was unlikely, but cutting off the remaining utilities would happen without a doubt. Big businesses couldn't care less about poverty, they just wanted the money.

"I forgot to bring a charger for my mobile, have you got one?" asked Liam.

"There's one down there."

Siobhan pointed to a vacuum cleaner tangled up in a knot of various cords, its telescopic tube pointing to the ceiling, on the end, an eye with luscious eyelashes posing as a brush. A conceptual piece straight out of the Tate Modern. The plaque might read, *The Intricate World of Mrs Mahoney's Fractured Brain.* Liam reached beyond the simulated innards, careful not to electrocute himself on the cluster bomb of synapses. Her mobile was like his, a cheap burner, with the right sized adaptor. He painstakingly untangled the cables, freeing the charger.

Liam eventually escaped into his old bedroom, now a junk room with barely room to move. After removing various bits and pieces piled up on top of his bed—an unopened, boxed plastic Christmas tree, an ironing board, bags of clothing—he laid some sheets and blankets, climbed in and plugged in his mobile, charging it up, hoping Maya had messaged him.

The phone immediately lit up with a cacophony of consecutive beeps telling him there were a ton of messages and voicemails.

The first text was from Maya and read, *Liam, please tell me you're okay. Call me now! URGENT!!!*

The next message also from Maya read, *Please, please call me Liam, I beg you!*

There was a message from Daniel: *Liam. Are you okay? Your caravan has burnt down and we're all worried that you were inside. Please call us.*

Liam read this again, his heart racing, blood draining from his face, dizzy and lightheaded, gawping at the phone with utter disbelief. He listened to his voice messages, the first one from Daniel:

Some lunatic is on his way to your caravan, you need to be aware as he looks rather insane. It's Maya's ex-boyfriend. I think I ought to call the police or maybe Maya... Anyway, call me when you get this message.

The next message was from Maya, crying, asking him to call her. In the background, he could hear men shouting and sirens. Pretty much all the other messages were from Maya, crying, wondering if he was alive.

Liam listened to all the messages until he got to the last one which was cut short due to his voicemail being full. It was from Maya:

Liam, where are you? Please say you're okay. You should have come to London with me, then I'd know you're alive. You have to be alive. I want you to know I... Maya had run out of space to finish the message.

Liam was in a state of shock. It had been bad enough losing Maya without an ex-jealous-lover coming along, intent on murder. If not for visiting his mum, he'd be a charred corpse in a body bag right now. A consolation maybe, but life, even when saved from the clutches of death, still needed somewhere to live. And somewhere wasn't just anywhere. Each nail, every lick of paint, all the planed pieces of timber had been thought out, chosen carefully. Components that over time had sprouted roots, winding their way into the rich, humus earth below, mooring the caravan into the woodland glade, bobbing lightly on a calm sea of nature.

He wasn't cut out for travelling, nor for the paper chain lifestyle of town life: he was a mossy, rolling stone. The caravan, a perfect carapace, freedom to spin the wheels, gamble a ramble, the life of the rover, but Liam preferred to stay put, firmly anchored to one place—it was the choice that liberated him.

Now it was gone, a pile of ashes. With it being a sixties caravan, the structure and insides were mainly wooden, cinders would be all that remained. Into the bargain, the harrowing truth of no insurance. Not even a bank account. The gardening was all cash in hand, his bank, an old biscuit tin under the bed in which around four thousand pounds was hidden, all gone, as well as chainsaws, solar panels, leisure batteries, tools, the personal stuff with sentimental value, old photos, stuff he'd made.

All that remained was the pushrod used to cycle to the station to get the train up north and his van, which was due for the scrap yard.

A feeble rat-a-tat-tat roused him from his anguish. Looking up from his mobile, smudging the evidence from the corner of his eye with his finger, his mother's face peeped around the door.

"Are you okay, you look upset?"

He wanted to tell her everything but couldn't.

He briefly told her about the caravan and Troy without going into detail, playing it down, concealing the sunken weight in his chest, needing to protect her, as had always been the way. Even at school when bullied, he'd never told his mum: her emotional state rested on a hair trigger and Liam had enough to deal with without psychotic episodes. He'd done enough damage by disappearing. He said everything was insured, though inside, he wondered where he was going to stay. He could stay at his mum's, but a few days was as much as he could handle.

"My God, Liam, you're lucky to be alive. You could be dead. To think if you hadn't come here! God is certainly looking out for you."

Oh, the paradox, thought Liam.

Should he be grateful for being alive despite losing everything?

In his mind, circling, sharklike, was a killer *Why me?* Waiting for an opportune moment to sink its teeth into his ankles, born under an inauspicious star, nothing good came his way; if it did, it was briskly snatched away by a tyrant God, taunting, *You deserve nothing good in your life.*

"Good ol' God, eh? Always got an eye out for me." Liam had to see the humour in such irony, to escape a darker, self-pitying place he couldn't afford to go to right now. "I need to make a phone call, is that ok?"

"Of course you can, love."

His mum, softened by his news, left the room. Maya answered straight away.

"Liam?"

"Hi."

Liam held the phone away from his ear as Maya screamed with joy.

"Fuck! Liam, you're alive!"

"Yup! Nowhere to live and everything burnt to the ground along with every penny I had, but I'm alive?"

"You're alive! That is so fucking amazing!" The joy and relief in Maya's voice was sonic balm to his writhing soul.

"I can't get over it. We were all at the police station a few hours ago, and everyone thought you were dead. I knew you weren't, I had a gut feeling."

"How bad is the damage?"

"Seriously bad, it's all gone. I'm so sorry, Liam. My dad will pay for everything as we're totally to blame."

"Who's to blame?"

"Well, me really, for not recognising what an utter nutcase Troy was, and my mum is for telling him where you lived. Where are you? God I am so, so happy! You're alive! That's just the best thing ever. Where are you?"

"I'm at my Mother's. I got here a few hours ago."

Liam explained what had happened.

"That's so cool you've gone to see your mum. She must be so happy. How long are you there for? When can I see you?"

There was a long pause.

"Liam? Hello?"

"I'm not sure what to say. I still feel the same. I can't cope with you seeing other guys, Maya. I respect that this is where you are, but for me..."

"Liam, my message said I want to be with just you. I want to give it a go. I think we're a good fit."

That must have been the last message that was cut short.

"Hmmm, is that when you thought I was dead?"

Maya laughed. "No, no, no! I spoke to my guru who helped me get a clearer picture. I want to give it a go. Me and you. I decided this before the fire, honestly. What do you think?"

A whirlwind was tossing everything around in his head: did Maya just say she wanted to have a monogamous relationship with him? The weird thing was, rather than a sense of joy, a tremor of panic crossed his belly. Wanting commitment was easier when it wasn't on offer.

"But what about the distance? I live in Falindon and you're in London."

"True, but it's not that far, and we could just give it a try and see how it goes. You've got to admit we're a fucking amazing fit, why end it now!"

Her exuberance was a dimmer switch brightening his loins to a soft glow. Maybe the universe was telling him it was time to move forward. Maybe God was looking down on him after all.

"Wow, I'm lost for words. I must admit, I'm feeling a bit scared."

"Of what?"

"It becoming real, the two of us, a couple—am I allowed to say that, will we be official?"

"What does that mean, being a couple? We don't have to put ourselves into a box. Let's call it something else, like *awake together-ness* or *conscious beings* or how about *intimate creatures in search of enlightened connection?*"

"Bit long-winded."

"True, how about *sexual humans in transformation*—because that's what it's all about."

"How'd ya mean?"

"Sex and relationships, it's all about transformation. That's what I want in a relationship, transformation, spiritual growth, and sex is the alchemical cauldron."

"Right, but it's still a bit long-winded though. What's the anagram?"

"You mean the acronym? *Sexual Humans in Transformation.* Oh, shit!"

"What?" Liam spurted into laughter. "SHIT, we're now in a SHIT relationship."

"Hmmm, not sure that's going to work."

"Well, it suits you."

"Cheeky git, how do you mean?"

"You love swearing," said Liam with a little hesitance.

"Fuck off you twat, I do not."

They both laughed.

"Shit's not too bad, you get good shit and bad shit. Good shit is like compost, it makes relationships thrive, and bad shit is toxic to a relationship," said Maya.

"Right on, sister!" said Liam, and with that they agreed that they were now in a SHIT relationship. Good shit, of course!

THIRTY-FIVE

Liam

Venturing into the sunless living room the next morning, Liam was instantly assaulted by the pervading stench of cigarettes. His mum, with her signature roll-up, sat staring into space, complexion the colour of an old, grey filing cabinet that resided in the spare room. Still in her dressing gown, legs akimbo, knickers for all to see like a little girl, unashamed or unaware, somewhere else.

"Morning," he said, eyeing her, trying to discern her mental state the way he always had.

She didn't answer.

"How yer doing?"

"Surviving."

He hated that term; right then he hated her, the heavy energy that oozed from her draining him. It was like ingesting one of her antipsychotics.

"Right. I'm going to try and sort out your benefits."

"You do that, love," Siobhan said, removing a tiny bit of tobacco from her lip and wiping it on her dressing gown.

Narrow shards of light catching the smoke sneaked through cracks between the newspaper-taped windows, infiltrating the room like marble lasers.

Liam started by calling the crisis team who were friendly enough but suggested he phone social services who informed him that it was the welfare benefits office he needed who, in turn, didn't appear to comprehend such words as *paranoia, social anxiety, medication, agoraphobia, dissociation, mental illness, psychotic episodes,* or *overwhelming fear of everything and in desperate need of help,* and concluded he should phone her GP who informed him that it was definitely social services he needed to speak with. And around it went until five hours later it was agreed that someone from the crisis team would visit to assess the situation and bring the appropriate forms to be filled out. A clear case of systemic madness. No wonder she was struggling; in fact, it raised the question, was there such a diagnosis as *lost in a bureaucratic hell syndrome?* Which of course, even though you'd have a fractured skull from banging your head against a brick wall, would still mean you're eligible for work.

The rest of the day he spent cleaning the flat, brushing away silky spider threads wagging like horse tails on the walls, wiping away layers of archaic dust from every surface. He'd read that dust mainly consisted of dead skin cells, a fact that once known couldn't be eradicated, some possibly his own from prior to leaving home, maybe even his father's judging by its dense layer.

Cleaning was a befitting distraction as the prospect of his cindered home raged at the back of his mind. He tore newspaper from the windows, opening them, allowing in something other than the smell of cigarettes. Hung across her brow, a crinkled banner, declaring her fear of intrusion. He promised there were no cameras attempting to sneak in to spy on her, that a meds review was essential, reassuring her she wouldn't end up in hospital. Eyes suspicious, her mouth jerked into a thin, crooked smile.

By late afternoon, the atmosphere was penetrating his bones, his mum straddling two worlds; he needed to re-enter collective reality, to stand in its remnant stability. Her fidgeting, chain smoking, talking about the neighbours in a way suggesting she knew them more than was probably the case were all distorting his perception. She didn't ask about the caravan, probably for the best, nor did she ask about Maya. Liam had to accept that other people were minor parts in his mother's drama, the script penned, the set designed by an unknown force in her fractured brain.

He cycled into town, buying flowers and chocolates, something he did only for girlfriends and his mum. His off-the-cuff plan was to stay there for a few days with a play-it-by-ear approach, heading back south as soon as the psyche team had visited and the meds were in order. Next on his list was seeing Auntie Maureen and Uncle Mick, knowing he'd be dealing with more fallout from not contacting them either.

Why had he gone underground and hidden from the very same people who'd given him so much? When he got back to his mum's in the evening, he gave her the flowers and chocolates before setting about cooking them both a meal.

A few more days passed, psych team came and went, meds and disability allowance sorted. The Tories hadn't yet managed to entirely dismantle the crumbling health care system, a saving grace.

As for reconnecting the phone, she'd just have to wait until her benefits started coming through again. Guilt really did pin him down over this. He would have happily paid, but what could he do, he didn't have any money either. A good son should have money in the bank, not ashes in a biscuit tin. Thankfully, he was able to top up her pay-as-you-go mobile with five pounds.

It couldn't be said she had her life back—it wasn't a Disney film, which would never be the case, her life bent out of shape by mental health would always be there, but now it was propped up like an amputee hobbling around on stilts.

When the phone had been working, it turned out her mum had started to call occasionally after years of incommunicado. With the Catholic Church sexual abuse scandals in Ireland, like many other Catholic churchgoers, their Catholicism became carte blanche, more lapsed than devout, their faith, along with the cloth, now in tatters. Liam had still never met them as they'd never had the decency to visit their daughter since he'd sprung from her womb.

His mum was forever glancing over, commenting on how she was reminded of her da when young, the same blue eyes, the same full lips, becoming doleful about how her folks had missed out on their beautiful grandson and how, in return, he too had no grandparents. According to his mum, Liam's father had completely rejected his parents, never once contacting them whilst she was with him, referring to his own father as a *knacker. The apple doesn't fall far from the tree,* his mum would say. Liam needed her to know his return was proof he hadn't completely inherited his father's genes. It was rare he asked about his father, having never known him, but the comment made a few days earlier about *yer man being a waste of space* had left a little sting in his heart—okay, he may be a prick, but it was still his father, even if only biologically.

It had been embarrassing having a father who was never there, indicating Liam's soul was somehow disfigured, like he might not be worth being there for. He knew logically this was bollox, but when his mum confirmed he wasn't interested even now, not even asking, *And how's Liam?* this hurt. It was unclear whether it was out of anger or curiosity that he decided to text his father. He did know, though, he certainly wouldn't be calling him *Dad* to his face, ever.

The text read, *Hi. It's Liam. I'm at my mum's Siobhan's and she said she'd phoned you. I wounded if you'd be up for meeting up? Liam.*

He quickly hit the send button.

The thought of dying in the caravan having not met his own father didn't sit well.

Obviously, there was no memory of being with him as a baby, just the photo, the dead eyes, the happy baby. His mum holding the camera, fretful to capture a happy family moment from a man whose spirit had already abandoned the house.

As soon as sent, regret piled in, noticing predictive text had put *wounded* instead of *wondered* which, as apt as it was, was not how Liam wanted to come across.

If corrected and resent, he worried this would emphasise the *wound*ed even more; contrary to this was an internal angry cry: *Yes, you fucking wounded me, you arsehole!* It was left it as it was.

Liam waited, waited and waited some more for a reply, and after five hours, nada. He checked and double-checked that it had been sent, which made no sense as his phone already showed it had been received.

"I told you, Liam, yer man's not worth it. What man walks out on his child and doesn't even bother to contact him. Ever! Awful, absolutely awful! He doesn't deserve you, and you deserve so much better."

"I'm just curious, that's all. I need to know what he's like."

"He's a stoner."

"He might have changed?"

"Oh, love." His mum pushed out her bottom lip, suggesting she could see the disappointment behind his philosophical veneer. "He sounded like Ozzy Osbourne."

"Ozzy who?"

"Yer man was into Black Sabbath, Ozzy Osbourne was the singer, an alcoholic, though actually, he stuck around for his kids. You'd think he might've learnt something. Your childhood was tough, Liam, no doubt about that, but if he'd have stuck around, you might've ended up like him. He's not got one single thing that deserves your love. All he thinks about is himself. He was too bloody handsome, and I was too shy and gullible. If I'd have been more confident, I'd have got myself a decent man, but I have no regrets because you're here." She continued. "I have all my difficulties too and what man is going to put up with that? Plus, I'm forty-seven now. Men my age want women who are still in their thirties. It's not easy, Liam."

What a stupid idea sending a text. The lifeless phone balanced on the edge of the table, suicidal. It had made things worse. He was tempted to send another text: *Wanker!* or *Fuck you!* But resisted, determined not to pick at the wound and instead to let it scab over.

His mum continued talking. The smoke, the pain, the same-old-same-old tugged at him, pulling him down further into his childhood. Before long, he was hearing all about her troubles. He listened patiently, empathising, eventually dragging himself to bed, drained. He looked at his phone—still nothing.

The next day, Liam cycled to Mick and Maureen's who lived on the edge of Barnsley. When Mick opened the door, Liam, standing there with his bike, did a double-take: what had formerly been a grand sunflower rising towards the skies was now wilted and brittle, curved in its final composition. In the few years since his last visit, Mick had gone from old to ancient. Nonetheless, his affection had weathered well.

Smiling generously, careful not to lose his balance, Mick patted Liam on the arm and welcomed him in.

Mick shouted to Maureen who then came downstairs, taking each step carefully whilst holding tight to the banister, legs slightly bowed, the keel of her body giving way to the weight of time. It was hard to see them looking like they did. He'd never known them looking young, but this was a new kind of old.

"I'll stick kettle on, shall ah?" said Mick.

"Aye, an' get us some o' that cake as well," Maureen responded. "Well, look at thee, lad! By 'eck tha's grown. Go on, teck a seat."

Liam sat down on the couch in their compact living room, a September sun bursting through net curtains, lighting up a galaxy of dust particles. There was the familiar musky smell mingled with wood polish and boiled potatoes, but there was an extra odour distinctly connected to being old.

Mick and Maureen's house had always been there, reliable, predictable, safe. They were simple in their ways, not asking for much in life: a decent home, a holiday to Scarborough or Whitby each year and good health. Neither smoked nor drank alcohol except on special occasions.

Mick wandered back in, a man on a tightrope, tea set rattling on the tray. He placed it down on a square wooden coffee table and gingerly crouched towards his armchair, until he was finally nuzzled in. After catching his breath, he offered Liam a piece of sliced cake on a plate.

"Help thee sen, lad."

"Thanks." Liam bit into the sweet, sticky cake, cosy hints of nutmeg and cinnamon making him wistful. "Mmm, delicious," he said, exaggerating his pleasure so his appreciation wouldn't go unnoticed.

"Did you make this, Maureen?"

"Of course I did, love. When I knew you were coming, ah thought, what's our Liam like most? An' ah know 'ow much ya love me cakes."

"Awe, thanks Maureen, I do. Always the best cakes in town."

"So, lad, what's tha' bin up ta?" chipped in Mick.

Liam told them about his gardening job, making it sound more impressive than it was. He told them about the caravan but decided not to mention it being burnt to the ground as he knew they'd offer him money which he wouldn't be comfortable taking and they'd be uncomfortable with him not taking, so keeping quiet was the easiest option. He told them about Maya.

"Ooh, she sounds right posh, yer should marry 'er, lad, settled for life then," said Mick, laughing.

"Dunt be a silly old fool," chimed Maureen. "What d'ya like about her, love?"

Liam took another bite of cake. It was true, he really did like Maureen's cakes.

"We get on well together, we just click, we're into similar things. Not sure, it's hard to say."

"Is she good-looking?" asked Mick.

"I think she is, yeah, but beauty's in the eye of the beholder, but yeah, she's pretty gorgeous."

"That's good then," said Mick.

"So, what's your secret?" asked Liam, looking at them both.

"No one else would have him 'cept me, an' ah couldn't leave him now, it'd be like throwing a puppy out. Plus, he has his uses," joked Maureen

"Charming that is, an' what might they be then?" said Mick, eyes sparkling.

"Not quite sure, I'll 'ave to think about that one. Come to think of it, what are you good for?"

All three of them chuckled and drank more tea and ate more cake.

Mick was eighty-nine and Maureen was eighty-seven, and yet they were both still reasonably sharp. Maureen had spent her life teasing Mick, commenting on how useless he was, how daft he was, how no one else would have him, how she'd had an army of men to choose from, but she gave him a chance because, being a plumber, he could at least fix the plumbing if it went wrong. Mick always smiled and found it amusing: he enjoyed the attention even if it was derogatory. Liam suspected Maureen's blatant put-downs were contrarily her way of showing Mick how much she loved him and that Mick, in his own paradoxical way, felt loved. Neither of them questioned Liam's disappearance. Maybe they felt like they had no right to, but Liam knew they had every right and for this reason brought it up.

"I'm sorry that I didn't get in touch."

"You don't have to explain, love, we understand," said Maureen. "You needed some time to be on your own. It's normal."

"How'd you mean?"

"You grew up looking after yer mum and it should've bin t'other way round, so me and Mick weren't surprised when ya buggered off. We were pleased you'd managed to get away but were worried that you weren't safe or summat'd happened to ya. Isn't that right, Mick?"

"Aye that's right an' all, just glad you're okay and we get to see ya before we pop our clogs."

"Ah, don't be thinking like that, you're still both young'uns," said Liam with a wink.

"Aye that's right, I reckon we should go out tonight, go to a night club or summat like that. Eh?" said Maureen. All three chuckled some more.

Liam stayed there all day. In the evening, Maureen switched on the TV to watch Eastenders and Mick fell asleep in the chair. During Eastenders, Liam asked her if she knew how often he'd been in foster care when he was young.

"Oh love, why'd you want ta be thinking about that?"

"Just curious."

"I reckon it was twice or a bit more, then me and Mick were granted permission to tek care of ya when ya mum had her struggles."

"Where was my dad?"

"God only knows, but ya don't want to be thinking about him, he's not worth it."

"Yeah, that's what Mum says."

"Let's not talk about it, eh, it'll ruin a nice evening."

"Sure."

They watched some more Eastenders. Soft snores purred from Mick.

"Did you know him?"

"No one knew Paddy, he never let anyone in. You'd ask him summat, but you never got a straight answer back. A secretive beggar he was. I can't abide with a man who doesn't stick around for his young'uns. The only person who knew Paddy was Paddy."

Liam saw himself as a tad secretive and not comfortable when others got too close—was he like his dad, he wondered?

"Am I like him?"

Maureen was incredulous. "What! You like Paddy? Don't be daft. You're nowt like him."

Maureen had been quick to answer. Maybe she did think he could be a little more open.

"What about to look at?"

"That's true, ya do tek after him in that area, but personality you're like chalk and cheese."

Liam dropped the subject: he could see Maureen was getting uncomfortable. He asked her about her garden and gave some advice on being more organic—it was nice to come back to the lighter topics. Liam wanted to thank Maureen for what she'd done but felt shy mentioning it. Maureen had been the mum and Mick had been the dad he'd needed. They'd given him enough to survive all the shit that had been thrown at him. They'd been reliable and loving throughout his childhood even if sometimes a bit too strict.

"I'd better be off, it's starting to get dark."

Maureen threw a cushion at Mick which startled him out of his snooze.

"Weck up, ya dozy lump! Our Liam's off."

Both Maureen and Mick struggled to their feet and, at a snail's pace, made it to the door. Liam hugged Maureen and gave her a kiss on her cheek, feeling her cold, wrinkly skin on his lips. He then shook hands with Mick—he wanted to hug him but knew this would make him feel uncomfortable.

"Give 'im a hug, yer big softie!" said Maureen to her husband. "It's twenty-fourteen, men do that kinda thing now. Yer might never see 'im again."

Both men hugged, and even with the awkward rapid patting of each other's backs, it still felt good to have done it, a new experience.

"Love yer both," said Liam as he cycled away, waving them goodbye. There was a sadness and a joy in his heart all the way to his mother's as he thought how lucky he'd been to have had Mick and Maureen in life.

THIRTY-SIX

Liam

Flicking through old CDs, Liam pulled out Eminem, sticking it on to play whilst packing, relishing the angry patter that once barricaded his ears from the din of chaotic home life. Eminem, fatherless, trailer trash like himself, except now there wasn't even a trailer.

The time had come to head back south; in order to survive, dosh was needed. His mum's meds now altered appeared to be doing the trick. Maybe it was just wishful thinking affecting Liam's ability to see straight, but she did seem a little perkier, though not to the point of getting dressed. He was dying to set light to that awful dressing gown and tell her to put some clothes on, get out and meet people, socialise, be in the world. Big words coming from someone whose own social life was about as exciting as a country lane bus stop at four in the morning. She must go out sometimes otherwise how would she eat or smoke, he reasoned.

The need to leave was ramping up along with the force field that held him there, the escalating tension set to catapult him into the stratosphere.

Liam promised he'd phone regularly and that she could phone him anytime, and if she was struggling, got too paranoid or the voices became too much, she should definitely call him. What else could he do? Being an only child meant everything rested on him. Siobhan was smiling—maybe she could see his guilt with her hypersensitivity and was trying to be more the grown up.

The van would be his home until he managed to sort out another caravan. Maya had tried persuading him to move in with her in London, but Liam told her he wasn't a city person, and, in the end, he knew London would drive him crazy.

* * *

Back at Bentley Farm, he pushed his bike down the track and through the woodland. There it was, his old home now a blackened pile of ashes and molten metal. The roof and walls gone except for some insubordinate remnant panels making their last stand. Stripy blue and white tape that cordoned off the scene rustled in a cool autumnal breeze pushing its way through the trees.

Kicking through the cremated corpse that could have been him, Liam scoured the cinders, making out the odd possession that had managed to retain some shape: some pots and pans, the fireplace, the tiny butler sink he'd managed to find on eBay in mint condition, now a fissured black crack of lightning running across it's enamel sky like a film negative. Where the bed had been, he found the biscuit tin. Opening it, he tipped out his life savings, watching the worthless ashes scatter to the floor.

The caravan had been a part of him, an extension of his identity.

It hadn't been just a place to live, it was who he was, which begged the question, who was he now? He thought about nature with its hurricanes that came to places like Louisiana and wiped out whole areas, or the recent wildfires in Australia, or the floods in Bangladesh and all the people that were left dispossessed, and now he felt like one of them. He'd hoped, like an Egyptian Pharaoh, that his most precious objects would end up going with him into death, but the afterlife did not care for the material, only souls were wanted, and this meant the journey was always alone. Around the caravan, the nearby oak leaves were scorched and crinkled, their gnarled, old bodies defiant in comparison to what had once been stuff on a busy production line, now crumbled, their fleeting moment gone, forever.

Graham Bentley had told Liam over the phone that he'd get rid of the wreckage within the next week. It'd be like it never even existed except for those who'd seen it. Liam would never forget it. Not just the wood, the tiles and paint but the space between them, the space he'd occupied, the space that had held him. It crossed his mind that maybe that space was still there and the objects that defined it were illusionary.

Maybe the burning of the caravan had been right, maybe it was time to move on, to go back to the world of people where evenings were spent in pubs, night clubs, evening classes, dinner parties or barbecues with friends, watching TV with a partner or family, but not alone. There'd been too much time alone. Meeting Daniel and Maya, he'd been reminded of the importance of connection. Being connected to nature was all well and good but being connected to other human beings went deeper. He'd been cut off from other human beings too long.

In Daniel, he'd received something no other man had shown. His father still hadn't replied to his text. Liam could think up various reasons as to why this might be, but the truth was his father had never made the effort, and for this, Liam wouldn't be sending him another text. Liam had often wondered what it would be like to have a father. Daniel welcomed Liam despite the obvious unlikelihood of their friendship, and that unconditionality had touched Liam's core.

He threw his bike in the back of his van and drove up the track towards the road, knowing that he'd be unlikely to pass through these gates again. This chapter of his life had come to an end and his future was now up in the air, as was always the case, but more often veiled by routine and familiarity. As he approached the entrance, he saw a figure loitering around the farm gate, the bright autumn sky turning whoever it was into a silhouette. Then, as he approached, the stiff, upright, statuesque gait of Meredith became distinct.

* * *

Meredith

It wasn't Liam's fault he reminded her of a life not lived, a life unclaimed. Obedience and servitude to austere conventionality and antiquarian ideas of marriage had taken their toll. Liam's virility was a reminder of the potency squashed and packed in tightly beneath, fit to burst. Light infiltrating the cracked veneer had been a slap in the face, but the red palm print left on her cheek hadn't belonged to Liam. This wasn't some Einsteinian equation, but Meredith had been too in the woods to work it out, the redness on her cheek was shame.

Liam had done nothing untoward and had not deserved such cold wrath. She was being a tempestuous aristocrat. This was the twenty-first century, and the idea of him as the roaming gypsy sleeping with the lord and lady's daughter was the stuff of medieval folk songs, surely not the modern age? And anyway, it wasn't just about Maya, it had begun when she'd first set eyes on him. When Daniel had taken a liking to him, yet Liam had been respectful and courteous, and for this, he had good reason to be bitter and hateful towards her, but the only time he'd shown her animosity was when she threw him out.

As he approached her at the gate, his face had a look of exasperation. Understandably.

"Graham said you were here. I asked him if he'd kindly call me when you came."

"Right," said Liam. "Here I am."

"Yes, well, I just wanted to … hum, you know."

Meredith scrambled to find the right words. This was the first time she'd spoken to him without animosity, his eyes looking straight into hers. It was as though he could see her blackened heart. She turned her head, looking back towards the car as if something was there, something she'd forgotten.

"Don't worry, Meredith, it wasn't you who burnt my home down."

Meredith initially had been bewildered with how what she'd pictured as a rusty, old caravan could be equated with a home. She hadn't known what the caravan meant to him. It was Maya who revived her sensibility. Maya had described to Daniel just how beautiful the caravan was, letting her know that every inch had been carved out by Liam's own artisan hands, that no amount of money could buy what Liam had created, only time, patience and love could do that. Daniel, too, had relayed these images to Meredith. This had been his home and now it was just a pile of cinders that would give itself up to the wind and rain, and here Liam was being kind to her, Meredith who was surely at fault. His kindness felt cruel. She struggled with the pain of a heart trying to prize itself open against her will. She just wanted to formally apologise, hand him over some money and be off on her way.

"It was that idiot Troy who did it, and you weren't to know he was a homicidal pyromaniac," said Liam, still looking squarely into her face.

He was making the whole thing even more gruelling for Meredith. Why was he being so understanding? It would be easier if he just shouted at her, called her some nasty names, and then she could throw the money at him and feel good about herself, but he was so infuriatingly reasonable. Worst of all, she had the unusual sense of liking him. She was beaten by her heart and had no choice but to surrender to its softening, yet the words in her mouth became cumbersome gobstoppers as she attempted to articulate herself.

"Why aren't you angry with me, Liam?" It felt strange to call him by his name. "I've been horrendous to you. I don't deserve you being nice to me. I told Troy where you were, really, my intentions were not good."

"I don't need to be angry with you, I know you don't like yourself, and I'm guessing that's because you've had a hard life. Maybe I'm wrong, but that's how I see it."

His words could be construed as trite, something Maya might say, but they wormed their way in. Pangs of grief took her by surprise, annoying tears unanticipated were quickly swallowed back into their ducts.

Liam continued. "The thing is, you think that no one can see you, but your eyes, your voice, your brow, the way you stand, reveals everything. We're all naked really, but we just don't know it. Here I am acting like I know better, but the truth is, I'm just as scared as you are."

"I'm not scared," Meredith said, her voice squeakier than she'd like.

"Fair enough," said Liam.

As he went to open the gate, a distinct power, like a gust of warm air, crossed over her body.

"Me and Daniel agreed that we'd like to give you something for your loss, and we wondered if thirty thousand pounds would suffice?"

Liam held still; a discernible coolness fell away from him.

"Sorry, I don't get you?"

"We'd like to offer you thirty thousand pounds for your inconvenience."

"Do you think I'm going to try and sue you? That's not my thing. I wouldn't do that. I wouldn't even know how to do that."

"That's not the reason. It's an apology. I know how much your caravan meant to you, I was being ... you know..." Meredith couldn't find the right word.

Liam, again, looked her directly, his face softer like a child. Meredith had disarmed him. A couple of tears trickled over his cheek. Meredith felt awkward.

"I would never take thirty thousand pounds from you. I am so touched, but that's way too generous." He cried a bit more. "That kind of money is unreal to me," he said, looking at her with watery eyes.

"Liam, we have more money than you can imagine. Yes, thirty thousand is a lot of money, but what I did was outrageous, I should not have told Troy where you live."

"What I'd really like is for you to accept me as someone who is going out with your daughter and who is friends with Daniel, Meredith."

"Nothing I've done so far has managed to stop you doing whatever you please."

"True, but it'd just be a bit more pleasant. You never know, you may even get to like me."

"You'd prefer me liking you than thirty thousand pounds?"

"Yes."

"Okay."

"And maybe fifteen thousand to cover the caravan and hassle?"

"Done!"

"Shall we shake on it?" Liam said, reaching out a hand.

Meredith put her hand out to meet his. His calloused palm felt warm and friendly. She could have almost smiled, but this would take a bit more time. She then went into her bag and brought out the money. She counted out fifteen bundles of notes and then another five and passed them to Liam.

"I'd feel better if you took twenty."

Liam smiled and thanked her.

"See you soon," she said as she left to get in her car.

"See you soon," replied Liam.

She then stopped, turned round and walked back to Liam, giving him the rest of the money.

"Just take it. Don't argue, you deserve it, and you will get far more out of it than we will."

* * *

Liam

Liam took the money. He wanted to hug Meredith, not just because he felt grateful, but because he could see she'd been short of them in her life. Her body was crying out to be touched and loved and held. He should have a word with Daniel, he thought to himself.

As Meredith drove away, Liam looked back down the farm track and it felt right to be leaving. If he was honest, he had to admit to himself that really he'd been mildly depressed for the last few years and it had been Daniel and Maya that had helped release him from this. Everything felt right. *So where to now,* he thought, and it was obvious really, he'd go stay with Maya in London for a few days and see how that panned out.

Part Three

THIRTY-SEVEN

Meredith

Meredith's thick-layered arms brushed against Colin as they strolled through Richmond Park. A bitterly cold winter's day, each encased in scarves, hats, gloves and heavy, warm coats.

The past five years had been quite the journey.

Wanting to hide, she hoped he wouldn't notice the lines that mapped her story, dark rings beneath the eyes, the tightness in her lips, a new deepening gauntness in her cheeks. Colin's hair was snowy white, but he'd aged well, retaining handsome features, body upright and solid, eyes still smouldering sensually when falling on her. Feeling old, she wondered if now he saw her as grotesque.

They meandered around the park, slightly awkward, politely conversing, cordially catching up. Colin was on his second marriage with two grown-up daughters to his first wife. He ran a printing company and had become reasonably wealthy, investing in properties just at the right time.

The sky, a clear artic blue, the sun low, yet at its peak when he eventually asked why Meredith had wanted to meet up. It probably wasn't the right moment to mention tantra, but it had been in the spirit of truth and integrity, a cornerstone of tantra, that she'd confessed to Daniel her fantasies about Colin. Tantric retreats with Daniel had become their new go-to, prompting a more open, honest side in Meredith and quite the saucy sausage in Daniel.

Daniel had gallantly suggested she arrange to meet Colin in the hope of putting the old demon to bed—figuratively not literally, he'd emphasised. Meredith worried that it may be the latter.

Girding her loins, she wondered aloud how the relationship might have gone should they have stayed together, Colin listening sensitively.

She talked about how those times had been difficult for her, how she hadn't known who she fully was back then, how her parents controlled her and she couldn't break free. As she spoke, her words began to flow, reconnecting to the young Meredith who was passionate and alive.

"All those years ago, and I never forgot you," she ended, looking away shyly.

"Well, yeah, I do think we had a bit of a laugh," said Colin, which quite frankly was not what she'd anticipated.

"Oh, and that time when we took the boat out," said Meredith excitedly—the image of them making love on the deck had always managed to fire up her engines.

"What boat?"

"My parents' boat."

"Hmm, where exactly?"

"On the south coast, near Worthing."

"Well, I've been on so many boats, they all blur into one. But must have been good then, eh?" He laughed, giving Meredith a cheeky little wink.

The tapestry into which such memories were woven with golden thread was now a rag, unfit for cleaning shoes.

Such a beastly annihilation of what she'd remembered as a transcendental union of two souls meeting: after making love, Colin had told her that he'd felt like the *happiest man in the world and hoped they would always be together*. How could he forget saying that? Had they been just random, meaningless, post coitus-fuelled, but ultimately, empty words?

"Well, yes, granted it was a while ago," Meredith threw back, abashed.

"Oh, but I do remember how you used to get pissed as a newt sometimes and we had sex in your old man's garage, remember that?"

Reduced to a posh tart, Colin's uncouth manner had escaped her memory.

"It was once! And I wasn't drunk!"

"Weren't you? Oh, sorry! And what about that time we came here?"

"Where?"

"Richmond Park."

"What did we do?"

"You know..."

"No, I haven't the foggiest."

"Oh? Oh! Maybe I'm getting it mixed up, my memory is a bit knackered these days."

They decided to change the subject to something more recent. Colin spoke about his first wife, how she was *a bit of a leech*, how she'd squeezed thousands in maintenance out of him for the kids by taking him to court, yet her new husband was minted which made it totally out of order that he should have to cough up so much bread, though he insisted he loved his girls, Jacklyn and Ashley. Meredith was now wanting to get away. She realised just how attractive and decent Daniel was. What made her hold onto such a fantastical idea of Colin for all this time when all she could see now was a man with a distinct lack of sophistication. Ironically, she'd remembered thinking of Colin metaphorically, as being like a stilton, an acquired taste full of earthy, rustic tang, but now he struck her as a tasteless, rubbery cheese slice not fit for toasting.

"Now I remember, we did go to this park," said Colin.

Meredith worried she was about to hear in graphic detail some sordid sexual act amongst the stags and wild Canadian geese.

"We came with my sister and Ryan, who'd just been born, and I asked you if you reckoned you'd ever fancy having kids, and you said, *Never in a million years*, that *children were like little aliens* to you and then you said *they even repulsed* you and I remember thinking, *Flippin' 'eck, that's a bit strong, innit!* I'd forgotten all about that. D'you remember? That might've been our first row."

They climbed Sawyers Hill where, from the top, the city loomed in the distance, the banking capital zigzagging its glass and steel lifeline across the horizon, contrasting with the bucolic quaintness of Richmond, both sculpted and manicured into aesthetically appropriate shapes that belied an underbelly of something more sinister. Like Jekyll and Hyde, different parts of the same psyche.

Meredith felt the chill of a northerly wind.

"Well, I was a teenager. Who wants children at that age? All that pressure on young women is ridiculous. In those days, you had a child and you were stuck at home all day, thank God it's changed. I wanted to see the world, have some fun before becoming tied down."

"So, did you?"

Meredith looked towards some scattered leaves beneath her feet that hadn't managed to rot back into the earth. She took a deep inhalation of the cold, fresh winter air as she decided how to answer.

"I got married and became a mother and a wife."

"Oh, so you had kids then, anyway?"

"Yes, a girl and two boys."

"So, what changed your mind then?"

"Becoming pregnant, I had no choice."

"Regrets?"

Meredith had been plagued her whole life with regrets, but now, here she was talking to the one regret that it just so happened had transformed itself over the last hour into a sense of relief, and *thank God I did what I did*—the only regret now was regret itself.

"No," she said. Then she thought about her daughter and how she'd resented Maya's freedom.

"Yes," she said, contradicting herself, "I regret, not being there more for my children."

Colin looked at her and understood. He smiled and said, "Yeah, I know what you mean."

They walked a bit more, went to a café, had some tea, made their excuses and said goodbye.

THIRTY-EIGHT

Liam

Strapped in a harness, soothed by Liam's heartbeat and the rhythmical rise and fall of his chest, Leaf slept peacefully, thank God—only half an hour earlier, it had been the end of the world as far as she was concerned. Sipping his café con leche, Liam leant back in his chair, people watching, enjoying the respite. This was their first trip away from El Mundo Livre since before the birth in February. Rowan, wearing a bright red Ninja costume, was chasing pigeons in the plaza, his power to make them fly away bringing ecstatic cries of joy.

Staying in London had only meant to be for a week or two. People started offering gardening work, and then other bits came in here and there, and a year passed, then Maya found herself pregnant. At that time, everything was happening. Corbyn became leader of the Labour party, receiving the biggest mandate any political leader had ever received in UK politics. For the first time in decades, there was hope for young people who were fed up with neoliberalism. Of course, the media wasn't having any of it—unlike other new leaders who were graced with an initial celebratory welcome, Corbyn was immediately vilified.

His desire to reduce military spending, keeping in line with the rest of Europe, and using the billions it would save for the NHS, education, housing, welfare and the rest, were not taken well by the establishment.

Then came the referendum: the English, unlike the Scots, chose to leave the European Union, winning by three percent. Liam voted Remain, but the truth was he didn't know enough about it, probably like the twenty-six percent who didn't vote at all.

It was time to get out of England. Not just to escape the façade of democracy but that the crazy, consumeristic, techno-dominant world of London was no place for a child to grow up. Rowan, like a young billy goat, ended up being born in the Portuguese mountainous village, hidden away amongst bleached, prehistoric boulders. There were fifteen adults in *El Mundo Livre Comunidad*, mostly all in their thirties and early forties with seven children all under the age of ten. They'd even started an Extinction Rebellion group since reading about the demos in England.

The spring air was cool. Maya was wearing a handknitted cardigan, a book propped in her hand: *Janet and John Behind the Garden Shed: How to talk to children about sex.*

"Fuck, did you know, in Holland they start talking to their kids about sex from birth and that they don't just call yonis vaginas, they name all the different parts. How fucking cool is that?"

"Wow, that is cool. I wouldn't mind reading that after you," said Liam, knowing he'd probably never find the time.

"You should, it's fucking mind-blowing."

Maya disappeared back into the book.

Bilbao was halfway between Le Nid and El Mundo Livre. It was a large town, the mountains not too far away juxtapositioned with state-of-the-art twenty-first-century architecture. The plaza was alive with tourists in the Siete Calles. They were sat outside a café bar.

"Eu gostaria de um sorvete!" said Rowan, running over to the table.

"Later, when vovó e vovô get here," said Liam.

It was rare that Rowan got the kind of treats most kids took for granted. He'd been looking forward to ice cream and a trip to a toy store with his grandparents all week.

Traditional Spanish Arabesque music tapered through the air like paisley smoke, suitable for the Basque country and satiating the tourist appetite, inciting them to feel like they'd arrived somewhere authentically exotic.

The plaza was a hive of busyness. A swarm of varied creatures searching for trinkets and snake oils to enhance their lives, only to gather dust and fail the claims made on the bottle.

Watching them at a distance, there was a lofty detachment. *Mañana* summed Liam up—tranquillo, dreamy, anthropologist, inquisitively observing the minutiae of each facial expression, body's gait, energetic pace. The human animal was fascinating in its unusual shape. A miracle that each of us made it, infinite to one chance, from those ancestral amoebae mating through the eons of evolution, always the odds stacked against us, here we all were for our moment in time.

And then, mid-reverie, Liam plummeted back to earth as the strangest of apparitions materialised, transforming the crowd back into an amorphous throng of sightseers and shoppers. Wearing a black beret, lips cherry red, matching flamenco dress ruffling to the floor, over the shoulder a fine black lace shawl, wild and elegant like a Siamese fighting fish released back into the ocean, Daniel sashayed across the plaza. Beside him, looking tanned and pantheresque with her Dolce & Gabbana shades perched on her head, Meredith. She smiled as Maya looked up, Maya's jaw dropping to the floor as she eyed her father in his outlandish garb.

Liam was reminded of the nomadic Wodaabe tribe of Niger in Africa: tall, lean men proudly paraded themselves in their colourful, beaded clothes, exaggerated beatific smiles enhanced by make up for the women to judge the most appealing.

Rowan picked up on the shift of awareness.

"Vovô!"

"Hey amigo, como está?" said Daniel, opening his arms for Rowan to run into.

"You look funny, Vovô."

"What the fuck!"

"Maya, please, don't swear in front of Rowan."

"Mother, seriously, Dad! My God! Come on?"

Daniel appeared slightly diminished.

"I like it." Liam chimed. "You look amazing, Daniel."

"Thank you."

"I think Maya's a bit jealous," said Liam.

"Oh seriously!" Maya scoffed. "I'm just not sure why you didn't wear something a bit more subtle? It's hard enough that you're both now into tantra. I'm used to you being the epitome of drab and colourless, but this new out-of-the-closet look is just too much, honestly!"

"It took your father a lot of courage to do this, so can I suggest we all support him."

"A bit of a warning would have been useful!"

"I've mentioned it before."

"Yes, but I've never—"

Daniel interrupted, making a beeline for Leaf. "Is that her, then, can I have a look?"

Daniel and Meredith took a peek at the snoozing bundle harnessed to Liam. Daniel looked relieved having the attention off him momentarily until two Spanish teenage boys started laughing and pointing.

"Fuck off, malditos idiotas!" shouted Maya. They laughed some more and vanished into the hordes of people. "I'm sorry, Dad."

"Oh look, she's awake!" crooned Meredith.

Leaf looked up at all the smiling faces and burst into tears.

"Ok, I think she might want you." Liam passed Leaf to Maya who unbuttoned her cardigan and pulled up her T-shirt, giving her breast to Leaf who, without hesitation, instantly latched on to it, looking around as she sucked, curious.

Rowan whispered something into Maya's ear.

"Of course it's ice cream time," declared Maya, and they ordered various treats. Maya toned down the judgemental comments, possibly aware of Daniel's fragility. Soon everyone was eating ice cream and chatting.

"Well, gosh, it's rather remarkable how we're all here. Can I propose a toast? Here's to us," said Daniel, raising a spoonful of mint choc chip ice cream. "Cheers!"

There was a unanimous *Cheers* around the table with a raising of spoons.

After a while, Rowan asked, "When is it time to go to the toy shop?"

"Maybe the boys could go off together, sorry ... erm ... boys and those who aren't quite sure," said Maya.

"My pronouns are still *he, him* and *his*."

"That's good to know, so me and Mum will hang out here, yeah?"

It was odd to hear Maya call Meredith, *Mum*—it had always been *Mother*.

"Sounds like a plan. What d'ya reckon, Rowan, me, you and Granddad do a trip to the toy shop?"

Rowan jumped in the air with excitement.

* * *

Meredith

Meredith wasn't used to being alone with Maya and was surprised at Maya's invitation, but Meredith had done a lot of work on herself and was in a better place, which may also have something to do with surviving the turbulent whitewater rapids of menopause without HRT—a major triumph. And now, from the still, glasslike surface water, she reached out and caressed Leaf's tiny, silken scalp.

"Exquisite. You are such a perfect, tiny bundle of loveliness." Leaf, finding Meredith's finger, tried to suck on it.

"Ooh, I think little missy would like another feed." Maya dutifully supplied the goods.

"You make a great mother, I'm so proud of you."

"Oh God, I'm exhausted all the time. I haven't had a decent night's sleep for years, and my nipples are traumatised. She's lucky to be alive—sometimes I feel like killing her!"

"Oh, that sounds terribly difficult, dear. You're considerably more patient than I ever was."

"Hmm. What was Grandma like?"

"Mother had very little to do with me. I was brought up by nannies pretty much until boarding."

"What was the nanny like?"

"They were mostly nice, they came and went. Milly was the nicest. I had her from about six until eight. She was so warm, Scottish. I loved Milly. She's probably dead now."

"That's sad."

"So how is it with you and Liam? Hope he's not tiring you out too much." Meredith laughed.

"Oh God, Mother, puh-leeeese! I really can't get used to your crudeness or cheesy double entendres. It's bad enough seeing Dad dressed like he is—there's only so much I can take."

"I'm teasing you, dear."

"Well, I can do without it, it's not easy—there is no happy ever after. We argue a lot, I bitch to him about missing London and he's a grumpy git in the mornings, but we still always end up liking each other. We have some amazing rows, Italian style—we ham it up to the max. It's all part of the SHIT relationship programme. We teach people how to have conflict that doesn't involve getting stuck in *verbal circles* or passive aggression."

"Maybe your father and I could come on a workshop."

"No fucking way, I'd rather die!"

Meredith laughed uproariously.

"What's so funny?"

"You. Your honesty, so straightforward. You're so different to me—how did that happen?"

"We're not as different as you think. I often find myself thinking I'm becoming more and more like you, which is scary."

"Am I that bad?"

"Worse."

"In what way?"

"...actually, you've improved."

"Thank you."

"Massively. But my life wasn't easy either. Thank Christ for Nannie Dot."

Meredith pulled a sad face.

* * *

Liam

Liam and Rowan walked beside Daniel, an entourage shadowed by a flamenco diva's peacock feathers. All around, passers-by gawped and whispered. There he was, centre stage of some Almodóvar movie. Liam, in supporting role, enthused about Daniel being brave, but Daniel was in a tizzy, having none of it.

"Good grief, I'm not sure I can cope with this much longer. I'm beginning to think I should have stuck to wearing a simple blazer and trousers."

"How come you chose today to strut your stuff, as it were?"

"I thought it would be fun. I'm thinking now it was rather an unwise decision. Everyone appears to be staring at me."

Surely Daniel must have known wearing a dress that could be seen from the moon would inevitably draw attention. Was it the little boy inside him wanting to hog the limelight, fearing being left out?

"Didn't you expect that?"

"I don't know what I expected, I just wanted to be free of my fear. I've always been someone who blended in. I wanted a change."

"You've got to be like Rowan in his ninja costume, walk proud, believe you are that ninja warrior, be that feisty gypsy."

"I feel foolish. I keep seeing my reflection in the shop windows and I look preposterous!"

"It's paranoia, you look fantastic, but you'd look even better if you allowed yourself to feel proud. You don't get many shrinking violet flamenco dancers."

"But I'm a man not a woman."

"And gypsies are persecuted and treated like vermin, but they still know how to have a good time and say *fuck it* to all those that put them down. Maybe that can be your affirmation—*Fuck it!*"

Rowan piped up. "Yeah, fuck it!"

Liam laughed. "Go Rowan! See, me and Rowan are on your side."

Daniel smiled, though judging by his scrunched-up brow, he was clearly uncomfortable with Rowan's use of the F-word.

Daniel pulled himself upright. "Fuck it!" and exhaled. "Fuck it! You know, that does feel rather good. Fuck it! Fuck it! Just fuck it!"

Arriving at the crazily busy toy shop, Rowan headed straight for the Lego section.

Daniel had grown two inches taller since his *fuck it* affirmations, parading himself as star of the show, finally treading the boards, affecting a more flirtatious manner towards his curtain call, the stalls being a mixture of harangued-looking parents worried about price tags, craving a siesta, children who had just possibly landed in nirvana depending on the amount of cash their guardians were willing to part with. As far as Liam was concerned, it was the theatre of the grotesque; he wanted out of there, away from the great plastic mountains that would inevitably end up in a landfill.

At last, they escaped. In tow, one very excited little boy and his five-hundred-piece *Lego Ninja Temple of Fire* and Daniel constantly chanting *Dash it!* having decided he couldn't quite get comfortable swearing in front of his grandson. Strolling back in the direction of the others down busy streets, Rowan spontaneously closed his eyes and began walking very slowly, each step meticulously taken, arms outstretched in front, the sea of oncoming pedestrians parting as he walked towards them.

"I'll bet you can't do this. I've got special powers that make me be able to see with my eyes closed."

"Wow, that's amazing, Rowan, how do you do it?" said Liam, admiring Rowan's ability to readily trust and embrace each new moment.

"Why don't you both have a go, it's easy," encouraged Rowan.

"I think one of us needs to keep his eyes open, just in case," said Daniel.

"Vovô, you can do that."

"How about I keep my eyes open and you and Grandad walk with your eyes closed?" Liam chipped in.

Rowan became excited at this idea.

Daniel, madly flapping, jumped in. "Oh, but, I do think it would make much more sense for me to keep *my* eyes open and you and Rowan do the superhero stuff!"

"Nah," said Liam. "How about I hold your hand and you hold Rowan's hand and I lead?"

Rowan beamed with shouts of approval.

"I think I feel conspicuous enough without inviting more attention."

"Fuck it, Grandad!" shouted Rowan, taking hold of his hand which thankfully, rather than overloading the heady combination, was the magic, mesmerising word to which Daniel's eyes clenched shut in childish play.

Liam took hold of Daniel's spare hand.

Daniel's firm grip was warm, dissembling a concealed barrier. Shaking hands had always been Daniel's preferred way of greeting, whereas Liam was more of a hugger, yet even to Liam, this type of connection between the conduits of the heart was dangerously more advanced on the intimacy spectrum.

Walking through the hustle and bustle of vendors, shoppers and buskers, there was no place to hide: the anthropologist was now the observed as people smiled, moving aside for the idiosyncratic Brits. Liam played with the power he'd been granted, gathering pace, weaving his way like a snake through the undergrowth of normality. The mass of concentration on Daniel's face weighed against Rowan's exuberance. Increasing speed, Liam forced the eccentric troupe into a gallop. A complete surrender to trust was the only thing left. Daniel's dress, like wings, flapped behind him. He began to giggle, perhaps like a child believing that because their eyes are closed, no one can see them, or perhaps because there was no time to think, so he was no longer able to worry. It was strange seeing him laugh— something else that was new.

Rowan's spontaneous magic was so cool. Adults may write fairy tales, but children know how to live them without all the self-conscious palaver getting in the way. Daniel wasn't doing too bad either, this unlikely man who'd invited Liam into his life, flying down the street, choosing to trust the darkened space, the not knowing where he was going, with the gall to show up in his *fuck it* regalia.

Giddy with the locomotive cavorting into chaos, they eventually reached the others, greeted by the bloodcurdling screams of Leaf.

"Just in time. She needs changing," said Maya, passing Liam the screaming bundle from hell.

Leaf was not shy in letting everyone know how pissed off she was. Her face shrivelled up like a dried prune, tonsils a boxer's punch-ball bouncing back and forth at the back of her gummy mouth. "Shit, we didn't get any disposable nappies."

"I know, I did mention it last night, but you started pontificating about the environment again."

Liam couldn't think. The screech of her cry made him want to throttle her, his own daughter: how could he think like that? Logically, he knew it ended, but this didn't always help. He and Maya had had quite a few rows about whose turn it was to get out of bed in the middle of the night. How could he feel so full of love one minute and like a killer the next?

The changing mat had already been laid on the bench alongside the bag of baby paraphernalia. Removing the onesie, Liam gagged, the overpowering stench causing his stomach to lurch. The others evacuated the contaminated area, as though fleeing a nuclear fallout. Leaf continued to warble at a level designed to torture anyone with a pair of ears. Earplugs would have come in handy for carrying out such complex operations. Undoing the Velcro, it was difficult to know what to do with the reusable cloth nappy covered in mustardy yellow poo. This is where being green and ethical really didn't pay. What difference was it really making? It would be better to stop flying or driving. With a baby wipe, the poo was cleared away, a new nappy administered and the onesie reinstated.

Wrinkles were ironed out and replaced with a face that was easier to love, the high pitch had lowered a few octaves, reaching a receding whimper and breathless stutter, her system slowly regulating. The toxic waste was sealed away in a Ziploc bag, and Leaf was bolted back onto Liam's torso via the harness.

"I think it's probably better to head back," said Liam, approaching the others, whereupon it was decided to do one last walk along the estuary.

Talking evaporated into the still air and there was calm, except for Rowan who was having a quiet conversation with himself. Leaf struggled to keep her eyes open. To the left of the path, the architectural splendour of the Guggenheim Museum glinted through the trees.

The silence was soon interrupted with a dull, recurring vibration pulsating against Liam's leg. Taking the mobile from his pocket, the low reverberating sound alerted the others. Lit up on the screen came the name, *Paddy Wanker*, the moniker Liam chose to call his father. It had been over five years since he'd sent the text, to which a reply never came. Unable to believe his eyes, he tapped the green phone icon on the screen to accept the call.

"Hello."

"Hello, is that yer man, Liam?" came a strong Irish lilt.

"Speaking."

"Hi."

A heavy, weighted breath billowed down the line, voices chatting in the background like a party. Lost for words, Liam waited, paralysed. A raging river running wild throughout his body. The suspense excruciating.

Daniel, Meredith and Maya stood quietly, waiting, whilst Rowan climbed on a small wall. Liam sensed their intrigue, turning away towards the river, desperate to hide. This phone call was too personal, scraping at the bone; he wasn't ready to let others get this near.

"Is that Paddy?" he whispered, unable to stand more silence.

Maya quickly moved towards him, her mouth opening fishlike, eyes round with astonishment. She took his arm, silently mouthing, *What the fuck!* Liam, taking a gulp of air, frowned, shaking his head, palm extended, blocking her intrusion. He was dangling over a precipice. Meredith and David loitered by a rail, signalling to Maya to join them.

A cough broke the silence on the other end of the phone, the kind made when in an awkward position. The man tells someone to *shut the fuck up a minute* and clears his throat.

"Sorry, no, Liam, I'm sorry … erm, it's not. I'm your dad's brother, Michael."

"Oh, right."

A seagull lets out a cry, hovering over the choppy, grey, rolling swell of water.

"I'm really sorry, Liam, but I've got some bad news. I'm afraid your dad's passed away. I found your number on his phone. I never even knew he had a son, but it said *Liam*, with *son* in brackets. I asked around just to be sure. None of us, his family, had seen him for over thirty years, he just disappeared."

"Oh, right," Liam repeated, dumbstruck. He felt like a character in a movie where the camera zooms in whilst in retreat.

"The funeral's next Tuesday at the Liverpool crematorium."

"Right." Liam still couldn't find any words. Too much to process. This man, the most significant man in his life, who'd spawned him, whose genes he shared, who abandoned him at a time he was most needed, never making contact, was dead. Abandoning him one last time, a cruel joke bringing bitter tears that jammed up in his throat like bad medicine.

"I won't be there. Thanks for letting me know. I've got to go now, sorry."

He tapped the red icon to end the call, his arm dropping to his side, a limp, dead weight. What was he meant to feel? Sad? Angry? Confused? Numb? Bitter? Hurt? Lost? Lost. Always lost.

"Who was it?"

"My father's brother. My father's dead."

"Oh no, how awful."

Sometimes, in the middle of the night when it was a struggle to sleep, his father would come to the foreground. One day he'd meet him, maybe he'd track him down when the time was right, just out of curiosity. He fantasised about what he'd be like, they'd chat, and his father would be sorry for all those years of not getting in touch, he'd want to be involved with Rowan and Leaf. He'd have his reasons for not getting in touch and there'd be shame and grief, and then another voice would come in, an uglier, less sympathetic voice telling him he was worthless. The same voice that plagued his mother. This voice, twisted with hate, reduced him to something worse than nothing.

"How did he die?" asked Daniel.

"Don't know."

"When's the funeral?" asked Meredith.

"Next week."

"Will you be going?" asked Maya.

"No."

As the world drifted away, its ashes scattering in the wind. Skin held no memory of a father's touch, only a longing for something unknown.

Rowan came over and took hold of Liam's hand.

"Are you sad, Daddy?"

Rowan's love and concern was unbelievably genuine and pure.

"I am, yes. Very sad."

"But you have me, and Maya and Leaf, and your daddy wasn't very nice."

Liam choked back the rising grief. Wiping his eyes, he looked down at his son, seeing a boy whom he knew had a father who loved him more than anything in the world, and from this he was gifted solace.

THIRTY-NINE

Troy

Troy was scribbling down some words on a piece of paper, half listening to the TV in his cell. The newsreader was waffling on about some flu in China, as if anyone gave a shit.

The cell wasn't too bad really, better than the bedsit in Tottenham—at least here he had proper mates.

It was lucky the guy in the caravan hadn't snuffed it. His solicitor told the court Troy had known there was no one in the caravan, and when he'd told the police that Satan was in there, it was a turn of phrase, like a bad spirit that needed exorcising. So, the attempted murder charge was dropped, as was all the Christian bollox. God had been useless. In fact, God didn't exist. There was no God. We're all masters of our own fate. We live and then we die, and that's it. Fuck trying to please others. Soon, he'd be out, free!

Jezza never once visited. Five years and not a word. What kind of therapist is that? A shit kind, that's what! There were only four weeks left to go and then those big iron doors would open, and freedom. The five years had crept by slower than a tortoise on crutches. All that proving you were rehabilitated, fit to go back into society. Doing stupid classes like how to write haikus. Meanwhile, Jezza was there with his stupid, fucking family in his nice, smug and cosy house, patting himself on the back. *Well, he won't be thinking that in a few weeks' time, will he!*

Troy looked at the words and was satisfied.

We are all lifers

Serving time in our prisons

Waiting for release

The End

ACKNOWLEDGEMENTS

The people I'd like to thank most of all are those who gave their precious time to reading the early drafts and gave me honest feedback, without them the book would not be what it is. So, in no particular order, I'd like to thank Kate Iwi, Emily Hannah, Jenny Anderson, Debbie Macnamara, Hannah Cox, Shaun Packham, Giovanni Jacobs, Judy Judge, Nicky Ferry and Leisa De Burca. I'd also like to thank Gillian Bains for her wonderful copy edit, Katie Evelyn for suggestions with the back cover blurb, Stefan Prodanovic for his help with the cover design, Nimra Bukhari for her superb formatting design, and my son River, for his ever-present support and encouragement.

J. L. Dent was raised in a working-class home in Leeds and has lived in communes, squats and the street. His interest in countercultural movements inspired a period as a stand-up punk poet. Dent is currently employed as a psychotherapist and writes in his spare time. He lives in Stroud and has a teenage son. *How to Have a SHIT Relationship* is his debut novel.

A WORD FROM THE AUTHOR

Your voice truly matters. So, if you enjoyed this book, it would mean the world to me if you would take a couple of minutes to leave a heartfelt review on Amazon or Goodreads. As Indie authors we need all the support we can get, so your feedback is always greatly appreciated. Thank you so much for your time.

Printed in Great Britain
by Amazon